Shalimar *the* Clown

By the same author

FICTION

Grimus
Midnight's Children
Shame
The Satanic Verses
Haroun and the Sea of Stories
East, West
The Moor's Last Sigh
The Ground Beneath Her Feet
Fury

NON-FICTION

The Jaguar Smile
Imaginary Homelands
Step Across This Line

PLAYS

Haroun and the Sea of Stories
(with Tim Supple and David Tushingham)
Midnight's Children
(with Tim Supple and Simon Reade)

ANTHOLOGY

The Vintage Book of
Indian Writing (co-editor)

Shalimar *the* Clown

A NOVEL

SALMAN RUSHDIE

Jonathan Cape
London

Published by Jonathan Cape 2005

2 4 6 8 10 9 7 5 3 1

Grateful acknowledgement is made to the following for permission to reprint previously published material:

W. W. NORTON & COMPANY, INC.: Excerpts from 'Farewell' from *The Country Without a Post Office* by Agha Shahid Ali, copyright © 1997 by Agha Shahid Ali. Reprinted by permission of W. W. Norton & Company, Inc.

CYBERSPACE INMATES: Excerpt from 'Things Will Get Better' by Leon Bell and from 'My Best Friend' by Dusty Ray Spencer. Both poems appeared on the Cyberspace Inmates website located at http://www.cyberspace-inmates.com. Reprinted by the kind permission of Cyberspace Inmates.

First published in Great Britain in 2005 by
Jonathan Cape
Random House, 20 Vauxhall Bridge Road,
London SWIV 2SA

Random House Australia (Pty) Limited
20 Alfred Street, Milsons Point, Sydney,
New South Wales 2061, Australia

Random House New Zealand Limited
18 Poland Road, Glenfield, Auckland 10, New Zealand

Random House South Africa (Pty) Limited
Endulini, 5A Jubilee Road, Parktown 2193, South Africa

The Random House Group Limited Reg. No. 954009
www.randomhouse.co.uk

A CIP catalogue record for this book is available from the British Library

ISBN 0-224-06161-5
ISBN 0-224-07784-8 (Trade paperback edition)

Papers used by Random House are natural, recyclable products made from wood grown in sustainable forests; the manufacturing processes conform to the environmental regulations of the country of origin

Book design by Dana Leigh Blanchette

Printed and bound in Great Britain by William Clowes Ltd, Beccles, Suffolk

In loving memory of my Kashmiri grandparents

Dr. Ataullah and Amir un nissa Butt

(Babajan and Ammaji)

I am being rowed through Paradise on a river of Hell:
Exquisite ghost, it is night.
The paddle is a heart; it breaks the porcelain waves . . .

I'm everything you lost. You won't forgive me.
My memory keeps getting in the way of your history.
There is nothing to forgive. You won't forgive me.
I hid my pain even from myself; I revealed my pain
only to myself.
There is everything to forgive. You can't forgive me.
If only somehow you could have been mine,
what would not have been possible in the world?

—AGHA SHAHID ALI,
The Country Without a Post Office

A plague on both your houses.

—MERCUTIO, IN *Romeo and Juliet*,
BY WILLIAM SHAKESPEARE

India

At twenty-four the ambassador's daughter slept badly through the warm, unsurprising nights. She woke up frequently and even when sleep did come her body was rarely at rest, thrashing and flailing as if trying to break free of dreadful invisible manacles. At times she cried out in a language she did not speak. Men had told her this, nervously. Not many men had ever been permitted to be present while she slept. The evidence was therefore limited, lacking consensus; however, a pattern emerged. According to one report she sounded guttural, glottal-stoppy, as if she were speaking Arabic. Night-Arabian, she thought, the dreamtongue of Scheherazade. Another version described her words as science-fictional, like Klingon, like a throat being cleared in a galaxy far, far away. Like Sigourney Weaver channelling a demon in *Ghostbusters.* One night in a spirit of research the ambassador's daughter left a tape recorder running by her bedside but when she heard the voice on the tape its death's-head ugliness, which was somehow both familiar and alien, scared her badly and she pushed the erase button, which erased nothing important. The truth was still the truth.

These agitated periods of sleep-speech were mercifully brief, and when they ended she would subside for a time, sweating and panting, into a state of dreamless exhaustion. Then abruptly she would awake again, convinced, in her disoriented state, that there was an intruder in her bedroom. There was no intruder. The intruder was an absence, a negative space in the darkness. She had no mother. Her mother had died giving her birth: the ambassador's wife had told her this much, and the ambassador, her father, had confirmed it. Her mother had been Kashmiri, and was lost to her, like paradise, like Kashmir, in a time before memory. (That the terms *Kashmir* and *paradise* were synonymous was one of her axioms, which everyone who knew her had to accept.) She trembled before her mother's absence, a void sentinel shape in the dark, and waited for the second calamity, waited without knowing she was waiting. After her father died—her brilliant, cosmopolitan father, Franco-American, "like Liberty", he said, her beloved, resented, wayward, promiscuous, often absent, irresistible father—she began to sleep soundly, as if she had been shriven. Forgiven her sins, or, perhaps, his. The burden of sin had been passed on. She did not believe in sin.

So until her father's death she was not an easy woman to sleep with, though she was a woman with whom men wanted to sleep. The pressure of men's desires was tiresome to her. The pressure of her own desires was for the most part unrelieved. The few lovers she took were variously unsatisfactory and so (as if to declare the subject closed) she soon enough settled on one pretty average fellow, and even gave serious consideration to his proposal of marriage. Then the ambassador was slaughtered on her doorstep like a halal chicken dinner, bleeding to death from a deep neck wound caused by a single slash of the assassin's blade. In broad daylight! How the weapon must have glistened in the golden morning sun; which was the city's quotidian blessing, or its curse. The daughter of the murdered man was a woman who hated good weather, but most of the year the city offered little else. Accordingly, she had to put up with long monotonous months of shadowless sunshine and dry, skin-cracking heat. On those rare mornings when she awoke to cloud cover and a hint of moisture in the air she stretched sleepily in bed, arching her back, and was briefly, even hopefully, glad; but the clouds invariably burned off by noon and then there it was again, the dishonest nursery blue of the sky that made the world look childlike and pure, the loud impolite orb blaring at her like a man laughing too loudly in a restaurant.

In such a city there could be no grey areas, or so it seemed. Things were what they were and nothing else, unambiguous, lacking the subtleties of drizzle, shade and chill. Under the scrutiny of such a sun there was no place to hide. People were everywhere on display, their bodies shining in the sunlight, scantily clothed, reminding her of advertisements. No mysteries here or depths; only surfaces and revelations. Yet to learn the city was to discover that this banal clarity was an illusion. The city was all treachery, all deception, a quick-change, quicksand metropolis, hiding its nature, guarded and secret in spite of all its apparent nakedness. In such a place even the forces of destruction no longer needed the shelter of the dark. They burned out of the morning's brightness, dazzling the eye, and stabbed at you with sharp and fatal light.

Her name was India. She did not like this name. People were never called Australia, were they, or Uganda or Ingushetia or Peru. In the mid-1960s her father, Max Ophuls (Maximilian Ophuls, raised in Strasbourg, France, in an earlier age of the world), had been America's best-loved, and then most scandalous, ambassador to India, but so what, children were not saddled with names like Herzegovina or Turkey or Burundi just because their parents had visited those lands and possibly misbehaved in them. She had been conceived in the East—conceived out of wedlock and born in the midst of the firestorm of outrage that twisted and ruined her father's marriage and ended his diplomatic career—but if that were sufficient excuse, if it was okay to hang people's birthplaces round their necks like albatrosses, then the world would be full of men and women called Euphrates or Pisgah or Iztaccíhuatl or Woolloomooloo. In America, damn it, this form of naming was not unknown, which spoiled her argument slightly and annoyed her more than somewhat. Nevada Smith, Indiana Jones, Tennessee Williams, Tennessee Ernie Ford: she directed mental curses and a raised middle finger at them all.

"India" still felt wrong to her, it felt exoticist, colonial, suggesting the appropriation of a reality that was not hers to own, and she insisted to herself that it didn't fit her anyway, she didn't feel like an India, even if her colour was rich and high and her long hair lustrous and black. She didn't want to be vast or subcontinental or excessive or vulgar or explosive or crowded or ancient or noisy or mystical or in any way Third World. Quite the reverse. She presented herself as disciplined, groomed, nuanced, inward, irreligious, understated, calm. She spoke with an English accent. In her behaviour she was not heated, but cool. This was the persona she wanted, that she had constructed with great determination. It was the only version of her that anyone in America, apart from her father and the lovers who had been scared off by her nocturnal proclivities, had ever seen. As to her interior life, her violent English history, the buried record of disturbed behaviour, the years of delinquency, the hidden episodes of her short but eventful past, these things were not subjects for discussion, were not (or were no longer) of concern to the general public. These days she had herself firmly in hand. The problem child within her was sublimated into her spare-time pursuits, the weekly boxing sessions at Jimmy Fish's boxing club on Santa Monica and Vine where Tyson and Christy Martin were known to work out and where the cold fury of her hitting made the male boxers pause to watch, the biweekly training sessions with a Clouseau-attacking Burt Kwouk look-alike who was a master of the close-combat martial art of Wing Chun, the sun-bleached blackwalled solitude of Saltzman's Moving Target shooting gallery out in the desert at 29 Palms, and, best of all, the archery sessions in downtown Los Angeles near the city's birthplace in Elysian Park, where her new gifts of rigid self-control, which she had learned in order to survive, to defend herself, could be used to go on the attack. As she drew back her golden Olympic-standard bow, feeling the pressure of the bowstring against her lips, sometimes touching the bottom of the arrow shaft with the tip of her tongue, she felt the arousal in herself, allowed herself to feel the heat rising in her while the seconds allotted to her for the shot ticked down towards zero, until at last she let fly, unleashing the silent venom of the arrow, revelling in the distant thud of her weapon hitting its target. The arrow was her weapon of choice.

She also kept the strangeness of her seeing under control, the sudden otherness of vision that came and went. When her pale eyes changed the things she saw, her tough mind changed them back. She did not care to dwell on her turbulence, never spoke about her childhood, and told people she did not remember her dreams.

On her twenty-fourth birthday the ambassador came to her door. She looked down from her fourth-floor balcony when he buzzed and saw him waiting in the heat of the day wearing his absurd silk suit like a French sugar daddy. Holding flowers, yet. "People will think you're my lover," India shouted down to Max, "my cradle-snatching Valentine." She loved the ambassador when he was embarrassed, the pained furrow of his brow, the right shoulder hunching up against his ear, the hand raised as if to ward off a blow. She saw him fracture into rainbow colours through the prism of her love. She watched him recede into the past as he stood below her on the sidewalk, each successive moment of him passing before her eyes and being lost forever, surviving only in outer space in the form of escaping light-rays. This is what loss was, what death was: an escape into the luminous wave-forms, into the ineffable speed of the light-years and the parsecs, the eternally receding distances of the cosmos. At the rim of the known universe an unimaginable creature would someday put its eye to a telescope and see Max Ophuls approaching, wearing a silk suit and carrying birthday roses, forever borne forward on tidal waves of light. Moment by moment he was leaving her, becoming an ambassador to such unthinkably distant elsewheres. She closed her eyes and opened them again. No, he was not billions of miles away amid the wheeling galaxies. He was here, correct and present, on the street where she lived.

He had recovered his poise. A woman in running clothes rounded the corner from Oakwood and cantered towards him, appraising him, making the easy judgements of the times, judgements about sex and money. He was one of the architects of the postwar world, of its international structures, its agreed economic and diplomatic conventions. His tennis game was strong even now, at his advanced age. The inside-out forehand, his surprise weapon. That wiry frame in long white trousers, carrying not much more than five per cent body fat, could still cover the court. He reminded people of the old champion Jean Borotra: those few old-timers who remembered Borotra. He stared with undisguised European pleasure at the jogger's American breasts in their sports bra. As she passed him he offered her a single rose from the enormous birthday bouquet. She took the flower; and then, appalled by his charm, by the erotic proximity of his snappy crackle of power, and by herself, accelerated anxiously away. Fifteen–love.

From the balconies of the apartment building the old Central and East European ladies were also staring at Max, admiringly, with the open lust of toothless age. His arrival was the high point of their month. They were out en masse today. Usually they gathered together in small street-corner clumps or sat in twos and threes by the courtyard swimming pool chewing the fat, sporting inadvisable beachwear without shame. Usually they slept a lot and when not sleeping complained. They had buried the husbands with whom they had spent forty or even fifty years of unregarded life. Stooped, leaning, expressionless, the old women lamented the mysterious destinies that had stranded them here, halfway across the world from their points of origin. They spoke in strange tongues that might have been Georgian, Croatian, Uzbek. Their husbands had failed them by dying. They were pillars that had fallen, they had asked to be relied upon and had brought their wives away from everything that was familiar into this shadowless lotus-land full of the obscenely young, this California whose body was its temple and whose ignorance was its bliss, and then proved themselves unreliable by keeling over on the golf course or face down in a bowl of noodle soup, thus revealing to their widows at this late stage in their lives the untrustworthiness of existence in general and of husbands in particular. In the evenings the widows sang childhood songs from the Baltic, from the Balkans, from the vast Mongolian plains.

The neighbourhood's old men were single, too, some inhabiting sagging sacks of bodies over which gravity had exerted far too much power, others grizzle-chopped and letting themselves go in dirty singlets and trousers with unbuttoned flies, while a third, jauntier contingent dressed sharply, affecting berets and bow ties. These natty gents periodically tried to engage the widows in conversation. Their efforts, with yellow glints of false teeth and melancholy sightings of slicked-down vestiges of hair beneath the doffed berets, were invariably and contemptuously ignored. To these elderly beaux, Max Ophuls was an affront, the ladies' interest in him a humiliation. They would have killed him if they could, if they had not been too busy staving off their own deaths.

India saw it all, the exhibitionist, desirous old women pirouetting and flirting on the verandahs, the lurking, spiteful old men. The antique Russian super, Olga Simeonovna, a bulbous denim-clad samovar of a woman, was greeting the ambassador as if he were a visiting head of state.

If there had been a red carpet on the premises she would have rolled it out for him.

"She keeps you waiting, Mr Ambassador, what you gonna do, the young. I say nothing against. Just, a daughter these days is more difficult, I was a daughter myself who for me my father was like a god, to keep him waiting unthinkable. Alas, daughters today are hard to raise and then they leave you flat. I sir am formerly mother, but now they are dead to me, my girls. I spit on their forgotten names. This is how it is."

All of which was spoken while turning a rooty potato in her hand. She was known to one and all in this her final neighbourhood as Olga Volga, and was by her own account the last surviving descendant of the legendary potato witches of Astrakhan, a fully fledged, honest-to-goodness enchantress, able by the subtle use of potato sorcery to induce love, prosperity or boils. In those distant places and long-gone times she had been the object of men's admiration and fear; now, thanks to the love of a sailor, since deceased, she was marooned in West Hollywood wearing outsized denim overalls and on her head a scarlet kerchief with white spots to cover her thinning white hair. In her hip pocket a spanner and a screwdriver with a Phillips head. Back then she could curse your cat, help you conceive or curdle your milk. Now she changed lightbulbs and peered into faulty ovens and collected the monthly rents.

"As to myself, sir," she insisted on informing the ambassador, "I live today neither in this world nor the last, neither in America nor Astrakhan. Also I would add neither in this world nor the next. A woman like me, she lives someplace in between. Between the memories and the daily stuff. Between yesterday and tomorrow, in the country of lost happiness and peace, the place of mislaid calm. This is our fate. Once I felt everything was okay. This I now don't feel. Consequently however I have no fear of death."

"I too am a national of that country, madam," he interrupted her gravely. "I too have lived long enough to acquire citizenship there."

She had been born a few miles east of the Volga River delta, within sight of the Caspian Sea. Then in her telling of it came the history of the twentieth century, shaped by potato magic. "Of course hard times," she said, to the old ladies on their balconies, to the old gentlemen by the pool, to India wherever and whenever she could corner her, right now to

Ambassador Max Ophuls on his daughter's twenty-fourth birthday. "Of course poverty; also oppression, dislocation, armies, servitude, today's kids they got it easy, they know nothing, I can see you are a man of sophistication who has gotten around some. Of course dislocation, survival, the necessity to be cunning like a rat. Am I right? Of course somewhere a man, a dream of elsewhere, a marriage, children, they don't stay, their lives are their own, they take them from you and go. Of course war, a husband lost, don't ask me about grief. Of course dislocation, hunger, deception, luck, another man, a good man, a man of the sea. Then a journey across water, the lure of the West, a journey across land, a second widowhood, a man will not last, present company not included, a man is not built to endure. In my life men were like shoes. I had two of them and they both wore out. After that I learned you could say to go barefoot. But I did not ask men to make things possible. Never I have asked this. Always it was what I knew that brought me what I wanted. My potato art, yes. Whether food, whether children, whether travel papers or work. Always my enemies failed and I in glory triumphed. The potato is powerful and all things may by it be accomplish. Only now comes the creeping of the years and even the potato it cannot turn back time. We know the world, am I right? We know how it ends."

He sent the driver up with the flowers and waited for India below. The new driver. India noted in her careful dispassionate way that this was a handsome man, even a beautiful one, fortysomething, tall, as graceful in his movement as the incomparable Max. He walked as if across a tightrope. There was pain in his face and he did not smile although the corners of his eyes were creased with laugh lines and he was staring at her with an unlooked-for intensity that felt like an electric shock. The ambassador did not insist on uniforms. The driver wore an open white shirt and chinos, the anti-uniform of the sun-blessed in America. The beautiful came to this city in huge pathetic herds, to suffer, to be humiliated, to see the powerful currency of their beauty devalued like the Russian rouble or Argentine peso; to work as bellhops, as bar hostesses, as garbage collectors, as maids. The city was a cliff and they were its stampeding lemmings. At the foot of the cliff was the valley of the broken dolls.

The driver dragged his gaze away from her, looking down towards the floor. He came, he said in halting reply to her enquiry, from Kashmir. Her heart leapt. A driver from paradise. His hair was a mountain stream. There were narcissi from the banks of rushing rivers and peonies from the high meadows growing on his chest, poking out through his open collar. Around him there raucously echoed the sound of the *swarnai.* No, that was ridiculous. She was not ridiculous, would never permit herself to sink into fantasy. The world was real. The world was as it was. She closed her eyes and opened them again and there was the proof of it. Normalcy was victorious. The deflowered driver waited patiently by the elevator, holding the door. She inclined her head to thank him. She noticed that his hands were bunched into fists and trembling. The doors closed and they began to descend.

The name he went by, the name he gave her when she asked, was Shalimar. His English was not good, barely functional. He would probably not have understood that phrase, barely functional. His eyes were blue, his skin colour lighter than hers, his hair grey with a memory of fair. She didn't need to know his story. Not today. Another time she might ask him if those were blue contacts, if that was his natural hair colour, if he was making a statement of personal style, or if this was a style imposed on him by her father who had known all his life how to impose, with such charm that you accepted the imposition as your own idea, as authentic. Her dead mother came from Kashmir also. She knew this about the woman about whom she knew little else (but surmised much). Her American father had never passed a driving test but loved buying cars. Therefore, drivers. They came and went. They wanted to be famous of course. Once, for a week or two, the ambassador had been driven by a gorgeous young woman who left to work in the daytime soaps. Other drivers had flickered briefly to life as dancers in music videos. At least two, one female, one male, had been successful in the field of pornographic cinema and she had run into their naked images late at night in hotel rooms here and there. She watched pornography in hotel rooms. It helped her sleep when she was away from home. She also watched pornography at home.

Shalimar from Kashmir escorted her downstairs. Was he legal? Did he have his papers? Did he even have a driving licence? Why had he been employed? Did he have a major penis, a penis worthy of late-night hotel viewing? Her father asked her what she wanted for her birthday. She looked at the driver and briefly wanted to be the kind of woman who could have asked him pornographic questions, right there in the elevator, within seconds of their first meeting; who could have talked dirty to this beautiful man, knowing that he would not have understood a word, that he would have smiled an employee's assenting smile without knowing what he was agreeing to. Did he take it in the ass? She wanted to see his smile. She didn't know what she wanted. She wanted to make documentary films. The ambassador should have known, should not have needed to ask. He should have brought her an elephant to ride down Wilshire Boulevard, or taken her skydiving, or to Angkor Wat or Machu Picchu or Kashmir.

She was twenty-four years old. She wanted to inhabit facts, not dreams. True believers, those nightmarish dreamers, grabbed at the corpse of the Ayatollah Khomeini, as once other true believers in another place, in India whose name she bore, had bitten off chunks of the cadaver of St Francis Xavier. One piece ended up in Macao, another in Rome. She wanted shadows, chiaroscuro, nuance. She wanted to see below the surface, the meniscus of the blinding brightness, to push through the hymen of the brightness, into the bloody hidden truth. What was not hidden, what was overt, was not true. She wanted her mother. She wanted her father to tell her about her mother, to show her letters, photographs, to bring messages from the dead. She wanted her lost story to be found. She didn't know what she wanted. She wanted lunch.

The car was a surprise. Max customarily went in for big classic English vehicles but this was something else entirely, a silver luxury speedmobile with batwing doors, the same futuristic machine in which people were time-travelling in the movies that year. To be chauffeur-driven in a sports car was an affectation unworthy of a great man, she thought, disappointed.

"There's no room for three people in this rocket ship," she said aloud. The ambassador dropped the keys into her hand. The car closed round the two of them, ostentatious, potent, wrong. The handsome driver, Shalimar from Kashmir, remained on the sidewalk, diminished into an insect in her wing mirror, his eyes like shining swords. He was a silverfish, a locust. Olga Volga the potato witch stood beside him and their dwindling bodies looked like numerals. Together they made the number 10.

She had felt the driver wanting to touch her in the elevator, felt his tearful yearning. That was puzzling. No, it was not puzzling. What was puzzling was that the need did not feel sexually charged. She felt herself transformed into an abstraction. As if by wanting to put his hand on her he hoped to reach out to someone else, across unknown dimensions of sad memory and lost event. As if she were just a representative, a sign. She wanted to be the kind of woman who could ask a driver, who do you want to touch when you want to touch me. Who, when you abstain from touching me, is not being touched by you? Touch me, she wanted to say to his uncomprehending smile, I'll be your conduit, your crystal ball. We can have sex in elevators and never mention it. Sex in transit zones, in places like elevators that are between one place and the next. Sex in *cars.* The transit zones traditionally associated with sex. When you fuck me you'll be fucking her, whoever she is or was, I don't want to know. I won't even be here, I'll be the channel, the medium. And the rest of the time, forget it, you're my father's employee. It'll be a *Last Tango* kind of thing without obviously butter. She said nothing to the aching man, who would not have understood anyway unless of course he would, she really had no knowledge of the level of his language skills, why was she making assumptions, why was she making this stuff up, she sounded ridiculous. She exited the elevator and let her hair down and went outside.

This was the last day she and her father would ever spend together. The next time she saw him it would be different. This was the last time.

"It's for you," he said, "the car, you can't be such a puritan that you don't want it." Space-time was like butter, she thought, driving fast, and this car the warm knife slicing through it. She didn't want it. She wanted to feel more than she felt. She wanted somebody to shake her, scream in her face, strike her. She was already numb, as if Troy had fallen. Yet things were good. She was twenty-four years old. There was a man who wanted to marry her and other men who did not, who wanted less. She had her first subject for a documentary film and there was money, enough to begin work. And her father was right beside her in the passenger seat as the DeLorean flew up the canyon. It was the first day of something. It was the last day of something else.

They ate hungrily in a high canyon lodge watched over by rows of antlered heads. Father and daughter, alike in their appetites, their high metabolic rates, their love of meat, their slender high-toned bodies. She chose venison to defy the watching heads of dead stags.

"O beast, I eat your ass."

This invocation she offered up aloud, to make him smile. He chose venison also but as an act of respect, he said, to give their absent bodies meaning. "This flesh whereof we eat is not their true flesh but the flesh of others like them, through whom their own lost forms may be conjured up and honoured." More proxies, she thought. My body in the elevator and now this meat on my plate.

"I'm a little freaked out by your driver," she said. "He looks at me as if I'm someone else. Are you sure about him? He checked out okay? What sort of name is that, Shalimar. Sounds like a club on La Brea with exotic dancers. Sounds like a cheap beach resort, or a trapeze artist in a circus. Oh, please," she raised an impatient hand before he condescendingly attempted to tell her the obvious, "spare me the horticultural explanation." She pictured the other Shalimar, the great Mughal garden of Kashmir, descending in verdant liquid terraces to a shining lake that she had never seen. The name meant "abode of joy". She set her jaw. "It still sounds like a candy bar to me. Also, by the way, speaking of names, I wanted to finally tell you, mine is pretty much a burden. This foreign country you made me carry around on my shoulders. I want to be some other name and smell as sweet. Maybe I'll use yours," she decided before he could reply. "Max, Maxine, Maxie. Perfect. Call me Maxie from now on."

He shook his head dismissively and ate his meat, not understanding that it was her way of begging him to stop mourning the male child he'd never had, to give up that old-fashioned sadness which he carried everywhere he went and which both wounded and offended her, because how could he allow his shoulders to sag beneath the weight of the unborn son sitting up there jeering at his failure, how could he permit himself to be tormented by that malicious incubus when she was standing right in front of him filled with love, and was she not his living image, was she not an altogether finer and worthier creature than any nonexistent boy? Her colouring and her green eyes might be her mother's, and her breasts certainly were, but almost everything else, she told herself, was the ambassador's legacy. When she spoke she failed to hear her other inheritance, the other, unknown cadences, and heard only her father's voice, its rise and fall, its mannerisms and pitch. When she looked in the mirror she blinded herself to the shadow of the unknown and saw only Max's face, his body type, his languid elegance of manner and form. All along one wall of her bedroom were mirrored, sliding closet doors and when she lay on her bed and admired her naked body, turning and turning it, striking attitudes for her own delight, she was frequently aroused, actually turned on, by the notion that this was the body her father would have had if he had been a woman. This firm jawline, this stalk of a neck. She was a tall young woman and her height was his gift, too, given in his own proportions; the relatively short upper body, the long legs. The spinal scoliosis, the slight curvature which hooked her head forward, giving her a hawklike, predatory air: that, too, came from him.

After he died she went on seeing him in her mirror. She was her father's ghost.

She did not mention the matter of the name again. The ambassador by his demeanour gave her to understand that he was doing her a favour by forgetting a piece of embarrassing behaviour, forgiving her by forgetting it, the way one forgives a urinating baby or a teenager who lurches home drunk and vomitous after passing an exam. Such forgiveness was irritating; but she in her turn let it go, making her behaviour the mirror of his. She mentioned nothing that mattered or rankled, not the childhood years in England during which thanks to him she had not known her own story, nor the woman who had not been her mother, the buttoned woman who had raised her in the aftermath of scandal, nor the woman who had been her mother, and of whom it was forbidden to speak.

They finished lunch and walked for a spell in the mountains, hiking like gods across the sky. It was not necessary to say anything. The world was speaking. She was the child of his old age. He was almost eighty years old, ten years younger than the wicked century. She admired him for the way he walked, without a hint of frailty in his gait. He could be a bastard, had in fact been a bastard more often than not, but he possessed, was possessed by, the will to transcendence, the interior power that enabled mountaineers to climb eight-thousand-metre peaks without oxygen, or monks to enter suspended animation for implausible numbers of months. He walked like a man in his prime; in, for example, his fifties. If the hornet of death were buzzing nearby right now, this demonstration of clock-stopping physical prowess would surely draw its sting. He had been fifty-seven when she was born. He walked as if he were younger than that now. She loved him for that will, felt it like a sword within herself, sheathed in her body, waiting. He had been a bastard as long as she could remember. He was not built to be a father. He was the high priest of the golden bough. He inhabited his enchanted grove and was adored, until he was assassinated by his successor. To become the priest, however, he also had had to murder his predecessor. Maybe she was a bastard too. Maybe she, too, could kill.

His bedtime stories, told on those unpredictable occasions when he had been at her childhood bedside, were not stories exactly. They were homilies such as Sun Tzu the philosopher of war might have delivered to his offspring. "The palace of power is a labyrinth of interconnecting rooms," Max once said to his sleepy child. She imagined it into being, walked towards it, half-dreaming, half-awake. "It's windowless," Max said, "and there is no visible door. Your first task is to find out how to get in. When you've solved that riddle, when you come as a supplicant into the first anteroom of power, you will find in it a man with the head of a jackal, who will try to chase you out again. If you stay, he will try to gobble you up. If you can trick your way past him, you will enter a second room, guarded this time by a man with the head of a rabid dog, and in the room after that you'll face a man with the head of a hungry bear, and so on. In the last room but one there's a man with the head of a fox. This man will not try to keep you away from the last room, in which the man of true power sits. Rather, he will try to convince you that you are already in that room and that he himself is that man.

"If you succeed in seeing through the fox-man's tricks, and if you get past him, you will find yourself in the room of power. The room of power is unimpressive and in it the man of power faces you across an empty desk. He looks small, insignificant, fearful; for now that you have penetrated his defences he must give you your heart's desire. That's the rule. But on the way out the fox-man, the bear-man, the dog-man and the jackal-man are no longer there. Instead, the rooms are full of half-human flying monsters, winged men with the heads of birds, eagle-men and vulture-men, man-gannets and hawk-men. They swoop down and rip at your treasure. Each of them claws back a little piece of it. How much of it will you manage to bring out of the house of power? You beat at them, you shield the treasure with your body. They rake at your back with gleaming blue-white claws. And when you've made it and are outside again, squinting painfully in the bright light and clutching your poor, torn remnant, you must persuade the sceptical crowd—the envious, impotent crowd!—that you have returned with everything you wanted. If you don't, you'll be marked as a failure forever.

"Such is the nature of power," he told her as she slipped towards sleep, "and these are the questions it asks. The man who chooses to enter its halls does well to escape with his life. The answer to the question of power, by the way," he added as an afterthought, "is this: Do not enter that labyrinth as a supplicant. Come with meat and a sword. Give the first guardian the meat he craves, for he is always hungry, and cut off his head while he eats: pof! Then offer the severed head to the guardian in the next room, and when he begins to devour it, behead him too. Baf! *Et ainsi de suite.* When the man of power agrees to grant your demands, however, you must not cut off his head. Be sure you don't! The decapitation of rulers is an extreme measure, hardly ever required, never recommended. It sets a bad precedent. Make sure, instead, that you ask not only for what you want but for a sack of meat as well. With the fresh meat supply you will lure the bird-men to their doom. Off with their heads! Snick-snack! Chop, chop, until you're free. Freedom is not a tea party, India. Freedom is a war."

The dreams came to her still as they had come to her child-self: visions of battle and victory. In sleep she tossed and turned and fought the war he had lodged within her. This was the inheritance she was sure of, her warrior future, her body like his body, her mind like his mind, her Excalibur spirit, like his, a sword pulled from a stone. He was quite capable of leaving her nothing in the way of cash or goods, quite capable of arguing that disinheritance was the last thing of value he had to give her, the last thing he needed to teach and she to learn. She turned away from thoughts of death and looked out across the blue hills to the orange late-afternoon sky melting idly into the warm, sluggish sea. A cool breeze caught at her hair. In 1769, somewhere down there, the Franciscan Fray Juan Crespi found a freshwater spring and named it Santa Monica because it reminded him of the tears shed by the mother of Saint Augustine when her son renounced the Christian Church. Augustine returned to the Church, of course, but in California the tears of Saint Monica still flowed. India was contemptuous of religion, her contempt being one of the many proofs that she was not an India. Religion was folly and yet its stories moved her and this was confusing. Would her dead mother, hearing of her godlessness, have wept for her, like a saint?

In Madagascar they periodically hauled the dead out of their graves and danced with them all night. There were people in Australia and Japan for whom the dead were worthy of worship, for whom ancestors were sacred beings. Everywhere you went a few of the dead were studied and remembered and these were the best of the dead, the least dead, living in the world's memory. The less celebrated, less advantaged dead were content to be kept alive within a few loving (or even hating) breasts, even in a single human heart, within the frontiers of which they could laugh and chatter and make love and behave well and badly and go to Hitchcock movies and vacation in Spain and wear embarrassing dresses and enjoy gardening and hold controversial opinions and commit unforgivable crimes and tell their children they loved them more than life. The deadness of India's mother, however, was of the worst and deadest kind. The ambassador had entombed her memory under a pyramid of silence. India wanted to ask him about her, desperately wanted it every time they met and through all the moments they spent together. The wanting was like a spear in her belly. But she never managed it. The deadly dead woman her mother had become was lost in the ambassador's silence, had been erased by it. This was stone death, death walled up in the Egyptian burial chamber of his silence along with her artifacts and foibles and everything that might have allowed her some small measure of immortality. India could have hated her father for this refusal. But then she would have had nobody to love.

They were watching the sun set into the Pacific through the beautifully dirty air and the ambassador was mumbling verses under his breath. He had been an American for most of his life but French poetry was still where he went for sustenance.

"Homme libre, toujours tu chériras la mer! La mer est ton miroir. . . ." After he saved her life, he had guided her reading; by now she knew what he had wanted her to know. She knew this. O free man, you will always love the sea. The sea's your mirror; you contemplate your soul in its surges as it endlessly unrolls. So he was thinking about death, too. She returned him Baudelaire for Baudelaire. *"Le ciel est triste et beau comme un grand reposoir; Le soleil s'est noyé dans son sang qui se fige."* And again: "*Le soleil s'est noyé dans son sang qui se fige . . . Ton souvenir en moi luit comme un ostensoir!"* The sky is sad and beautiful like a great, a great what, some sort of altar. The sun has drowned in its own congealing blood. The sun has drowned in its own congealing blood. Your memory shines in me like, damn it, *ostensoir.* Oh, right: a monstrance. Again with the religious imagery. New images urgently needed to be made. Images for a godless world. Until the language of irreligion caught up with the holy stuff, until there was a sufficient poetry and iconography of godlessness, these sainted echoes would never fade, would retain their problematic power, even over her.

She said it again, in English: "Your memory shines in me."

"Let's go home," he murmured, kissing her on the cheek. "It's getting chilly. Let's not overdo it. I'm an old guy now."

It was the first time she had heard him acknowledge his infirmity, the first time in her experience that he had conceded the power of time. And why had he kissed her then, spontaneously, when there was no need to do so. That, too, was an indication of weakness, a misjudgement, like the gift of the vulgar car. A sign of slipping control. They were no longer in the habit of demonstrating their affections to each other, except perfunctorily. By such samurai abstinence did they give each other proofs of their love.

"My time is being swept away," the ambassador said. "Nothing will remain." He foretold the Cold War's accelerated ending, the Soviet Union's house-of-cards collapse. He knew that the Wall would fall and that the reunification of Germany could not be held back and would happen more or less overnight. He foresaw the invasion of Western Europe by the elated job-hungry Ossis in their Trabants. Ceauşescu's Mussoliniesque ending, and the elegiac presidencies of the writers, of Václav Havel and Arpad Goncz, these too he foresaw. He closed his mind to other, less palatable possibilities, however. He tried to believe that the global structures he had helped to build, the pathways of influence, money and power, the multinational associations, the treaty organizations, the frameworks of co-operation and law whose purpose had been to deal with a hot war turned cold, would still function in the future that lay beyond what he could foresee. She saw in him a desperate need to believe that the ending of his age would be happy, and that the new world which would come after would be better than the one that would die with him. Europe, free of the Soviet threat, and America, free of the need to remain permanently at battle stations, would build that new world in friendship, a world without walls, a frontierless newfound land of infinite possibility. The doomsday clock would no longer be set at seven seconds to midnight. The emerging economies of India, Brazil and a newly opened-up China would be the world's new powerhouses, the counterweights to the American hegemony of which he had always, as an internationalist, disapproved. When she saw him surrender to the utopian fallacy, to the myth of the perfectibility of man, India knew he could not have long to live. He looked like a tightrope walker trying to keep his balance even though there was no longer a rope beneath his feet.

The weight of the inexorable bore down on her, as if the gravitational force of the earth had suddenly increased. When she was younger they had often touched. He could place his lips against any part of her body, her hand, her cheek, her back, and find a bird in there and make it speak. Birdsong burst from her skin under the magic pressure of his mouth, soaring, celebratory. Until the age of eight she would climb him like an Everest. She had learned the story of the Himalayas on his knee, the story of the giant proto-continents, of the moment when India broke off from Gondwanaland and moved across the proto-oceans towards Laurasia. She closed her eyes and saw the huge collision, the mighty mountains crumpling up into the sky. He taught her a lesson about time, about the slowness of the earth: *the collision is still happening.* So if he was a Himalaya, if he too had been caused by the smashing together of great forces, by a clash of worlds, then he, too, was growing still. The collision in him was also still taking place. He was her mountain-father and she his mountaineer. He held her hands in his and up she came until she was straddling his shoulders, her groin against his neck. He kissed her stomach and she somersaulted backward off his shoulders to the floor. One day he said, No more of that. She wanted to cry but controlled herself. Childhood was over? Very well, then, it was over. She would put aside childish things.

The freeway home was empty, shockingly empty, as if the world were ending, and while they were floating along in that asphalt void the ambassador again began to speak volubly, the words crowding out of him like traffic, trying to make up for the absence of the cars. Volubility came easily to Max Ophuls, but it was just one of his many techniques of concealment, and he was never more hidden than when he seemed most open. For the greater part of his life he had been a burrower, a man of secrets, whose job it was to uncover the mysteries of others while protecting his own, and when by choice or necessity he spoke the use of paradox had long been his preferred disguise. They moved down the empty freeway so swiftly that it seemed they were standing still, with the ocean to their right and the city beginning to twinkle to their left, and it was of the city that Max decided to speak because he knew he had already said too much about himself, shown too much, like an amateur. So now he praised the city, commended it precisely for the qualities that were commonly held to be its greatest faults. That the city had no focal point, he professed hugely to admire. The idea of the centre was in his view outdated, oligarchic, an arrogant anachronism. To believe in such a thing was to consign most of life to the periphery, to marginalize and in doing so to devalue. The decentred promiscuous sprawl of this giant invertebrate blob, this jellyfish of concrete and light, made it the true democratic city of the future. As India navigated the hollow freeways her father lauded the city's bizarre anatomy, which was fed and nourished by many such congealed and flowing arteries but needed no heart to drive its mighty flux. That it was a desert in disguise caused him to celebrate the genius of human beings, their ability to populate the earth with their imaginings, to bring water to the wilderness and bustle to the void; that the desert had its revenge on the complexions of its conquerors, drying them, ingraining lines and furrows, provided those triumphant mortals with the salutary lesson that no victory was absolute, that the struggle between earthlings and the earth could never be decided in favour of either combatant, but swung back and forth through all eternity. That it was a hidden city, a city of strangers, appealed to him most of all. In the Forbidden City of the Chinese emperors, only royalty had the privilege of remaining occult. In this brilliant burg, however, secrecy was freely available to all comers. The modern obsession with intimacy, with the revelation of the self to the other, was not to Max's taste. An open city was a naked whore, lying invitingly back and turning every trick; whereas this veiled and difficult place, this erotic capital of the obscure stratagem, knew precisely how to arouse and heighten our metropolitan desires.

She was used to such soliloquies, his fugues on themes of this or that; used, also, to his habit of half-humorous perversity. But now his praise-song seemed to cross a frontier and bear him away from her into a shadow. When he claimed to admire the city's powerful gangs for the thrilling casual potency of their violence and the tag artists for their transient encrypted graffiti; when he praised the earthquakes for their majesty and the landslides for their reproof to human vanity; when with no apparent irony he celebrated the junk food of America and waxed lyrical about the new banality of diet cola; when he admired the strip malls for their neon and the chain stores for their ubiquity; when he declined to criticize the produce on sale in the farmers' markets, the visually delightful apples that tasted like cotton puffs, the bananas made of pulped paper, the odourless flowers, calling them symbols of the inevitable triumph of illusion over reality that was the single most obvious truth about the history of the human race; when he, who had been a model of probity in his own public (though not sexual) life, admitted to secret feelings of admiration for a corrupt local official because of the flamboyant daring of his corruption and, contradicting himself, cynically lauded a second corrupt local official for the sneaky, decade-long subtlety of his crimes, then India began to see that in the depths of the old age whose effects he had so heroically concealed, even from her, he had lost his hold on joy, and that failure had eaten at him from within, eroding his ability to discriminate and to make moral judgements, and if things continued to deteriorate along these lines, he would eventually become incapable of making any choices at all, restaurant menus would become mysteries to him, and even the choice between getting out of bed in the morning and spending the daylight hours between the sheets would become impossible to make. And when the final choice stymied him, the choice between breathing and not breathing, then he would surely die.

"I used to long for your good opinion," she told him, to silence him. "But now that I'd have to share it with all this shit I'm not so sure I want it any more."

They got back to her apartment building and the driver was waiting, eyes still ablaze, standing exactly where she had last seen him, as if he hadn't moved all day. Flowers grew out of the concrete sidewalk at his feet and his hands and clothes were red with blood. What? What was that? She blinked and squinted and of course it was not so, he was flowerless, spotless, waiting patiently as a good employee should. Also, he had been busy in their absence. He had made his way up to Woodrow Wilson Drive and brought down the ambassador's Bentley. Look: there it was, large as life. Why hadn't she seen it right away? Why did such moments come to her; whence this hallucinatory curse? Had she done something to annoy Olga Simeonovna and been placed under a potato spell born in the Volga River delta centuries ago, when goblins walked the earth? But she didn't believe in potato magic either. She was overtired, she thought. Things would settle down if she could just get a good, uninterrupted night's sleep. She promised herself a pill at bedtime. She promised herself a clean, uncluttered life. She promised herself ease, an end to turbulence. She promised herself to be content with the humdrum reassurances of the everyday.

"Where'd you find him, anyway, your Mughal gardener," she asked her father, who didn't seem to be listening. "Shalimar," she insisted. "The driver with the phoney name. His poor English. Did he pass the written test?"

The ambassador waved a dismissive hand. "Stop worrying about it," he said. That made her worry about it. "Happy birthday," he added, dismissing her. *"Un bisou."*

After the assassination, India, watching television, would see Gorbachev getting off a plane in Moscow, having survived the attempted Communist coup against him. He looked shaken, imprecise, blurry at the edges, like a watercolour smudged by rain. Somebody asked him if he intended to abolish the Communist Party and in his shock at the question, his confusion, his indecision, she saw his weakness. The Party had been Gorbachev's cradle, his life. And he was being asked to abolish it? No, his whole body said, trembling, fuzzy, how can I, I will not; and at that moment he became irrelevant, history swept past him, he turned into a bankrupt hitchhiker on the verges of the freeway he had built in his glory days, watching the wild cars, the Yeltsins, roaring past him into the future. For the man of power, too, the house of power can be a treacherous place. In the end he, too, must fight his way out of it, past the swooping bird-men. He emerges empty-handed and the crowd, the cruel crowd, laughs. Gorbachev looked like Moses, she thought, the prophet unable to enter the Promised Land. And that was when he began to look like her father watching the sunset.

On another day, one of the timeless days after Max's murder, she saw another vision of him. In South Africa a man walked out of prison after a lifetime sequestered from the public gaze. Nobody really knew what this Lazarus was going to look like. The only photograph the papers ever printed had been taken decades earlier. The man in that picture was heavy-set, a raging bull, a Mike Tyson look-alike. A flame-eyed revolutionary. But this man was tall and slender and walked with gentle grace. When she saw that silhouette, long and skinny as a Spielberg alien, walking to freedom with the klieg lights behind it, she knew she was seeing her father, raised from the dead. Emotion leapt up in her; but resurrections don't happen, they really don't, and it wasn't her father. As the glare of the lights stopped flooding the camera lens India understood that she was looking at an allegory of the future, the future her father had not wanted to imagine. Mandela, metamorphosed from firebrand into peacemaker, with wicked Winnie at his side. Morality and immorality, the beatified and the corrupted, walked towards the cameras, hand in hand, and in love.

In the capital city of the billion-dollar industries of film, television and recorded music Max Ophuls never went to the movies, detested television drama and comedy, owned no sound system, and happily foretold the coming end of these temporary perversions, which, he predicted, would shortly be abandoned by their devotees in favour of the infinitely superior appeal of the immediacy, spontaneity and continuity of live performance, the thrilling power of the physical presence of the performer. In spite of this melancholically purist position the ambassador frequently descended from his ivory tower on the mountaintop road named after the president who died dreaming of a league of united nations, and like the Assyrian in the poem who came down like a wolf on the fold, occupied, under cover of night, the penthouse suite he maintained in one of the city's best hotels. It was widely held that many ladies with big careers in the despised forms had been entertained there. When they asked him why he refused to see their movies he replied devotedly that he was experiencing the thrilling power of their live performances instead, and nothing they could do on screen could equal what they were doing with such immediacy, spontaneity, continuity and presence right there in the famous hotel.

On the day before Max's death the first bad portent manifested itself in the form of a contretemps with an Indian movie star. In the beginning Max had had no idea she even was a film actress, this girl with the skin the colour of scorched earth, the well-concealed body and the demure manner of a disciple walking in the footsteps of a great *rishi.* She began following him around the lobby of the great hotel day after day until he demanded to know her business and was told in the low voice of the deep fan, the heart fan, that she had been drawn into his gravitational field just as the planet Venus had been sucked into its orbit around the sun and she asked for nothing better than to be allowed to move around him at a respectful distance for, perhaps, the rest of her life. Her name, Zainab Azam, meant nothing to him, but at his age he had no wish to look so beautiful a gift horse in the mouth. In his suite after their first lovemaking she suddenly spoke with detailed knowledge and boundless admiration about his long-past ambassadorship to India, when he had coined the saying *India is chaos making sense* which was now to be found in all books of quotations and which was used on an almost weekly basis by some Indian public figure or other, always with pride. She told him that he was the Rudyard Kipling of ambassadors, the only one of all the envoys in all the embassies down all the years who had truly understood

India, and she was his reward for that understanding. She asked for nothing, refused his gifts, disappeared into an inaccessible dimension of her own for most of every day but always returned, demure and self-effacing as ever until she undressed, after which she was a fire and he her slow but eager fuel. What are you doing with an old reprobate like me, he asked her, shocked into self-deprecation by her beauty. Her reply was so obviously a lie that it was a good thing his vanity reasserted itself in the nick of time and whispered in his ear that he should accept it humbly as the unvarnished truth.

"Worshipping you," she said.

She reminded him of a woman who had been dead to him for over twenty years. She reminded him of his daughter. She could only have been two or three years older than India, four or five years older than India's mother when he saw her for the last time. Max Ophuls found himself imagining in an idle moment that the two young women, his daughter and his sexual partner, might meet and become friends, but that was a possibility he discarded with a swift shudder of revulsion. Zainab Azam was the last lover of his long life and fucked him as if she were trying to erase all the many women who had gone before. She told him nothing about herself and did not appear to mind that he never asked. This state of affairs, which the ambassador considered close to ideal, persisted splendidly until the evening before the last day, when Max made his brief, ill-advised return to public life.

The question that nobody could answer in the days after the assassination was why, after the long years of the self-denying ordinance that had removed him from the banalizing, hollowing-out effects of the public eye, Max Ophuls chose to go on television to denounce the destruction of paradise in the florid language of a fading age. On an impulse he had telephoned an acquaintance, the West Coast's most celebrated late-night talk-show host, to ask if he might appear on the programme as soon as possible. The great media celebrity was both astonished and delighted to accommodate him. The talk-show host had long wanted Max on his show because of his fabled gifts as a raconteur. Once at the home of Marlon Brando the famous television personality had been entranced by Max Ophuls's anecdotal genius—by his stories of how Orson Welles would arrive at and depart from restaurants through their kitchens, to ensure that while he was amazing his dining companions by ordering nothing but a plain green salad the kitchen staff were filling his waiting limousine with boxes full of profiteroles and chocolate cake; and of Chaplin's Christmas dinner for the Hispanics of Hollywood, at which Luis Buñuel had solemnly, in the spirit of surrealism, completely dismantled Chaplin's Christmas tree; and of a visit to Thomas Mann, exiled in Santa Monica with the air of a man guarding the crown jewel of himself; and of a drunken night's carousing with William Faulkner; and of Fitzgerald's despairing transformation into the hack scenarist Pat Hobby; and of the improbable liaison between Warren Beatty and Susan Sontag, which allegedly took place on an unspecified date in the parking lot at the In-N-Out Burger eatery on Sunset and Orange.

By the time the ambassador, an amateur of local history, had launched into an account of the subterranean lives of the mysterious lizard people who supposedly dwelt in tunnels below Los Angeles, the talk-show host had become possessed by the idea of getting this reclusive extrovert to reveal himself on television, and had pursued him down the years with a fidelity that bore a close resemblance to unrequited love. That a man who despised the movies was also an encyclopedia of Hollywood lore was enjoyably odd; when the man in question had also lived a life as rich as Max Ophuls's—Max, the Resistance hero, the philosopher prince, the billionaire power-broker, the maker of the world!—this made him irresistible.

The talk show had been recorded in the late afternoon, and things did not go as the famous host had planned. Ignoring all invitations to repeat his most enjoyable anecdotes, Max Ophuls launched instead into a political diatribe on the so-called Kashmir issue, a monologue whose excessive vehemence and total lack of wit distressed his interlocutor more than he was able to express. That Ophuls of all men, this brilliant storyteller of infinite charm, should finally emerge from the shadows into the redemptive and validating light of television, but then turn at once into a ratings-sapping current-affairs bore, was unimaginable, unbearable, and yet it was happening right before the studio audience's suddenly soporific eyes. The talk-show host had the feeling that he was watching the drowning of one reality, the reality in which he lived, by a sudden flood from the other side of the world, an alien deluge in response to which his beloved viewers would form a flood of their own, pouring over in the midnight hour of the show's transmission to the channel where his bitter rival, the other talk-show host, the tall bony gap-toothed one from New York, would be dancing in a rain of gold.

"We who live in these luxury limbos, the privileged purgatories of the earth, have set aside thoughts of paradise," Max was roaring into the camera in a series of high-flown locutions, "yet I tell you that I have seen it and walked by its fish-rich lakes. If thoughts of paradise do occur to us, we think of Adam's fall, of the expulsion from Eden of the parents of humanity. However, I have not come to speak of the fall of man, but the collapse of paradise itself. In Kashmir it is paradise itself that is falling; heaven on earth is being transformed into a living hell." Thus, in the unambassadorial language of a gospel-pulpit fire-eater, which was a world away from the veiled verbiage of diplomacy and came as a shock to everyone who knew and admired the habitual suavity of his speech, Max ranted about fanaticism and bombs at a time when the world was briefly full of hope and had little interest in his killjoy news. He lamented the drowning of blue-eyed women and the murder of their golden children. He railed against the coming of cruel flames to a distant city made of wood. He spoke too of the tragedy of the *pandits,* the Brahmins of Kashmir, who were being driven from their homeland by the assassins of Islam. The rapes of young girls, the fathers set alight, burning like beacons prophesying doom. Max Ophuls could not stop speaking. Once he had begun it was plain that a great tide had risen in him which would not be denied. Across the face of the celebrated talk-show host on whose programme this diatribe was delivered, and for whom the legendarily media-shy Ambassador Ophuls's agreement to be interviewed had represented the culmination of a decade-long pursuit, there now spread a red choleric glow, in which the fury of a disappointed lover mingled with the panic of an entertainer who could hear the future, the sound of channels being changed all over America round about midnight.

After Max's host finally managed to break into his guest's soliloquy and terminate the interview, he briefly considered both suicide and murder. He committed neither solecism, contenting himself, instead, with television's best revenge. He thanked Max for his fascinating views, guided him courteously to the exit, and then personally supervised the editing of the Ophuls interview; which he cut, to shreds, to the bone.

That night in Max's hotel suite the ambassador and Zainab Azam watched a greatly abbreviated version of the paradise monologue, and it was probably true that the heavy cuts had changed the sense of what was said, that this truncated remnant had tilted the balance of the argument and distorted the ambassador's meaning, but at any rate when Max's image faded from the screen his lover rose from their bed for the last time in her life, quivering with anger, cured of both worship and desire. "I didn't mind that you didn't know a damn thing about me," she told him, "but it's too bad you had to prove you were dumb about something that really matters." Then she let fly a fusillade of dirty words that earned Max Ophuls's respect, so much so that he forbore to mention that it was strange that someone suddenly claiming to be speaking as an outraged Muslim should have so foul a mouth; nor did he argue that her behaviour in recent weeks had not indicated that matters devotional often featured prominently in her thoughts. He understood that the cause of her anger was his "bias" towards the Hindus, and that it would do him no good to explain that his equal and fervently expressed horror at the slaughter of innocent Muslims had been deleted from the programme by the vindictive scissors of the network apparatchiks, because the rage of religion had risen up in her and the very rarity of her ardour made it impossible to quell.

As to the truth about herself, which she believed she had so carefully concealed from him, he knew it all, had discovered her identity weeks ago from the chauffeur who went by the name of Shalimar. Back home in India there were tens of millions of men who would have cut off their right ears or little fingers for the privilege of five minutes of Zainab Azam's company. She was the hottest box-office star in that distant firmament, a sex goddess such as the Indian cinema had never seen, and was consequently unable to leave her design-magazine home in the Pali Hill district of Bombay without a phalanx of bodyguards and a convoy of armoured limousines. In America, where nobody then knew that the Indian movies existed, she had found her freedom, and during the affair with Max Ophuls she had revelled in her luxurious anonymity, in his beautiful unknowing, which was why he had never revealed to her that he knew everything there was to know, for example about the broken heart she was nursing and for which he was no more than a temporary palliative, and about the gangsterish movie-star boyfriend who had broken that heart as insouciantly as he crashed and wrote off vintage American motorcars, Stutz Bearcats, Duesenbergs, Cords. Even now at the end of the affair old Max Ophuls in his generosity allowed her to go on believing in the cloak of secrecy beneath which she had permitted herself to do so much that had been so pleasurable in his bed.

He called the chauffeur and asked him to drive the lady home. It is probable that this telephone call sealed his fate, or rather that what had been waiting to happen was finally precipitated by the anger that spilled out of Zainab Azam into the driver's ears. After the assassination, when she was briefly under suspicion as the possible perpetrator of a crime of passion, the great movie star remembered the fellow's last words to her. "For every O'Dwyer," he had said in excellent Urdu as she got out of the car, "there is a Shaheed Udham Singh, and for every Trotsky a Mercader awaits."

Because she was wallowing in the tar pits of her own anger Zainab had not taken this boastful statement seriously. The name Mercader meant nothing to her anyway. The story of the death of Trotsky was not among her personal golden treasury of tales, but as for the story of the man who murdered the imperialist lieutenant-governor who had sanctioned the Amritsar massacre, the story of Udham Singh who went to England and waited for six years and then shot O'Dwyer at a public meeting, this was well known. It didn't occur to Zainab that the driver was being serious. Men were always trying to ingratiate themselves with her, after all, and yes, maybe she had said something to the effect that Max Ophuls was a bastard and she wished he was dead, but that was just her way of talking, she was an artist of passion, a hot-blooded woman, and how else should such a woman speak of a man who had proved himself unworthy of her love? She herself was incapable of murder, she was a woman of peace and also, excuse me, a star, there was the responsibility to her public to consider, a person in her position had to set an example. So soulful was her deposition, so vast and innocent were her eyes, so profound was her guilty horror at the thought that the assassin had confessed his crime to her before he committed it, and that if she had been paying attention to the confession she could have saved a human life, even if it was only the life of a human worm like Max Ophuls, so self-evidently genuine was her self-criticism, that the police officers investigating the crime, hard, cynical men inured to the wiles of American movie queens, became her loyal fans for life and spent substantial portions of their spare time learning Hindustani and hunting down videos of her movies, even the early terrible ones when she was to be frank a little on the chubby side.

The second portent came on the morning of the murder, when Shalimar the driver approached Max Ophuls at breakfast, handed him his schedule card for the day, and gave in his notice. The ambassador's drivers tended to be short-term appointees, inclined to move on to new adventures in pornography or hairdressing, and Max was accustomed to the cycle of acquisition and loss. This time, however, he was shaken, though he did not care to show it. He concentrated on his day's appointments, trying not to let the card tremble. He knew Shalimar's real name. He knew the village he came from and the story of his life. He knew the intimate connection between his own scandalous past and this grave unscandalous man who never laughed in spite of the creased eyes that hinted at a happier past, this man with a gymnast's body and a tragedian's face who had slowly become more of a valet than a mere driver, a silent yet utterly solicitous body servant who understood what Max needed before he knew it himself, the lighted cigar that materialised just as he was reaching for the humidor, the right cuff-links that were laid out on his bed each morning with the perfect shirt, the ideal temperature for his bathwater, the right times to be absent as well as the correct moments to appear. The ambassador was carried back to his Strasbourgeois childhood years in a Belle Époque mansion near the old synagogue, since destroyed, and found himself marvelling at the rebirth in this man from a distant mountain valley of the lost traditions of service of the pampered prewar culture of Alsace.

There seemed to be no limits to Shalimar's willingness. When the ambassador, to test him, mentioned having heard that the Prince of Wales made his valet hold his penis while he urinated, to control the direction of the flow, the man whose real name was not Shalimar inclined his head an inch or so and murmured, "I also, if you wish." Later, after what had to happen had happened, it became clear that the assassin had deliberately drawn his victim almost as close as a lover, had effaced his own personality with the strategic discipline of a great warrior in order to study the true face of the enemy and learn his strengths and weaknesses, as if this vicious killer had been gripped by the need to know as intimately as possible the life he planned so brutally to terminate. It was said in court that such despicable behaviour proved the murderer to be a person so inhumanly cold-blooded, so calculatingly icy of heart, so fiendishly diseased of soul that it would never be safe to return him to the company of civilized men.

The schedule card did begin to tremble in Max's hand in spite of all his efforts to restrain it. Once, in the interregnum between the scandal that had deprived him of his Indian ambassadorship and his appointment to the covert ambassadorial-level job that remained a secret even from his daughter until after his death, Max Ophuls had lost his way. The sudden shapelessness of his days, after long years in which they would be planned and programmed in fifteen-minute segments, shook and bewildered him, until his secretary had the brainwave of reinstating the little daily appointment cards to which he had grown so accustomed, and filling them with things to do. Gone, inevitably, were his appointments with ministers and captains of industry, his invitations to upper-echelon conferences and his ambassadorial receptions for visiting notables. This was a humbler schedule—eight a.m., get up, go to bathroom, eight-twenty, walk dog, eight-thirty, read newspaper—but it restored a semblance of shape, and Max Ophuls held on to that shred with intense determination and slowly pulled himself out of the depression that had threatened to claim his life. Ever since his recovery from that minatory bout of mental illness Max Ophuls made sure there would always be a little white card waiting for him each morning, the little white card that meant that the universe had not descended into chaos, that the laws of men and nature still held sway, that life had direction and purpose, and that the inchoate outlaw void could not swallow him up.

Now the void was yawning again. It was Shalimar's arrival in Max's life that had reawakened Kashmir in him, had brought back that paradise from which he had been expelled long years before. It was in a way for Shalimar, or rather for the love they had once shared, that Max had found his way to the television studios to deliver his last oration. It was on account of Shalimar, then, that he had lost Zainab Azam. And now Shalimar too was leaving. Max had a vision of his open grave, of a rectilinear black hole huddling in the ground, as empty as his life, and felt the darkness measuring him for his shroud. "We'll discuss this nonsense later," he said, affecting nonchalance even though sudden terror had risen in his throat like bile. He tore up the schedule of the day's events. "I'm going to see India. Get the goddamn car."

When they were on Laurel Canyon the Himalayas began to rise around them, at high speed, like special effects. This was the third portent. Unlike his daughter and her mother Max Ophuls did not possess the gift or curse of occasional second sight and so when he saw the white eight-thousand-metre giants smashing up into the sky, bearing away the neighbourhood's split-level homes, designer pets and exotic plant life he trembled with fear. If he was seeing visions it meant that trouble was coming. It would be extreme in nature and would not be long delayed. The murderous illusion of the Himalayas persisted for a full ten seconds, so that the Bentley seemed to be skidding down a spectral ice-valley towards certain destruction, but then as if in a dream a traffic light reared up out of the snow and guided by that red beacon the whole city came back unscathed. Max's throat felt sore and raw, as if he had caught a chill in the thin Karakoram air. He pulled out his silver hip-flask, gulped down a burning mouthful of whisky and called his daughter on the phone.

It had been months since India had seen him but she had made no reproach. These hiatuses were not unusual. Max Ophuls had saved her life once but these days his sense of family was weak and his need for contact with his own blood was intermittent and easily satisfied. He was happiest when immersed in worlds of his own making or discovery, busying himself in these years of his retirement with the revised version of his classic book on the nature of power which India had received in the form of bedtime stories, and lately on a bizarre quest—one that his daughter at first dismissed as the obsession of an old fellow with too much time on his hands—for the rumoured tunnel complexes of those apocryphal lizard people of Los Angeles whose subterranean lives he had once conjured up at dinner with the famous talk-show host, and which led him in his expensive chauffeur-driven vehicles into some unsavoury neighbourhoods whose armed gangs he and Shalimar had at least once been obliged to flee at high speed. The ambassador had always been insatiably curious, and also possessed a dangerous, abiding belief in his own indestructibility, so that in the course of his lizard odyssey around South Central Los Angeles and the City of Industry he commanded Shalimar to stop the car outside the gates of an embattled high school past which even police cars would fearfully accelerate at certain times of day, and using field glasses through a wound-down window he commenced in his penetrating voice to forecast who amongst the emerging youngsters would end up in jail and who would go to college, until the driver, seeing the weapons emerging from their hiding places, the unsheathed knives like sharks, the unholstered snouts of the handguns, decided without waiting to be told to floor it and get out of there before the bad guys could start up their motorbikes and hunt them down.

When India heard her father's voice on the telephone, however, she understood that it was not the usual, confident Max Ophuls, dipped at birth like Achilles in the magic waters of invulnerability, who was coming to pay her a visit. Her father's voice sounded hoarse and weak, as if it were finally buckling under the weight of all Max's eight decades, and there was a new note in it, a note so unexpected that it took India a moment to realize that it was fear. She herself was in a preoccupied frame of mind that morning. Love of all things was pursuing her and she had an aversion to being hunted in general and to love in particular. Love was coming after her in the form of the young man in the neighbouring apartment, literally the boy next door, an idea so comical that it would have been endearing had she not erected steel walls of plate armour against the very concept of being endeared. She had begun to think she would have to move house to escape this inescapably claustrophobic assault. She could not remember his name even though he told her repeatedly that it was easy because it rhymed. "Jack Flack," he said. "See? You'll never forget it. You'll never get me out of your mind. You'll think of my name in bed, in the bathtub, driving the freeways, at the grocery store. You might as well marry me. It's inevitable. I love you. Face the facts."

It had probably been a mistake to have sex with him but he was undeniably attractive in an average sort of corn-fed white boy way and he had caught her at a susceptible time. He was the average perfected, the ordinary made super-ordinary, the boy next door raised to the Platonic ideal of boy-next-doorness, and as a result you saw him on giant billboards everywhere in that city dedicated to idealization, his flaxen hair and innocent eyes, his face free from history or pain, he wore alligator shirts here and Stetsons there and underpants in a third place and on all of the billboards he was wearing his super-averagely attractive, super-averagely goofy smile, his body glistening like a young god's, *le dieu moyen,* the average god of average folks, who had not been born or grown up or suffered life in any way at all, but had sprung like Athena fully formed from the aching head of some middle-of-the-road Zeus.

To be super-average in America was a gift one could parlay into a fortune, and the boy next door was taking his first steps down that jewelled runway, just preparing to take off and fly. No, she realized, she would not have to move house, after all. *He* would move out soon, first into the luxury Fountain Avenue apartment of his glorious averageness, then into the Los Feliz mansion, the Bel Air palazzo, the thousand-acre Colorado ranch that all super–boys next door deserved. "What's your name again?" she asked him after they had sex, and he was amused by the question in his super-average way. "Ha! Ha! That's a good one!" If Clark Kent had not secretly been Superman this is who he would have been. "Jock Flock," he reminded her when he stopped laughing. "This name is burned into your memory. This name is repeating in there, over and over, on a loop, like some song you can't forget. It's driving you crazy. You're saying it in the shower. Over and over. Jake Flake, Jake Flake. This thing is stronger than your will. You don't have a chance. Give in now."

He wanted her to marry him right away. "The only sensible way to love is to love conditionally," she warned him, backed off. "What you're asking sounds a little too unconditional for me." When he didn't understand her he had a way of beaming at her vacuously, patronizingly. This aroused her most violent instincts. "Just think about it, okay?" he requested. "Think, Mrs Jay Flay. Think how much you like the sound of that. You like it *so much.* You can't fight it if you think about it. Just do me a favour. Don't act without thinking." This from a prominent practitioner of the unexamined life. She had to work hard to restrain herself from slapping him across his homely, handsome face.

Ever since Joe Flow's proposal she had been wandering the corridors of the apartment building in a daze of irritation and confusion. She ran into the great denim-shelled ovoid of the sorceress Olga Simeonovna. "What's up, beauty," Olga Volga gruffly enquired, fingering her customary potato. "You look like your cat dies only you don't got no cat." India squeezed a smile and in her perplexity blurted out her trouble to the Russian super. "It's the boy next door," she confessed. Olga looked contemptuous. "That nancy schmancy what's-his-name? Rick Flick?" India nodded. Olga Volga prepared to go on the warpath. "He been bothering you honey? You say the word and he's outa here on his little tushy we have to look at supersized up there on the side of the Beverly Center. I mean, I'm sorry, keep it to yourself, Dickie, nobody wants to see."

India shook her head, came out with it. "He proposed." Olga quivered all over, a low-grade earthquake rippling across her flesh. "You serious? You and Nick? Nick and you? Okay, wow." India found herself bridling at the disbelief in the super's voice. "Well, don't sound *that* surprised. Why shouldn't someone want to marry me?" Olga placed a great blue-veined slab of arm on India's shoulder. "No, of course not because of you, my darling, my gorgeous. It's just that Mick? Always, until today, I totally thought he was guy." "Guy?" "Of course guy. Like everyone round here. Big guy neighbourhood, just my luck, huh. The Mister Softee van man across the street, calls himself *The Emperor of Ice Cream,* right there on the side of his van he puts it, who does he think he fooling, you know? *Totally* guy. Guy dog walkers also, guy waiters in the cafeterias, guy gyms a girl like you goes there and gets no whistles from nobody, guy Hispanic construction teams, guy electricians and plumbers, guy mail carriers, guy girls hand in hand on the sidewalk, guy guys tanning all day on sunbeds by the pool then going upstairs to do shit doggy style and I'm supposed to ignore this. Perverts everyplace only now we must call them happy boys and girls. What is so guy about perversion, explain me? About this crime against God's plan what is so cheerful, please?"

India's head ached. Insomnia was still her most attentive, cruellest lover, demanding and possessing her selfishly whenever it chose to do so. Light-heartedness was beyond her today. A man of middling quality was trying to marry her and there was something wrong with her father's voice on the phone. There was no time for Olga Simeonovna's mock-bigotry. The Russian super was as broad of mind as she was of behind, and her ritual fulminations were soaked in European irony. She pretended that in the privacy of her little apartment she was trying to alter her neighbours' sexual orientation by casting potato spells but in fact she was majestically uninterested in what went on behind closed doors. Sex, doggy or bitchy fashion, missionary or convert style, was no longer a concern of hers. In love, however, she continued to affect an interest. "Say him yes, my gorgeous. Sure, why not. You will be very happy, ten per cent probability minimum, and if not, bah. Marriage I remember from when it was God's great sacrament, the unbreakable promise, but I am extinct Russian dinosaur. Marriage now is what, car rental. Thank you for using our service, we'll pick you up, when you're done with the vehicle we'll take you home again. Get all the insurance you can get up front, loss damage waiver, whatever, and the risk is nothing. You crash the car, you walk away without nothing to pay. Go for it, baby, who you gonna save it for? They don't make no glass slippers no more. They already closed the factory. They don't make no princes neither. They shot the Romanovs in a cellar and Anastasia too is dead."

Everywhere was now a part of everywhere else. Russia, America, London, Kashmir. Our lives, our stories, flowed into one another's, were no longer our own, individual, discrete. This unsettled people. There were collisions and explosions. The world was no longer calm. She thought of Housman in Shropshire. *That is the land of lost content.* For the poet, happiness was the past. It was that other country where they did things differently. England, England. *An air that kills.* She had had an English childhood too, but she did not remember it as a golden place, she had no sense of a better before. For her that disenchanted after-land was where she had lived all her life. It was all there was. Contentment, contentedness, content, these variant forms were the names of dreams. If he could offer her such a dream, her suitor, maybe it would be a greater gift than love. She went back to her apartment to consider his proposal, damn it, what was his fucking name. Judd Flood.

Another beautiful day. The road where she lived, leafy, bohemian, moved through the indolent light, dawdling, taking its time. The city's greatest illusion was of sufficiency, of space, of time, of possibility. Across the hall from her apartment Mr Khadaffy Andang's door was open as usual, standing about two feet ajar, affording a glimpse into a darkened vestibule. The silver-haired Filipino gentleman had lived in the building longer than anyone else. India had once surprised him at the washing machines when she returned from a rare late night out, and had herself been surprised to see how nattily turned out he was in that predawn hour: the silk dressing-gown, the cigarette holder, the perfume, the slicked-back hair. After that, on occasion, they talked while the laundry was being done. He told her about the Philippines, about his home province of Basilan, a word that meant "iron trail". Once there had been a legendary ruler there, he said, Sultan Kudarat, but then the Spanish came and overthrew him, and the Jesuits came too, just like the discovery of California. He told her about Yakan weddings and Samal fisherfolk's stilt-houses and the wild ducks of Malamawi. He said that it had been a peaceful place but now there was trouble between Muslims and Christians and he had come away from that, he and his wife wanted only to make their life good, but unfortunately that had not been his fate. Still, in America, life was *la dolce vita,* wasn't it, even for the people for whom it wasn't. He accepted his fate, he said, and then the laundry was ready. She was touched by this sweet, shuffling gentleman and looked forward to their talks, even telling him something of her own life, overcoming her natural reserve.

Sometimes in the lobby there were fashionable mail-order catalogues waiting for him. Yet, as Olga Simeonovna confirmed, he rarely left the building except to buy essential groceries and supplies. His wife, the wife he had brought to America in search of a good life, had left him some years ago for a loan company repo man. India imagined the music of the Filipino language, of its insults. She thought of it as a softer, more flowing Japanese. A language of rolling, curvaceous obloquies, like woodwinds. "He keeps himself ready," Olga confided, "in case Mrs Andang returns. That's why the open door policy. But she won't be coming back." The repo man had pals in the insurance game. "They fixed her up good. She's covered from dollar one all the way up the wazoo. Health, teeth, accidents. She has now her comfort zone. This Mr Andang was unable to provide. At her age such things signify." In spite of which Mr Andang left his door ajar. The city sang its love songs, deluding him, making him hope.

The ambassador's Bentley was turning in to the street. There were parking restrictions in force on India's side of the street because it was the day the garbage trucks came to collect the trash. The sidewalk was broad. India's building had an entry-phone system. All this slowed things down, increased his window of vulnerability. There were procedures Max Ophuls knew intimately from his days in the secret job, the job whose name could not be spoken, the job that didn't exist except that it did, but the ambassador was not thinking about those procedures. He was thinking about his daughter and how strongly she would disapprove of his just-terminated liaison with the woman who looked like her, who looked like her mother as well as her. The procedures required advance men to precede him, to block off a parking space right in front of the venue, to pre-enter the address and secure it, to hold the door open. Any professional in this area knew that the so-called principal was easiest to attack in the space between the door of his vehicle and the door of the location he planned to enter. But the threat assessment against Max Ophuls was not high nowadays and the risk assessment was lower. Threat and risk were not the same. Threat was a general level of presumed danger, while the level of risk was particular to any given activity. It was possible for the threat level to be high while at the same time the risk attached to a given decision, for example a last-minute whim to go and see your daughter, could be negligibly low. These things had once been important. Now he was just an old man investigating a cock-and-bull story about underground lizard people, a sexually inactive individual, recently rejected by his lover, a father paying an unpremeditated house call on his child. This was within established safety parameters.

Like any other professional in this field, Max knew that there was no such thing as complete security. The videotape of the shooting of President Reagan was the illustrative tool that best demonstrated this. Here was the president moving from building to car. These were the positions of the members of the security detail. All of the positions were ideal. Here came the assailant. These were the reaction times of the officers in the team. The times were extraordinary, the officers' responses exceeding what was expected of them. The president was not shot because of a mistake. There had been no mistake. But the president had been shot. POTUS was down. The most powerful man in the world, surrounded by the planet's security elite, was not secure between the door of the secure building and the door of the armoured car. Security was percentages. Nothing was ever one hundred per cent.

And nothing on earth could protect you against the inside job, the loyal traitor, the protector turned assassin. Ambassador Max Ophuls allowed Shalimar the driver to open the car door for him, crossed the sidewalk and dialled his daughter's code. Upstairs in her apartment the entry-phone rang. India picked it up and heard a voice she had only heard once before in her life, on the tape recorder she had left running by her bedside to capture her sleep-talk night-language. When she heard that gurgling, incoherent, choking noise she recognized it as the voice of death and began to run. Everything around her became very slow while she ran, the motion of the trees outside the windows, the noises of people and birds, even her own movements seemed to be in slow motion as she hurled her body down the sluggish stairs. When she arrived at the glass double doors to the outside world she saw what she knew she would see, the huge splash of blood across the glass, the thick drag of blood down towards the ground, and the body of her father, Ambassador Maximilian Ophuls, war hero and holder of the Légion d'Honneur, lying motionless and soaked in a darkening crimson lake. His throat had been slashed so violently that the weapon, one of his own Sabatier kitchen knives, which had been dropped beside his corpse, had all but severed his head.

She didn't open the door. Her father wasn't there, just a mess that needed cleaning up. Where was Olga? Somebody needed to inform the janitor. There was work for a janitor to do. Moving steadily, her back straight and her head held high, India called and entered the elevator. In the elevator she stood with her hands clasped in front of her like a child reciting a poem. When she was back in her apartment she shut and locked the front door. In the little vestibule beneath a round mirror there stood a wooden Shaker chair, and she sat down on it, her hands still clasped and resting now on her lap.

She wanted the noise to stop, the shouting, the braying sirens. This was a quiet neighbourhood. She closed her eyes. The telephone was ringing which didn't matter. There was a knocking, then a louder knocking at her door which didn't matter either. A kitchen knife belonged in a kitchen and had no business on the sidewalk. An investigation was called for. This was not a matter for her. She was just the daughter. She was just the illegitimate but only child. She didn't even know if there was a will. It was important to go on sitting down. If she could keep sitting here for a year or two it would be all right. Sometimes the joy takes a long time to come around again.

It was a big day. A man had proposed marriage. The poster boy had proposed. Soon there would be a ring and all the customary et cetera. Right now he had climbed across from his balcony to hers and was outside her sliding glass doors yelling honey honey. Honey open up it's me it's Jim. This was a matter for the police. She had work to do. When your work went well it gave you perspective, you could see things as they were, the distortions were minimized, the otherness went away. The driver with blood on his hands and great spreading scarlet stains on his clothes. She remembered seeing that, had made herself un-see it. She could have saved her father and had not done so. There had been portents. She had seen flowers at Shalimar's feet, flowers growing from the sidewalk where he stood, also on his chest, bursting through his shirt. It was not her business to believe these things, the things she saw when her eyes betrayed her. It was not her place to save her father. It was her place to sit perfectly still until the joy came around.

Alouette, gentille alouette,
Alouette, je te plumerai.

She sat straddling her father's shoulders, facing him, and they sang. *Et le cou! Et le cou! Et la tête! Et la tête! Alouette! Alouette! Ohhhh* . . . and she somersaulted backwards away from him, somersaulted away, her hands in his hands, her hands in his hands, her hands forever and nevermore in his.

Boonyi

There was the earth and there were the planets. The earth was not a planet. The planets were the grabbers. They were called this because they could seize hold of the earth and bend its destiny to their will. The earth was never of their kind. The earth was the subject. The earth was the grabbee.

There were nine grabbers in the cosmos, Surya the Sun, Soma the Moon, Budha the Mercury, Mangal the Mars, Shukra the Venus, Brihaspati the Jupiter, Shani the Saturn, and Rahu and Ketu, the two shadow planets. The shadow planets actually existed without actually existing. They were heavenly bodies without bodies. They were out there but they lacked physical form. They were also the dragon planets: two halves of a single bisected dragon. Rahu was the dragon's head and Ketu was the dragon's tail. A dragon, too, was a creature that actually existed without actually existing. It was, because our thinking made it be.

Until he found out about the shadow planets Noman Sher Noman had never understood how to think about love, how to give names to its effects of moral illumination and tidal fluctuation and gravitational pull. The moment he heard about the cloven dragon many things became clear. Love and hate were shadow planets too, noncorporeal but out there, pulling at his heart and soul. He was fourteen years old and had fallen in love for the first time in the village of Pachigam where the travelling players lived. It was his time of glory. His apprenticeship was over and he had taken his professional name. He wanted to set Noman the child aside and be his new adult self. He wanted to make his father proud of Shalimar the clown, his son. His great father, Abdullah, the headman, the *sarpanch,* who held them all in the palm of his hand.

It was the pandit Pyarelal Kaul who taught him about grabbing and it was the pandit's green-eyed daughter Bhoomi whom he loved. Her name meant "the earth", so that made him a grabber, Noman supposed, but cosmological allegory didn't account for everything, it didn't explain, for example, her interest in grabbing him back. Except on performance days when there were audiences within earshot she never called him Shalimar, preferring the name he had been born with, even though she disliked her own name—"my name is mud," she said, "it's mud and dirt and stone and I don't want it," and asked him to call her "Boonyi" instead. This was the local word for the celestial Kashmiri chinar tree. Noman would go out into the pine forests above and behind the village and whisper her name to the monkeys. "Boonyi," he murmured also to the hoopoes in the high flower-strewn meadow of Khelmarg, where he first kissed her. "Boonyi," the birds and monkeys solemnly replied, honouring his love.

The pandit was a widower. He and Bhoomi-who-was-Boonyi lived at one end of Pachigam in the village's second-best dwelling, a wooden house like all the other houses but with two floors instead of one (the best house, which belonged to the Nomans, had a third level, a single large room in which the *panchayat* met and all the village's key decisions were taken). There was also a separate kitchen house and a toilet hut at the end of a little covered walkway. It was a dark, slightly tilting house with a pitched roof of corrugated iron, just like everyone else's only a little larger. It stood by a talkative little river, the Muskadoon, whose name meant "refreshing" and whose water was sweet to drink but freezing cold to swim in because it tumbled down from the high eternal snows where the bare-chested, naked-breasted Hindu deities played their daily thunder-and-lightning games. The gods didn't feel the cold, Pandit Kaul explained, on account of the divine heat of their immortal blood. But in that case—Noman wondered but did not dare to ask—why were their nipples always erect?

Pandit Kaul didn't like his name either. There were far too many Kauls in the valley already. For an uncommon man it was demeaning to bear so everyday a surname, and it surprised nobody when he announced that he wanted to be called Pandit Kaul-Toorpoyni, Pandit Kaul of the Cold Water. That was too long to be practical, so he dropped the hated Kaul altogether. But Pandit Pyarelal Toorpoyn, which is to say, Pandit Sweetheart Coldstream, didn't stick either. In the end he gave up and accepted his nomenclatural fate. Noman called the pandit Sweetie Uncle, though they were not connected by blood or faith. Kashmiris were connected by deeper ties than those. Boonyi was the pandit's only child, and as she and Noman approached their fourteenth birthday they both discovered that they had been in love for their whole lives and it was time to do something about it, even though that was the most dangerous decision in the world.

They sat by the Muskadoon with the pandit while he prattled of the cosmos because he was a man who liked to talk and it was a way for them to be together, speaking to each other in the silent careful language of forbidden desire while they listened to Pyare her father babbling away as fluently as the garrulous river at his back. Noman's fingers stretched towards Boonyi's and hers yearned for his. They were several yards apart, sitting on smooth boulders by the riverside, bathed in the relentless clarity of mountain sunlight beneath the unbroken sky that shone above them blue as joy. In spite of the distance their yearning fingers were invisibly entwined. Noman could feel her hand curling around his, digging its long nails into his palm, and when he stole a look at her he could tell by the light in her eyes that she could feel his hand too, warming hers, rubbing at her fingertips, because the extremities of her body were always cold, her toes and fingers and earlobes and the points of her new breasts and the tip of her Greek nose. These places required the attention of his warming hand. She was the earth and the earth was the subject and he had grabbed it and sought to bend its destiny to his will.

Like many men who prided themselves upon their ability to resist spiritual fakery and mumbo-jumbo charlatanism of all kinds, Boonyi's father the pandit had a sneaky love of the fabulous and fantastic, and the notion of the shadow planets appealed to him powerfully. In short he was wholly under the spell of Rahu and Ketu, whose existence could only be demonstrated by the influence they exercised over people's daily lives. Einstein had proved the existence of unseen heavenly bodies by the power of their gravitational fields to bend light, and Sweetie Uncle could prove the existence of the cloven heavenly dragon-halves by their effects on human fortunes and misfortunes. "They churn our insides!" he cried, and there was a little thrill in his voice. "They hold sway over our emotions and give us pleasure or pain. There are six instincts," he added parenthetically, "which keep us attached to the material purposes of life. These are called Kaam the Passion, Krodh the Anger, Madh the Intoxicant, e.g. alcohol, drug et cetera, Moh the Attachment, Lobh the Greed and Matsaya the Jealousy. To live a good life we must control them or else they will control us. The shadow planets act upon us from a distance and focus our minds upon our instincts. Rahu is the exaggerator the intensifier! Ketu is the blocker the suppressor! The dance of the shadow planets is the dance of the struggle within us, the inner struggle of moral and social choice." He wiped his brow. "Now," he said to his daughter, "let's go and eat." The pandit was a jolly-bodied man who liked his food. Pachigam was a village of gastronomes.

Shalimar the clown watched them go and had to fight to stop his feet from following. It wasn't just the shadow planets that tugged at his feelings. Boonyi acted on him too, she worked her magic on him every minute of the day and night, dragging at him, pulling, caressing and nibbling him, even when she was at the opposite end of the village. Boonyi Kaul, dark as a secret, bright as happiness, his first and only love. Bhoomi by the Cold Water, great kisser, expert caresser, fearless acrobat, fabulous cook. Shalimar the clown's heart was pounding joyfully because it was about to be granted its greatest desire. In the lusty silence during the pandit's monologue they had decided that the moment had come to consummate their love, and in an exchange of wordless signals had briskly settled the hour and the place. Now it was time to prepare.

That evening, while she braided her long hair for her lover, Boonyi

Kaul thought about the blessed Sita in the forest hermitage at Panchavati near the Godavari River during the wandering years of Lord Ram's exile from Ayodhya. Ram and Lakshman were away hunting for demons that fateful day. Sita was left alone, but Lakshman had drawn a magic line in the dirt all the way across the mouth of the little hermitage and warned her not to cross it or to invite anyone else to do so. The line was powerfully enchanted and would protect her from harm. But the moment Lakshman had left, the demon king Ravan showed up disguised as a wandering mendicant dressed in a tattered ochre cloth and wooden sandals, and carrying a cheap umbrella. He did not talk like a holy beggar, however, but effusively praised, in sequence, Sita's skin, her scent, her eyes, her face, her hair, her breasts and her waist. He said nothing about her legs. Her legs would have been concealed from view, of course, and although a great *rakshasa* like Ravan would surely have been able to see through cloth he could not admit it, because if he had praised her lower body his salacious hidden nature would have been revealed instantly. Boonyi Kaul's almost-fourteen-year-old legs were already long and slender. She wanted to know about Sita Devi's legs and was frustrated that they were never described.

She wanted to know, too, whether it was in spite of or because of his lecherous, flattering speech that Sita invited Ravan in disguise to come indoors and rest. It was a question of some importance because once Sita had invited the stranger to cross the magic line its power was broken. Moments later Ravan resumed his true multiheaded form and carried Sita off to his kingdom of Lanka, abducted her against her noble will in the flying chariot drawn by the green mules. The great eagle Jatayu, old and blind, tried to save her, killing the mules in the air and making the chariot fall to earth, but Ravan picked up Sita and leapt unharmed to the ground and when tired Jatayu attacked him he cut off the eagle's wings.

Surely the whole epic conflict could not simply be Sita's fault, Boonyi Kaul thought. "Jatayu, you have died for me," Sita cried out. That was true. But how could the responsibility for everything that followed the abduction, the eagle's fall, the countrywide search for the missing princess, the mighty war against Ravan, the rivers of blood and mountains of death, be laid at the door of Ram's revered wife? What a strange meaning that would give to the old story—that women's folly undid men's magic, that heroes had to fight and die because of the vanity that had made a pretty woman act like a dunce. That didn't feel right. The dignity, the moral strength, the intelligence of Sita was beyond doubt and could not so trivially be set aside. Boonyi gave the story a different interpretation. However much Sita's family members sought to protect her, Boonyi thought, the demon king still existed, was hopelessly besotted by her, and would have to be faced sooner or later. A woman's demons were out there, like her lovers, and she could only be coddled for so long. It was better to be done with magic lines and to confront your destiny. Lines in the dirt were all very well but they only delayed matters. What had to happen should be allowed to happen or it could never be overcome.

And so who was this boy, the son of the village headman, the new pratfalling clown prince of the performing troupe, the lover she was preparing to meet in the upper sheep meadow above the village at midnight? Was he her epic hero or her demon king, or both? Would they exalt each other or be destroyed by what they had resolved to do? Had she chosen foolishly or well? For certainly she had invited him to cross a powerful line. How handsome he was, she mused tenderly, how funny in his clowning, how pure in his singing, how graceful in the dance and gravity-free on the high rope, and best of all how wonderfully gentle of nature. This was no warrior demon! He was sweet Noman, who called himself Shalimar the clown partly in her honour, because they had both come into the world on the same night in the Shalimar garden almost fourteen years ago, and partly in her mother's, because she had died there on that night of many disappearances when the world began to change. She loved him because his choice of name was his way of honouring her deceased mother as well as celebrating the unbreakable connection of their birth. She loved him because he would not—he could not!—hurt any living soul. How could he cause her harm when he would not harm a fly?

Her hair was ready and her body was oiled. Rahu the intensifier had worked upon Kaam the passion and her body pulsated with its need. She had become a woman two years ago—early as usual, she thought; ever since her premature birth she had done things ahead of time—and was strong enough for whatever was to come. Through the moonless dark the scent of peach and apple blossom made her eyelids heavy. She sat on her bed and rested her head on the windowsill and closed her eyes. Soon enough her mother came to her as she had known she would. Her mother had died giving her birth but came to her most nights in dreams, letting her in on womanly secrets and family history and giving her good advice and unconditional love. Boonyi did not tell her father this because she didn't want to hurt his feelings. The pandit had tried to be both father and mother to her all her life. In spite of his unworldly nature he treated her as an inestimable treasure, as the pearl of great price his beloved wife had left behind for him as a going-away present. He had learned the secrets of child rearing from the women of the village, and from the beginning insisted on doing everything himself, preparing her compound and wiping her arse and waking up to tend to her whenever she screamed until the neighbours begged him to get some sleep, warning him that he had better let them help out unless he wanted the poor girl to grow up without even one parent to lean on for support. The pandit relented, but only very occasionally. As she got older he taught her to read and write and sing. He skipped with her and let her experiment with kohl and lipstick and told her what to do when she began to bleed. So he had done his best, but a girl's mother is her mother even if she existed without actually existing, in the noncorporeal form of a dream, even if her existence could only be proved by her effect on the one human being whose fate she still cared to influence.

The pandit's deceased wife had been named Pamposh after the lotus flower, but, as she confided to her dozing daughter, she preferred the nickname Giri, meaning a walnut kernel, which Firdaus Begum, Abdullah Noman's yellow-haired wife, Firdaus Butt or Bhat, once gave her as a mark of friendship. One summer day in the saffron fields of Pachigam Firdaus and Giri were gathering crocuses when a rainstorm came at them like a witch's spell out of a clear blue sky and soaked them both to the bone. The sarpanch's wife was a foul-mouthed woman and let the cackling rain know what she thought of it but Pamposh danced in the downpour and cried out gaily, "Don't scold the sky for giving us the gift of water."

That was too much for Firdaus. "Everyone thinks you have such a sweet nature, so open, so accepting, but you don't fool me," she told Pamposh or Giri while they sheltered dripping under a spreading chinar. "Sure, I can see how quickly and easily you smile, how you never have a harsh word for anyone, how you face every hardship with equanimity. Me, I wake up in the morning and I have to start fixing everything I see, I need to shake people up, I want everything to be better, I want to clean up all the shit we have to deal with every day of this gruelling life. You, by contrast, act like you take the world as it is and are happy to be in it and whatever happens is just fine by you. But guess what? I'm onto you. I've worked out your little act of an angel in paradise. It's brilliant, no question about that, but it's just your shell, your hard walnut shell, and inside you're a completely different girl and it's my guess that you're far from contented. You're the most generous woman I know, if I mention once that I like this or that shawl you'll make me take it, even if it came down to you from your great-grandmother in your trousseau and it's an heirloom one hundred and fifty years old, but secretly, in spite of all that, you're a miser of yourself."

It was the kind of speech that either destroys a friendship forever or pushes it to a new level of intimacy, and it was typical of Firdaus to gamble everything on one throw of the dice. "I guess I saw through her too that day," Pamposh Kaul told her daughter Boonyi as she dreamed, "and I caught sight of the incredibly loyal and loving woman under her act of a hard-hearted bitch. Also, she was the only woman in the village who might just be able to understand what I wanted to say." So Pamposh confided her deepest secrets to Firdaus, amazing her. Until that moment the headman's wife, like everyone else, had thought of Pamposh as the perfect wife for the pandit, because she had her feet planted firmly on the ground while his head was always getting a soaking in the middle of some metaphysical cloud. Now Firdaus discovered that Pamposh possessed a secret nature far more fantastic than her husband's, that her dreams were far more radical and dangerous than anything Firdaus had ever been able to come up with in spite of all her world-shaking ambitions.

In the matter of lovemaking Kashmiri women had never been shrinking violets, but what Pamposh confided to Firdaus made her ears burn.

The sarpanch's wife understood that hidden away inside her friend was a personality so intensely sexual that it was a wonder the pandit was still able to get up out of bed and walk around. Pamposh's passion for the wilder reaches of sexual behaviour introduced Firdaus to a number of new concepts that simultaneously horrified and aroused her, although she feared that if she attempted to introduce them into her own bedroom Abdullah, for whom sex was a simple relief of physical urges and not to be unduly prolonged, would throw her out into the street like a common whore. Although Firdaus was the older of the two women by a few years she found herself in the unaccustomed position of awestruck student, enquiring with stammering fascination into how and why such and such a practice achieved the desired results. "It's simple," Pamposh replied. "If you trust each other you can do anything and so can he and believe me it feels pretty good." What was even more remarkable about Pamposh's revelations was the sense that she was not following her husband's desires but leading them. When she moved on from sex itself to sexual politics and began to explain her broader ideas, her utopian vision of the emancipation of women, and to speak of her torment at having to live in a society that was at least a hundred years behind the times she had in mind, Firdaus held up her hand. "It's bad enough that you have filled my head with stuff that will give me nightmares for weeks," she said. "Don't upset me with any more of your notions today. The present is already too much for me. I can't cope with the future as well."

Pamposh Kaul in her daughter's dreams went into all the things Firdaus Noman had not wanted to hear, told her about the unshackled future that shone on the horizon like a promised land she could never enter, the vision of freedom that had eaten away at her all her life and destroyed her inner peace, although nobody knew it because she never stopped smiling, she never dropped her lying façade of contented calm. "A woman can make every choice she pleases just because it pleases her, and pleasing a man comes a poor second, a long way behind," she said. "Also, if a woman's heart is true then what the world thinks doesn't matter one jot." This made a big impression on Boonyi. "That's easy for you to say," she told her mother. "Ghosts don't have to live in the real world."

"I'm not a ghost," Pamposh replied. "I'm a dream of the mother you want me to be. I'm telling you what's already in your heart, what you want me to confirm."

"That's true," said Boonyi Kaul, and began to stretch and stir. "Go to him," her mother said, and faded into nothing.

Boonyi slipped out of the house and made her way up the wooded hillside to Khelmarg, the meadow where sometimes by moonlight she practised archery, spearing arrows into innocent trees. She had a gift for the bow but tonight was for different sport. There was no moon. There were a few lights shining from the Indian army camp across the fields, a few glowing lanterns and cigarette tips, but even the soldiers were mostly asleep. Her father was certainly asleep and snoring his buffalo snores. She was wearing a dark kerchief around her head and a full-length dark *phiran* over a long dark shirt. There was a chill in the air but the loose robe was warm enough. Under the phiran her little *kangri* of hot coals sent long fingers of heat across her stomach. She wore no other garments or undergarments. Her bare feet knew the path. She was a shadow in search of a shadow. She would find the shadow she was looking for and he would love and protect her. "I will hold you in the palm of my hand," he had said, "the way my father held me." Noman, also known as Shalimar the clown, the most beautiful boy in the world.

At that moment the most beautiful boy in the world was doing what he did whenever he needed to calm down and concentrate on what really mattered: he was climbing a tree. Trees had featured prominently both in his professional education and in his inner life. One night at the age of eleven Noman had been unable to sleep because of his uncertainties about the nature of the universe, on which subject his parents had arguments so spectacular that the whole village gathered outside their house to listen and take sides, arguments about the precise location of the heavenly paradise and whether or not in the future men would get there by spaceship, and about the probability or improbability of there being prophets and holy books on other planets, and consequently about whether or not it was blasphemous to hypothesize the theoretical existence of little green-skinned bug-eyed prophets receiving holy writ in the incomprehensible languages of Mars or of the creatures who lived on the unseen far side of the moon. Noman didn't know how to choose between his father's modern-day open-mindedness and his mother's occultist threats which usually had something to do with snake charms, so that even though there was a rainstorm brewing he escaped through the back door and climbed the tallest chinar in the Pachigam district to think. He wasn't stupid enough to step out onto the rope that night. He hung there madly in the wind and rain while all around him branches shook and broke. The universe flexed its muscles and demonstrated its complete lack of interest in quarrels about its nature. The universe was everything at once, science and sorcery, what was occult and what was known, and it didn't give a damn. The storm's fury grew. He saw dead men's hands flying past his face, catching at him from their airy graves. The wind screamed and meant to kill him but he screamed back into its face and cursed it and it couldn't take his life. Years later when he became an assassin he would say that it might have been better if he hadn't lived, better if his life had been carried off that day in the rotting teeth of the gale.

Just outside the village there was a stand of ancient chinar trees clawing gracefully at the sky. A tightrope stretched between two of the oldest trees, and now, in preparation for his assignation with Boonyi, Shalimar the clown was strolling across it, tumbling, pirouetting, prancing so lightly that it seemed he was walking on air. He had been nine years old when he learned the secret of airwalking. In this green glade beneath a sun-pierced dome of leaves he stepped barefoot out of his father's grasp and flew. On that first flight the tightrope was barely eighteen inches off the ground but the exhilaration was as great as anything he felt later in his professional life when he stepped out from a high branch and looked down twenty feet to where his open-mouthed admirers clapped and gasped. His feet knew what to do without being told. His toes curled round the rope, gripping hard. "Don't think of the rope as a safety line through space," his father had said. "Think of it as a line of gathered air. Or think of the air as something preparing to become rope. The rope and the air are the same. When you know this you will be ready to fly. The rope will melt away and you will step out onto the air knowing that it will bear your weight and take you wherever you may want to go." Abdullah Sher Noman was initiating his son into a mystery. A rope could become air. A boy could become a bird. Metamorphosis was the secret heart of life.

After his first walk it proved impossible to keep Noman off the rope and gradually it rose higher and higher until he was flying at the level of the treetops. He practised in all weathers and at all times of the day and night and his father, Abdullah, never stopped him, never reined him in, even when Firdaus Begum, the great man's wife and Noman's ferocious mother, threatened to bewitch them both and turn them into water snakes and trap them in a glass bowl in the kitchen if that was what it took to protect her son from his damn fool of a father who didn't care if Noman fell headfirst to the ground and got himself smashed into a thousand pieces like a mirror. Snakes loomed large in Firdaus Begum's worldview and therefore in her family's too. "Snake wriggle, world jiggle," she liked to say, meaning that the great serpents burrowing away down by the roots of the mountains caused earth tremors when they moved. She knew many snake secrets. Under the shivering Himalayas, she said, there was a lost city where the snakes hoarded gold and precious stones. Malachite was a snake favourite and its possession bestowed good fortune on the possessor; but only if the stone had been found, not bought. "You can't buy snake luck," she warned. In general if a snake got in the house it was to be considered a blessing, something to be grateful for, and not only because it might gobble up the household mice. You should take a stick and flick it out of the door or window, by all means, because luck was not something to be pushed; but you should do it with respect and not attempt to crush its head. Snake protection was a thing all houses needed, and if you didn't have a snake to protect you then you'd better have some malachite stones instead.

(The first time Noman heard the pandit rhapsodizing about the sky-dragons Rahu and Ketu he marvelled at the secret affinity between his beloved's father and his own, standoffish mother. Dragons, lizards, snakes, the sinuous scaly worms of earth and air; it seemed like the whole world had magical monsters on the brain.)

Firdaus had a lazy right eye and people said behind her back that once you had been fixed by that lidded sidelong look you knew that she must be part snake herself. Noman sometimes suspected that it was because of his mother's serpentine concerns that he slithered so well up, down and along things like trees and ropes. Now all his thoughts were coiling around this girl, Boonyi, to whom he planned to bring good luck for all the days of their lives. The words *Hindu* and *Muslim* had no place in their story, he told himself. In the valley these words were merely descriptions, not divisions. The frontiers between the words, their hard edges, had grown smudged and blurred. This was how things had to be. This was Kashmir. When he told himself these things he believed them with all his heart. In spite of this he had not told his father or mother about his feelings for the pandit's child. He had rarely kept secrets from his father—with his mother he had always been more guarded, because she scared him in a way that his father did not—and he felt guilty about the great secret he was hugging to himself up here in the trees. But nobody, not even the three other clowns, who were also his older brothers and his closest friends, knew what he was planning to do tonight.

Boonyi, whose first love and greatest gift was dancing, could walk the high rope too, but for her it was just a rope. For young Noman it was a magic space. "One day I'll really take off," he told her after their first kiss. "One day I won't need the rope at all. I'll just walk into empty air and hang there like a cosmonaut without a suit. I'll stand on my hands, on my feet, on my head, and there won't even be anything to stand on." She was impressed by his air of total certainty and even though she knew his words were the craziest kind of foolishness she was greatly moved by them. "What makes you so sure?" she asked. "My father made me believe it," he replied. "He raised me nestling in the palm of his hand and my feet never touched the ground."

In the palm of his father's hand it wasn't soft or cushiony as a rich man's hand might have been, but hard and used and knowing. It was a hand that knew what the world was and it did not shield you from the knowledge of the hardships in store. But it was a strong hand nevertheless and could protect you from those hardships. As long as Noman stayed in the valley of its skin nothing could touch him and there was nothing to fear. His father raised him in the palm of his hand for he was the most precious jewel Abdullah ever possessed, or so the sarpanch said when his older boys Hameed, Mahmood and Anees weren't listening, because a man in his position, a leader, should never lay himself open to the charge of favouritism. Still Noman in the palm of Abdullah's hand knew his father's secret, and kept it. "You are my lucky charm," Abdullah told him. "With you beside me I am invincible." Noman felt invincible too, for if he was his father's magic talisman then his father was also his. "My father's love was the first phase," he told her. "It carried me as far as the treetops. But now it's your love I need. That's what will let me fly."

There was no moon. The white furnace of the galaxy burned across the sky. The birds were sleeping. Shalimar the clown climbed the wooded hill to Khelmarg and listened to the river flow. He wanted the world to remain frozen just as it was in this moment, when he was filled with hope and longing, when he was young and in love and nobody had disappointed him and nobody he loved had died. Regarding death, his mother believed in a snaky afterlife but his father's eternity had wings. When Noman was a little boy of six his bad-tempered grandfather Farooq had ended his long, grumbling life in an uncharacteristically cheerful mood. "At least I won't have all of you screwing things up all around me to worry about any more," he said. Farooq's idea of love was to grab Noman's young cheek and pinch and twist it as hard as he could.

"Babajan thinks I'm ugly," Noman complained.

"Of course he doesn't," his father unconvincingly replied.

"If he didn't think I was as ugly as a *bhoot,*" said Noman conclusively, "he wouldn't keep trying to rip my face off with his claws."

In spite of Grandfather Farooq's bad attitude to Noman's physiognomy the boy was unnerved by the funeral rites. Grandfather Farooq was buried with bewildering speed, consigned to the earth six hours after his expiry, but he was mourned at devastating and tedious length. To comfort and invigorate Noman, Abdullah explained that after death the souls of their family members entered the local birds and flew around Pachigam singing the same songs they used to sing back when they were people. As birds they sang with the same level of musical talent they had possessed in their earlier human life, no more, no less. Noman didn't believe him and said as much. His father replied seriously. "Just let me die and then look out for a hoopoe with a voice like a broken exhaust pipe. When you hear that hoopoe croaking and cracking that will be me singing my favourite I-told-you-so song." Abdullah laughed and it was true that he sounded exactly like the split exhaust pipe of his old truck, and his singing voice was even worse than his laugh. It was also true that "I told you so" was Abdullah Noman's favourite song, because he was cursed with the curse of knowing too much and the double curse of being unable to avoid pointing this out even though it made Firdaus Begum threaten to hit him on the head with a stone.

"You won't die," Noman told him. "You won't die, ever, ever."

When he was a boy his father could find birds all over him. Abdullah kissed Noman's cheek, his stomach or his knee and at once the child could hear birdsong right there where his father's puckered lips touched his skin. "I think there's a bird in your armpit," Abdullah would say and Noman would wriggle with delight, trying to stop him, not wanting him to stop, and Abdullah would wrestle his way in there and suddenly, hey presto, there were the piercing tweets coming out of Noman's armpit too. "Maybe," his father said as he moved menacingly towards his face, "that birdy wants to escape through your nose."

Abdullah Sher Noman was indeed a lion, as the honorific *sher* which he had eventually taken as his middle name suggested. Ever since his young days people in Pachigam had said that there were two lions in Kashmir. One was Sheikh Abdullah, of course, Sher-e-Kashmir himself, the unquestioned leader of his people. Everyone agreed that Sheikh Abdullah was the valley's real prince, not that Dogra maharaja living in the palace on the slopes above Srinagar that afterwards became the Oberoi Hotel. The other lion was Pachigam's very own headman, Abdullah Noman, whom everybody admired and, in a loving and respectful way, also somewhat feared, not only because he was the boss but also because he possessed a stage presence so commanding in its heroism, so fiercely valiant for truth, that some of the more unsavoury members of their audiences around the valley had been known to leap to their feet and confess to unsuspected crimes without even waiting for the climax and finale of the play.

Abdullah wasn't tall but he was strong, with arms as thick as any blacksmith's. He was wide of shoulder, profuse of hair, and the Indian soldiers in the camp treated him with as much respect as they could summon up. He was also a formidable actor-manager who led the travelling players wherever they went, and greatly beloved of women too, though Firdaus Begum was all the lioness he required. "He gave me his same, leonine middle name," Shalimar the assassin wrote many years later, "but I do not deserve to bear it. My life was going to be one thing but death turned it into another. The bright sky vanished for me and a dark passage opened. Now I am made of darkness, but a lion is made of light." He wrote this on a flimsy sheet of lined prison notepaper. Then he tore the paper to bits.

The official name of their village, Pachigam, lacked any apparent meaning; but some of its older inhabitants claimed that it was a latter-day corruption of Panchigam, which is to say "birdville". In the vexed debate on whether or not birds were transfigured human souls this etymological rumour proved nothing or everything depending on your inclination. When Shalimar the clown found Boonyi Kaul waiting for him in the Khelmarg meadow, however, that debate was no longer uppermost in his mind. Another debate was raging there instead. Standing before him, oiled of skin and with wildflowers scenting the carefully braided hair that hung kerchief-free around her shoulders, was the girl he loved, waiting for him to make her a woman and in doing so make himself a man. Desire rose in him, but so did a counterforce he had not expected: restraint. The shadow dragons were fighting over him, Rahu the exaggerator and Ketu the blocker battling for mastery of his heart.

He looked into Boonyi's eyes and saw the telltale dreaminess there, warning him that she had smoked *charas* to give her the courage to be deflowered. In the subtly suggestive movements of her lips, too, he could discern the cryptic seductiveness of her condition. "Boonyi, Boonyi," he mourned, "you've burdened me with a responsibility I don't know how to discharge. Let's, you know, caress each other in five places and kiss in seven ways and make out in nine positions, but let's not get carried away." In reply, Boonyi pulled her phiran and shirt off over her head and stood before him naked except for the little pot of fire hanging low, below her belly, heating further what was already hot. "Don't treat me like a child," she said in a throaty voice that proved she had been unsparing in her drug abuse. "You think I went to all this trouble just for a kiddie-style session of lick and suck?" When he heard the unexpected coarseness of her speech Shalimar the clown surmised that she must have been very afraid indeed of what she had agreed to do, which was why she had needed to derange herself so completely. "Okay, it's not going to happen," he said, and the conflict within him grew so great, the two halves of the dragon churned up his insides so completely, that he was physically sick. Boonyi laughed hysterically at the sight. "You think that's going to put me off?" she gasped between the sobs of laughter, and pulled him down on top of her. "Mister, you'll have to try a lot harder than that to get yourself out of this."

Never afterwards did Boonyi Kaul utter a word of regret or recrimination for what she did in the meadow of Khelmarg, even though the events of that night set her on the road that led to an early death. She never reproached herself or Shalimar the clown for their choice, which was really hers. Shalimar the clown had been wrong about that too. She had not smoked the charas to abdicate responsibility but to be sure of seizing her opportunity; nor was she afraid of what she had chosen to do. The dragon's head had won her over long ago. The spirit-killing tail had no power over her.

"God," she said when it was over, "and *that's* what you *didn't* want to do?"

"Don't leave me," he said, rolling over onto his back and panting for joy. "Don't you leave me now, or I'll never forgive you, and I'll have my revenge, I'll kill you and if you have any children by another man I'll kill the children also."

"What a romantic you are," she replied carelessly. "You say the sweetest things."

Before Shalimar the clown and Boonyi were born there had been the villages of the actors and the villages of the cooks. Then times changed. The Pachigami performers of the traditional entertainments known as *bhand pather* or clown stories were still the undisputed player kings of the valley, but Abdullah the genius—young Abdullah, in his prime—was the one who made them learn how to be cooks as well. In the valley at times of celebration people liked a bit of a drama to watch but there was also a demand for those who could prepare the legendary *wazwaan,* the Banquet of Thirty-Six Courses Minimum. Thanks to Abdullah the villagers of Pachigam were the first to provide a rounded service which offered both sustenance for the body and pleasure for the soul. As a result they didn't have to share the feast-day cash emoluments with anyone. There were other villages that specialized in the Thirty-Six-Courses-Minimum banquet, the most famous of which was Shirmal, just a mile and a half down the road; but as Abdullah pointed out it was easier to study recipes than to hold an audience in the palm of your hand.

He did not institute this radical change in the village's lifestyle unopposed. Firdaus Begum told him it was a damn-fool scheme that would ruin the village financially. "Look at all the stuff we have to buy—all the copper haandis, the grills, the portable tandoor ovens, just for a start!—and then there is the cost of learning the food and practising," she protested. "Is there any reason, theoretically speaking," Abdullah had roared ruminatively at Firdaus Begum one cold spring day—he had forgotten long ago that it was possible to lower one's voice when speaking—"why actors should not be able to fry spices and boil rice into something other than a soggy mush?" Firdaus Begum bridled at his tone. "Is there any good explanation, by the same token," she bawled back at him, "of why the sarus cranes aren't flying upside down?"

Her dissident voice was in the minority, however, and after the policy started showing signs of being a success the leading cookery village of Shirmal took a leaf out of Pachigam's book and tried to put on comedy dramas to accompany their food. However, their amateurish stage show was a bust. Then one night war was declared between the rivals. The men of Shirmal staged a raid on Pachigam, aiming to steal the great cauldrons and to break the ovens in which the travelling players had learned to cook the noblest delicacies of the region, the *roghan josh,* the *tabak maaz,* the *gushtaba,* but the Pachigam men sent the Shirmalis home crying with broken heads. After the pot war it was tacitly accepted that Pachigam was at the top of the entertainment tree, and the others got hired only when Pachigam's tellers of clown stories and cookers of banquets were too busy to offer their services.

The pot war horrified everyone in Pachigam even though they had come out on the winning side. They had always thought of their neighbours the Shirmal villagers as being more than a little weird, but nobody had imagined that so outrageous a breach of the peace was possible, that Kashmiris would attack other Kashmiris driven by such crummy motivations as envy, malice and greed. Firdaus Begum's friend, the ageless Gujar tribal woman and prophetess Nazarébaddoor, sank into an uncharacteristic gloom. Nazarébaddoor was the most optimistic of seers, whom people liked to visit in her mossy-roofed forest hut in spite of its damp smell of fornicating livestock because she invariably foretold happiness, wealth, long life and success. After the pot war her vision darkened. "This is the first pebble that starts the avalanche," she said, shaking her toothless head. Then she went into her odorous little hut, drew a wooden screen across the entrance, and retired forever from the art of divination. Nazarébaddoor had taken her name—"evil eye, begone!"—from a character out of the old stories, a beautiful princess who was in love with the hero Prince Hatim Tai and whose touch could avert curses, and she allowed the more gullible villagers to believe that she was in fact none other than that fabled immortal beauty, whom death had been unable to seize because her lucky touch kept getting her out of its clutches. "If it makes people happy," she confided in Firdaus, "I don't care if they believe I was once the Queen of Sheba."

To tell the truth, Nazarébaddoor didn't look much like the queen of anywhere. With her loose turban and her single golden front tooth she more closely resembled a marooned corsair. When she was young, she said, she had been blessed with flowing waves of auburn hair, gleaming white teeth and a blue left eye, but nobody could verify these claims because nobody in the neighbourhood could remember when Nazarébaddoor had been young. Her husband had offended her by dying without managing to leave her with so much as a single son to look after her in her declining years, which she considered the height of bad manners, and which had left her with a poor opinion of men in general. "If there's a way to propagate the human race without depending on men," Nazarébaddoor said to Firdaus, "lead me to it, because then women can have everything they want and dispense with everything they don't need." By the time news of artificial insemination arrived in the valley, however, she was long past child-bearing age, and could not have afforded the procedure even if she had been in the first red, white and blue flush of youth.

She had made the best of her life, tending her livestock, smoking her pipe, and surviving. The fortune-telling was a sideline that brought in a little extra, but prophecy was not Nazarébaddoor's main concern. Like the true Gujar woman that she was, her first love was the pine forest. Her most frequently repeated saying was, in Kashmiri, *Un poshi teli, yeli vun poshi,* which meant, "Forests come first, food comes second." She saw herself as the guardian of the trees of the Forest of Khel and had to be propitiated every autumn when the villagers of Pachigam and Shirmal, who both foraged there, needed to stock up on firewood before the coming of the winter snows. "You wouldn't want our children to freeze to death," the villagers pleaded, and eventually she would concede that human children mattered more than living wood. She would guide the village men to those trees that were closest to death and these were the only ones she would allow them to fell. They did what she said, fearing that if they did not she would bewitch them, blighting their crops and sending them a shaking sickness or a plague of boils.

She made her living selling buffalo milk and cheese, and her body and clothing smelled constantly of dairy products and ghee. This gave her the aroma of an ancient queen who took milk baths and made her flunkeys massage her in butter, even though she was as poor as mountain mud. The world outside the forest struck her as unreal and she did not like to go there more often than was necessary. "It was a long journey we made from Gujria," she liked to say, "and when you have made such a trek it is no longer necessary to go gadding about the place." The fact that the supposed migration of the Gujars from Gujria or Georgia had taken place fifteen hundred years earlier changed nothing. Nazarébaddoor spoke of the great trek as if it had happened just the other day and she herself had walked every step of the way, starting from the Caspian Sea and marching across central Asia, Iraq, Iran and Afghanistan, over the Khyber Pass and down into the Indian subcontinent. She knew the names of the settlements they had left behind in Iran, Afghanistan, Turkmenistan, Pakistan and India—Gurjara, Gujrabad, Gujru, Gujrabas, Gujdar-Kotta, Gujargarh, Gujranwala, Gujarat. She spoke with sorrow of the dreadful droughts that assailed Gujarat in the sixth century of the so-called Common Era, driving her ancestors out of the Forest of Gir and up into the verdant woods and meadows of the mountains of Kashmir. "Never mind," she told Firdaus. "Out of tragedy, something good showed up. We lost Gujarat, but lo and behold! We got, instead, Kashmir."

Firdaus Butt or Bhat as a young girl formed what became the lifelong habit of making her way up the forested slopes behind Pachigam to sit at the Gujar woman's feet, listening to Nazarébaddoor's inexhaustible stories and drinking salty pink tea and learning the knack of disconnecting her sense of smell, until she could switch it off like a radio and in the bland silence of its absence could drown in the sound of Nazarébaddoor's hypnotic voice without having her reverie interrupted by the scent of sheep shit or Nazarébaddoor's own frequent and extraordinary buffalo farts. The prophetess revealed that it was around the time of her arrival at puberty that she first discovered that she could avert small-scale disasters by prophesying good news. However, she resisted making the seemingly obvious menstrual connection. "If it had anything to do with that nonsense sent to make women's life hell, as if the world wasn't tough enough without it," she scoffed, "then it would have ended when I stopped bleeding, and that happened so long ago that it isn't polite to ask."

Nazarébaddoor remembered that long ago when she had been a young child she once found herself in the city in the company of her father for reasons which she could no longer bring to mind. In spite of the beauty of the streets of Srinagar with their overhanging wooden houses out of whose upper stories women could lean towards one another and exchange gossip, linen, fruit and perhaps even surreptitious kisses, in spite of the shining mirrors of the lakes and the magic of the little boats cutting across them like knives, the young Nazarébaddoor had felt horribly ill at ease. "So many people so close by," she explained. "It was offensive to me." Suddenly, and uncharacteristically, for she was a happy, sweet-natured child, not a rebel, the claustrophobic pressure of urban life became too much for her. She picked up a stone from the street and hurled it with all her might at the glass window of a shop selling *numdah* rugs. "I don't know why I did it," she told Firdaus years later. "The city seemed to be a kind of illusion, and the stone was a way of making it vanish so that the forest could reappear. Maybe that was it, but I really can't be sure. We are mysteries to ourselves. We don't know why we do things, why we fall in love or commit murder or throw a stone at a sheet of glass."

The thing young Firdaus loved best about Nazarébaddoor was that she talked to a girl exactly as she would to an adult, pulling no punches. "You mean," she asked wonderingly, "that one day I could cut off somebody's head and I wouldn't even know why I was doing it?" Nazarébaddoor farted noisily under her phiran. "Don't be so bloodthirsty, missy," she admonished. "And, by the by, the subject under discussion right now is not you. There is a stone in the air, flying towards its mark."

The moment the stone left her hand the young Nazarébaddoor regretted it. She saw her father's stunned eyes staring at her and for the first time in her life entered the trance of power. A form of blissful lethargy enveloped her and she felt as if the world had slowed down almost to the stopping point. "It won't break! The window won't break!" she heard her voice shouting out in the middle of that delicious stasis, and in that timeless period while the world stood still she saw the stone deviate slightly from its path so that when motion returned to the universe an instant later the missile struck the wooden window-frame of the numdah store and fell harmlessly to the ground.

After that she discovered the extents and limits of her powers by a process of trial and error. In the same year as the incident of the stone the rains failed and there was great concern in Pachigam. The child Nazarébaddoor overheard two villagers discussing the subject as they walked in the forest. "But will the rains come?" one asked the other, and the lovely slowness descended on Nazarébaddoor once more. "Yes," she answered loudly, astonishing the two men. "They will be here on Wednesday afternoon." Sure enough, after lunch on Wednesday it began to pour.

People started squinting at Nazarébaddoor with that mixture of suspicion and admiration which human beings reserve for those who can foretell the future. The path to her cottage began to be well trodden, by lovers asking if their sweethearts would return their love, by gamblers wondering if they would win at cards, by the curious and the cynical, the gullible and the hard-hearted. More than once there was a campaign against her in the village by people whose reaction to abnormality was to drive it away from their doorstep. She was saved by her discretion, by her refusal to speak if she didn't know the answer, because the visionary indolence which allowed her to push the future in the required direction could not be conjured up; it came when it pleased, and her own will seemed to have little to do with it. Only when she was sure of her ability to ensure a happy outcome would she gently murmur the good news into a supplicant's ear.

As she grew into womanhood her power began to fill her with doubts. The gift of affecting the course of events positively, of being able to change the world, but only for the best, ought to have been a source of joy. Nazarébaddoor was cursed with a philosophical cast of mind, however, and as a result even her innate good nature could not avoid being infected by a strain of melancholy. Difficult questions began to nag at her. Was it always a good thing to make things better? Didn't human beings need pain and suffering to learn and grow? Would a world in which only good things happened be a good world, a paradise, or would it in fact be an intolerable place whose denizens, excused from danger, failure, catastrophe and misery, turned into insufferably big-headed, overconfident bores? Was she damaging people by helping them? Should she just get her big nose out of everyone else's business and let destiny take whatever course it chose? Yes, happiness was a thing of great, bright value, and she believed herself to be promoting it; but might not unhappiness be as important? Was she doing God's work, or the devil's? There were no answers to such questions, but the questions themselves felt, from time to time, like answers of a sort.

In spite of her reservations, Nazarébaddoor continued to employ her gifts, unable to believe that she would have been given such powers if it wasn't okay to use them. But her fears remained. Outwardly she continued to behave with happy, outspoken, flatulent ease, but the unhappiness inside her grew; slowly, it's true, but it grew. Her greatest fear, which she shared with nobody, was that all the misfortune she was averting was piling up somewhere, that she was recklessly pouring out Pachigam's supply of good luck while the bad luck accumulated like water behind a dam, and one day the floodgates would open and the flood of misery would be unleashed and everyone would drown. This was why the pot war affected her so badly. Her worst nightmare had begun to come true.

Nazarébaddoor's friendship with the much younger Firdaus was the reason that nobody in Pachigam worried about Firdaus's lazy eye, and as a result Abdullah's wife was able to set up a nice little sideline in the sale of protective charms, such as chillies and lemons hung on strings, painted eyes, malachite, black streamers and teeth taken from the fierce *sur,* the wild boar of Kashmir, which you were well advised to hang around your children's necks. On wedding days people sent for Firdaus to line the happy couple's eyes with special kohl and to burn the propitiatory seeds of the white *isband* flower, also known as rue. During the ceremony Firdaus often dueted with Nazarébaddoor, and with a backing group of eunuchs summoned from the village of the singing castrati the two of them would sing their magic songs:

Lo, the wild young girl has her mild young guy,
Save them, God, from the evil eye.

After Nazarébaddoor immured herself in her cottage she stopped eating and drinking. Firdaus, heavily pregnant with the unborn Noman, went to her door with food and water and pleaded to be let in. She didn't dare to push the screen aside and force an entrance because that would be to draw bad luck down upon her own head. The two friends sat down on either side of the flimsy wooden screen, placed their lips against it and began the last conversation of their lives. "Live," Firdaus implored, "or you'll be leaving me to handle this shitty new world full of cookpots and anger all by myself." She heard Nazarébaddoor kissing the other side of the screen as if she were taking leave of a lover. "The age of prophecy is at an end," Nazarébaddoor whispered, "because what's coming is so terrible that no prophet will have the words to foretell it."

Firdaus lost her temper. "Okay, die if you want to," she said fiercely, placing defensive hands upon her swollen womb, "but to curse us all just because you've decided to go is just plain bad form."

For a while it didn't seem as if Nazarébaddoor's curse was going to come true. Pachigam was a blessed village, and its two great families, the Nomans and Kauls, had inherited much of the natural bounty of the region. Pandit Pyarelal had the apple orchard and Abdullah Noman had the peach trees. Abdullah had the honeybees and the mountain ponies and the pandit owned the saffron field, as well as the larger flocks of sheep and goats. That summer the weather was kind and the fruit hung heavy on the trees, the honey dripped sweetly from the combs, the saffron crop was rich, the meat animals fattened nicely and the breeding mares gave birth to their valuable young. There were many requests for the actors to perform the traditional plays. The dramatization of the reign of Zain-ul-abidin, the fifteenth-century monarch known simply as Budshah, "the great king", was especially in demand. The only dark cloud on the horizon was that relations with the village of Shirmal continued to be poor. Abdullah Noman was confident that his people would continue to defend themselves successfully against any further attacks but he was saddened by the estrangement, even though it had been his own idea to try and break the Shirmalis' local monopoly of the banquet market. He felt no guilt about his initiative. The world moved on and all enterprises had to adapt to survive. However, he felt bad about the damage to his friendship with the Shirmalis' *waza* or head chef, Bombur Yambarzal, and Firdaus of the unsparing tongue made him feel worse. "To put business before friendship is to displease God," she warned him. "We had enough to be going on with but in Shirmal they have it tougher; if they don't get hired to feed other people they will starve themselves."

Firdaus's pregnancy was weighing her down in those days and she spent most of her time in the company of the pandit's wife Pamposh a.k.a. Giri the walnut kernel, whose own pregnancy was a couple of months less advanced, and because all dreams are permitted to pregnant women they fantasized about the future lifelong friendship of their unborn children. The sweetness of these fantasies served only to intensify the force with which Firdaus attacked her husband for his behaviour towards the master cook of Shirmal. Pamposh, however, gently defended Abdullah. While the two women sat on the back verandah of Firdaus's home and looked out across the saffron fields towards Shirmal, Pamposh Kaul pointed out gently that the chef was a hard man to like. "Abdullah was the only one of us who even kept up a friendship with him," she said. "To try and love somebody who loves nobody but himself—well, it just goes to show what a generous man your husband is. Now that things have been broken off between them, that big fat waza doesn't have a single pal in the world."

As his name suggested, Bombur Yambarzal was part black bumblebee, part narcissus; he could sting when he chose to do so, and he was extremely vain. He ruled the roost in Shirmal because of his culinary mastery, but was widely disliked by his own kitchen brigade on account of his strutting manner of a parade-ground martinet and his repeated demands that all their pots be polished until he could see his reflection in them. As long as Shirmal village was the undisputed champion maker of the Banquet of Thirty-Six Courses Minimum, and Shirmalis provided gluttonous quantities of food at all important weddings and celebrations, Bombur Yambarzal ruled the roost, and everyone put up with his bee stings and narcissism. However, his influence waned as the village's income declined, and, as will be seen, the new mullah Bulbul Fakh's power began to grow. For this and much else Yambarzal blamed Abdullah Noman.

Out of admiration for his great skills as a chef and respect for his village headman status, Abdullah had long made an effort to remain on cordial terms with Bombur Yambarzal. At Abdullah's suggestion the two men had gone fishing for brook trout together from time to time, and spent occasional evenings drinking dark rum, and taken several mountain walks. Abdullah had begun to see glimpses of another, better Bombur beneath the bloated, preening surface that Yambarzal unfortunately presented to the world: a lonely man for whom cookery was his single passion in life, who approached it with an almost religious fervour and who demanded of others the same level of dedication he himself brought to his work, and who was therefore constantly and vociferously disappointed by the ease with which his fellow human beings were drawn away from the ecstatic devotions of the gastronomic arts by such petty distractions as family life, weariness and love. "If you weren't so hard on yourself," Abdullah had once told Bombur, "maybe you'd ease off on everyone else and run a happier outfit." Bombur bristled. "I'm not in the happiness game," he said sharply. "I'm in the banquet business." It was a statement that revealed the monomaniacal strain in the waza's personality, a characteristic he shared with the fanatical Mullah Bulbul Fakh, whose dreams became the two villages' nightmares.

After the pot war, contact between the two village headmen came to an acrimonious end, until messengers from the maharaja himself arrived in both Pachigam and Shirmal, demanding that to augment the staff of the palace kitchens they set aside their quarrels and pool their resources to provide food (and theatrical entertainment) at a grand Dassehra festival banquet in the Shalimar garden, a feast conceived on a scale not seen in the valley since the time of the Mughal emperor Jehangir. Firdaus Noman, who had picked up a little of Nazarébaddoor's prophetic ability the way one picks up an itch from a flea-ridden dog, at once concluded that bad trouble was on the way and the maharaja knew it. "He's partying like there's no tomorrow," she told Abdullah. "Let's hope that just goes for him, not us."

On the morning of Dassehra, at the end of the nine Navratri nights of singing paeans to Durga, Pandit Pyarelal Kaul awoke with a big smile on his face. "What's made you so happy?" Pamposh asked him, sulking. Her pregnancy was making her feel very ill that morning, so that her disposition was less than cheerful, especially as her husband's incessant hymn-singing, with which he persevered doughtily, not only when officiating at the village's small temple but also at home, had interfered severely with her sleep. "Doesn't matter how many love songs you sing to the goddess," Pamposh added sourly, "the only woman in your life is this big balloon." But the pandit's blithe spirits could not be deflated, even by his wife's bad mood. "Just consider for a moment!" cried Pyarelal. "Today our Muslim village, in the service of our Hindu maharaja, will cook and act in a Mughal—that is to say Muslim—garden, to celebrate the anniversary of the day on which Ram marched against Ravan to rescue Sita. What is more, two plays are to be performed: our traditional *Ram Leela,* and also *Budshah,* the tale of a Muslim sultan. Who tonight are the Hindus? Who are the Muslims? Here in Kashmir, our stories sit happily side by side on the same double bill, we eat from the same dishes, we laugh at the same jokes. We will joyfully celebrate the reign of the good king Zain-ul-abidin, and as for our Muslim brothers and sisters, no problem! They all like to see Sita rescued from the demon-king, and besides, there will be fireworks." Giant effigies of Ravan, his son Meghnath and his brother Kumbhakaran would be erected within the walls of the Shalimar Bagh, and Abdullah Noman as Lord Ram—a Muslim actor playing the part of a Hindu god—would shoot an arrow at Ravan, after which the effigies would be burned at the heart of a huge fireworks display. "Okay, okay," said Pamposh, doubtfully, "but I'll be the bloated girl in the corner, throwing up."

At the other end of Pachigam, Firdaus Noman awoke at dawn and noticed that her yellow hair had begun to darken. The baby was almost due and strange juices were running in her veins and because she was full of intimate forebodings the shadow lying on her hair seemed like one more bad omen. Abdullah had learned to trust his wife's instincts and went so far as to ask her if the Pachigam actors' troupe and kitchen brigade should stay home and let the royal command performance go to hell, but she shook her head. "Something shitty is beginning, like Nazarébaddoor said," she answered him, patting her distended womb. "That's for sure, but the person that's giving me the shivers right now is still inside here." It was the only time that Firdaus ever uttered what became the greatest secret of her life, a secret for which she had no rational explanation and to which, accordingly, she had no desire to give voice: that even before his birth her son, whom everyone loved the minute he was born, and whose nature was the sweetest, gentlest and most open of any human being in Pachigam, had started scaring her half to death.

"There's no need to worry," Abdullah reassured her, misunderstanding her. "We'll only be gone one night. Stay here with the boys"—that is to say, the five-year-old twins Hameed and Mahmood, and the two-and-a-half-year-old Anees—"and Pamposh will also wait by your side until we return. . . ." "If you imagine that Giri Kaul and I are going to stay home and miss out on such a gala evening," Firdaus interrupted, returning her attention to everyday matters, "then men are even more ignorant than I thought. Besides which, if the baby decides to come, don't you think I'd rather be with the women of the village, instead of staying back in an empty ghost-town?" Like all the women of Pachigam, Firdaus had a matter-of-fact view of childbirth. There was pain involved, but it had to be borne without a fuss. There were risks involved, but they were best faced with a shrug. As to timing, the baby would come when it came and its imminence was no reason for changing one's plans. "Besides," she added, conclusively, "who should run the show in a Mughal pleasure-garden if not a direct-line descendant of mighty Iskander the Great?" Abdullah Noman knew better than to go on arguing once Alexander the Great had entered the discussion. "Okay." He shrugged, turning away.

"If you two waddling hens are prepared to go behind a bush and lay your children like eggs while the grandees feast on chicken, there's no more to be said."

The Alexandrian fantasy of Firdaus Noman, which caused her to insist that her fair hair and blue eyes were a royal Macedonian legacy, had provoked her most vehement quarrels with her husband, who opined that conquering foreign monarchs were pestilences as undesirable as malaria, while simultaneously, and without conceding that his behaviour was in any way contradictory, revelling in his own theatrical portrayals of the arriviste pre-Mughal and Mughal rulers of Kashmir. "A king on stage is a metaphor, an idea of grandeur made flesh," he said, straightening the flat woollen hat which he wore every day like a crown, "whereas a king in a palace is usually a sot or a bore, and a king on a warhorse"—Firdaus bridled at this gibe, as he knew she would—"is invariably a menace to decent society." On the subject of the current Hindu maharaja of Kashmir, Abdullah had managed to preserve a position of diplomatic neutrality. "At present I don't care if he's a maharaja, a maharishi, a maha-lout or a *mahaseer* trout," he told the assembling villagers before the banquet at the Shalimar Bagh. "He's our employer, and the travelling players and wazwaan cooks of Pachigam treat all their employers like kings."

Firdaus's family had moved to Pachigam in her grandfather's time, carrying, on their sturdy little mountain ponies, the gunny sacks filled with gold dust with which her grandparents had purchased the fruit orchards and grazing meadows which she, as an only child, afterwards brought with her as her dowry when she married the charismatic sarpanch. Before the move her family had lived in the beautiful (but also bandit-infested) Peer Rattan hills to the east of Poonch, in a village named Buffliaz after Alexander the Great's legendary horse Bucephalus, who according to legend had died in that very spot centuries ago. In that hill town, as Abdullah Noman was well aware, Bucephalus was still revered as a semidivinity, and it was Firdaus's Buffliazi blood that had risen in her cheeks when her husband jeered dismissively at warhorses.

It was also possible to rile Firdaus by speaking dismissively of giant ants. The historian Herodotus had written about the gold-digging ants of northern India, and Alexander's scientists believed him. They were not foolishly gullible, these scientists, primitive as science was in those swordlike days: for example, they had swiftly disproved the racist Greek legend that Indians had black semen. (Best not to ask how.) Nevertheless, they believed in the prospector ants, and so did the villagers of the Peer Rattan. Alexander himself, according to the ancients of Buffliaz, had come to these mysterious hills because he had heard that giant, furry, antlike creatures were to be found in that locality, smaller than dogs but bigger than foxes, the size of a marmot, more or less, and in the construction of their outsized formicaries they dug up great heaps of gold-heavy earth. Once the Greek army, or at least its generals, found out that the gold-digging ants actually existed, many of them refused to go back home, settling in the region instead and leading the lives of the idle rich, raising miscegenated families amongst whom children with Grecian noses, blue or green eyes and yellow hair frequently coexisted with darker-haired, differently-nosed Himalayan siblings. Alexander himself stuck around long enough to restock his war chest and leave a few random by-blows behind; from whom there grew a series of accidental family trees, Firdaus's two-thousand-year-old ancestor being the first shoot of one such plant.

"My people, Iskander's progeny, knew the secret locations of the treasure-laden anthills," Firdaus would tell her infant son Noman as he grew, "but over the centuries the gold deposits dwindled. When they finally ran out we filled our gunny sacks with the last dusty remnants of that strange fortune and migrated to Pachigam, obliged by necessity to become actor-counterfeits of the magnificoes we once were." Firdaus Noman was a third-generation Pachigami and the wife of the headman, and in spite of her lazy eye and her tales of subterranean ant and snake cities she had the protection of Nazarébaddoor, so the village arranged to forget what everyone knew in her grandfather's time, namely that when a Mr Butt or Bhat comes to town at dead of night from a well-known bandit region and buys his way into the community by throwing money around and sleeps sitting up with a shotgun across his lap and uses a name that everyone suspects is not his own because he doesn't know how to spell it, you don't have to believe in furry, marmotlike, treasure-hunting ants to understand the situation.

Mr Butt or Bhat didn't say much to anyone in Pachigam at first. He just sat up every night guarding his sleeping wife and son and in the daytime his eyes looked like they would crack with silent pain. Nobody dared ask him any of the obvious questions, and after five or six years he calmed down and began to act as if he believed that whoever he was running from wasn't coming after him. After ten years he smiled for the first time. Maybe the bandit chief who had deposed him out there in Buffliaz had settled for his newfound power and didn't need to finish off his ousted rival. Maybe there really were giant treasure-hunting ants, but they had let him go. It was said in the ancient tales that the ants chased you if you stole their wealth, and woe betide the man or woman who didn't run fast or far enough. Death by ant horde was a terrible fate. It would be better to hang yourself or cut your own worthless throat. Mr Butt or Bhat had probably been afraid that the ant army would come after him, but his luck had held, they had lost his trail or found a new motherlode to mine and lost interest in his few pathetic bags of subterranean loot. Anyway, after fifteen years had passed the people who remembered Mr Butt or Bhat's arrival started dying off and when the old man himself breathed his last twenty-one years after he arrived in Pachigam, dying in bed like anyone else, without a shotgun in sight, people called it quits and stopped bitching about the family's shady past. Then Firdaus made her good marriage and after that the subject of the bandit gold became taboo and the ant story was the only one anyone ever told. To doubt this version was to be given the rough end of Firdaus's tongue and that was a lash only the sarpanch himself could withstand; even he sometimes reeled beneath the ferocity of her verbal attacks. But when Firdaus awoke on the day of the Shalimar banquet and saw that her hair had begun to darken she spoke clouded words about fearing her unborn son, who would be born later that night upon those numinous lawns. "He gives me the shivers," she repeated to herself both before and after the birth, because she saw something in his newly opened eyes, some golden glint of piracy, warning her that he, too, would have much to do in his burgeoning life with lost treasures, fear and death.

At the entrance to the Shalimar garden, beside the sumptuous lake bobbing with boats that resembled an eager audience waiting impatiently for the show to begin, beneath the whispering chinars and the gossiping poplar trees and in the silent eternal presence of the uncaring mountains, who were preoccupied by the gigantic effort of very slowly pushing themselves higher and higher into the virginal sky, the villagers of Pachigam herded together the animals they had brought for slaughtering, the chickens, goats and lambs whose blood would soon be flowing as freely as the garden's celebrated cascades, and unloaded their bullock carts and shouldered their loads of cooking utensils and theatrical props, their effigies and fireworks, while, as if for their entertainment, a tiny demagogue standing on an empty oil barrel made a startling claim, which he emphasized by beating a brightly painted stick vigorously against an enormous drum. "There is a tree in paradise," this little fellow cried, "that gives shelter and sustenance to all those in need. It has long been my belief that here—right here, in our unparalleled paradise on earth!—which, so as not to sound too boastful to the ears of outsiders, we choose to call Kashmir!—there exists a cousin of that celestial *tooba* tree. According to legend the location of the earthly tooba was revealed by holy *pirs* to the Emperor Jehangir and he built the Shalimar Bagh around it. To this day nobody knows which tree it is. Tonight, however, through the use of my personal magic, the truth will be revealed." He was a dark-skinned, glitter-eyed individual with a dancing moustache that seemed to lead a gymnastic life of its own above his mouthful of smiling white teeth, but even with the help of the oil barrel and the absurd cockaded turban on his head he didn't rise off the ground much higher than a full-grown man, and it occurred to Abdullah Noman that this was a man whose life's work was a form of revenge for the personal tragedy of his size: he had never fully appeared in the world and therefore wished to make parts of it dematerialise instead.

Firdaus saw more deeply. "He's ridiculous when he's banging his drum and yelling like that," she murmured to her husband. "But look at him in his brief moments of repose. Don't you think he suddenly looks like a man confident of his authority, calm, unafraid? If he'd just shut up he might convince us he isn't a cheap fraud."

"I am the Seventh Sarkar," shouted the little man, banging his drum. "Ladies and gents!—You see before you the Seventh-Generation Perpetrator Extraordinaire of Illusion, Delusion and Confusion!—In sum, of

Sorcery and Jadoo of every type!—And the Unique Exponent and Grand Master of the Most Ancient Form of Magic, known as Indrajal." Whereupon he banged his drum so hard that he tottered on his oil barrel and people began, unfortunately, to laugh. "Laugh as hard as you like," stormed the Seventh Sarkar, "but tonight, at the height of the evening's celebrations, after the banquet, the play, the dancing and the fireworks, I will make the Shalimar Bagh disappear completely for a period of three minutes minimum, and at that time, when the tree of paradise will be revealed, for only a heaven-tree is proof against my wiles, then!—ha!—we will see who is laughing then." With that he hopped off his oil barrel and, banging his drum with all his might, pushed his way through the mirthful Pachigami crowd.

Firdaus stopped him. "We mean no harm," she said. "We're entertainers too and if you pull off this trick, believe me, we'll be the ones applauding first, loudest and for the longest time." The Seventh Sarkar was greatly mollified upon hearing these words, but pretended not to be. "You think I haven't done things already?" he snorted. "Please! Peruse. Regard." From inside his shirt he pulled out a bundle of yellowing newspaper reports. The villagers crowded around. "SEVENTH SARKAR MAKES RUNNING TRAIN VANISH," he read, proudly, and, "POOF! BOMBAY'S FLORA FOUNTAIN MAGICKED AWAY." Then came his greatest credential. "TAJ MAHAL DISAPPEARS UNDER MAGIC SPELL."

These news reports changed the mood around him. Though he could barely be seen at the heart of the gathering crowd, he had grown greatly in stature. "What is it you do, then?" Abdullah Noman asked, somewhat gracelessly, for his disbelieving laugh had been the loudest of all. "I mean to say, what's the basis of your act? Some sort of mass hypnotism?" The Seventh Sarkar shook his head gaily. "No, no. Hypnotism totally not involved. I am simply able to keep things away from your eyes. Nothing supernatural or occultist, friends! It is all Science, the Science of the Perfect Illusion and of Mind Control." Many voices now clamoured for further details, but the Seventh Sarkar banged on his drum to silence them. "*Bas!* Enough! Shall I reveal my secrets in the public street even before I amaze you all? I say only this: that I have the willpower to create a Psychic Balance with the world around me, and this makes possible my Deeds. What is Indrajal? It is a theatrical representation of the wishful dream of living happily—for when you live happily, nothing seems impossible. But be still now my voice and babble no more! Already I have said too much. Perform your play, bhand-folk. Then watch a true master of the art of theatre go to work." Bang! Bang! And off he went, up into the terraced lawns. Pandit Pyarelal Kaul said to his wife, "You wait; by the end of the evening I will unlock the secret of this fancy vanishing trick." It was a night of dark absentings. Giri Kaul herself would be among those spirited away.

From the moment he entered the garden and found himself wading through high golden drifts of leaves Abdullah Noman began to suffer from misgivings about the event. It was an exceptionally cold October night. Snow had already begun to fall. "By the time the guests arrive in their finery we'll be in the middle of a blizzard and the air will ice people's lungs. Will there be enough braziers to keep the guests warm while they eat? And after that? Because a cold audience isn't easy to warm up. This is not the weather for a garden party. Not even *Ram Leela* and *Budshah* can overcome an obstacle like this snow."

Then the magic of the garden began to take hold. Paradise too was a garden—Gulistan, Jannat, Eden—and here before him was its mirror on earth. He had always loved the Mughal gardens of Kashmir, Nishat, Chashma Shahi, and above all Shalimar, and to perform there had been his lifelong dream. The present maharaja was no Mughal emperor, but Abdullah's imagination could easily change that, and as he stood at the centre of the central terrace and directed his people to their posts, as the theatre troupe went off to the highest terrace to build the stage for the performance of *Budshah,* while the chefs' brigade headed for the kitchen tents and began the interminable work of chopping, slicing, frying and boiling, the sarpanch closed his eyes and conjured up the long-dead creator of this wonderland of swaying trees, liquid terraces and water music, the horticulturalist monarch for whom the earth was the beloved and such gardens were his verdant love-songs to it. Abdullah drifted towards a trancelike state in which he felt himself being transformed into that dead king, Jehangir the Encompasser of the Earth, and something almost feminine came into his body, an imperial lassitude, the languorous sensuality of power. Where was his palanquin, he dreamily wondered. He should be carried up into the garden in a jewelled palanquin borne on the shoulders of wiry rope-sandalled men; why then was he on foot? "Wine," he murmured under his breath. "Bring sweet wine and let the music start."

There were times when Abdullah's powers of autosuggestion frightened his fellow actors. When he unleashed them he could, or so it seemed, resurrect the dead to inhabit his living flesh, an occultist feat far more impressive, but also more alarming, than mere performance. Now, as on all such occasions, the players of Pachigam brought his wife Firdaus to his side, to talk him back from the past. "The times are growing so dark," he told her distantly, "that we must try as best we can to cling to the memory of brightness." It was the emperor speaking, the emperor on his last journey hundreds of years ago, dying on the road to Kashmir without reaching the longed-for haven of his earthly paradise, his hymn-like garden of terraces and birds. Firdaus saw that the time for gentle measures was past and, what was more, she had news of her own to impart. She grabbed her husband roughly and shook him. Soft explosions of snow flew off his *chugha* coat and his beard. "Have you been smoking something?" she shouted, deliberately making her words as harsh as possible. "This garden has a big effect on small men. They start believing they are giants." The insult penetrated Abdullah's reverie and he began to return mournfully to the waking banality of himself. He was not the emperor. He was the help. Firdaus, who knew everything about him before he knew it himself, read his mind and laughed in his face. This increased his groggy dolour and heightened the colour in his cheeks. "If you want to prepare to play a king," she said more gently, "think about Zain-ul-abidin in the first play. Think about being Lord Ram in the second half of the programme. But right now there are more important lives to think about. Giri's baby is coming early, probably just because you said it would."

His head was clearing. Life-and-death matters were all around him. *In the middle of the fifteenth century the Sultan Zain-ul-abidin succumbed to a deadly Disease, viz. a poisonous Boil on the Chest, and would certainly have died, had it not been for the intervention of a scholarly Doctor, a Pandit whose Name was Shri Butt or Bhat. After Dr Butt or Bhat had cured the King of his Illness, Zain-ul-abidin told him he should ask for a very precious Gift, for had he not given the King himself renewed Life, the most precious of all Gifts? "I need nothing for myself," Dr Butt or Bhat replied, "but sire, under the Kings who came before you my Brothers were persecuted without end, and they are in need of a Gift at least as valuable as Life." The King agreed to cease the Persecution of the Kashmiri Pandits at once. In addition, he made it his Business to see to the Rehabilitation of their devastated and scattered Families, and allowed them to preach and practise their Religion without any Hindrance. He rebuilt their Temples, reopened their Schools, abolished the Taxes that burdened them, repaired their Libraries and ceased to murder their Cows. Whereupon a Golden Age began.*

Words reawakened in him and rushed out like panicky sheep. "Pamposh, hai! hai! Pamposh—where is she—what's happening—is she all right—the baby, will the baby live—where is Pyarelal, he must be wild—my God, didn't I tell you to stay back—*arré,* how did she, when did it, what should we do?"

His wife put her hand on his lips and loudly, for public consumption, jeered dismissively. "Listen to my great husband who holds the whole village in his hand," she said. "Listen to what one new baby turns him into—a panicky little boy." Then, so that nobody else could hear, she whispered into his ear in quite a different manner. "We have taken sheets and constructed a private delivery area behind the kitchen tents. There are enough women to do the needful. I can help with the baby and the others will keep an eye on the twins and little Anees. But Giri is not so well, and the blizzard doesn't help. There are doctors on the guest list and some of them live in nearby parts of Srinagar. Pyarelal has gone into the city to fetch one. Everything that can be done is being done. Leave it to me. There is enough on your plate just now."

Abdullah opened his mouth to speak, and Firdaus saw the words *I told you so* trembling on his lips. "Don't say it," she forestalled him. "Just don't even bother to try."

Abdullah Noman was himself again. Yes, the doctor would be brought and Pamposh and the baby would be saved. *The intervention of a scholarly doctor, a pandit,* just the way it was in *Budshah.* In the meanwhile there was cooking to supervise and a double bill of plays to prepare for. Abdullah strode about, pointing and ordering, smoothing points of liaison with liveried members of the maharaja's security guards, as well as service personnel and kitchen staff. The world resumed its familiar shape. On each of the terraces of the Shalimar garden, on either side of the central cascade of water, gaily coloured *shamiana* tents had been erected, and the royal household staff were spreading the Dogra *dastarkhans,* the floor-cloths surrounded by bolster cushions at which the banquet was traditionally served to guests sitting in groups of four. Abdullah was everywhere, satisfying himself that all was as it should be. The snow fell straight down in large feathery flakes. It was hard to tell if it was a benediction or a curse.

In a tent on the lowest terrace Bombur Yambarzal the waza of Shirmal confronted him with a face whose colours were anything but gay. In spite of the maharaja's requirement that their rivalries be set aside, this was not a man at peace with his neighbour. "It's the final humiliation," he snapped. "We—we, who are the unrivalled wazwaanis, longtime virtuosos of the *pulao,* maestros of *methi* chicken and artists of *aab gosh!*—we have been given the junior terrace, where the least important diners will come to eat. You interlopers—you pickpockets—you ignoramuses who think you can cook this food without even a waza to supervise you, let alone a *vasta waza,* a grand chef like myself!—have been ranked above us. The insult is apparent to all and will not be forgotten. I console myself that at least your rabble don't have access to the highest terrace either, because the household chefs threatened to walk out if they didn't get to feed the top tables. Clearly the maharaja was prepared to insult the whole village of Shirmal but felt obliged to butter up his cooks."

Abdullah Noman held his tongue. It was true that Pachigam was to feed the middle tier of guests, but later in the evening Abdullah's troupe of bhand pather actors would perform the history of Zain-ul-abidin, and then the *Ram Leela,* climaxing in the burning of the effigies and the fireworks, before the maharaja himself. "No point rubbing poor Bombur's nose in his misfortune," he thought, feeling one of his periodic twinges of guilty compassion for the waza of Shirmal; he inclined his head towards Yambarzal in a manner that was almost apologetic or at least deferential, and went on his way without returning hot words for hot, never suspecting that what lay ahead was not an evening of feasting and theatre but one of the great hinge moments of his life and also of the life of everyone and everything he loved, a night after which nothing in the world would continue down its expected path, rivers would change their courses, the stars would turn up in unexpected places in the sky, the sun might as well start rising in the north or south or any damn place, because all certainty was lost, and the darkening began, ushering in the time of horrors, which Abdullah's dreaming tongue had prophesied without consulting his brain. He went about his business, leaning into the snow, kicking drifts aside with his stout boots; and he was on his way to inspect the progress of the stage construction when Firdaus, staggering slightly, found him by the pond on the uppermost terrace. Exclamatory fountains burst upwards as she clutched his arm for support, as if the garden itself were shocked by the alteration in her demeanour. She looked much less in control of things than before, her face showed evidence of strain, and her lazy eye drifted uncertainly away to the side. "Okay," she said, and then winced and gritted her teeth, perspiring silently as a powerful contraction hit her, "so, I admit, the situation has become a little more complicated than we thought."

Two women gave snowbound birth behind the bushes, attended by a well-known local doctor and Sufistic philosopher, Khwaja Abdul Hakim, master of medicine both herbal and chemical, traditional and modern, Eastern and Western. But tonight his skills were useless; life arrived by itself, and death would not be denied. One boy child, one girl child, one trouble-free birth, one fatality. Firdaus Noman gave birth at speed, spitting out Noman Noman like a fruit pip. "Here you are, then, in a hurry," she whispered into the ear of her newborn boy, neglecting to make sure that the first word he heard was the name of God. "Your father is a shape-shifter who calls his sorcery acting and your mother's family of desperadoes is pretty suspicious, too, and nothing is at all normal about tonight; but just grow up normal anyway, okay, and don't give me any reason to be scared." Then Giri shrieked and Firdaus had to be restrained from jumping up to help her anguished friend. The women of Pachigam tended the living mother, swaddled and cared for the two healthy children and covered the dead woman's face. They would take the body home during the night on a bullock cart covered with blossom from the garden and tomorrow she would burn in a sandalwood flame. What was there to say about such things? They happened. They did not happen frequently enough to threaten the survival of the species, the statistics were improving all the time, but when it was your turn, you were one hundred per cent dead. There was grieving to be done and it would be done, as fully as was fitting. The pandit and his baby daughter needed the village's support and they would receive it. The village would close around them like a hand. The pandit would live on. His daughter would live on. Life continued. The snow would melt and new flowers would grow. Death was not the end.

The news of a fourth son was brought to Abdullah, whose pride in fatherhood had to be shelved for the moment, there being so much to be done before the guests arrived; and, besides, he was already preparing for the role of Zain-ul-abidin, metamorphosing into the old-time Sultan who represented for him everything that was best about the valley he loved, its tolerance, its merging of faiths. The pandits of Kashmir, unlike Brahmins anywhere else in India, happily ate meat. Kashmiri Muslims, perhaps envying the pandits their choice of gods, blurred their faith's austere monotheism by worshipping at the shrines of the valley's many local saints, its pirs. To be a Kashmiri, to have received so incomparable a divine gift, was to value what was shared far more highly than what divided. Of all this the story of Budshah Zain was a symbol. Abdullah closed his eyes and sank ever deeper into his favourite role. As a result he was unable to be present to comfort his friend the pandit when Pamposh Kaul died in the bloody mess of her daughter's premature birth.

A flight of winged shadows fled from the garden with her soul. Pyarelal wept beneath the illuminated trees while the Sufi philosopher embraced and kissed him, weeping as copiously as he. "The question of death," said the *khwaja* through his tears, "proposes itself, does it not, panditji, every day. How long do we have left, will it be kind or unkind when it comes, how much more work can we do, how much of life's richness will we experience, how much of our children's lives will we see, et cetera." Under normal circumstances, the opportunity to discuss ontology, to say nothing of the finer points of Sufi and Hindu mysticism, would have overjoyed Pyarelal Kaul. But nothing was normal that night. "She knows the answer now," he wept back in reply, "and what a bitter answer it is." The sobbing khwaja stroked the distraught widower's face. "You have a beautiful daughter," he said, choking. "The question of death is also the question of life, panditji, and the question of how to live is also the question of love. That is the question you have to go on answering, to which there is no answer except in the going on." Then there were no more words. They both wailed long and loud at the baleful, gibbous moon. Before there was a Mughal garden here this had been a jackal-infested place. The weeping of the two grown men sounded like jackals' howls.

Death, most present of absences, had entered the garden, and from that moment on the absences multiplied. It was dusk, and the appointed hour had arrived, the warm scents of the banquet were rising from the kitchens, and in spite of tragedy everything was ready on time; but where were the guests? It was cold, certainly, and perhaps that put some people off; the first few Dassehra revellers who did arrive were bundled up for warmth and looking dramatically unlike people who had come to have fun. But the expected flood of visitors never materialised, and, what was worse, many members of the royal household staff began to sneak quietly away, the bearers, the guards, even the chefs from the uppermost terrace, the maharaja's own chefs who had been preparing the food for his personal entourage.

How could the occasion be saved? Abdullah Noman rushed around the garden shouting at people but got few of the answers he needed. Beneath a Mughal pavilion he found the magician Sarkar with his head buried in his hands. "It's a catastrophe," said the Seventh Sarkar. "People are too afraid to come out in this snowstorm—and from what I've been hearing it's not only the snow that frightens them!—and so my greatest achievement will only be witnessed by a bunch of village buffoons."

The shamiana tents, their bright colours glowing in the light of the great heat-braziers and gay strings and loops of illuminations bouncing across the trees, stood almost empty as the evening darkened towards night, looking ghostly as they loomed out through the snow. Bombur Yambarzal, unnerved by the phantom banquet, sought Abdullah's advice. "What does that sorcerer mean, it's not only the snow? If people are too scared to show up," he said, almost timidly, the change in his demeanour an indication of the depth of his uncertainty, "do you think it's safe for us to stay?" Abdullah's heart was already in turmoil, the joy of Noman's birth warring in his breast with his feeling of despair at the death of sweet Pamposh. He just shook his head perplexedly. "Let's wait it out awhile," he said. "We should both send people into Srinagar to ask around. Things must become clearer than they are." Abdullah was not himself. There would be no performance of *Budshah* that night and he was trying to shake loose the shade of Zain-ul-abidin, pieces of whom were still stuck to his psyche. This was confusing. It was the second time that day that he had needed to exorcise the spirit of a king, and he was spent.

In the absence of the great majority of guests, all manner of rumours came into the Shalimar Bagh, hooded and cloaked to shield themselves against the elements, and filled the empty places around the dastarkhans: cheap rumours from the gutter as well as fancy rumours claiming aristocratic parentage—an entire social hierarchy of rumour lounged against the bolsters, created by the mystery that enveloped everything like the blizzard. The rumours were veiled, shadowy, unclear, argumentative, often malicious. They seemed like a new species of living thing, and evolved according to the laws laid down by Darwin, mutating randomly and being subjected to the amoral winnowing processes of natural selection. The fittest rumours survived, and began to make themselves heard above the general hubbub; and in the hissed or murmured noises emanating from these survivors, the loudest, most persistent, most puissant rumours, the single word *kabailis* was heard, over and over again. It was a new word, with which few people in the Shalimar Bagh were familiar, but it terrified them anyway. "An army of kabailis from Pakistan has crossed the border, looting, raping, burning, killing," the rumours said, "and it is nearing the outskirts of the city." Then the darkest rumour of all came in and sat down in the maharaja's chair. "The maharaja has run away," it said, contempt and terror mingling in its voice, "because he heard about the crucified man." The authority of this rumour was so great that it seemed to the appalled villagers of Pachigam and Shirmal that the crucified man materialised then and there on the lawns of the Mughal garden, nailed to the white ground, the snow around him reddening with his blood. The crucified man's name was Sopor and he was a simple shepherd. At a remote hillside crossroads in the far north the kabaili horde had come sweeping past him and his sheep and demanded to know the way to Srinagar. Sopor the shepherd lifted an arm and pointed, deliberately sending the invaders in the wrong direction. When, after a day-long wild goose chase, they realized what he had done, they retraced their steps, found him, crucified him in the dirt of the crossroads where he had misled them, let him scream for a while to beg God for the death that wouldn't come quickly enough for his needs, and when they were bored of his noise, hammered a final nail through his throat.

So much was new in those days, so much only half understood. "Pakistan" itself was a former rumour, a phantom-word that had only had a real place attached to it for two short months. Perhaps for this reason—its move across the frontier from the shadow-world of rumours into the "real"—the subject of the new country aroused the most furious passions among the rumours swarming into the Shalimar Bagh. "Pakistan has right on its side," said one rumour, "because here in Kashmir a Muslim people is being prevented by a Hindu ruler from joining their coreligionists in a new Muslim state." A second rumour roared back, "How can you speak of right, when Pakistan has unleashed this murderous horde upon us? Don't you know that the leaders of Pakistan told these cutthroat tribals that Kashmir is full of gold, carpets and beautiful women, and sent them to pillage and rape and kill infidels while they're at it? Is that a country you want to join?" A third rumour blamed the maharaja. "He's been dithering for months. The Partition was two months ago!—And still he can't decide who to join, Pakistan or India." A fourth butted in. "The fool! He has jailed Sheikh Abdullah, who has sworn off all communal politics, and is listening to that mullah, Moulvi Yusuf Shah, who obviously tilts towards Pakistan." Then many rumours clamoured at once. "Five hundred thousand tribals are attacking us, with Pak army soldiers in disguise commanding them!"—"They are only ten miles away!"—"Five miles!"—"Two!"—"Five thousand women raped and murdered on the Jammu border!"—"Twenty thousand Hindus and Sikhs slaughtered!"—"In Muzaffarabad, Muslim soldiers mutinied and killed their Hindu counterparts and the officer in charge as well!"—"Brigadier Rajender Singh, a hero, defended the road to Srinagar for three days with just 150 men!"—"Yes, but he is dead now, they slaughtered him."—"Raise his war cry everywhere! *Hamla-awar khabardar, ham Kashmiri hain tayyar!*"—*"Look out, attackers, we Kashmiris are ready for you!"*—"Sheikh Abdullah has been let out of jail!"—"The maharaja has taken his advice and opted for India!"—"The Indian army is coming to save us!"—"Will it be in time?"—"The maharaja held his last Dassehra Durbar at the palace and then hightailed it to Jammu!"—"To Bombay!"—"To Goa!"—"To London!"—"To New York!"—"If he's so scared what chance have we?"—"Run! Save yourselves! Run for your lives!"

As panic gripped the people in the Shalimar garden, Abdullah Noman ran to be with his wife and sons in the little makeshift screened-off maternity area Firdaus had had constructed in a corner of the Bagh. He found her sitting grim-faced on the ground, nursing the baby Noman, and beside her were Pandit Pyarelal Kaul and Khwaja Abdul Hakim, standing with bowed heads by the body of Pamposh. Pyarelal was singing a hymn softly. Abdullah could not speak for a moment. He was full of feelings of self-reproach at his own ignorance. He had known nothing, or next to nothing, of the trouble rushing down upon them. He was the sarpanch and should have known; how could he protect his people if he knew nothing of the dangers threatening them? He did not deserve his office. He was no better than Yambarzal. Petty rivalries and prideful self-absorption had blinded them both, and they had brought their people towards this terrifying conflict instead of keeping them safe and far away. Tears fell from his eyes. He knew they were tears of shame.

"Why are you singing that song of praise?" Firdaus's voice dragged him back into the world. She was glaring savagely at Pyarelal. "What do you have to thank Durga for? You worshipped her for nine days and on the tenth she took your wife." The pandit received the admonition without rancour. "When you pray for what you most want in the world," he said, "its opposite comes along with it. I was given a woman whom I truly loved and who truly loved me. The opposite side of such a love is the pain of its loss. I can only feel such pain today because until yesterday I knew that love, and that is surely a thing for which to thank whoever or whatever you like, the goddess, or fate, or just my lucky stars." Firdaus turned away from him. "Maybe we are too different, after all," she grumbled under her breath. Khwaja Abdul Hakim took his leave. "I do not think I will stay in Kashmir," he said. "I do not want to watch the sadness destroying the beauty. I have it in mind to give my land to the university and go south. Into India; always India; never into Pakistan." Firdaus's back was towards the khwaja. "You're lucky," she muttered without turning to wish him goodbye. "You're one of those who has a choice."

Abdullah asked for and received his swaddled baby boy. "We need to go," he told Firdaus and Pyarelal gently. "The rumours flying around here are making people crazy." All day, he thought, there have been kings and princes in my head. Alexander, Zain-ul-abidin, Jehangir, Ram. But it's our own prince's indecision that has unleashed this holocaust, and nobody can say whether or not India, that newly kingless land, can save us, or even if being saved by India is going to be good for us in the end.

A drum boomed immensely in the night, louder and louder, commanding attention. So potent was the drumming that it froze people in their tracks, it silenced the rumours and got everyone's attention. The little man, Sarkar the magician, was marching down the central avenue of the garden, hammering away at his mighty *dhol.* Finally, when all eyes were on him, he raised a megaphone to his lips and bellowed, "Fuck this. I came here to do something and I'm going to do it. The genius of my magic will triumph over the ugliness of the times. On the seventh beat of my drum, the Shalimar garden will disappear." He banged the drum, one, two, three, four, five, six times. On the seventh boom, just as he had foretold, the whole Shalimar Bagh vanished from sight. Pitch blackness descended. People began to scream.

For the rest of his life the Seventh Sarkar would curse history for cheating him of the credit for the unprecedented feat of "hiding from view" an entire Mughal garden, but most people in the garden that night thought he'd pulled it off, because on the seventh beat of his drum the power station at Mohra was blown to bits by the Pakistani irregular forces and the whole city and region of Srinagar was plunged into complete darkness. In the night-cloaked Shalimar Bagh the earthly version of the tooba tree of heaven remained secret, unrevealed. Abdullah Noman experienced the bizarre sensation of living through a metaphor made real. The world he knew was disappearing; this blind, inky night was the incontestable sign of the times.

The remaining hours of that night passed in a frenzy of shouts and rushing feet. Somehow Abdullah managed to send his family away on a bullock cart, which Firdaus had to share with the dead body of her friend and, next to deceased Pamposh, Pyarelal Kaul cradling his baby daughter and unstoppably singing praisesongs to Durga. Then by a lucky chance Abdullah collided with Bombur Yambarzal again. Bombur in the darkness was a quivering wreck of a man, but Abdullah managed to get him on his feet. "We can't leave our stuff here," he persuaded Yambarzal, "or both our villages will be crippled for good." Somehow the two of them rounded up a rump or quorum of villagers, half Shirmali, half from Pachigam, and this raggle-taggle remnant dismantled their special *wuri* ovens and hauled many dozens of pots full of feast-day food to the roadside. The portable theatre had to be dismantled as well, and the materials for the plays packed in great wicker panniers and taken down the terraces to the lakeside. All night the villagers of Shirmal and Pachigam worked side by side, and when dawn crept over the hills at the end of that dark night and the garden reappeared, the waza and the sarpanch hugged each other and made promises of unbreakable fellowship and undying love. Above them, however, the shadow planets Rahu and Ketu existed without actually existing, pulling and pushing, intensifying and suppressing, inflaming and stifling, dancing out the moral struggle within human beings while remaining invisible in the brightening heavens. And when the actors and cooks departed from the Shalimar Bagh they left behind the giant effigies of the demon king, his brother and his son, all filled with unexploded fireworks. Ravan, Kumbhakaran and Meghnath glowered across the trembling valley, not caring whether they were Hindus or Muslims. The time of demons had begun.

Man is ruined by the misfortune of possessing a moral sense," reflected Pandit Pyarelal Kaul by the banks of the loquacious Muskadoon. "Consider the superior luck of the animals. The wild beasts of Kashmir, to enumerate a few, include Ponz the Monkey, Potsolov the Fox, Shal the Jackal, Sur the Boar, Drin the Marmot, Nyan and Sharpu the Sheep, Kail the Ibex, Hiran the Antelope, Kostura the Musk Deer, Suh the Leopard, Haput the Black Bear, Bota-khar the Ass, Hangul the Twelve-Pointed Barasingha Stag, and Zomba the Yak. Some of these are dangerous, it's true, and many are fearsome. Ponz is a danger to walnuts. Potsolov is cunning and a danger to chickens. Shal's is a fearsome howl. Sur is a danger to crops. Suh is ferocious and a danger to stags. Haput is a danger to shepherds. The Ass, by contrast, is a coward and runs from danger; however you must remember in mitigation that he is an Ass, just as a jackal is a jackal and a leopard is a leopard and a boar has no option but to be boarish one hundred per cent of the time. They neither know nor shape their own nature; rather, their nature knows and shapes them. There are no surprises in the animal kingdom. Only Man's character is suspect and shifting. Only Man, knowing good, can do evil. Only Man wears masks. Only Man is a disappointment to himself. Only by ceasing to need the things of the world and relieving oneself of the needs of the body . . ."

And so on. Boonyi Kaul knew that when her father, a man with many friends because of his love of people and one too many chins because of his ever more voracious and perfectionist love of food, started mourning the failings of the human race and making ascetic recommendations for its improvement he was secretly missing his wife, who had never disappointed him, whose surprises had filled his heart, and for whom after fourteen years his body still ached. At such times Boonyi usually became extra demonstrative, trying to bury her father's grief beneath her love. Today, however, she was distracted, and could not play the dutifully loving daughter. Today, she and her Noman, her beloved clown Shalimar, sat listening to her father on their usual boulders, neither touching nor glancing at each other, both of them struggling to control the confessional smiles that kept creeping out onto their lips.

It was the morning after the great event in the high mountain meadow of Khelmarg. Boonyi, intoxicated by love for her lover, lounged with open sensuality on her rock, her arching body a provocation to anyone who cared to notice it. Her father, lost in melancholy, noticed that she was looking even more like her mother than usual, but failed, with the stupidity of fathers, to understand that this was because desire and the fulfilment of desire were running their hands over her body, welcoming it into womanhood. Shalimar the clown, however, was doubly agitated by her display; at once aroused and alarmed. He began to make small jerking downward movements of his fingers, as if to say calm down, don't make it so obvious. But the invisible strings connecting his fingertips to her body weren't working properly. The more insistently he pushed his fingers downward the higher she arched her back. The more urgently his hands pleaded for passivity the more languorously she rolled about. Later that day, when they were alone in the practice glade, both of them balancing high above the ground on the precarious illusion of a single tightrope, he said, "Why didn't you stop when I asked you?" At which she grinned and said, "You weren't asking me to stop. I could feel you fondling me here, pressing and squeezing and all, and pushing down on me here, hard hard, and it was driving me crazy, as you knew perfectly well it would."

Shalimar the clown began to see that the loss of her virginity had unleashed something reckless in Boonyi, a wild defiant uncaringness, a sudden exhibitionism which was tumbling towards folly—for her flaunting of their consummated love could bring both their lives crashing down and smash them to bits. There was irony in this, because Boonyi's daring was the single quality he most admired. He had fallen in love with her in large part because she was so seldom afraid, because she reached out for what she wanted and grabbed at it and didn't see why it should elude her grasp. Now this same quality, intensified by their encounter, was endangering them both. Shalimar the clown's signature trick on the high wire was to lean out sideways, increasing the angle until it seemed he must fall, and then, with much clownish playacting of terror and clumsiness, to right himself with gravity-defying strength and skill. Boonyi had tried to learn the trick but gave up, giggling, after many windmilling failures. "It's impossible," she confessed. "The impossible is what people pay to see," Shalimar the clown on the high wire quoted his father, and bowed as if receiving applause. "Always do something impossible right at the beginning of the show," Abdullah Noman liked to tell his troupe. "Swallow a sword, tie yourself in a knot, defy gravity. Do what the audience knows it could never do no matter how hard it tries. After that you'll have them eating out of your hand."

There were times, Shalimar the clown understood with growing concern, when the laws of theatre might not precisely apply to real life. Right now in real life Boonyi was the one leaning out from the high wire, brazenly flaunting her new status as lover and beloved, defying all convention and orthodoxy, and in real life these were forces that exerted at least as powerful a downward pull as gravity. "Fly," she told him, laughing into his worried face. "Wasn't that your dream, Mister Impossible? To do without the rope and walk on air." She took him deeper into the wood and made love to him again and then for a while he didn't care what followed. "Face it," she whispered. "Married or not married, you've passed through the stone door." The poets wrote that a good wife was like a shady boonyi tree, a beautiful chinar—*kenchen renye chai shihiji boonyi*—but in the common parlance the imagery was different. The word for the entrance to a house was *braand;* stone was *kany.* For comical reasons the two words were sometimes used, joined together, to refer to one's beloved bride: *braand-kany,* "the gate of stone." Let's just hope, Shalimar the clown thought but did not say, that the stones don't come smashing down on our heads.

Shalimar the clown was not the only local male to have Boonyi Kaul on the brain. Colonel Hammirdev Suryavans Kachhwaha of the Indian army had had his eye on her for some time. Colonel Kachhwaha was just thirty-one years old but liked to call himself a Rajput of the old school, a spiritual descendant—and, he was certain, a distant blood relation—of the warrior princes, the old-time Suryavans and Kachhwaha rajas and ranas who had given both the Mughals and the British plenty to think about in the glory days of the kingdoms of Mewar and Marwar, when Rajputana was dominated by the two mighty fortresses of Chittorgarh and Mehrangarh, and fearsome one-armed legends rode into battle bisecting their enemies with cutlasses, crushing skulls with maces, or hacking through armour with the *chaunch,* a long-nosed axe with a cruel storklike beak. At any rate, England-returned Colonel H. S. Kachhwaha had a splendid Rajput moustache, a swaggering Rajput bearing, a barking British-style military voice, and now he was also commanding officer of the army camp a few miles to the northeast of Pachigam, the camp everyone locally called Elasticnagar because of its well-established tendency to stretch. The colonel wholeheartedly disapproved of this irreverent title, which in his ramrod opinion was far from commensurate with the dignity of the armed forces, and after arriving in post one year back had tried to insist that the camp's official name be used by all persons at all times, but had given up when he realized that most of the soldiers under his command had forgotten it long ago.

The colonel had a preferred nickname for himself, too. "Hammer", an English play on Hammir. A good, soldierly name. He practised it sometimes when he was alone. "Hammer Kachhwaha." "Hammer by name, hammer by nature." "Colonel Hammer Kachhwaha at your service, sir." "Oh, please, dear fellow, just call me Hammer." But this attempted self-naming failed just as the battle against Elasticnagar had, because once people heard his surname they inevitably wanted to shorten it to Kachhwa Karnail, which is to say "Colonel Turtle" or "Tortoise". So Tortoise Colonel he became, and was forced to look for his metaphors of self-description closer to the ground. "Slow and steady wins the race, eh, what?" he practised; and "Tortoise by name, damned hard-shelled by nature." But somehow he could never bring himself to say, "My dear chap, just call me Turtle," or, "I mostly go by Tortoise, don't you know—but it's just plain Torto to you." His testudinarious fate further soured a mood which had already been ruined by his father on his thirtieth birthday, when the newly promoted colonel was on home leave in Jodhpur before taking up his posting in Kashmir. His father was in fact the Rajput of the old school that his son aspired to be, and his birthday gift to Hammirdev was a set of two dozen golden bangles. Ladies' bangles? Hammir Kachhwaha was confused. "Why, sir?" he asked, and the older man snorted, jingling the bangles on a finger. "If a Rajput warrior is still alive on his thirtieth birthday," grunted Nagabhat Suryavans Kachhwaha in tones of disgust, "we give him women's bangles to express our disappointment and surprise. Wear them until you prove they aren't deserved." "By dying, you mean," his son sought clarification. "To win favour in your eyes I have to get myself killed." His father shrugged. "Obviously," he said, neglecting to discuss why there were no bangles on his own arms, and spat copious betel juice into a handy spittoon.

So Colonel Kachhwaha of Elasticnagar was well known not to be a happy man. The men of his command feared his martinet tongue, and the locals, too, had learned that he was not lightly to be crossed. As Elasticnagar grew—as soldiers flooded north into the valley and brought with them all the cumbersome matériel of war, guns and ammunition, artillery both heavy and light, and trucks so numberless that they acquired the local name of "locusts"—so its need for land increased, and Colonel Kachhwaha requisitioned what he needed without explanation or apology. When the owners of the seized fields protested at the low level of compensation they received, he answered furiously, his face turning shockingly red, "We've come to protect you, you ingrates. We're here to save your land—so for God's sake don't give me some sob story when we have to bally well take it over." The logic of his argument was powerful, but it didn't always go down well. This was not finally important. Outraged by his continued failure to die in battle, the colonel was unquiet of spirit, and as livid as a rash. Then he saw Boonyi Kaul and things changed—or might have changed, had she not turned him down, flatly, and with scorn.

Elasticnagar was unpopular, the colonel knew that, but unpopularity was illegal. The legal position was that the Indian military presence in Kashmir had the full support of the population, and to say otherwise was to break the law. To break the law was to be a criminal and criminals were not to be tolerated and it was right to come down on them heavily with the full panoply of the law and with hobnailed boots and *lathi* sticks as well. The key to understanding this position was the word *integral* and its associated concepts. Elasticnagar was integral to the Indian effort and the Indian effort was to preserve the integrity of the nation. Integrity was a quality to be honoured and an attack on the integrity of the nation was an attack on its honour and was not to be tolerated. Therefore Elasticnagar was to be honoured and all other attitudes were dishonourable and consequently illegal. Kashmir was an integral part of India. An integer was a whole and India was an integer and fractions were illegal. Fractions caused fractures in the integer and were thus not integral. Not to accept this was to lack integrity and implicitly or explicitly to question the unquestionable integrity of those who did accept it. Not to accept this was latently or patently to favour disintegration. This was subversive. Subversion leading to disintegration was not to be tolerated and it was right to come down on it heavily whether it was of the overt or covert kind. The legally compulsory and enforceable popularity of Elasticnagar was thus a matter of integrity, pure and simple, even if the truth was that Elasticnagar was unpopular. When the truth and integrity conflicted it was integrity that had to be given precedence. Not even the truth could be permitted to dishonour the nation. Therefore Elasticnagar was popular even though it was not popular. It was a simple enough matter to understand.

Colonel Kachhwaha saw himself as a man of the thinking kind. He was famous for possessing an exceptional memory and liked to demonstrate it. He could remember two hundred and seventeen random words in succession and also tell you if asked what the eighty-fourth or one hundred and fifty-ninth word had been, and there were other such tests that impressed the officers' mess and gave him the air of a superior being. His knowledge of military history and the details of famous battles was encyclopedic. He prided himself on his storehouse of information and was pleased with the consequent, irrefutable thrust of his analyses. The problem of the accumulating detritus of quotidian memories had not yet begun to distress him, although it was tiresome to remember every day of one's life, every conversation, every bad dream, every cigarette. There were times when he hoped for forgetfulness as a condemned man hopes for mercy. There were times when he wondered what the long-term effect of so much remembering might be, when he wondered if there might be moral consequences. But he was a soldier. Shaking off such thoughts, he got on with his day.

He thought of himself, too, as a man of deep feeling, and consequently the ingratitude of the valley weighed heavily upon him. Fourteen years ago, at the behest of the fleeing maharaja and the Lion of Kashmir, the army had driven back the kabaili marauders but had stopped short of driving them out of Kashmiri territory, leaving them in control of some of the high mountainous areas to the north, Gilgit, Hunza, Baltistan. The de facto partition that resulted from this decision would be easy to call a mistake if it were not illegal to do so. Why had the army stopped? It had stopped because it had decided to stop, it was a decision taken in response to the actual situation on the ground, and it followed that that was the proper decision, the only decision, the decision with integrity. All very well for armchair experts to query it now, but they hadn't been there, on the ground, at the time. The decision was the correct decision because it was the decision that had been taken. Other decisions that might have been taken had not been taken and were therefore wrong decisions, decisions that should not have been taken, that it had been right not to take. The de facto line of partition existed and so had to be adhered to and the question of whether it should exist or not was not a question. There were Kashmiris on both sides who treated the line with contempt and walked across the mountains whenever they so chose. This contempt was an aspect of Kashmiri ingratitude because it did not recognize the difficulties faced by the soldiers at the line of partition, the hardships they endured in order to defend and maintain the line. There were men up there freezing their balls off and occasionally dying, dying of the cold, dying because they intercepted a Pak sniper's bullet, dying before they were given golden bangles by their fathers, dying to defend an idea of freedom. If people were suffering for you, if they were dying for you, then you should respect their suffering and to ignore the line they were defending was disrespectful. Such behaviour was not commensurate with the army's honour to say nothing of national security and was therefore illegal.

It was possible that many Kashmiris were naturally subversive, that they all were, not just the Muslims but the meat-eating pandits as well, that it was a valley of subversives. In which case they were not to be tolerated and it was right to come down hard. He resisted this conclusion even though it was his own, even though there was something ineluctable about the process of thought that led to it, something almost beautiful. He was a man of deep feeling, a man who appreciated beauty and gentleness, who loved beauty, and who accordingly felt great love for beautiful Kashmir, or who wished to feel love, or who would feel love if he were not prevented from doing so at every turn, who would be a true and sincere lover if he were only loved in return.

He was lonely. In the midst of beauty he was mired in ugliness. If it were not subversive to say that Elasticnagar was a dump then he would have said that it was a dump. But it could not be a dump because it was Elasticnagar and so by definition and by law and so on and so forth. He went into a corner of his mind, a small subversive corner that didn't exist because it shouldn't, and he whispered into his cupped hands. Elasticnagar was a dump. It was fences and barbed wire and sandbags and latrines. It was Brasso and spit and canvas and metal and the smell of semen in the bunkhouses. It was a smudge on an illuminated manuscript. It was debris floating on a glassy lake. There were no women. There were no women. The men were going crazy. The men were masturbating like crazy and there were stories of crazy assaults on crazy local girls and when they were able to visit the crazy brothels of Srinagar the crazy wooden houses shook with their crazy exploding lust. There were many Elasticnagars now and they were getting bigger and bigger and some of them were up in the high mountains where there weren't even goats to fuck so he shouldn't be complaining, even in the little subversive corner in his head that didn't exist because by definition and et cetera, he should be proud. He was proud. He was a man of integrity, honour and pride and where were the goddamn girls, why wouldn't they come near him, he was a single male of wheatish complexion and good family who personally had no communalist-type Hindu-Muslim issues, he was a secularist through and through, and anyway it wasn't as if he was talking about getting married, the question didn't arise, but how about a cuddle for your commanding officer, how about a kiss or a goddamn caress?

It was like that bit in *The Magnificent Seven* where Horst Buchholz discovers that the villagers have been hiding their women from the gunmen they've hired to defend them. Except hereabouts the women weren't hidden away. They just looked through you with their ice-blue eyes their golden eyes their emerald eyes their eyes of creatures from another world. They floated by you on the lakes wearing their scarlet head scarves their burgundy their cobalt head scarves concealing the dark or yellow flame of their hair. They were squatting down on the prows of their little boats like birds of prey and they ignored you as if you were plankton. They didn't see you. You didn't exist. How could they even think about kissing you cuddling you kissing you when you didn't exist? You were living or so it seemed on a shadow planet. You were the creature from another world. You existed without actually existing. Your existence could only be perceived through your effects. The women could see Elasticnagar which was an effect and because they thought it was ugly even though it was illegal to think so they assumed that the invisible men who lived there must be ugly too.

He was not ugly. His voice barked like a British bulldog but his heart was Hindustani. He was unmarried at thirty-one but nothing should be deduced from that. Many men were not prepared to wait but he was resolved to do so. The men under his command cracked and went to brothels. They were of lower calibre than he. He contained his seed, which was sacred. This required self-discipline, this remaining within the bounds of the self and never spilling across one's frontiers. This building of inner embankments, of dikes, like the Bund in Srinagar. When he walked on the Bund at the edge of the Jhelum he felt he was walking on the defences of his heart.

He felt full to bursting of his need, of his unholy unfulfilled need, but he did not burst. He held himself in and told nobody his secret. This was his secret, which he attributed to all that was pent up in him, all that was dammed: *his senses were changing.* There was a bug in the system. His senses were shifting sands. If you devoted too many of your resources to fortifying one front line you left yourself open to an attack on another front. His desires had been reined in and so his senses were playing tricks. He barely had the words to describe these deceptions, these blurrings. He saw sounds nowadays. He heard colours. He tasted feelings. He had to control himself in conversation lest he ask, "What is that red noise?" or criticize the singing of a camouflaged truck. He was in turmoil. Everybody hated him. It was illegal but that didn't stop them. People said terrible things about what the army did, its violence, its rapaciousness. Nobody remembered the kabailis. They saw what was before their eyes, and what it looked like was an army of occupation, eating their food, seizing their horses, requisitioning their land, beating their children, and there were sometimes deaths. Hatred tasted bitter, like the cyanide in almonds. If you ate eleven bitter almonds you died, that's what they said. He had to eat hatred every day and yet he was still alive. But his head was whirling. His senses were changing into one another. Their names didn't make sense any more. What was hearing? What was taste? He hardly knew. He was in command of twenty thousand men and he thought the colour gold sounded like a bass trombone. He needed poetry. A poet could explain him to himself but he was a soldier and had no place to go for *ghazals* or odes. If he spoke of his need for poetry his men would think him weak. He was not weak. He was contained.

The pressure was building. Where was the enemy? Give him an enemy and let him fight. He needed a war.

Then he saw Boonyi. It felt like the meeting of Radha and Krishna except that he was riding in an army Jeep and he wasn't blue-skinned and didn't feel godlike and she barely recognized his existence. Apart from those details it was exactly the same: life-changing, world-altering, mythic, religious. She looked like a poem. His Jeep was enveloped in a cloud of khaki noise. She was with her girlfriends, Himal, Gonwati and Zoon, just like Radha with the milky gopis. Kachhwaha had done his homework. Zoon Misri was the olive-skinned girl who liked to claim descent from the queens of Egypt even though she was only the daughter of the outsized village carpenter Big Man Misri and Himal and Gonwati were the tone-deaf children of Shivshankar Sharga who had the best singing voice in town. The four of them were practising a dance from one of the bhand plays. Looked like they were playing at being milkmaids, which would be perfect. Kachhwaha didn't know much about dancing but the dance was all perfume and the look of her was emerald. He was on his way to meet the panchayat of Pachigam to discuss important and difficult issues of resources and subversion but his need spoke to him and he told the driver to stop and got out by himself.

The dancers stopped and faced him. He felt at a loss. He saluted. That was a misstep. That didn't go down well. He asked to speak to her alone. It came out as a barked command and her girlfriends scattered like breaking glass. She faced him. She was thunder and music. His voice stank of dog turds. He had hardly begun to speak when she guessed his meaning, saw him naked. His hands moved involuntarily to cover his genitals. You are the *afsar,* she said, Kachhwa Karnail. He flushed. He did not know how to speak his heart. The officer, yes *bibi.* The officer who—after a lifetime of waiting—of building dams—of saving himself—who profoundly wishes. Who hopes—who most fervently yearns . . . He said nothing, and she bridled. Have you come to arrest me, she demanded. Am I a subversive, then. Do I need to be beaten on the soles of my feet or electrocuted or raped. Do people need to be protected against me. Is that what you have come to offer. Protection. Her contempt smelled like spring rain. Her voice showered over him like silver. No, *bibi,* not that way, he said. But she knew the truth already, his burgeoning hangdog desire. Fuck off, she told him, and fled, into the woods, along the stream, anywhere but where he stood on the outskirts of Pachigam with the embankments crumbling around his soul.

Back in Elasticnagar he allowed his anger to claim him, and began to lay plans to descend on Pachigam in force. Pachigam would suffer for Boonyi Kaul's insulting behaviour, for metaphorically slapping her better's face. The liberation movement was starting up in those days and the idea was to nip it in the bud by strong preemptive measures. Kashmir for the Kashmiris, a moronic idea. This tiny landlocked valley with barely five million people to its name wanted to control its own fate. Where did that kind of thinking get you? If Kashmir, why not also Assam for the

Assamese, Nagaland for the Nagas? And why stop there? Why shouldn't towns or villages declare independence, or city streets, or even individual houses? Why not demand freedom for one's bedroom, or call one's toilet a republic? Why not stand still and draw a circle round your feet and name that Selfistan? Pachigam was like everywhere else in this sneaky, dissembling valley. There were tendencies there on which he had been too soft for too long. He had leads: suspects, targets. Oh, yes. He would come down hard. And he had a reliable informer in the village, a subtle, ruthless and skillful spy, eating breakfast on most days right in Boonyi Kaul's house.

Pandit Gopinath Razdan, an exceedingly thin man with a deep furrow between his eyebrows, the reddened gums of an addict of *paan* and the air of one who expected to find much to be dissatisfied with wherever he went, arrived at Boonyi's door wearing narrow gold-rimmed spectacles and a pinched expression, carrying an attaché case full of Sanskrit texts and a letter from the education authorities. He wore citified Western dress, a cheap tweedy jacket with its collar turned up against the crisp breeze, and grey flannel trousers with a coffee stain above the right knee. He was a young man, about the same age as Colonel H. S. Kachhwaha, but he took pains to look older. His lips were pursed, his eyes were narrowed, and he leaned upon a furled umbrella with at least one visibly broken spoke. Boonyi disliked him on sight and before he had opened his bony face she told him, "You must be looking for someone somewhere else. There is nothing here for you." But of course there was.

"Everything is in order, please be assured," said Pandit Gopinath Razdan, jerking his head to the side and emitting a long red stream of betel juice and saliva; and there was hauteur in his voice, even though he spoke with the bizarre accent of Srinagar which not only omitted the ends of some words but also left out the occasional middles. *Ev'thing is in or'er, plea' be assur'.* "I am presenting myself—*I am prese'ing mysel'*—at your goodfather's own behest." Bustling out from the kitchen came Pandit Pyarelal Kaul, smelling of onions and garlic. "Dear cousin, dear cousin," fussed Pyarelal, casting shifty glances at Boonyi, "I wasn't expecting you until next week at the earliest. I am afraid you have taken my daughter by surprise." Gopinath was sniffing the air disapprovingly. "If I did not know better," he said in his skeletal voice, "I would think that was a Muslim kitchen you have back there." *Know be'er. Musli' ki'en.* Boonyi felt a great snort of laughter blowing through her nostrils. Then a huge surge of irritation welled up in her and the impulse to laugh was lost.

Pyarelal slapped Gopinath heartily on the back; whereupon he, the city slicker, winced, might even be said to have recoiled. "Ha! Ha! dear chap," Boonyi's father explained. "We're all of a jumble here in Pachigam. Ever since I got bitten by the cooking bug I've been slowly introducing pandit cooking into the wazwaan—a radical change, but one of great symbolic importance, I'm sure you will agree!—so that now we for example offer our clients the garlicless *kabargah* rack of ribs, and even there are dishes made with asafoetida and curds!—and in return for everyone's willingness to go along with my innovations, I thought it was only fair to start using lashings of onions and garlic in some of my own food, just the way our Muslim brothers like it." A faint shudder coursed through Gopinath's etiolated frame. "I see," he stated faintly, "that many barriers—*ma'y ba'iers*—have fallen down around here. Much, sir, for a man like myself—*my'elf*—to ponder."

Boonyi had listened to this exchange with growing impatience and bewilderment. Now she burst out, "Pon'er, is it? Daddy, who is this to come here from the city and immediately start pon'ering over us?"

It transpired that Gopinath was the new schoolteacher. Pyarelal, fearing Boonyi's reaction, had hidden from her his decision to give up the pandit's traditional role of educator and concentrate on his cooking instead. As the years passed the kitchen had moved ever closer to the centre of his life. In the kitchen where once Pamposh had reigned he felt in communion with her departed beauty, felt their souls blending in his bubbling sauces, their vanished joy expressing itself in vegetables and meat. This much Boonyi knew: cooking was his way of keeping Pamposh alive. When they ate his food they swallowed her spirit too. What Boonyi had not noticed, however, because children need their parents only to be their parents and accordingly pay less attention than they should to their elders' dreams, was that cooking gradually became more than therapy for Pyarelal. The kitchen released an unsuspected artistry in him and in that village of actors who had taken up cooking as a sideline his growing mastery gave him a new, central part to play. More and more, when Pachigam people went off to a wedding to prepare the Banquet of Thirty-Six Courses Minimum, the pandit took a leadership role. His saffron-flavoured pulao was a miracle, his gushtaba meatball mixture was pounded until it acquired the softness of a baby's cheek. Wedding guests clamoured for his *dum aloo,* his chicken with almonds, his fenugreek-scented cottage cheese and tomatoes, his lotus stems in gravy, his red chili *korma,* and the closing, delicious sweetness of the *firni,* and cardamom tea. Women came up to him and asked slyly for his wazwaan recipes, at which the innocent fellow, ever ready to help, began to spell them out until his fellow cooks shouted him down and shut him up. After that he devised a standard response to all requests for the secrets of his culinary sorcery. "Ghee, madams," he would say with a grin. "Nothing else to it. Use much and much of real, *asli,* ghee."

Boonyi was naturally well aware of her father's growing importance in the preparation of the Thirty-Six Courses Minimum, but it had never occurred to her that this would lead to his making such a dramatic career move. Badly off balance, she lost her head completely. "If teaching isn't that important to you," she burst out at miserable Pyarelal, "then learning isn't that important to me. If my father the great philosopher wants to turn into a tandoori cook, then maybe I'll find something to turn into as well. Who wants to be your daughter? I'd rather be somebody's wife."

It was her wildness talking, the impulsive uncontrolled thing that Shalimar the clown had begun to fear. When she saw Pyarelal's face fall and Gopinath's ears prick up she at once regretted that she had hurt the man who had loved her most ever since the day of her birth, and in addition that she had said far too much in the presence of a stranger. What she didn't know was that Pandit Gopinath Razdan, Pyarelal's distant cousin, was also a secret agent, and had been sent to Pachigam to sniff out certain subversive elements in this village of artists—for artists were natural subversives, after all. His orders were to report his findings covertly and in the first instance to Colonel H. S. Kachhwaha at Elasticnagar, who would evaluate the quality and value of the intelligence and recommend any course of action that might be required. Nobody in Pachigam suspected Gopinath of having a secret identity because the identity that he made apparent was so hard to take that it was impossible to believe he had an even more problematic self concealed beneath it. The children he taught with an asperity and severity that was the exact opposite of Pyarelal's jolly prattling gave him the nickname of "Batta Rasashud". *Batta* was another word for pandit and *rasashud* was an extremely bitter herb given to children who were infested with *aam,* that is to say, roundworms. When he discovered this, because teachers always discover the rude names by which they are known, his temper got even worse. He was living in a bedroom upstairs from the schoolroom and at nights the villagers would hear crashes and oaths emanating from it, so that many of them suspected that the angry pandit was possessed by a demon who came out of his body at night and flew around like a trapped bird.

Pyarelal felt responsible for his distant cousin and believed in his good-natured way that a little human companionship and family feeling would improve the man's temperament. Boonyi dissented strongly. "Once the milk has curdled," she argued, "it never tastes sweet again." In spite of her objections, Pyarelal Kaul assured Gopinath that he was always welcome at their table. Thus Boonyi had to breakfast and often dine with the spy, which suited Gopinath fine, because Colonel Kachhwaha's interest in her made her an important topic for his regular reports. And inevitably, given the unusual degree of access to her that he enjoyed, it was only a matter of time before the angry pandit became besotted with Boonyi Kaul as well. His paan habit increased dramatically, but the betel-nut addiction failed to mask his new, deeper dependency on the presence in his life of a fourteen-year-old girl. In the small schoolhouse where he taught children of all ages in a single room, he quickly saw that Boonyi Kaul was a lazy student, clever but idle, whose detachment from her education was in part a deliberately anti-intellectual reaction against being her learned father's child, in part a protest against Pyarelal's withdrawal from school, and mostly the consequence of an immature belief, rooted in her highly eroticized self-image, that she already knew everything she would need to get men to do whatever she desired. It was easy to see why so sexually confident a child had inflamed the passions of poor confused Colonel Tortoise, but Gopinath had thought himself to be made of sterner stuff. The speed of his surrender to her charms engendered in his breast the same feelings of disgust he normally reserved for the sick and the maimed. And her obvious feelings for Noman Sher Noman who called himself Shalimar the clown nauseated the schoolteacher even more than his own infatuation, and distracted him from his original purpose in Pachigam, the secret pursuit of Shalimar the clown's brother, the third son of Abdullah and Firdaus. Gopinath temporarily downgraded that project and focused instead on the sarpanch's fourth and youngest boy, whom he privately resolved to destroy.

At the age of nineteen the twin eldest sons of Abdullah and Firdaus Noman, Hameed and Mahmood, were gentle, gregarious fools whose only interest in life was to make each other laugh. Accordingly they had contentedly lost themselves in the comic fictions of the bhand pather, and were so immersed in their imaginary world, in creating burlesque versions of pratfalling princes and clumsy gods, cowardly giants and devils in love, that the real world lost its charm for them, and perhaps alone of all Kashmiris they became immune to its natural beauty. The third boy, Anees, was introspective and morose, as if he expected little good to come of his life. He performed the clown antics required of him with an unblinkingly melancholy face that divided audiences. Most reacted with hilarity to his mournful air, but a minority, unexpectedly touched by his sadness in a place they did not expect a mere clown-story to reach, a sequestered place in which they guarded their own sadnesses about their beleaguered lives, were disturbed by him, and felt happy when he left the stage. As his seventeenth birthday neared Anees began to display a growing skill with his hands, casually creating miniature marvels of paper-chain cutout figures and fantastical creatures made out of twisted silver paper taken from the insides of cigarette packs. He whittled wood into tiny wonders, such as owls with latticed bodies inside which other, tinier owls could be seen. It was this gift that brought him to the attention of the local liberation front commander, and one star-filled night Anees was brought by two fighters with scarves around their faces to the wooded hill where Nazarébaddoor's old cottage stood rotting and empty. Here he was asked by a man he could not see if he would like to learn to make bombs. Okay, Anees shrugged. At least this meant that his melancholy life was likely to be short. When he said this he was wearing his longest and most lugubrious face and the liberation front commander standing in the shadows was mysteriously seized by an inappropriate urge to laugh, which he only partially managed to resist.

On the day of her denunciation, Boonyi was with her friends at their afternoon dance practice by the banks of the Muskadoon. "Look," said Zoon the carpenter's daughter, pointing to a rocky outcrop where Gopinath stood watching them. "If it isn't Mr Bitterherb himself." The spy made his way down the rocks, chewing his paan, his umbrella tapping on the stone, and Boonyi suddenly saw through his fogeyish pose. "This is not a crabby little duffer at all, but a very dangerous man," she warned herself, but it was too late. Gopinath had already seen everything he needed to see. To wooded groves and moonlit mountain meadows he had followed Shalimar the clown and Boonyi. Eight-millimetre movie film had been exposed, and still photographs taken also. They had never suspected his presence, never heard his footfall. He, by contrast, had seen more than enough. Now he stood before Boonyi, spat out betel juice and dropped his mask. His body straightened, his voice strengthened, and his face changed—his furrowed brow smoothed itself out, his expression was no longer narrow and pinched but calm and authoritative, and he plainly didn't need (and so removed) his spectacles; he looked younger and steelier, a man to be reckoned with, a man it might be advisable not to cross. "That boy is trash—not worthy of you," he said, loudly and clearly. "And the trashy things you were doing with him are unworthy of any decent girl." *Wor'y. U'wor'y.* The accent at least had been genuine. Zoon, Gonwati and Himal became stiff with curiosity and horror. "You will be angry with me now," the spy went on, "but later, when we are married, you may be pleased to have at your side a man of real mettle, not a lecherous boy." The girl shook her head in disbelief. "What have you done?" she asked. "I have put an end to sin," the spy replied. Boonyi's thoughts raced. Her friends had closed in around her, pressing their bodies loyally against hers, forming a wall against the alien attack. Catastrophe was close.

"The panchayat is meeting at this moment in emergency session, to consider the evidence I have laid before it," said Gopinath. "The sarpanch, your father and the others will soon decide your fate. You are disgraced, of course, your face is blackened and your good name is dirt, and that is your own doing; but I have informed them that I am prepared to restore your honour by taking you as my wife. What choice does your father have? What other man would be so generous towards a fallen woman? Repent now and thank me later, when your senses are your own again. Your lover is finished, of course, he is branded forever as a varlet and a dastard, but I snap my fingers at him as should you—as you will, when you enter into your only possible destiny, namely your inevitable life with me."

Repen' and than' me whe' your se'ses are your ow'. It was a remarkable proposal of marriage and after making it the transformed Gopinath did not wait for his beloved's reply, but walked off some distance along the bank of the Muskadoon and sat down perhaps a hundred yards away, pretending that he didn't have a care in the world. In reality he knew that he would be in boiling hot water with his superiors, having revealed his spying abilities to everyone in Pachigam and simultaneously turned himself into the most hated man in the village. His serious purposes were undone, he would have to withdraw immediately from his post at the school and from the village itself, and it would be far harder for the authorities to plant a second agent inside a community that would henceforth be on its guard against traitors and spies. In short, Gopinath had gambled everything on Boonyi, had been willing to sacrifice his secret career in return for capturing a wife who would never reciprocate his love, who would in fact detest him for painting her scarlet and puncturing her dreams of love. He stared into the fast-flowing waters and contemplated the tragedy of desire.

An air of calamity was rapidly enveloping the village. The fruit orchards, saffron fields and rice paddies lay empty and untended as those who habitually laboured there downed tools and gathered outside the Noman residence where the panchayat was meeting. No food was cooked in the villagers' kitchens that afternoon. Children ran barefoot hither and yon, gleefully shouting out ill-founded rumours of banishment and suicide. Boonyi and her three friends huddled together, arms around one another, in an inward-facing circle of misery from which loud wails and sobs of anguish escaped constantly. Even the livestock had divined that something was wrong; goats and cattle, dogs and geese displayed the kind of instinctive or premonitory agitation that is sometimes seen in the hours before an earthquake. Bees stung their keepers with unwonted ferocity. The very air seemed to shimmer with concern and there was a rumble in the empty sky. Firdaus Noman came for Boonyi, running with an ungainly lolloping gait, panting heavily, and screamed abuse at the judas Gopinath sitting calmly by the riverside. "Carbuncle!" she cursed him. "Clovenhoof! Bad-smell buttock! Little penis! Dried-up *brinjal!*" The object of her wrath, the *zaharbad,* the *pedar,* the possessor of the smelly *mandal,* the wee *kuchur,* the *wangan hachi,* neither turned nor flinched. "*Wattal-nath Gopinath!*" Firdaus screamed—that is to say, mean-spirited, low-life, degraded Gopinath—and Boonyi's friends broke away from their circle to take up the chant. "Wattal-nath Gopinath! Gopinath Wattal-nath!" Through the village went that cry, taken up by the eager children, until the whole village, almost all of whose residents were by now gathered outside the sarpanch's home, was shouting. "Wattal-nath Gopinath! Little penis, bad-smell buttock, dried-up brinjal, clovenhoof! Gopinath Wattal-nath, go!"

"Damn you too," Firdaus said more conversationally to Boonyi. "Come on, you stupid oversexed child. I'm taking you back to your father's house and there you'll stay until what's done is done and your fate is known." "We're coming too," cried Zoon, Himal and Gonwati. Firdaus shrugged. "That's your concern. But I will be locking you four wretches in." Boonyi did not argue and made her way home, chaperoned by her beloved's irate mother. "Where is Noman?" she asked Firdaus in a small voice. "Shut up," Firdaus answered loudly. "That is nothing to do with you." Then in a low fast murmur she went on, "His brothers have taken him away, up to Khelmarg, to stop him from cutting off Pandit Gopinath Razdan's fat head." Boonyi replied more heatedly, and certainly more lewdly, than her situation warranted. "Anyway, they shouldn't make me marry that snake. The first time he's asleep I'll cut off his kuchur and stuff it into his evil little mouth." Firdaus slapped her hard across the face. "You'll do as you are told," she said. "And that was for the dirty talk, which I will not tolerate." Faced with the incandescent fury of Firdaus Noman, neither Boonyi nor her friends dared to remind her where that day's bad language had come from in the first place.

Once they were inside Boonyi's home, Firdaus stopped pretending to be angry and made the girls a pot of salty pink tea. "The boy loves you," she said to Boonyi, "and even though you have behaved like a disgusting slut, that love counts with me." One hour later a boy knocked at the door to tell them that the panchayat had reached its decision and their presence was required. "We're coming too," said Himal, Gonwati and Zoon again, and again Firdaus did not demur. They made their way to the steps of the sarpanch's residence where the panchayat members stood solemn-faced. Shalimar the clown was there with his brothers surrounding him and Boonyi's heart thumped when she saw his face. There was a murderous darkness on his brow that she had not seen before. It frightened her and, worse than that, it made him look unattractive to her for the first time in her life. All the villagers were gathered around this little tableau and when they saw Firdaus approaching with Boonyi and her girlfriends a silence fell. Pandit Pyarelal Kaul was standing beside Abdullah Noman and the two fathers' faces were the grimmest on display. "I'm done for," Boonyi thought. "They're going to pack me off to that bastard sitting like a cold fish by the river, waiting to have me handed over on a plate—me, Boonyi Kaul, whom he could never otherwise have won."

She was wrong. Abdullah Noman the sarpanch spoke first, followed by Pyarelal, and the other three members of the panchayat, Big Man Misri the carpenter, Sharga the singer, and the frail old dancing master Habib Joo, also made brief remarks, and their verdict was unanimous. The lovers were their children and must be supported. Their behaviour was worthy of the strongest censure—it had been licentious and rash and filled with improprieties that were a disappointment to their parents—but they were good children, as everybody knew. Abdullah then mentioned *Kashmiriyat,* Kashmiriness, the belief that at the heart of Kashmiri culture there was a common bond that transcended all other differences. Most bhand villages were Muslim but Pachigam was a mixture, with families of pandit background, the Kauls, the Misris, and the baritone singer's long-nosed kin—*sharga* being a local nickname for the nasally elongated—and even one family of dancing Jews. "So we have not only Kashmiriness to protect but Pachigaminess as well. We are all brothers and sisters here," said Abdullah. "There is no Hindu-Muslim issue. Two Kashmiri—two Pachigami—youngsters wish to marry, that's all. A love match is acceptable to both families and so a marriage there will be; both Hindu and Muslim customs will be observed." Pyarelal added, when his turn came, "To defend their love is to defend what is finest in ourselves."

The crowd cheered and Shalimar the clown broke out into a broad smile of disbelieving joy. Firdaus went up to Abdullah and whispered, "If you had made any other decision I would have kicked you out of my bed." (Later that night, when they lay in that bed in the dark, she was in a more reflective mood. "The times are changing," she said softly. "Our children aren't like us. In our generation we were straightforward folk, both hands on the table in plain view at all times. But these youngsters are trickier types, there are shadows on the surface and secrets underneath, and they are not always as they seem, maybe not always even what they think they are. I guess that's how it has to be, because they will live through times more deceptive than any we have known.")

Two panchayat members, Misri the carpenter and Sharga the baritone, the two largest and, along with the sarpanch, strongest men in Pachigam, were dispatched to the riverside to throw Gopinath Razdan out of town—Abdullah the sarpanch, fearing excessive violence, forbade his enraged sons to have anything to do with the ejection—but by the time the posse of two reached the Muskadoon the spy had already slipped away, and he was never seen in Pachigam again. Six months later, after a period of professional disgrace, he was assigned new duties in the village of Pahalgam, and was found dead one morning in the nearby mountain meadow of Baisaran. His legs had been blown off by some sort of homemade bomb and his head had been severed from his body by a single slash of a blade. The murder was never solved, nor did any clues lead back to anyone in the actors' village. Eventually the investigation ran out of steam and the official case file was closed. Colonel H. S. Kachhwaha had his strong suspicions, however, and his frustration grew. Not only had he been insulted by Boonyi Kaul, but the failure of his spy's mission had given him no shred of a pretext for the "descent in force" that he had planned for Pachigam. The colours of his world continued to darken, and he made a note that the village of actors was still earmarked for special attention, a decision whose medium- and long-term consequences would be grave.

For a time after the departure of the spy, however, the mood in Pachigam was celebratory. Pandit Pyarelal Kaul agreed to resume his teaching duties, to shoulder the dual burdens of education and gastronomy as long as his strength lasted; and preparations for the nuptials of

Boonyi and Shalimar the clown began. However, snags soon started cropping up. The detailed wedding arrangements proved more problematic than Abdullah, with his plan for an idealistic, multifaith ceremony, had foreseen. This was because of the arrival of the families. From Poonch, from Baramulla, from Sonamarg, from Tangmarg, from Chhamb, from Aru, from Uri, from Udhampur, from Kishtwar, from Riasi, from Jammu, the two clans gathered; aunts, cousins, uncles, more cousins, great-aunts, great-uncles, nephews, nieces, yet more cousins and in-laws descended on Pachigam until all the village's houses were badly overcrowded and many minor relatives had to sleep under the fruit trees and trust to luck regarding rain and snakes. Almost all the new arrivals had strong ideas and expectations about the proceedings, and many of them were openly scornful of the sarpanch's ecumenical scheme. "What, she won't convert to Islam?" the doubters from the groom's side demanded, and the bride's people retorted, "What, there will be meat served at the feast?" All over the village and in the surrounding fields and pastures the arguments raged. The only thing generally agreed was that the traditional Muslim Thap ceremony, when the young couple meet in a public place to decide if they want to go ahead with the match, was unnecessary. "They have thapped each other long ago," said a wicked aunt's tongue, and there was laughter from wicked uncles, cousins, great-aunts, great-uncles, further cousins and so on.

Then came the argument over the Livun ceremonies of the Hindus, when, the Kauls insisted, the two families' houses should be ritually cleansed. "Let the Kauls cleanse their idolatrous home if they need to," said a hard-line old Muslim granny, "but our people's place is already perfectly clean." Nobody objected to frequent wazwaan banquets, naturally, and the veg/nonveg disputes were relatively easily resolved when Pandit Pyarelal Kaul, in spite of his abiding love for meat, agreed to banish all trace of it from his kitchen, while the Nomans, who had built a new brick-and-mud wuri oven in their backyard, offered daily menus that were carnivore's delights. At the actual wedding, it was agreed after much haggling, separate groups of chefs would prepare both cuisines, chicken to the left, lotus to the right, goat meat on one side, goat cheese on the other. Music, too, was agreed on without too much dispute. The *santoor,* the *sarangi,* the *rabab,* the harmonium were nonsectarian instruments, after all. Professional *bachkot* singers and musicians were hired and ordered to alternate Hindu *bhajans* and Sufi hymns.

The question of the bride's clothes was far thornier. "Obviously," said the groom's side, "when the *yenvool,* the wedding procession, comes to the bride's house, we will expect to be welcomed by a girl in a red *lehenga,* and later, after she is bathed by her family women, she will don a *shalwar-kameez.*"—"Absurd," retorted the Kauls. "She will wear a phiran just like all our brides, embroidered at the neck and cuffs. On her head will be the starched and papery *tarang* headgear, and the wide *haligandun* belt will be round her waist." This standoff lasted three days until Abdullah and Pyarelal decreed that the bride would indeed wear her traditional garb, but so would Shalimar the clown. No tweed phiran for him! No peacock-feathered turban! He would wear an elegant *sherwani* and a *karakuli topi* on his head and that was that. Once the clothes issue had been resolved, the *mehndi* ceremony, a joint custom, was quickly settled. Then came the matter of the wedding itself and at that point the entire entente cordiale came close to collapse. To many Muslim ears, the other side's suggestions were appalling. Blow a conch shell if you will, cried the Islamic aunts and great-aunts and cousins and so on, exchange all the gifts of nutmeg you desire, but a *purohit,* a priest, performing *puja* before idols? Sacred fire, sacred thread? The newlyweds to be treated as Shiva and Parvati and worshipped as such? Hai-hai. Such superstition would never do. The Kauls retreated in high dudgeon. All dialogue between the two households ceased. "Families," sighed Firdaus Noman in despair, "are the narrow-minded, low-grade cause of all the discontent on earth."

That night there was a full moon. Pachigam had divided into two camps, and long years of communal harmony were at risk. Then, on an impulse, the baritone Shivshankar Sharga came out into the main street and began to sing love songs, songs of the love of the gods for men, and of men for God, songs of the love between fathers and daughters, mothers and sons, songs of love requited and unrequited, courtly and passionate, sacred and profane. His daughters Himal and Gonwati, the tone-deaf duo, sat at his feet under strict instructions not to open their mouths no matter how much the music moved them. When he started singing the village was still in the grip of its plague of bad temper, and there were cries of "Shut up, we're trying to sleep," and "Nobody's in the mood for these damned sentimental songs." But slowly his voice worked its magic. Doors opened, lights came on, sleepers came in from the fields. Abdullah and Pyarelal met by the singer and embraced. "We'll have two wedding days," Abdullah said. "First we'll do everything your way and then we'll do it all again in the way we know." A single shrewish aunt called out, "Why their way first?" but her carping cry was swiftly followed by a stifled gurgle, as her husband put his hand over her bad mouth and dragged her away to bed.

It was all settled. Pandit Pyarelal Kaul dug the aluminum box containing his wife's wedding jewels out of the place in the backyard where he had buried them soon after her death and brought them to Boonyi lying wide awake in bed. "Here is everything that remains of her," he told his daughter. "These jewels in this box and the greater jewel shining in this bed." He left the box on the mattress, kissed her cheek and left. Boonyi remained wide awake, staring furiously at the nocturnal ceiling, willing the walls of the house to dissolve so that she could rise up into the night sky and escape. For at the very moment in which the village had decided to protect her and Shalimar the clown, to stand by them by forcing them to marry, thus condemning them to a lifetime jail sentence, Boonyi had been overwhelmed by claustrophobia and had seen clearly what she had been too deeply in love with Shalimar the clown to understand before, namely that this life, married life, village life, life with her father chattering away by the Muskadoon and with her friends dancing their gopi dance, life with all the people amongst whom she had spent every one of her days, was not remotely enough for her, didn't begin to satisfy her hunger, her ravenous longing for something she could not yet name, and that as she grew older her life's insufficiency would only grow harder and more painful to bear.

She knew then that she would do anything to get out of Pachigam, that she would spend every moment of every day waiting for her chance, and when it came she would not fail to pounce upon it, she would move faster than fortune, that elusive will-o'-the-wisp, because if you spotted a magic force—a fairy, a djinni, a piece of once-in-a-lifetime luck—and if you pinned it to the ground, it would grant you your heart's desire; and she would make her wish, *get me away from here, away from my father, away from this slow death and slower life, away from Shalimar the clown.*

Two years later a gaunt man with a long straggling beard, beautiful pale eyes that seemed to look right through this world into the next one, and skin the colour of rusting metal, suddenly showed up in Shirmal village wearing a long, threadbare woollen coat and a loosely tied black turban, with all his worldly goods tied up in a bundle like a common vagabond, and began preaching hellfire and damnation. He spoke the language harshly, like a foreigner, like someone unused to speaking at all. The words seemed to be torn from his throat like pieces of rough skin, causing him much physical pain. Shirmalis, like all the people of the valley, were unused to blood-and-thunder preachers of this type, but they gave him a hearing, because of the legends of the iron mullahs that were circulating in those days.

Kashmiris were fond of saints of all types. Some of these even had military associations, such as the Bibi Lalla or Lalla Maj, the daughter of the commander of the armies of Kashmir in the fourteenth century. Many were miracle workers. The story currently doing the rounds was both military and miraculous. The Indian army had poured military hardware of all kinds into the valley, and scrap metal junkyards sprang up everywhere, scarring the valley's pristine beauty, like small mountain ranges made up of malfunctioning truck exhausts, jammed weaponry and broken tank treads. Then one day by the grace of God the junk began to stir. It came to life and took on human form. The men who were miraculously born from these rusting war metals, who went out into the valley to preach resistance and revenge, were saints of an entirely new kind. They were the iron mullahs. It was said that if you dared to knock on their bodies you would hear a hollow metallic ring. Because they were made of armour they could not be shot but they were too heavy to swim and so if they fell into water they would drown. Their breath was hot and smoky, like burning rubber tires, or the exhalations of dragons. They were to be honoured, feared and obeyed.

That day in Shirmal, Bombur Yambarzal, the vasta waza, was the only man who dared interrupt the mendicant preacher's tirade. He confronted the strange *faqir* in the street and demanded to know his name and business. "My business is God's business," the fellow replied. In that first exchange the newcomer was reluctant to answer to any name at all. Eventually, under pressure from Bombur, he said, "Call me Bulbul Shah." Bulbul Shah, as even Bombur knew, was a fabled saint who had come to Kashmir in the fourteenth century (the time of Bibi Lalla). He was a Sufi of the Suhrawardy order named Syed Sharafuddin Abdul Rehman, known as Bilal after the Prophet's muezzin—an honorific title that got corrupted to Bulbul, or "nightingale". His origins were disputed. He may have come from Tamkastan, in ancient Iran, or from Baghdad, or, most probably, from Turkistan; he may have been a refugee from the Mongols or he may not. He did, however, succeed in converting to Islam the Ladakhi usurper Rinchin or Renchan or Rencana, who had seized the throne of Kashmir in 1320, and began the process of conversions by which Kashmir became a Muslim state. At any rate, he had been dead for six hundred years, and certainly was not standing in front of Yambarzal now smelling like dragon's breath.

"That's nonsense," Bombur told the wanderer in his customarily haughty manner. "Be off with you. We don't want any trouble, and you, standing here in the middle of our little town and yelling your head off about the punishments of hell—you look like trouble to me." "There are big infidels," replied the stranger, calmly, "who deny God and his Prophet; and then there are little infidels like you, in whose belly the heat of faith has long since cooled, who mistake tolerance for virtue and harmony for peace. You must let me stay or kill me, and I leave the choice to you. But understand this: I am the bellows who will rekindle your fire."

"Of course we won't kill you," said Yambarzal, discomfited. "What sort of people do you think we are?" "Weaklings," the stranger answered in his alarming, rasping voice. Bombur flushed, and called out loudly to the growing crowd, "Give this beggar some food to eat and he'll pretty soon be on his way." This was a misjudgement. The supposed reincarnation of Bulbul Shah had come to stay, and many ears wanted to hear what he had to tell them, especially because his response to Yambarzal's dismissive remark was to remove the turban from his head, clench his right hand and rap his knuckles smartly on the bald dome of his head. Everybody present heard the hard metallic clang and many women and several men dropped instantly to their knees.

After that there was a new power in Shirmal. The iron mullah was given shelter in one Shirmali home after another, and within a year the character of the village had changed, and the cooks in whose hearts new passions were blazing had grouped together to build the inspirational Bulbul a mosque. The iron mullah never spoke of his origins, never said in what seminary or at the feet of which master he had received religious instruction; indeed he never said a word about his life before the day he arrived in Shirmal to change everything forever. He even allowed the village children to rename him. The Kashmiri love of nicknames and penchant for good-natured honesty meant that the children had soon dubbed him Bulbul Fakh, "Bulbul bad-odour", because of his sulfurous smell. So Maulana Bulbul Fakh he became, accepting the name without demur, as if he had just come into the world, simultaneously innocent and ferocious, created particularly for this village, and it was the villagers' right to call him whatsoever they chose, like parents naming a newborn child.

Relations between Shirmal and Pachigam had been good ever since Bombur Yambarzal and Abdullah Noman had embraced each other on the night of the Shalimar Bagh débâcle. Their periodical fishing expeditions had started up again, and on those occasions when a client with sufficient resources called for the outsized version of the wazwaan, the "super-wazwaan" or Banquet of Sixty Courses Maximum, the two villages would pool their resources and cooperate. Abdullah even offered to send some of his people over to give the Shirmalis acting lessons if they wanted to continue to seek employment as purveyors of portable theatre, but Yambarzal declined the offer, going so far as to make a self-deprecating remark. "We can't pretend to be people we're not," he said, "so we'll just stick with who we are." There was something a little back-handed in this compliment but Abdullah decided not to notice, partly because it was a pleasant day and the fish were jumping, and partly because he had come to understand that Yambarzal was not much more highly strung or egotistical than many artists—including some of his own troupe of performers—but was unquestionably better at putting his foot in his mouth. Bombur was definitely mellowing, however. Lately he had even managed to praise "that new pandit waza of yours" for "having the taste in his hands", which was a compliment so high that when Abdullah repeated it to Pyarelal the pandit could not prevent himself from blushing with pride.

The two villages were still rivals in the feasting game, so some tension remained, and sharp words would sometimes be said. Bombur Yambarzal in his worst moments still blamed Abdullah Noman for taking away some of the wazwaan income on which Shirmal's economic well-being and his, Bombur's, personal standing depended. "If it wasn't for Pachigam and that Hindu cook," the voice of evil whispered in his ear, "you'd be the undisputed vasta waza again and that would make you, not Bulbul Fakh, unchallenged top dog in Shirmal." The overall decline in festive occasions had hit both Pachigam and Shirmal hard. Kashmiris felt a lot less like celebrating these days. There were weeks, even months when Abdullah Noman believed that the days of the bhand pather were numbered, that nobody wanted the traditional clown stories any more, and that it would be impossible to compete with the vans travelling to even the most remote towns and villages with projectors, screens and reels of the latest motion pictures in the back. Bombur Yambarzal was similarly worried that the Kashmiri love of gourmandizing might not be transmitted to the next generation. But even though the gaps between performances were lengthening, bookings for Pachigam's bhand plays did still arrive; and, as for mass-catering cookery, that was also still required. Even the Indian army could not prevent families from arranging marriages, and there was also the occasional love match, this being the 1960s, after all, and so, thanks to the optimistic insistence of the human race in general on getting hitched, even in bad times, and also to Kashmiris' continuing expectation that weddings would be celebrated with week-long displays of gluttony on the grandest possible scale, nobody in the business of producing the Banquet of Thirty-Six Courses Minimum was likely to starve just yet. However, eighteen months after the appearance of Bulbul Fakh the iron mullah, over seventeen years of more or less pleasant co-operation between Shirmal and Pachigam came to an abrupt and ugly end.

The summer of 1965 was a bad season. India and Pakistan had already engaged in battle, briefly, in the Rann of Kutch far away to the south, but now the talk was all about war over Kashmir. The rumble of convoys was heard, and the overhead roar of jets. Threats were made—*force will be met with overwhelming force!*—and counterthreats offered in return—*aggression will not be countenanced or permitted to succeed!* There was a hammering, a howling, a dark cloud in the air. Children in playgrounds postured, menaced, attacked, defended, fled. Fear was the year's biggest crop. It hung from the fruit trees instead of apples and peaches, and bees made fear instead of honey. In the paddies, fear grew thickly beneath the surface of the shallow water, and in the saffron fields, fear like bindweed strangled the delicate plants. Fear clogged the rivers like water hyacinth, and sheep and goats in the high pastures died for no apparent reason. Work was scarce for actors and chefs alike. Terror was killing livestock, like a plague.

The new mosque built for Bulbul Fakh in Shirmal was a simple enough structure. The roof was wooden and the walls were of whitewashed earth. There were two simple windowless rooms at the back where he now lived. No provision had been made for ladies to attend prayers. The one striking feature stood in the mosque's main hall, where, in Bulbul Fakh's honour, a frightening-looking scrap-metal pulpit had been erected, complete with a bank of truck headlights (nonfunctional), bent fenders spearing upwards like horns, and a snarling radiator grille. The floors, more traditionally, were covered in numdah rugs. One Friday in late August the iron mullah climbed into his ominous pulpit and made a declaration of war of his own. "There is the enemy from outside," he declared in his cold, rust-covered voice, "and then there is the enemy hiding in our midst." The enemy within was Pachigam, a degenerate village where, in spite of a substantial Muslim majority among the residents, only one member of the panchayat was of the true faith, whereas three appointed elders—three!—were idol worshippers, and the fifth was a Jew. Furthermore, a Hindu had been named as chief waza of the wazwaan, and had started using curds in the food. And above all—O final, irrefutable proof of Pachigam's moral perfidy!—there was its wholehearted support for the wanton, lascivious, whorish, debauched, ungodly, idolatrous, four-year-long liaison between Bhoomi Kaul better known as Boonyi and Noman Sher Noman alias Shalimar the clown.

Colonel Kachhwaha in Elasticnagar heard about the sermon soon enough. Such a sermon was worse than improper. It was seditious. Such a sermon called for the sternest response: an arrest, a jail sentence of seven years minimum. Colonel Kachhwaha had heard the absurd stories about the so-called iron mullahs and these stories needed to be knocked on the head and to the devil with hollow metallic sounds. This Fakh fellow was not miracle but man and needed to be taught a lesson and taken down a peg. This Fakh fellow was a pro-Pak communalist bastard and dared to preach about enemies within the state when he himself was the incarnation of that foe. Yes, strong measures were called for. Iron fist against iron priest. Quite so. And yet, and yet.

The Hammirdev Kachhwaha of August 1965 was a very different fellow from the tongue-tied ass who had allowed Boonyi Kaul to cheek him so outrageously four years earlier: on the one hand he was a seasoned commander, planning eagerly for battle, and on the other hand there were the deepening sensory and mnemonic disorders. His father had passed away so it was no longer incumbent upon the son to die to gain the parent's approval. On the day in the autumn of 1963 when he heard the news of Nagabhat Kachhwaha's demise, Tortoise Colonel took off the golden bangles of humiliation, had his driver take him all the way to the Bund in Srinagar, stood with his back to the city's great stores, Cheap John, Suffering Moses and Subhana the Worst, and hurled the gleaming circlets far out into the sluggish brown waters of the Jhelum. He felt like Sir Bedivere returning Excalibur to the lake, except that the bangles had been a symbol of weakness, not of strength. At any rate, in this case there was no arm clothed in white samite, mystic, wonderful, emerging to receive what was thrown. The bangles scattered noiselessly on the sluggish surface of the river and quickly sank. Tall poplars faintly swayed, and reddened autumnal chinar leaves fluttered a farewell. Colonel Kachhwaha saluted briefly and crisply, performed a smart about-face and marched forward into a newer, more confident future.

The number of men under his command had grown. Elasticnagar had stretched so wide that people were beginning to call it Broken-Elasticnagar. The war drums were beating and the troop transport aircraft were flying a nonstop relay service and the eager glitter-eyed *jawans* were pouring in. Kachhwaha was one of the chief supervisors of the major statewide operation that was sending hundreds of thousands of soldiers to the front lines. Now he had received his own marching orders. Elasticnagar's boss was going to war. He was going to smash the enemy with maximum force, and survival was permissible. Returning as a war hero was permissible. Returning as a decorated war hero and enjoying the attentions of excited young women back home was not only permissible but actively encouraged. Colonel Kachhwaha in jodhpurs smacked a riding crop against his thigh in anticipation. Since his father's death he had begun to dream of going home in triumph and having the pick of the women, the beautiful Rajput women of the kohl-rimmed flashing eyes, the gorgeous Jodhpuri women waiting in their mirrored halls, opening wide their arms for their conquering local hero, dressed in clouds of organza and lace. These women were women of his own kind, desert roses, women who appreciated a warrior, women quite unlike the foolish girls of Kashmir. Unlike, for example, Boonyi. He did not permit himself these days to think about Boonyi Kaul even though reports reached his ears of her extraordinary, blossoming beauty. At eighteen she would be in full flower, she would have entered into the first flush of womanhood, but he would not allow himself to consider that. His restraint was laudable. He congratulated himself upon it. In spite of many provocations he had not persecuted her village of bohemians and suspicious types, in spite of her insult to his honour. He would not wish it said of him that H. S. Kachhwaha pursued vendettas while on duty, that his conduct had been in even the smallest way unbecoming. He had shown himself to be above such matters. Discipline was all. Dignity was all. Boonyi was nothing to him, nothing compared to the waiting Rajput girls, even though he did not know their names, had not seen their faces, met them only in his dreams. These dream women were the ones he wanted. Any one of them was worth ten Boonyis.

He was a soldier and so he tried to compartmentalise, to put his disorders in a box in the corner of the room and to go on functioning normally. When they spilled out it was regrettable but his troops had grown accustomed to the jumbling of his senses, the strangeness of his descriptions. Nowadays his fellow officers reacted normally when told that they had rigid vermilion voices and the soldiers on parade kept silent when he congratulated them on smelling like jasmine blossoms and the cooks at

Elasticnagar knew just to nod wisely when he told them that the lamb korma wasn't pointy enough. The condition could be said to be under control. The problem of memory, of excessive remembering, was not. The accumulation grew every day more oppressive and it became harder and harder to sleep. It was impossible to forget the cockroach that had crawled out of the shower drain six months earlier, or a bad dream, or any one of the thousands of hands of cards he had played in his military life. The weather of the past piled up in him, names and faces jostled for space, and the overload of unforgotten words and deeds left him wide-eyed with horror. Time was supposed to soothe all pain wasn't it but the knife of his late father's disapproval refused to grow dull with the passing months. He now believed that the two problems, the two bugs in the system, were somehow connected. He did not seek medical help for his troubles because any diagnosis of mental problems, however slight, would certainly be a reason for removing him from his command. He could not return home as a head case. There would be no dream girls then. And memory was not madness was it, not even when the remembered past piled up so high inside you that you feared the files of your yesterdays would become visible in the whites of your eyes. Memory was a gift. It was a positive. It was a professional resource.

And so, to return to the matter at hand, this mullah, this Bulbul Fakh, was quite unacceptably denouncing a neighbouring village for its tolerance, was stirring things up, inciting violence and advocating a firebrand Islam that was positively un-Kashmiri and un-Indian as well. However, he made a good point when he condemned the hussy and her fancy boy, that couple who had chosen to fly in the face of every decent social and religious convention and who had been defended for it by people who should have known better, people among whom a number of suspected subversives probably lurked. These liberation-front-wallahs were nationalist subversives rather than religious fanatics and between them and the iron mullahs there was little love lost. So why not just stand back, eh? Resources were not infinite and time was pressing and one could not be everywhere and there was a war to fight. It was not so much a matter of turning a blind eye as of the proper prioritizing of goals. Why not let two kinds of subversive wipe each other out, and allow the young whore to reap the whirlwind for her misdeeds? If some sort of cleanup operation was required later, the forces left behind to police the district would be fully capable of handling that situation. Maulana Bulbul Fakh's turn would come. Yes, yes. The thing to do was to do nothing. That was the statesmanlike choice.

Colonel Hammirdev Kachhwaha in his office put his legs up on his desk, closed his eyes and surrendered for a time to the internal whirl of the system, submerging his consciousness in the ocean of the senses, listening like a boy with a shell at his ear to the unceasing babble of the past.

It was almost eighteen years since the death of the Gujar prophetess Nazarébaddoor, but that didn't stop her from intervening in local affairs when the need arose. Numerous residents of the region reported her visits, which usually took place in dreams, and whose purpose was usually to warn ("Don't marry your daughter to that boy—his cousins in the north are dwarfs," she advised a drowsy goat farmer on a hillside near Anantnag) or to commend ("Snap up that girl for your boy before someone else does, because her firstborn is destined to be a great saint," she commanded a boatman sleeping in his *shikara* on Lake Gandarbal, causing him to jerk awake and fall out of the boat). In death Nazarébaddoor appeared more cheerful than she had been in the last days of her life, and she admitted to several of those who had seen her in visions that death suited her.

"The hours are better," she said, "and you don't have to worry about the animals." When she appeared to Bombur Yambarzal, however, all her old gloominess was back. The bulbous waza awoke in the dark to see her one-toothed face leaning down close to his, and he felt the cold breath of the dead upon his cheek. "If you don't do something double-quick," she said, "Bulbul Fakh's civil war will burn both your villages down." Then she drew back and became one with the darkness and he awoke all over again, alone in his bed and sweating. A few seconds later he heard the Maulana's voice raised in the *azaan.* The dawn call to prayer was also, on this occasion, a call to arms.

Wherever information is tightly controlled, rumour becomes a valued alternative source of news, and according to rumour the whole tribe of iron mullahs was summoning Kashmiris to arms that day, calling upon them to arise and rid the land of the alien Indian troops and of the pandits too. But Bombur Yambarzal had not heard any such rumour. For him this was not a national but a personal matter. He rolled out of bed and ran, wobbling, heaving, panting and sweating, all the way to the main village kitchens where the wazwaan was prepared. There he girded himself for battle. Once he was ready, and had caught his breath, he walked much more deliberately down the main street of Shirmal towards the mosque at the far end of the village, in a manner that might almost have been called kingly except that this was a king with kitchen knives and cleavers stuck in his belt, with kitchen kettles and cookpots strung around his body in place of armour, and with a big kitchen saucepan on his head. The fresh blood of slaughtered chickens dripped from him, he had smeared it over his hands and face and over all the kitchen equipment too, and had brought along a small leather wineskin full of even more blood, to make sure the effect wasn't lost ahead of time. He looked simultaneously horrifying and ridiculous, and the village's women and children, who had been waiting anxiously for the men to emerge from the mosque and announce their decision regarding the attack on Pachigam, began to laugh and cry at the same time, not knowing which was the more appropriate response. Bombur Yambarzal stiffened his back and raised his head up proudly and led a parade of astonished women and children to the door of the mosque.

When he reached it he drew from his belt, as if they were swords, a pair of great metal spoons, and began to bang on his armour, making a noise that would have raised the dead had the dead not preferred to remain peacefully underground and ignore the appalling racket. The men of Shirmal poured out of the mosque with zealotry in their eyes, and behind them came a considerably irritated Maulana Bulbul Fakh. "Look at me," shouted the waza Bombur Yambarzal. "This thickheaded, comical, bloodthirsty moron is what you have all decided to become."

For years afterwards the men of Shirmal spoke of Bombur Yambarzal's great, and unusually selfless, feat. By turning their familiar world of pots and pans into an effigy of horror, by sacrificing his own much-treasured dignity and pride, by insulting them with the weapon of himself, he awoke them from their strange waking sleep, the powerful hypnotic spell woven by the harsh seductive tongue of Bulbul Fakh. No, they would not arise against their neighbours, they told him, they would remain themselves, and the only creatures they would slaughter would be animals meant for tables at which people were celebrating moments of private joy. When Bulbul Fakh saw that he had lost the day, that his knifelike clarity had been blunted by Yambarzal's obfuscating creation of a comic grotesque, he went without a word into his residential quarters and came out with nothing more than the ragged bundle he had carried on the day of his arrival in Shirmal. "You blockheads aren't ready for me yet," he said. "But the war that is beginning will be long, and necessary, too, because its enemy is godlessness, immorality and evil, and thanks to the corrupt heart of man in general and unbelieving *kafirs* in particular that is a war that cannot easily be brought to an end. When your hearts are open to me, at that time I may return."

Bombur Yambarzal had never married and now that he was past fifty he no longer expected to find a bride. But in the eyes and faces of some of the matrons who watched him as he marched clanging and dripping back to the kitchens to take off the silly armour of righteousness and peace, he saw something he had not seen in women's eyes and faces before: that is to say, affection. The widow of a recently deceased sub-waza, Hasina Karim, known as Harud, "Autumn", on account of her red-tinged hair, a handsome woman with two grown sons to take care of her material needs but nobody to fill her bed, accompanied him without being asked and helped him take off his pots and pans and wash the chicken blood from his skin. When they were done Bombur Yambarzal attempted for the first time in his life to flatter a member of the opposite sex. "Harud is the wrong name for you," he told her, meaning to continue, "They should call you Sonth, because you look as young as the Spring." But anxiety made his mouth foolish, and *sonth,* to his great discomfiture, came out as *sonf.* "Because you look as young as aniseed" was an idiotic remark, obviously. Embarrassed, he flushed deeply. "I like it that you're clumsy with compliments," she consoled him, seriously, touching his hand. "I never trusted men who were too smooth with words."

In spite of the waza's boldness, there was a tragedy that day. Unknown to everyone except Bulbul Fakh, three young men, the sparsely bearded Gegroo brothers, Aurangzeb, Alauddin and Abulkalam, a trio of disaffected, layabout young rodents whom Bombur did not trust to do much at banquets except wash the dishes, had slipped out of the mosque the back way and headed for Pachigam, looking for trouble, and giving themselves courage from a bottle of dark rum of which Bulbul Fakh would most certainly have disapproved. Much later that night, under cover of darkness, they slipped back into Shirmal and locked themselves into the empty mosque. They were just in time. Before dawn broke, the immense figure of Big Man Misri the carpenter arrived in Shirmal on horseback, with axes in his belt and rifles slung across his shoulders. "Gegroos!" he yelled as he galloped into town, rousing all those villagers who were still asleep. "You have met my daughter, and now you must meet your God."

Zoon Misri had been raped. She had been on her way to Khelmarg to gather flowers when it happened. She had been dragged off the hill path into the forest and held down on the rough ground and brutalized, and even though a sack had been thrown over her head she had easily identified her three assailants by their whiny, nasal Gegroo voices, which were unmistakable even though the brothers were horribly drunk. "If we can't get the blasphemous whore herself," she heard Aurangzeb say, "then her prettiest friend will do fine." "Too fine," Alauddin had assented, "she was always too stuck up to look back at the likes of us," and the youngest, Abulkalam, concluded, "Well, Zoon, we see you now." After the rape her assailants ran off giggling. She found the strength to walk, bruised and torn, down the hill to Pachigam, where in a frighteningly level voice she confided all the details of the assault to Boonyi, Gonwati and Himal, not daring to tell her father (her mother being some years deceased), and even though they comforted her and bathed her and told her she had no reason to be ashamed she said she could not imagine remaining alive with them inside her, with the memory of their intrusion, with their seed. Boonyi, dreadfully weighed down by the feeling that Zoon had suffered in her stead, that the wounds inflicted on her friend had been meant for herself, was the one who told the carpenter the news. Big Man Misri did little to relieve her of this burden. As he saddled his horse he told her, "The three of you keep her alive. It's up to you. Get it? If she dies I'll be asking you why." Then he vanished into the night as fast as his horse could take him.

When the Gegroo brothers sobered up they realized that as a consequence of their stupidity their lives had suddenly become worthless, and their only hope was to remain within the sanctuary of the mosque until the army or the police showed up and restrained Zoon's father from crucifying them, chopping them to bits or whatever else he might be planning by way of revenge. Big Man Misri did indeed have a number of vile fates in mind for each of the three Gegroos, and when he informed the gathering Shirmalis of the nature of the ratty brothers' crime nobody had the heart to dissuade him. However, the consensus of opinion was that the carpenter should not violate the sanctity of the mosque. Big Man Misri tethered his horse to a tree and shouted to the Gegroo brothers, "I'll be waiting here whenever you decide to come out, even if it takes me twenty years."

Aurangzeb, the eldest Gegroo, attempted bravado. "It's three to one and we're heavily armed," he yelled back. "You'd better look out for yourself." "If you come out one at a time," mused Big Man Misri, "I'll slice you like kababs. If you all come out I'll certainly get two of you before you get me, and you don't know which two that will be." "Besides," added Bombur Yambarzal, angrily, "it isn't three against one. It's you three little shits against every able-bodied man in these parts." The men of Shirmal had ringed the building to make escape impossible. After a few hours a jeepload of military police did arrive and warned all present that violence would not be tolerated, a warning which everyone ignored. "By the way," Bombur shouted to the terrified Gegroos, "no food or drink will be brought to you. So let's see how long you last."

The sky screamed as invisible warplanes scarred it with savage white lines. There were battles beyond the border near Uri and Chhamb, where Colonel Kachhwaha, unaware of the siege of Shirmal, was earning his battle spurs. The war between India and Pakistan had begun. It lasted for twenty-five days. During every minute of that time, except for the small intervals required for him to perform his natural functions behind a nearby bush, Big Man Misri like a rock squatted outside the door of Bulbul Fakh's mosque with his saddle by his side. Food was brought to him from the kitchens of Shirmal, and a kindly young village syce stabled, fed and exercised his horse. A steady stream of visitors from Pachigam brought him news of Zoon, who was living with the Nomans, acting quiet and docile, and even smiling once or twice. The men of Shirmal took turns sitting with Big Man, and the police, too, worked shifts. And gradually the voices emanating from inside the mosque fell silent. The Gegroos had threatened, complained, cajoled, wept, ranted, quarrelled, apologized and begged, but they had not emerged.

After twenty-five days the sky stopped shrieking overhead. "Peace," said Bombur Yambarzal to Hasina Karim, and a bloodstained peace it was; the silent sky over Shirmal felt like death. "Are they still alive? What do you think?" Bombur asked Big Man Misri, and the carpenter came slowly to his feet, swaying with exhaustion, like a soldier coming home from a war. "They always were gutless cutlets," he said, knowing he was speaking the Gegroos' epitaph. "They died like rats in a trap."

Big Man made sure that all exits from the windowless structure were securely padlocked before he gave up his vigil, and he took away the keys. The military police—that is, the weary duty officer in his dusty Jeep—protested without much enthusiasm. "Go home now," Big Man told him. "No crime has been committed by any living person." "And if they are alive?" the officer asked. "Then," answered Big Man, "all they need to do is knock." But no such knock was ever heard. The little mosque at the end of the village remained padlocked and unused. The great events of a single powerful day, the defeat of Bulbul Fakh by Bombur Yambarzal and his saucepans, and the crime of the Gegroo brothers and their decision to immure themselves in this building until they died, had somehow pushed the mosque out of the villagers' consciousness, as if it had literally moved farther away from their homes. Wilderness reclaimed it. Trees marched out of the wood and captured it; creepers and thornbushes bound and guarded it. Like a castle under a fairy-tale curse it vanished from sight and eventually the wooden roof rotted and caved in, and the bolts on the doors rusted, the cheap padlocks fell away, and the memory of the Gegroo brothers was also eaten up, leaving behind a village superstition so powerful that nobody ever set foot in the place of their death by cowardice and starvation; and that was how things remained until the day of the dead brothers' return. That day, however, would not come for more than twenty years, and in the meanwhile Zoon

Misri lived quietly on, and was slowly nursed back to something like her former self, though a certain lightness of spirit had been lost forever. No man ever came to ask for her hand in marriage. That was how things were. Nobody could defend it but nobody could change it either. And nobody understood that the only thing keeping Zoon alive was the disappearance of the Gegroo brothers into their vanished tomb, which permitted her to agree with herself that they had never existed and the thing that they had done had never been done. The day of their return from the dead would be the last of her life.

When he returned to Elasticnagar from the war of 1965, Colonel Hammirdev Kachhwaha was once more a changed man. His father's death had briefly liberated him from the jail of unfulfilled expectations, but the experience of war had imprisoned him again, and this was a dungeon from which he would never escape. Military action had been a disappointment to Tortoise Colonel. War, whose highest purpose was the creation of clarity where none existed, the noble clarity of victory and defeat, had solved nothing. There had been little glory and much wasteful dying. Neither side had made good its claim to this land, or gained more than the tiniest patches of territory. The coming of peace left things in worse shape than they had been before the twenty-five days of battle. This was peace with more hatred, peace with greater embitterment, peace with deeper mutual contempt. For Colonel Kachhwaha, however, there was no peace, because the war raged on interminably in his memory, every moment of it replaying itself at every moment of every day, the livid green dampness of the trenches, the choking golf ball of fear in the throat, the shell bursts like lethal palm fronds in the sky, the sour grimaces of passing bullets, the iridescence of wounds and mutilations, the incandescence of death. Back in Elasticnagar, he immured himself in his quarters and pulled down the blinds and still the war would not cease, the intense slow motion of hand-to-hand combat in which the glassy fragility of his own pathetic, odorous life might be shattered at any moment by this bayonet that knife this grenade that screaming black-greased face, where this twist of the ankle that swivel of the hip this duck of the head that jab of the arm could summon up the darkness welling out of the cracks in the jagged earth, the darkness licking at the bodies of the soldiers, licking away their strength their legs their hope their legs their dissolving colourless legs. He had to sit in this darkness, his own soft darkness, so that other darkness, the hard darkness, would not come. To sit in soft darkness and forever be at war.

His soldiers were on edge. They were counting their dead and nursing their wounded and the high voltage of war continued to flow in their veins. They had fought a war for people who were ungrateful, who didn't deserve to be fought for. A fantasy of the enemy was spreading through the majority community in the valley, a dream of an idyllic life on the other side, in the religious state. You could not explain things to these people. You could not explain the measures taken for their protection in peace as well as war. For example it was not permitted for non-Kashmiris to own land here. This enlightened law did not exist on the other side where many people were settling whose culture was not Kashmiri culture. Wild mountain men, fanatics, aliens were coming in there. The laws here protected the citizenry against such elements but the citizenry remained ungrateful, continued to call for self-determination. Sheikh Abdullah was saying it again. Kashmir for the Kashmiris. The idiotic slogan was repeated everywhere, painted on walls, pasted on telegraph poles, hanging in the air like smoke. Maybe the enemy had the right idea. The population was unsuitable. A new population should be found. The valley should be emptied of all these people and refilled with others, who would be grateful to be here, grateful to be defended. Colonel Kachhwaha closed his eyes. The war exploded on the screen of his eyelids, its shapes coalescing and blurring, its colours darkening, until the world was black on black.

Acting on his instructions the army began to make routine sweeps through the villages. Even in routine sweeps, it had to be emphasized, accidents could happen. And, in fact, the level of violence accidentally rose. There was talk of accidental shootings, accidental beatings, the accidental use of cattle prods, one or two accidental deaths. In Shirmal where Bulbul Fakh had been based everyone was suspect. There were long interrogations and these sessions were not marked by the gentleness of the questioners. There were problems in Pachigam as well, even though the presence of three pandits in the panchayat counted for something. Abdullah Noman, who for years had held the village in the palm of his hand, found himself in the unfamiliar position of having to depend on Pyarelal Kaul, Big Man Misri and Shivshankar Sharga to put in a good word for his family and himself. The Nomans were on a list. The shameless intermarriage of Abdullah's youngest son and Boonyi Kaul was frowned on in the highest circles. Moreover, Anees Noman had disappeared. Firdaus told the soldiers he was visiting relatives in the north but this explanation was not believed. Anees Noman's name was on another list.

Boonyi Kaul Noman and Shalimar the clown were living with Abdullah and Firdaus. On the night that Anees left home the brothers quarrelled badly. At the end of the argument Anees said, "The trouble with you is this marriage of yours that stops you from seeing straight." Boonyi and Shalimar the clown had no children because Boonyi claimed to be too young to start a family. Anees in a parting shot did not fail to point out that this was suspicious behaviour on her part. Then, knowing he had said too much, he opened the back door and disappeared into the darkness. "He should stay out there," said Shalimar the clown to nobody in particular. "It isn't safe for him in here any more." Later that night when everyone was in bed Abdullah and Firdaus Noman spoke to each other of disillusion. Up to now they had tried to believe that their beloved Kashmiriness was best served by some kind of association with India, because India was where the churning happened, the commingling of this and that, Hindu and Muslim, many gods and one. But now the mood had changed. The union of Boonyi their friend's daughter and Shalimar the clown their own sweet boy, which they had held up to the world as a sign, felt like a falsely optimistic symbol, and their fierce defence of that union was beginning to look like some kind of futile last stand. "Things are growing apart," Firdaus said. "Now I know why Nazarébaddoor feared the future and didn't want to live to see it come." Unsleeping, they stared at the ceiling and feared for their sons.

On the same night, at the other end of the village, in his empty house by the Muskadoon, Pandit Pyarelal Kaul also lay awake, also grieving, also afraid. But when the thunderbolt hit Pachigam, it wasn't Hindu-Muslim trouble that brewed up the storm. The problem wasn't caused by the creeping madness of Tortoise Colonel or the latent danger of the iron mullah or the blindness of India or the accidental sweeps or the crescent shadow of Pakistan. Winter was approaching when it happened. The trees were almost bare and the nights were drawing in and a cold wind blew. Many of the village women were beginning their winter work, the painstaking embroidery of shawls. Then, just as the bhands of Pachigam were packing away their props and costumes until the spring, an envoy from the government in Srinagar came to inform them that there would be an extra command performance that year.

The American ambassador, Mr Maximilian Ophuls, was coming to Kashmir. He was a scholarly gentleman who evidently took a strong interest in all aspects of Kashmiri culture. He and his entourage would be staying at the government guesthouse at Dachigam, a spacious lodge set below a steep hill where the barasingha deer walked like kings. (But at this time of year the stags would have lost their mighty horn racks and would be girding themselves for the winter like everyone else.) Ambassador Ophuls's personal aide, Mr Edgar Wood, had specially asked for an evening of festivities during which the Banquet of Sixty Courses Maximum would be eaten, a santoor player from Srinagar would play traditional Kashmiri music, leading local authors would recite passages from the mystical poetry of Lal Ded as well as their own contemporary verses, an oral storyteller would tell tales selected from the gigantic Kashmiri story-compendium *Katha-sarit-sagar,* which made the *Arabian Nights* look like a novella; and, by particular request, the famous bhands of Pachigam would perform. The war had hit Pachigam's earnings badly and this late commission was a bonanza. Abdullah decided to offer a selection of scenes from the company's full repertoire, including, fatefully, the dance number from *Anarkali,* a new play devised by the group after the immense success of the film *Mughal-e-Azam,* which told the story of the love of Crown Prince Salim and the lowly but irresistible *nautch* girl Anarkali. Prince Salim was a popular figure in Kashmir, not because he was the son of the Grand Mughal, Akbar the Great, but because once he ascended to the throne as the emperor Jehangir he made it plain that Kashmir was his second Anarkali, his other great love. The role of the beautiful Anarkali would be played as usual by the best dancer in Pachigam, Boonyi Kaul Noman. Once Abdullah Noman had announced this decision, the die was cast. The invisible planets trained their full attention on Pachigam. The approaching scandal began to hiss and whisper in the chinar trees like a monsoon wind. But the leaves of the trees were still.

When Boonyi met Maximilian Ophuls's eyes for the first time he was applauding wildly and looking piercingly at her while she took her bow, as if he wanted to see right into her soul. At that moment she knew she had found what she had been waiting for. I swore I'd grab my chance when it showed up, she told herself, and here it is, staring me in the face and banging its hands together like a fool.

Max

In the city of Strasbourg, a place of charming old quarters and pleasant public gardens, near the charming parc des Contades, around the corner from the old synagogue on what is now the rue du Grand Rabbin René Hirschler, at the heart of a lovely and fashionable neighbourhood peopled by delightful and charming folk, there stood the ample and, yes, undeniably charming mansion house, a *petit palais* of the Belle Époque in which Ambassador Maximilian Ophuls, a man famed for possessing what a newspaper editorialist once described as "dangerous, possibly even lethal quantities" of charm, grew up in a family of highly cultured Ashkenazi Jews. Max Ophuls himself agreed with the leader writer's jaundiced assessment. "To be a Strasbourgeois," he was fond of saying, "was to learn the hard way about the deceptive nature of charm."

When he was appointed by Lyndon Johnson to succeed John Kenneth Galbraith as ambassador to India nearly two years after the Kennedy assassination, Max Ophuls went so far as to say—he was speaking at a Rashtrapati Bhavan banquet in his honour, hosted by the philosopher-president Sarvepalli

Radhakrishnan soon after Ophuls's presentation of his diplomatic credentials—that it was because he came from Alsace that he hoped he might be able to understand India a little, since the part of the world where he was raised had also been defined and redefined for many centuries by shifting frontiers, upheavals and dislocations, flights and returns, conquests and reconquests, the Roman Empire followed by the Alemanni, the Alemanni by Attila's Huns, the Huns by the Alemanni again, the Alemanni by the Franks. Even before the year acquired four digits Strasbourg had belonged first to Lotharingia and then to Germania, had been smashed up by nameless Hungarians and reconstructed by Saxons called Otto. Reformation and revolution were in its citizens' blood, which counter-reformation and reaction spilled in its charming streets. After the Thirty Years' War weakened the German Empire, the French made their move. The Frenchification of Alsace, which Louis XIV began, led in turn to de-Frenchification in 1871, after the Prussians starved and burned the city through the brutal winter of 1870. So there was Germanification, but less than forty years later there was de-Germanizing too. And then came Hitler, and Gauleiter Robert Wagner, and history stopped being theoretical and musty and became personal and malodorous instead. New place-names became a part of Strasbourg's story and the story of his family as well: Schirmeck, Struthof. The concentration camp, the extermination camp. "We know all about being part of an ancient civilization," Ambassador Ophuls said, "and we have suffered our share of slaughter and bloodletting as well. Our great leaders, and our mothers and children, too, have been taken from us." He bowed his head, momentarily unable to speak, and President Radhakrishnan reached over and took his hand. Everyone was suddenly in a heightened emotional state. "The loss of one man's dream, one family's home, one people's rights, one woman's life," said Ambassador Maximilian Ophuls, when he could resume, "is the loss of all our freedoms: of every life, every home, every hope. Each tragedy belongs to itself and at the same time to everyone else. What diminishes any of us diminishes us all." Few people paid much attention to these rather too generalized sentiments at the time; it was the handclasp that stuck in the mind. Those few seconds of undefended human contact caused Max Ophuls to be seen as a friend of India, to be gathered to the national bosom even more enthusiastically than his admired predecessor had been. From that moment Max's popularity soared, and as it became evident to everyone with the passage of time that he was in fact a great enthusiast for most things Indian, the relationship deepened towards something not unlike love. It was for this reason that the storm of scandal, when it broke, was so horrifyingly ferocious. The country felt more than mere disappointment in Max Ophuls; it felt jilted. Like a scorned lover, India turned on the charming cad of an ambassador and tried to break him into charming little bits. And after his departure, his successor, Chester Bowles, who tried for many years to tilt American policy away from Pakistan and towards India, was nevertheless given an altogether rougher ride.

Like most people from his part of the country, the young Max Ophuls had been raised to distrust Paris. His parents, Anya Ophuls and Max senior, owned an apartment at 8, avenue du Bois, but they rarely used the place, except when business necessitated the unwelcome journey west, and they invariably returned home as soon as possible with their eyebrows lifted high in fastidious disdain. Max junior himself had spent some years in Paris after graduating from the University of Strasbourg with brilliant degrees in economics and international relations, and had almost been seduced. In Paris he added the law to his accomplishments, established a reputation as a dandy and a ladykiller, affected spats and carried a cane, and demonstrated an astonishing technical skill as a spare-time painter, making Dalís and Magrittes of such subtle brilliance that they fooled the art dealer Julien Levy when he visited Max's studio apartment after a long drunken night at the Coupole. "Why are you wasting your time with law and money when you should dedicate your life to being a forger?" Levy shrieked when the deception was revealed. He was the lover of Frida Kahlo and exhibitor of the magic realist Tchelitchew, and in those days he was also in a permanent rage because his plan to build a Surrealist pavilion in the shape of a giant eye in the middle of the New York World's Fair had just been turned down. "These aren't forgeries," Max Ophuls said, "because there are no originals." Levy was silenced and examined the pictures more closely. "There's only one thing wrong with them," he said. "I'll bring the artists over to sign them one of these days, and then they will be complete." Max Ophuls was flattered, but he knew that art was not the world for him. He was right about this; about his future membership in the world of forgers, however, he was incorrect. History, which was his true métier, the real profession to which he would devote his life, would for a time value his skills as a faker above his talents in other fields.

Paris wasn't his place, either. Soon after the Levy visit he stunningly declined the offer of a partnership in one of the city's most illustrious legal practices and announced that he was going home to work with his father. This was a refusal as preposterous as the original offer, his astounded Parisian friends said, startled into agreeing with his envious enemies: he was far too young to have been offered so great an honour in the first place, and in the second place he was evidently too stupid or—much worse—too provincial to accept it. He returned to Strasbourg, where he divided his time between working as a junior professor of economics at the university—the vice-chancellor, the great astronomer André-Louis Danjon, was "mightily impressed" with him, and called him "one of the coming fellows, the Next People"—and helping his ailing, consumptive father with the family printing business. Within a year the catastrophe of Europe brought that age of the world to an end.

Decades had passed since those times, but Paris lingered in the ambassador's Americanized memory as a series of flickering images. It was present in the way he held a cigarette, or in the slow drift of smoke reflected in a gilded mirror. Paris was his own fist hammering on a café table to emphasize a political or philosophical point. It was a glass of cognac beside his morning coffee and tepid brioche. That innocent-uninnocent city was a prostitute, was a gigolo, was sophisticated infidelity in the guilty-unguilty afternoons. It was too beautiful, flaunting its beauty as if begging to be scarred. It was a certain precise mixture of tenderness and violence, love and pain. *Everyone in the world has two fatherlands, his own and Paris,* a Parisian filmmaker told him back then. But he didn't trust it. It seemed . . . he struggled for the right word . . . weak. The weakness of Paris was the weakness of France, which would make possible the dark metamorphosis that was beginning, the trumping of subtlety by crudity, the shriveled victory of wretchedness over joy.

It was not only Paris that changed, obviously. His beloved Strasbourg metamorphosed too, from river jewel into cheap Rhinestone. It turned into tasteless black bread and too many rutabagas and the disappearances of friends. Also the sneer of conquest above the collar of a grey uniform, the living death of collaboration in the eyes of the beautiful showgirls, the stinking gutter finales of the dead. It became rapid capitulation and slow resistance. Strasbourg, like Paris, shape-shifted and was no longer itself. It was the first paradise he lost. But in his heart he blamed the capital, blamed it for its arrogant weakness, for presenting itself to the world—to him—as a vision of high civilization which it did not have the force to defend. The fall of Strasbourg was a chapter in its back-and-forth frontier history. The fall of Paris was Paris's fault.

When Boonyi Noman danced for him in the Dachigam hunting lodge in Kashmir he thought of those feathered dead-eyed showgirls wreathed in Nazi cigar smoke, flaunting their gartered thighs. The clothes were different but he recognized the same hard hunger in her stare, the readiness of the survivor to suspend moral judgement in the presence of imagined opportunity. But I'm not a Nazi, he thought. I'm the American ambassador, the guy in the white hat. I'm for God's sake one of the Jews who lived. She swung her hips for him and he thought, And I'm also a married man. She swung her hips again and he ceased to think.

He was a Frenchman with a German name. His family's printing presses operated under the name Art & Aventure, a name they had borrowed, in French translation, from Jean Gensfleisch of Mayence, the fifteenth-century genius whose own Strasbourg workshop had been called Kunst und Aventur when, in 1440, he invented the printing press and became known to the world as Gutenberg. Max Ophuls's parents were wealthy, cultured, conservative, cosmopolitan; Max was raised speaking High German as easily as French, and believing that the great writers and thinkers of Germany belonged to him as naturally as the poets and philosophers of France. "In civilization there are no borderlines," Max senior taught him. But when barbarism came to Europe, that erased borderlines as well. The future Ambassador Ophuls was twenty-nine years old when Strasbourg was evacuated. The exodus began on September 1, 1939; one hundred and twenty thousand Strasbourgeois became refugees in the Dordogne and the Indre. The Ophuls family did not leave, although their household staff disappeared overnight without giving notice, silently fleeing the exterminating angel, just as the Kashmiri palace servitors would abandon the royal Dassehra banquet in the Shalimar gardens eight years later. The workers at the printing presses also began to desert their posts.

The university was moving to Clermont-Ferrand in the Zone Sud, outside the area of German occupation, and vice-chancellor Danjon urged his budding young economics genius to accompany them. But Max the younger would not leave unless he could get his parents to a place of safety as well. He tried hard to persuade them to join the evacuation. Wiry, graceful, their white hair cropped short, their hands the hands of pianists, not printers, their bodies leaning intently forward to listen to their son's absurd proposition, Max senior and his wife, Anya, looked more like identical twins than a married couple. Life had made them into each other's mirrors. Their personalities, too, had shaded into each other, creating a single, two-headed self, and so complete was their unanimity in all matters, both great and small, that it was no longer necessary for either to ask the other what they wished to eat or drink, or what their opinion might be on any subject of concern. At present they were seated side by side on carved wooden chairs in a six-hundred-year-old restaurant near the Place Kléber—an absolutely charming and historical spot—feasting heartily on *choucroute au Riesling* and caramelized lamb shoulder in a beer and pine honey sauce, and gazing on their brilliant son, their onliest golden child, with a mixture of profound love and gentle, but genuine, contempt. "Max junior isn't eating," Max senior mused with an air of wonderment, and Anya replied, "The poor boy has lost his appetite on account of the political situation." Their son urged them to be serious and they immediately put on their gravest expressions with every appearance (and none of the substance) of obedience. Max took a deep breath and launched into his prepared speech. The situation was desperate, he said. It was only a matter of time before the German army attacked France and if the border country should go the way of Poland the family's German name would not protect them. Theirs was a well-known Jewish household in a strongly Jewish neighbourhood; the risk of informers was real and had to be faced up to. Max senior and Anya should go away to their good friends the Sauerweins' place near Cro-Magnon. He himself would go to Clermont-Ferrand and teach.

They would have to lock and seal the Strasbourg house and the printing works and simply hope for the best. Was that agreed?

His parents smiled at their son the lawyer and his skilfully marshalled arguments—and these were identical smiles, cocked up to the left a little, smiles affording no glimpses of ageing teeth. They put down their utensils in unison and clasped their pianist's hands in their laps. Max senior gave a little glance at Anya and Anya gave a little glance back, offering each other the right of first reply. "Son," Max senior finally began, pursing his lips, "one never knows the answers to the questions of life until one is asked." Max was familiar with his father's circumlocutory philosophizing and waited for the point to arrive. "You know what he means, Maxi," his mother took over. "Until you have back pain you don't know your tolerance for back pain. How you're going to tolerate not being so young any more, you won't know until you grow old. And until danger comes a person doesn't know for sure how a person's going to think about danger." Max senior picked up a breadstick and bit it in half; it broke with a loud crack. "So now this question of peril has been posed," he said, pointing the remaining half of the stick at his son and narrowing his eyes, "and so now I know my answer."

Anya Ophuls drew herself up in a rare show of disunity. "It's my answer also, Maximilian," she corrected her husband mildly. "I think this slipped your mind a moment." Max senior frowned. "Sure, sure," he said. "Her answer as well, I know her answer as well as I know my own, and my mind, excuse me, nothing slips it. My mind, excuse me, is a fist of steel." Max junior thought it was time to press a little. "And what is that answer?" he asked as delicately as possible, and his father with a loud short laugh forgot his irritation and smacked his palms together as hard as he could. "I discover that I am a stubborn bastard!" he cried, coughing hard. "I discover bloody-mindedness in myself, and mulishness to boot. I will not be chased from my home and my business! I will not go to Sauerwein's and be made to look at his trembling old man's paintings and eat quenelles of pike. I will stay in my house and run my factory and face the enemy down. Who do they think they are dealing with here? Some common inky-fingered ragamuffin from the streets? Maybe I'm on my last legs, young fellow, but I stand for something in this town." His wife tugged at the sleeve of his coat. "Oh, yes," he added, sinking faintly back into his seat and dabbing a napkin at his brow. "And your mother. She's a stubborn bastard too." Then came a series of coughs and expectorations into a silk kerchief that declared the subject closed.

"In that case, I won't raise this with you again," said Max junior, admitting defeat. "On one condition. If the day arrives when I have to come to you and say, today it's time to run, on that day I want you to run without any argument, knowing that I will never say such a thing to you unless it is the simple truth." His mother beamed with unqualified pride. "See how he drives a hard bargain, Maximilian, isn't that so," she cried. "He leaves us no honourable choice except to agree."

Professor Max Ophuls informed vice-chancellor Danjon that family responsibilities obliged him to remain in Strasbourg. "What a waste," Danjon replied. "If you should choose to stay alive before they kill you, come and see us. Although it is possible that we will not be spared, either. I fear that this will be an L=0 eclipse." In the 1920s André Danjon had devised a scale of luminosity, the so-called Danjon scale, to describe the relative darkness of the moon during a lunar eclipse. L=0 meant total blackness, a complete absence of the reflected earthshine that could give the eclipsed moon a residual colour ranging from a deep grey to a bright copper-red or even orange. "If I'm right," Danjon told Max, "you and I are simply choosing to die in different towns during the general blackout."

From that day forward each of the three Ophulses kept a small bag packed in a closet, but otherwise went about their work. In the absence of domestic help, most of the Belle Époque mansion was dust-sheeted and closed up. They ate meals together in the kitchen, moved extra desks into Max senior's library to construct a three-person office, kept their own bedrooms clean and dusted, and maintained one small living room in which to receive their dwindling list of guests. As for Art & Aventure, two of the famous firm's three Strasbourg presses were closed down at once. The third, on the quai Mullenheim, a smaller art-book facility—both letterpress and photogravure—where for many generations volumes dedicated to the finest artists in Europe had been produced to the highest standards in the world, was the scene of the Ophulses' last stand. At first all three of them went in every day and manned the machines.

However, contracts were being cancelled constantly, so that soon enough the parents were obliged angrily to "retire", and Max junior went to the print shop alone. Every call from a grand publisher from the capital deepened Max's scorn for the weakness of Paris. He remembered his mother shouting into the telephone, "What do you mean, this is no time for art? If not now, when?"—and then staring fire-eyed at the silent receiver in her hand as if it were a traitor. "He hangs up," she said to the room at large. "After twenty years' business, without so much as goodbye." The death of courtesy appeared to distress her more than the collapse of the family business. Her coughing husband moved at once to comfort her. "Take a look on the shelves," he said. "You see that army of volumes? That army will outlast whatever iron men come clanking across our lives."

When Max junior, hiding behind a burned-out truck just over a year later, saw the treasures of Art & Aventure's backlist being tossed onto a bonfire outside the burning synagogue, his father's words came back to him. If he had been able to discuss the burning books with Max senior the old man would probably have shrugged and quoted Bulgakov. *Manuscripts don't burn.* Well, maybe they do and maybe they don't, thought orphaned Max in the incandescent night; but people, of course, will blaze away nicely, given a decent chance.

Strasbourg had become a ghost town, its streets ragged with absences. It was still charming, naturally, with its medieval half-timberings, its covered bridges, its pleasing aspects and riverside parks. As he prowled the largely deserted alleys of the Petite France district, the future Ambassador Ophuls told himself, "It's as if everyone went away for August, and any day now it will be time for *la rentrée* and the place will be bustling again." But in order to believe that one had to ignore the broken windows, the evidence of looting, the feral dogs in the streets, many of them abandoned pets driven insane by abandonment. One had to ignore the ruination of one's own life. There were traditional, time-honoured ways of doing this, and during the course of that year in which his family lost everything Max Ophuls did not ignore tradition. He frequented the few brothels and drinking dives that were still in business; they welcomed him in, glad of the trade, and offered him their best goods at bargain prices. The melancholy strain that had been lying dormant in his personality revealed itself in those months, inducing periods of Churchillian depression during which he considered ending his life more than once, and was only prevented from doing so by the knowledge that he would profoundly disgust his parents. As the year 1940 moved forward, a year in which all the news was bad, he walked the city streets and squares, alleys and embankments at high speed, hour after hour, with his head down, his hands jammed deep into the pockets of a double-breasted serge greatcoat, and a dark blue beret pulled low over his frowning brow. If he moved fast enough, like an American comic-book superhero, like the Flash, like a Jewish Superman, maybe he could create the illusion that the people of Strasbourg were still there. If he moved fast enough maybe he could save the world. If he moved fast enough maybe he could break through into another universe in which everything wasn't so full of shit. If he moved fast enough maybe he could outpace his own anger and fear. If he moved fast enough maybe he could stop feeling like a helpless fool.

These thoughts were interrupted one May afternoon by a violent collision. As usual, he hadn't been looking where he was going, and on this occasion there was someone in the way, a surprisingly small woman, so small that at first he thought he had knocked over a child. A parcel wrapped in string and brown paper dropped from the small woman's hands as she fell, and the brown paper tore. Her companion, a big shambling fellow as oversized as she was tiny, helped her to her feet and hurriedly retrieved the torn parcel, carefully taking off his own raincoat and wrapping the parcel in it. He also picked up and dusted off his companion's fallen hat, with its single upright feather, placing it carefully, even lovingly, back on her head of marcelled black hair. The fallen woman had not cried out, nor did the big man seek to remonstrate with Ophuls for his clumsiness. They simply gathered themselves together and moved on. It was as if they were phantoms, ill-assorted phantoms surprised that they still possessed solidity, mass, volume, that people were still able to collide with them and knock them down, rather than passing through their bodies with nothing more than a small icy shudder of subconscious recognition.

When they had taken a dozen steps away, however, they stopped and looked back over their shoulders without turning their bodies. They saw

Max staring after them and were covered in a kind of spectral embarrassment. Ghosts were probably always surprised to be seen, Max supposed. The woman was nodding furiously and the man, slowly, as if in a dream, turned and walked back towards Max. He's going to hit me after all, Max thought, and wondered whether he should take to his heels. Then the man reached him and spoke, carefully, in a low voice: "You are the printer?" With those four words he gave Max Ophuls back a sense of purpose in life.

You are the printer. Even before the fall of the Maginot Line, the first stirrings of what would become the Resistance were making themselves felt. The couple with the brown paper parcel, whom he would only know by the work-names of "Bill" and "Blandine", were his first links to that world. Their group would later start calling itself the Seventh Column of Alsace, but for the moment it was just Bill and Blandine and a few like-minded associates, doing what they could to prepare for the coming unpleasantness. Yes, he was the printer, Max affirmed. Yes, he was a Jew. Yes, he would help. "Time is short," Bill said. "Escape routes are being built. Identity documents must be printed. However many possible. The need is very great. Your parents included. You included also." Max looked at the parcel. "These are adequate," Bill said, grimacing. "But not guaranteed to pass. Work of a higher standard is required." Bill's manner was always courteous and deferential. Blandine was the sharp-tongued one of the pair. "Do you actually know how to do what we need," she asked Max that first time, looking unblinking into his eyes, "or are you just a pampered milord who underpays his workers and spends the money on whores?"

Her enormous lover looked discomfited and shifted his feet. "But no, my dearest, be good, the gentleman is going to be of assistance. Please excuse her, sir," he said to Max. "The communism burns hot in her, the class war and autonomy and such." Ever since Gouraud's Fourth Army brought Strasbourg back under French control in November 1918, the local communists had favoured the autonomy of Alsace from both France and Germany, whereas socialists had favoured a rapid assimilation with France. How obsolete both positions looked now, how pathetic the passions they had so recently aroused. Max glared back at Blandine. "Yes," he told her, not knowing if he was telling the truth, suddenly determined to prove himself unworthy of her scorn. "I can print any damn thing you want me to." She spat into a gutter. "Good," she said. "Then there's work to be done."

If he moved fast enough maybe he could break through into another universe. He had been granted his wish. Julien Levy had been right. Max turned out to have a real gift for forgery, the painstaking miniaturist zeal of a monk illuminating a Bible, that enabled him to create plausible counterfeits of whatever was required and make good his boast. When the materials provided by Bill and Blandine were inadequate—when the paper had the wrong sort of coarseness or the ink was fractionally the wrong colour—he scavenged and scrounged tirelessly until he came up with the goods. On one occasion he actually broke into a deserted art-supplies store and took what he needed, promising himself that if liberation ever came he would return and repay the owner, a promise that, as he recorded in his book of wartime memoirs, he faithfully kept. As he forged and printed the documents—one by one, at snail's pace, always by night, alone in the pressroom, with the shutters locked, and by the light of no more than a single small lantern—he felt he was also forging a new self, one that resisted, that pushed back against fate, rejecting inevitability, choosing to remake the world.

Often, as he laboured, he had the sense of being the medium, not the creator: the sense of a higher power working through him. He had never been a religious man, and tried to rationalize this feeling away; yet it stubbornly persisted. A purpose was working itself out through him. He could not give it a name, but its boundaries were far greater than his own. When he had contact with Bill or Blandine and handed over the identity cards and doctored passports he spoke in effusive, optimistic words about what they were doing. Bill was monosyllabic at best in responding to such torrents, until Max learned the lesson of his silences and did his best to restrain himself. Blandine was, as ever, cuttingly to the point. "Oh, shut up," she said. "To listen to you, one would think we were on the verge of overthrowing the Third Reich, instead of just hoping to prick the beast's behind here and there and maybe save a few wretched souls as well."

It was four o'clock in the morning of the fifteenth of June, 1940. Paris had fallen. The French military command had believed that tanks could not pass through the heavily wooded hill country of the Ardennes and that the German advance could therefore be resisted at the immense Maginot Line defence system in Lorraine. This was a mistake. Along the Line there was a well-dug-in force, also an extensive underground system of tunnels, railways, hospitals, kitchens and communications centres. While they waited for the German assault the French soldiers whiled away their subterranean days by painting trompe-l'oeil murals on the tunnel walls—tropical landscapes, rooms with chintz wallpaper and open windows looking out onto bucolic spring scenery, heroic crests bearing such mottoes as *They shall not pass.* Unfortunately, they did not need to pass. Panzer divisions commanded by Rommel and others invaded through the supposedly impassable Ardennes and reached the villages of Dinant and Sedan on the Meuse on May 12. On June 13 the government of France abandoned the capital to the aggressor. Outflanked and irrelevant, the French forces at the Maginot Line surrendered a few weeks later. Four years after that the tide of history would have turned and the Normandy landings would begin, but those four years would be a century long.

"I have to go," Blandine said, gathering up the papers Max had for her, without a word of thanks or of appreciation for the quality of the work. This was her way. But at the back door, as he let her out, she saw the first light of dawn slinking into the sky and trembled and leaned back against him. "The dawn before the darkness," she said, and turned, and kissed him. They stumbled back through the door into the room of the printing presses and had sex against one of the big dark green machines, without getting undressed. He had to lift her up to enter her and for a moment her feet in their high heels dangled awkwardly. Then she swiftly wrapped her legs around his waist and squeezed. He saw that her height was a matter of sensitivity. To compensate for it she remained almost savagely composed at all times. Even during their congress the hat with the feather remained firmly planted on her head. Four days later the Nazi flag flew over the Cathedral and the darkness began.

The city's charm was no defence. It ran deep, there were subterranean tunnels of charm underground, subterranean charm hospitals and charm canteens in case of need, and so there were those who had allowed themselves to believe that nothing much would change, the Germans had been here before, after all, and this time as on previous occasions the city would bewitch them and shape them to its ways. Max senior and Anya Ophuls succumbed slowly to this fantasy of a Maginot Line of charm, and their son despaired of them. Gauleiter Wagner, he pointed out, was not a charming man. His parents put on serious expressions and nodded gravely. All of a sudden, when he hadn't been looking, they had become very old and frail, deteriorating sharply with the same simultaneity with which they had lived the greater part of their married lives. They had always belittled their difficulties, but in the past their lightness had had an undercurrent, a knowing, ironic intelligence. That undercurrent had disappeared. What remained was a sort of foolishness, a forgetting, happy sort of unwisdom. They laughed a great deal and whiled away the days playing card and board games in the shrouded house, behaving as if the times were not out of joint, as if it were an excellent idea that the house was largely shuttered up and the population had fled and the street names were being Germanized and the speaking of the French language and the Alsatian dialect had been forbidden. "Well, dear, we do all speak Hochdeutsch, don't we, so there's no difficulty, is there," Anya said when Max junior brought her the language news. And when Wagner's minions banned the wearing of the beret, calling it an insult to the Reich, old Max told his son, "I never thought it suited you anyway; wear a trilby instead, there's a sensible fellow," and returned to his game of solitaire.

Some days, Max thought his parents believed they could behave the Nazis out of existence, could make them disappear by simply treating them as if they weren't there. At other times it was clear that they were losing their hold on things, slipping out of the world and into a region of dreams, sliding charmingly and uncomplainingly towards senility and death.

The university district was as deserted as the rest of the city but a couple of bars somehow managed to stay open. One of these was Le Beau Noiseur, and as the desire for resistance grew among the city's remaining residents this became one of the places where interested parties met. Bill, Blandine, Max and a few others were regulars. Afterwards the innocence and openness of those early days would strike everyone as the height of insanity. The group openly referred to itself as *les noiseurs,* "the squabblers". Yet in spite of such foolhardiness its members managed surprising feats. After the French surrender Blandine, for example, became an ambulance driver and visited several internment camps near Metz, where French soldiers were being interrogated before being released and sent home. Nobody paid this tiny woman in uniform much attention, with the result that as she distributed food and medicines she was able to learn a good deal about German troop and supply movements. The problem was that she didn't know who to give the information to; which did nothing to sweeten her disposition. Her irritability was greater than ever, her tongue sharper, and most of her worst barbs were aimed at Max. The clumsy, hurried episode at the print shop was never repeated, nor did she allude to it. It was evident now that she and Bill were married, though neither of them wore a ring. Max filed away the memory of the sexual encounter, and eventually managed to forget it altogether. Then, twenty years later, while he was researching the period for a book, he made the chance discovery that in the vicious death-throes of the Nazi phase, when the Allies were sweeping across France after the successful D-Day landings, Blandine—real name Suzette Trautmann—had been captured in a refitted garage basement trying to send messages to the liberating army on a ham radio set, and had been executed on the spot. In the breast pocket of her shirt was a passport-sized photograph of an unknown man. The photograph had not survived.

Suppose it was me in that photo, Max suddenly thought. Suppose all those tongue-lashings were inverted signs of love, coded pleas for me to do what she could not do herself: to tear her away from her marriage and make off with her into some impossible wartime Eden. He tried to set aside these speculations, which were only a form of vanity, he scolded himself. But the possibility of misunderstood love went on eating away at him. Blandine, Blandine, he thought. Men are fools. No wonder we made you so mad. That afternoon in the archives when he discovered Suzette Trautmann's fate he promised himself that if a woman ever sent him such signals again, if a woman were ever trying to say please, let's get out of here, please please let's run away and be together forever and to hell with the damnation of our souls, *please,* he would not fail to decipher the secret code.

He never found out what happened to Bill.

By the fall of 1940, the camps outside the city were being readied for guests, and, right on cue, the citizens of Strasbourg started returning to the city, under German instructions. Tens of thousands of young men, the so-called *malgré-nous,* were quickly pressed into front-line service in the German army. Max Ophuls understood that, paradoxically, now that everyone was home, however temporarily, it was time for him and his family to leave. The new homes being prepared near Schirmeck at Natzweiler-Struthof, intended for homosexuals, communists and Jews, sounded like a step down in the world. (The gas chamber being constructed down the road from the Struthof facility was still a secret.) It had not been possible to go to the printing works on the quai Mullenheim for some time now, and the family's money shortage had forced Max to pawn and sell quantities of the Ophuls jewelry and silver. These would be gone soon, and with them the best chance of escape, for which substantial finances would almost certainly be required. Silver was the easiest thing to fence; melted down and anonymous, it told no tales about its provenance. Jewelry carried with it the higher risk of being classified as a looter, a charge carrying the death penalty; so in those confused days before the underworld reestablished its systems, even spectacular pieces, offered in exchange for a pittance, might be refused by the city's ever-prudent pawnbrokers, those perpetual weathercocks of the winds of change. When the jewels could be fenced—jewels on whose true value the family could have lived for decades—the prices were so low that they barely paid for a week's worth of essential provisions. Possessions were the past, and the future was arriving rapidly, and nobody had time—or cash—for yesterdays.

Thus far the Art & Aventure works had not been raided or seized by the city's new authorities, but it was only a matter of time. Max did his best to conceal his forging materials from view, finding a number of ingenious hiding places both at the quai Mullenheim and at home, but a thorough search might easily uncover some damning cache, and after that . . . well, he preferred not to imagine what might happen after that. This increasingly uneasy and precarious state of affairs lasted until the spring of 1941. Then, one evening at Le Beau Noiseur, Bill told Max in whispers that an escape route had been readied for use, and that he and his parents had been selected to make the first run. Members of the faculty and student body of Strasbourg University—*les non-jamais*—had refused to return to the "Motherland", the Gross Reich, and had remained in internal exile in Clermont-Ferrand, in spite of the risk of being declared deserters by the Germans. The vice-chancellor, a certain Monsieur Dungeon, had somehow persuaded Vichy officialdom to maintain the Strasbourg University at this "external campus", and for the moment the Germans were prepared to let Pétain's people have their way. A history professor named Zeller, assisted by student and teacher volunteers, and with some help from the Clermont-Ferrand military governor, had spent the summer building a large "country cottage" at Gergovie, near the well-known Gallo-Roman excavations, about which Bill knew nothing except that they were well known. "You leave tonight," Bill said, passing him a piece of paper. "If your family can reach Gergovie, you will be contacted there and given new orders." Max Ophuls kept a poker face throughout this briefing, telling Bill nothing he did not need to know, keeping his university connections to himself. Gaston Zeller, he thought. It will be good to see his ugly mug again.

He left the café without looking back. At home his parents had taken the dust sheets off the grand piano in the main drawing room and Anya was playing from memory, smiling beatifically, even though the instrument was harshly out of tune. Max senior stood behind her, his hands resting lightly on her shoulders, his eyes closed, his expression distant and serene. Their son interrupted their reverie. "The day has come," he said. "It's time for us to run." The elderly couple looked as if the universe had quivered slightly; then his mother put on her sweetest smile. "Oh, but it's out of the question, dear," she said. "You know that our dear friend Dumas's son Charles receives his *bachot* tomorrow. We'll talk about going once that's done with."

This was a dreadful statement. Charles Dumas was thirty, the same age as the younger Max, and not in Strasbourg. The day of their *baccalauréat* graduations was long past. "But you promised," Max said, in great distress. "You said that if I ever came to you with this warning, you would do as I asked." His father inclined his head. "It's true we made a promise," he said. "And you rightly stress the importance of our having given our word. Thus two great principles are in conflict here: honesty and friendship. We prefer to be good friends to our friends, and stay here for their family's important day, even if that makes us dishonest in your eyes." "For God's sake," shouted Max the younger, "there's no such ceremony—you know perfectly well that all the schools and colleges have been closed since the evacuation, and even if they weren't, this isn't the right time of year. . . ." Anya Ophuls prepared to resume playing the piano. "Shh, shh, my darling, for goodness' sake," she admonished him. "It's just one day. The day after tomorrow we'll pick up those bags we packed and scurry off to wherever you see fit."

There was nothing for it but to acquiesce. On the piece of paper Bill had given Max at the bar was the location of the rendezvous point, a stable in a remote corner of the Bugatti estate in the village of Molsheim, and the word *Finkenberger,* which Max had always thought of as the name of a local wine, not a particular man. He took this to be the pseudonym of the *passeur,* the man who would be responsible for facilitating the run and getting the Ophuls family across enemy lines. That night, a moonless night which had no doubt been selected on account of its unusual darkness, Max bicycled twenty kilometres down the so-called wine road to Molsheim to inform M. Finkenberger that there would be a twenty-four-hour delay in the plan. The choice of meeting place was risky because the Bugatti factory was now in German hands; but then again, there were no risk-free places that fall. Molsheim, a beauty spot with old-world cobbled streets and leaning Geppetto houses, was so utterly charming that you expected to see blue fairies at its windows and the new Disney movie's already famous talking cricket on its hearths. Tonight, however, the tragedy of the Bugatti family lay over the village like a shroud, darkening the unmooned darkness until it felt like a blindfold. The closer Max came to the great estate the darker it grew, until he had to dismount from his bicycle and grope his way forward like a blind man.

Within the space of a single year the legendary car designer Ettore Bugatti, "Le Patron", had suffered the loss first of his son Jean—in an automobile accident—and then his father Carlo, who died just before the German invasion, as if reluctant to be a part of that future. Ettore had been living in Paris, and although he remained the company's engineering genius, Jean had for several years been in charge of the coachwork design, the distinctive curved fenders, the futuristic body shapes. After his son's death Ettore returned to the quasi-baronial Molsheim factory-estate, where all the buildings—even the pattern shop, the body shops, the foundry, the drafting room—boasted great, polished doors of oak and bronze. The Bugattis had lived in feudal splendour. There was a sculpture museum, a carriage museum, luxurious facilities for their Thoroughbred horses, a riding school. They kept prize terriers, prime cattle, racing pigeons. They had their own distillery, and housed clients in a spectacular residence, the Hotel of the Pure Blood. The grandeur of the private world he had built served only to twist the knife in Ettore's heart, magnifying the sudden emptiness of his life. Within a few months of his return he sold out to the Germans—was forced to do so—and left Molsheim with the air of a man emerging from a tomb. He moved his manufacturing operations to Bordeaux, but no Bugatti cars were ever built again; Ettore now made crankshafts for Hispano-Suiza aircraft engines. Less well known was his work with the Resistance, into which many of his former employees followed their benevolent but dictatorial boss. One such employee, the leathery old horse trainer now known to Max Ophuls as the *passeur* Finkenberger, was waiting at the end of a tiny wooded dead-end lane behind the stable, sitting on a fence post, smoking. Max stumbled down the lane, colliding with other fence posts and sadistic trees, trying not to cry out. The lighted tip of Finkenberger's cigarette was his beacon, and he swam towards it through the eyeless darkness like Leander in the Hellespont. When the horse man first spoke it was as if the night's curtain had been torn. Around the words, Max Ophuls began to be able to see or at least imagine a face, which to his great surprise turned out to be familiar. "Fuck me," were the waiting man's first words. "I know you, don't I? *Fuck.*"

Max Ophuls had been on close terms with Jean Bugatti, had learned to fly planes with him, performing daredevilry in the innocent prewar sky. They had also ridden the length and breadth of this formerly blessed countryside on golden stallions across brilliant summer afternoons. Tonight, exhausted, filled with trepidation, Max was rushed back to that happier time by the unmistakable, obscene tongue of the *passeur.* "Ophuls, Max," he said. "And sure, I know you, Finkenberger. Who could forget." The other offered a cigarette, which Max declined. "Everything's gone to fuck," the horse trainer confided. "Nazis want to use the shop to build guns, obviously. Cunts. But they like the dogs and horses and of course they want to drive the fucking cars. I see a 57-5 with that fucking swastika flying on the hood, I want to fucking throw up. Fucking gutter rats playing at being aristos. Fucking pond scum. And that hotel, I always thought the name was a mistake. They fucking love that place. Hotel of the Pure Blood. It's a fucking whorehouse now. Why are you alone, anyway? I was told three persons."

Max explained the problem and there was an abrupt change of mood. The darkness itself seemed to tighten, to gather itself into a pair of clenched fists. Finkenberger threw away his cigarette and, to judge by his breathing, seemed to be making an effort to suppress his rage. Finally he spoke. "Le Patron, he left Molsheim and fucked off to Paris because he thought the workers weren't grateful. Old school, he is. Take your fucking cap off when he comes by, touch the fucking forelock, bend the fucking knee, you catch my drift. And yeah, maybe there were those who weren't grateful for the chance to behave like fucking serfs, even if they did get houses and benefits and such. There were those who weren't too fucking grateful at all. Monsieur Jean was different. Common fucking touch. Had it in spades. Think yourself lucky you were his pal. If you weren't his pal and came to me saying what you're saying to me now I'd have told you to go fuck yourself. If you were one of Le Patron's high-falutin pricks I'd have told you what you could fucking do with your twenty-four-hour delay. Do you know how fucking hard it is to set this stuff up, the danger of using the radio, the number of people waiting for you down the road that have to be stood down and stood up again tomorrow, do you know the fucking danger you're putting them in? Fucking dilettante fuckers like you can't think about anyone else. But you're the lucky bastard, I say again, on account of Monsieur Jean, on account of his fucking beautiful fucking memory. Be here on time tomorrow the three of you or you can go fuck yourselves to death in the fucking synagogue on the fucking Sabbath day."

In Strasbourg there were fires burning, and helmeted goon squads in the street. Max Ophuls went carefully, on foot, pushing his bike, hiding in shadows. When he saw the flames licking at Art & Aventure the fear began pounding in him, kneading him like dough. Long before he reached home he knew what he would find, the broken door, the wanton damage, the shit on the Biedermeiers, the daubed slogans, the urine in the hall. If the house had not been torched it could only be because some Nazi high-up wanted it for himself. All the lights were on and nobody was home. He went through the rooms one by one, darkening them, returning them to the night, letting them mourn. In the library with the three desks the destruction was very great, the books scattered and torn, a mound of them burned in the middle of the rug, a great charred heap of wisdom that somebody had pissed on to put it out. Desk drawers hung open. Gashed paintings hung askew in broken frames. He had brought his parents' false papers home with him and had made the mistake of leaving them at home when he went on the errand that had temporarily saved him. The discovery of those documents increased his parents' peril and doomed him as well. Nobody was home but by the end of this night of looting the house would have passed into enemy hands, like the Hotel of the Pure Blood. Nazi whores would loll where once his mother lay. He should leave. He should definitely leave at once. There was nobody home but that would change. He found a bottle of cognac that had somehow been spared. It lay unbroken in a corner next to a chaise between blowing curtains. He pulled out the cork and drank. Time passed. No, it did not pass. Time stood still. Beauty passed, love passed, bloody-mindedness and mulishness passed. Time stood still with its hands up. Stubborn bastards faded away.

After the war he found out how their story had ended. He learned the numbers burned into their forearms, memorized them and never forgot. The record showed that they had been used for medical experimentation. They were old and losing their reason and good for nothing and so a use had been found for them. After lifetimes lived mainly in their now-enfeebled minds they ended up as mere bodies, bodies that reacted this way to pain, this way to greater pain, this way to the greatest pain imaginable, bodies whose response to being injected with diseases was of interest, of high scientific interest. So they were interested in learning? Very well then. They had helped the advancement of knowledge in a valuably practical way. They never made it to the gas chamber. Scholarship killed them first.

Drunk, close to physical collapse, Max Ophuls got back on his bicycle and made the twenty-kilometre wine road dash for the third time that night. When he got back to Molsheim he realized he had no idea how to find the *passeur,* no idea which of the many workers' cottages on the Bugatti estate might be his, didn't even remember his real name. The night was no longer absolute; a hint of future colour softened the black. More by luck than memory he found his way back to the small stable at the estate's edge, an interim sort of place, a way station for tired riders, and wheeled his bicycle inside and passed out on the muddy floor in one of the stalls. This was where Finkenberger found him several hours later, in broad daylight, and shook him roughly, shouting curses into the sleeper's ear. Max came awake fast and was frightened to find a horse nuzzling at him as if to determine whether he might be edible. Next to the horse's head was Finkenberger's head. Finkenberger by daylight was a jockey-sized gnome with a caustic face filled with bad and probably aching teeth. "You're one lucky fuck," he hissed at Max. "Gauleiter Wagner, the big cunt himself, was planning to ride here today, but it seems everybody wants twenty-four-hour delays right now." Then he read the look on Max's face and his manner changed. "Shit," he said. "Shit, I'm sorry. Oh, shit, shit, shit, shit, shit. I shit on myself for my insensitivity, I shit on their fascist grandmothers' graves, I wish them shit for dinner in hell for all eternity." He sat down in the mud and put his arm around Max, who was unable to cry. Then in a flash the *passeur* was all business, all questions and options. The escape route to the Zone Sud had been set up again, he had done that before going to sleep, but if the big roundups had begun the risk factor had risen, was maybe unacceptable. Yes, of course he was confident of the route, but only as confident as it was possible to be, because this would be the first time and the first time is never sure. And if the bastards were in the middle of a big operation then there could be no guarantees but of course everyone would do his best. "That sounds good," Max said bitterly. "Sure, let's do that." It was at that moment that Finkenberger the *passeur* had the idea that would make Max Ophuls one of the great romantic heroes of the Resistance: the Flying Jew.

At the beginning of the war Ettore Bugatti, along with the well-known aeronautical engineer Louis D. de Monge, designed a plane—the so-called Model 100—to break the world speed record, which a German Messerschmitt Me209 had raised to 469.22 miles per hour on April 26, 1939. As the threat of war grew Bugatti was given a contract to build a military version of the Racer, with two guns, oxygen cylinders and self-sealing fuel tanks. The plane was built in secret on the second floor of a Parisian furniture factory, but had never had the chance to fly. As the German armies marched on Paris, Ettore Bugatti had the plane lowered to the street, loaded it onto a truck and sent it out of the city and into hiding. "The Racer," Finkenberger whispered to Max Ophuls, grinning his snaggletoothed grin. "I know where she is. If you can fly her, take her."

She was hidden right under the enemy's nose, in a hay barn on the estate. She could fly at over five hundred miles an hour, or that, at any rate, was what her designers believed. She was powered by two Bugatti T50B auto-racing engines, had forward-swept wings and a revolutionary system of variable wing geometry, a system of self-adjusting split trailing edge flaps that responded to airspeed and manifold pressure and then automatically set themselves into any of six different positions: takeoff, cruise, high-speed dash, descent, landing, rollout. She was fast, fast, fast, and painted Bugatti blue. Finkenberger brought Max to the barn after darkness made it safe to move again, and the two men worked silently for an hour and a half removing the camouflage of hay and netting and revealing the Bugatti Racer in all her glory. She was still standing on the truck that had brought her out of Paris, like a greyhound in the slips. Finkenberger said he knew a stretch of straight road nearby that would serve as a runway. Max Ophuls marvelled at the Racer's streamlined bullet beauty. "She'll reach Clermont-Ferrand all right, but don't go crazy, okay? No need to go for the fucking speed record," Finkenberger said. "Now look and learn." So he was more than a horse trainer, Max realized. Finkenberger was explaining the aircraft's unorthodox engine/power arrangement, its canted engines, its counter-rotating propellers. The cooling system, the tail-fin control system: these, too, were innovations. "Nothing like her ever built," Finkenberger said. "One of a fucking kind."

"Can you authorize this?" Max Ophuls asked, his voice heavy with wonder, his thoughts already rushing skywards. "Her maiden flight will be an act of resistance," Finkenberger replied, the blue language disappearing as he revealed a previously hidden streak of emotional patriotism. "Le Patron would not wish it otherwise. Just take her, okay? Take her before they find her. She needs to escape as well."

The night flight of the Bugatti Racer from Molsheim to Clermont-Ferrand would become one of the grand myths of the Resistance, and in the whispered retelling it swiftly acquired the supernatural force of a fable: the impossible super-speed of the aircraft bulleting the black sky; the low-altitude streak towards freedom that only the most skilful and fearless pilot could have pulled off; the five-hundred-miles-per-hour barrier broken through for the first time in history as the world record was unofficially but unquestionably shattered, and, more important, reclaimed for France from the Germans, thus becoming a metaphor for the Liberation; the daring takeoff from a country road and the even more dangerous dark-of-the-moon landing on the grassy plain down which Julius Caesar's legions had marched toward the oppidum of Gergovia, where Vercingetorix, the chief of the Arverni, defeated them.

Some of this was certainly true, but in later years Maximilian Ophuls himself seemed prepared to allow the myths to embellish the truth. Had he really broken the record in spite of Finkenberger's warnings about fuel? Had he really flown at or near rooftop level all the way, or had he escaped radar detection by luck, and on account of the strong element of the unexpected in his dash? In his own memoir of the war years, Max Ophuls clarified nothing, speaking instead with a hero's modesty of his great good fortune and of the many helpers without whom, and so on. "I thought of Saint-Exupéry," he wrote. "In spite of the anxious situation I understood what he meant when he spoke in *Vol de nuit* of flying as a form of meditation. *That profound meditation in which one tastes an inexplicable hope.* Yes, yes. It was like that."

Here, again, an ungenerous reader might perceive a calculated merging of Max's own story with that of another beloved figure. In 1940 the writer and pilot Antoine de Saint-Exupéry played a heroic part in the battle of France, then left with his squadron for North Africa, and later reached New York. He was already famous as the author of *Night Flight,* but when Max Ophuls in his memoir went on to reference a later Saint-Exupéry book he was guilty of anachronism. At the time of his own flight to Gergovia, *Pilote de guerre,* published in English as *Flight to Arras,* was still being written, and even after its publication a year later and its considerable American success it was banned by the Vichy government and the Gallimard edition of 1942 was suppressed. It was therefore impossible for Max Ophuls in the Bugatti Racer to have had any knowledge of its contents. In spite of these awkward details, Max Ophuls unashamedly set down his airborne reflections on a text of which he could not then have been aware. *"War, for us, signified disaster. But was it the case that France, to spare itself a defeat, had refused to fight? I do not believe it."* Max reliving his own *vol de nuit* added approvingly, "As I whistled over the heads of my sleeping countrymen, I did not believe it either. France would soon awake." The error wasn't important. He got away with it. Even those critics who spotted the blunder said it was within the bounds of poetic licence. A hero was a hero and deserved to be cut a little slack. Max's book was highly praised and became a commercial success, notably in America. After all, by the end of the war Saint-Exupéry was dead, lost in action over Corsica, whereas Max Ophuls was a living flying ace and giant of the Resistance, a man of movie-star good looks and polymathic accomplishment, and in addition he had moved to the United States, choosing the burnished attractions of the New World over the damaged gentility of the Old.

Once he had landed, the aircraft was quickly concealed in the nearby forest by a small team of volunteers who were nicknamed the Gergovians and led by the redoubtable Jean-Paul Cauchi, the organizer of Combat Universitaire, also known as Combat Étudiant, the Resistance group based at the Strasbourg university-in-exile and answerable to Henri Ingrand, the Chief for Combat Region Six. Max was taken to the forest cottage where his colleagues vice-chancellor Danjon and the historian Gaston Zeller were waiting with a bottle of wine. As his personally forged papers were in the name of "Sebastian Brant" his arrival as part of the Strasbourgeois faculty would need some explanation. He would be described as a scholar from the south, and Danjon, who exercised an almost hypnotic power over the Nazi fellow travellers of Vichy, would square the paperwork. "But you took a stupid risk by giving yourself a well-known name," Danjon chided him. "One might almost say you yourself travelled here in an airborne ship of fools." The real Brant was the fifteenth-century Strasbourg author of *Stultifera Navis,* or *Das Narrenschiff* (1494), a satire of human follies illustrated in part by the young Albrecht Dürer. Ophuls spread his hands apologetically: yes, it was true, he had made an idiotic choice.

"It will pass muster," Zeller reassured him. "Nobody you need to worry about round here does any reading at all."

Not long after his arrival in Gergovie, Max acquired a second false identity. Hungry for revenge, he joined the Action Section of Combat Étudiant under the work-name "Niccolò" and learned about blowing things up. The first and only bomb he threw was built by an assistant named Guibert in the Institute of Chemistry, and its target was the home of Jacques Doriot, a Vichy stooge who ran the pro-Nazi Doriot Association. The explosion—the gigantic excitement of the moment of power, followed almost immediately by a violent involuntary physical reaction, a parallel explosion of vomit—taught him two lessons he never forgot: that terrorism was thrilling, and that, no matter how profoundly justified its cause, he personally could not get over the moral hurdles required to perform such acts on a regular basis. He was moved to the Propaganda Section and in the two years that followed went back to what he knew: the creation of false identities. "The reinvention of the self, that classic American theme," he would write in his memoir, "began for me in the nightmare of old Europe's conquest by evil. That the self can so readily be remade is a dangerous, narcotic discovery. Once you've started using that drug, it isn't easy to stop."

Forgery had become the section's most important task. As the Resistance became more unified and organized, and the numbers of men and women involved increased, false papers were the essentials without which nothing serious was possible. Combat Étudiant gradually built closer alliances with the intelligence networks of the Auvergne, George Charaudeau's Alibi network, Colonel Rivet's Kléber organization, and Christian Pineau's Phalanx; also with other action commandos, the Ardents whose symbol was the flame of Joan of Arc, the Mithridate and the ORA. This work took Cauchi away from Clermont-Ferrand for long periods and a surly, haughty fellow named George Mathieu deputized for him, actually becoming the acting head of Mithridate. Mathieu was a large man, all bones and teeth. His blue eyes were somewhat bulging and his blond hair was slicked down with macassar oil. He insisted on wearing a beret as a gesture of defiance, and was respected on account of his icy, military manner. His girlfriend Christiane worked in the Vichy offices, as the secretary of a certain Captain Burcez. This seemed like a valuable "inside" connection. At any rate, for a plurality of reasons, nobody questioned Mathieu's right to lead.

At that time many packages needed to be carried back and forth as the commando attacks grew in frequency and force, and as the German hunt for the Resistance intensified. Max Ophuls decided to stop asking himself what those packages might contain. The couriers needed documents to ensure their safe passage and it was his business to provide them. Then, after the Jews of Paris were rounded up, perhaps one thousand Jewish children escaped the death-trains to Auschwitz; false papers had urgently to be supplied if they were to be brought south to safety. Max Ophuls, whose work was praised by his immediate superior Feuerstein as well as the more exalted, though increasingly remote figures of Cauchi and Ingrand as the best they had seen, created many of these new identities, which he dispatched to their new owners via secret drop points from which they were collected by anonymous go-betweens. But perhaps the greatest contribution Max Ophuls made to the Resistance was sexual; although in order to pull off the feat he had to create yet another phoney self and inhabit it fully and, alas, somewhat painfully. He was the man who seduced the Panther, Ursula Brandt.

In November 1942 the Germans invaded the Zone Sud and at once the stakes rose. Until then students at the Strasbourg university-in-exile could play at resistance, but with the Germans established in Clermont-Ferrand it became a far more dangerous game. In all, one hundred and thirty-nine students and faculty members would die as a result of their involvement in Resistance activities. That November, SS captain Hugo Geissler set up a Gestapo "antenna" in Clermont-Ferrand. Its director was Paul Blumenkampf, who pretended to be a hearty, good-natured fellow. His immensely influential assistant made no such pretence. She was known as the Panther because she wore a coat of panther fur which she never removed, even on the hottest days of the year. Her particular expertise was infiltration, demolition from within; and her prize witness, her quisling, her inside man was none other than George Mathieu. Many Resistance groups—the Mithridate, the ORA—were smashed and their leaders seized thanks to Mathieu's treason. In a series of raids on these organizations, several university students were arrested, and Reichsführer-SS Himmler was finally able to authorize the attack on the university, against which Danjon's influence with Vichy, and Foreign Minister Ribbentrop's reluctance to overrule the puppets he had installed, had protected it for so long.

The assault on the university, which became known as the Great Raid, took place on November 25, 1943. The literature professor Paul Collomp, a good friend of Max Ophuls's, was shot dead trying to bar the attackers from the secretariat where the teachers' addresses were kept. A theology professor, Robert Eppel, whom Max had also befriended, was shot in the stomach in his own home. The traitor George Mathieu identified many students holding false identity papers. There were over 1,200 arrests. Max Ophuls escaped because of an instinct for self-preservation that had led him to deal with Mathieu on a strict need-to-know basis. Consequently the names Sebastian Brant and Max Ophuls could not be connected by the traitor to the Resistance operative and master forger Niccolò, and Max was safe for the moment. As a precaution, however, he moved out of Zeller's cottage, moved in with a pretty young law student named Angélique Strauss, one of the lovestruck young women of whom there would never be a shortage in his life, forged himself yet another new identity ("Jacques Wimpfeling," after yet another medieval humanist) and took a leave of absence from university duties.

The day after the attack André Danjon wrote a powerful letter of protest to the French prime minister Laval, a tirade in which more or less every sentence was a lie. He lied about the number of Jews at the university, and about the students' and faculty's involvement with the Resistance. In those years of eclipse his determination was like earthshine; it provided the only available light. As a result of his well-feigned outrage the university was allowed to remain open. Danjon then telephoned Max personally at Strauss's apartment. "It's the last act," he said. "The curtain has already begun to fall. You need to think about leaving France." During his sojourn in the cottage at Gergovie, Max Ophuls had passed his time discussing military history with Gaston Zeller and writing papers on international relations, which he himself feared were excessively utopian, and in which he speculated about the construction of a more stable world order in the aftermath of the defeat of Nazism, improbable as that sounded at the time. These papers, in which he foresaw the need for entities similar to those that would afterwards come into being as the Council of Europe, the International Monetary Fund and the World Bank, had been greatly admired by Danjon, who revealed that he had managed to have them smuggled to the Free French headquarters in London, where they had impressed de Gaulle. "You can do more for your country at the Général's side than you are doing here," Danjon said. "Get ready and we will prepare the run. I'm afraid you can't fly this time. Twice would be pushing your luck."

"Before I go," Max replied, "there's something I have to do."

The second legendary exploit of Max Ophuls during his Resistance years became known as "Biting the Panther". When people spoke of it their voices fell into the hushed tones reserved for the achievement of the ridiculously, beautifully impossible. Agent Niccolò, by now a senior figure in the unified resistance known as MUR—which had been created by the merging of Combat with the two other large armies of the Resistance, Franc-Tireur and Libération—simply disappeared from view. It was as if he, and Sebastian Brant, and Jacques Wimpfeling, and Maximilian Ophuls had all ceased to exist. In their place arrived a German officer, Sturmbahnführer Pabst, transferred from Strasbourg to assist Ursula Brandt's team in its investigations, with papers of authorization personally signed by Heinrich Himmler, whose antipathy to the university-in-exile was of long standing. It was a testament to the impostor's skill that the phoney Pabst aroused no suspicion: a tribute to the implacable force of his will, which simply did not permit anyone to entertain the thought that he might not be what he said. He spoke immaculate German, was notable for his utter devotion to the Reich, his papers were perfectly in order, and there could be no questioning the authenticity and force of the Reichsführer-SS's autograph. He was also, as the Panther noticed when he complimented her on the powerful, feline quality that made her nickname so appropriate, a man of immense personal charm and physical appeal. Ursula Brandt was a short, stocky woman to whom the term *pantherlike* could not truthfully be said to apply, but she received the compliment without demur. Within the week she and the Sturmbahnführer were lovers.

Brandt in bed revealed that she was pantherlike in one respect at least: she was fond of using her teeth and claws. Her lover stoically professed to enjoy this, and encouraged her not to restrain herself, but rather to give free rein to all her sexual proclivities, no matter how extreme. After their lovemaking the bedsheets would often be bloodstained, and Brandt would be afflicted by a strangled, stiff-backed contrition that made her unusually malleable. Thus in return for the shared secret of his nocturnal scars the nonexistent Sturmbahnführer gained almost unlimited access to the secrets of her office by day. During the month of their liaison the false Pabst was able to transmit a torrent of priceless intelligence information to the MUR. Then, when the agreed warning sign from the *maquis*—a small chalk circle with a dot in the centre, meaning "they're beginning to suspect you—get lost"—appeared one morning on the door of his lodgings, he quietly disappeared again.

This was the only known instance in the whole of World War II of a successful "reverse sting" on a Gestapo infiltration operation, and once the deception became known Ursula Brandt's position became untenable, and she, like her imaginary lover, disappeared from view. Reichsführer-SS Himmler was an unforgiving man.

In his memoir, Maximilian Ophuls reflected on the events of the Great Raid and his own revenge on one of its architects in a sombre passage. "Every moment of joy in the Resistance, every triumph, was marred by our knowledge of other tragedies. We were fortunate to be successful in the Panther operation, but as I look back on those days I think not of victory but of fallen comrades. I think, for example, of Jean-Paul Cauchi, our founder, our leader, who was arrested in Paris just two months before the D-Day landings and sent to Buchenwald. On April 18, 1945, at the very moment at which American troops were closing in on Buchenwald, he was vindictively killed by the camp's soulless German personnel. And I think with a little more satisfaction of the trial of George Mathieu, who was arrested in September 1944, claimed that he had turned traitor because Ursula Brandt had threatened to kill his pregnant girlfriend if he didn't, was found guilty, and was executed by firing squad on December 12. I have been an opponent of the death penalty all my life, but in the case of Mathieu I must confess that my heart rules my head."

And he also wrote, "Entering the Resistance was, for me, a kind of flying. . . . One took leave of one's name, one's past, one's future, one lifted oneself away from one's life and existed only in the continuum of the work, borne aloft by necessity and fatalism. Yes, a sort of soaring feeling possessed me at times, tempered by the perpetual knowledge that one could crash or be shot down at any moment, without warning, and die in the dirt like a dog."

It was only after his safe arrival in London that Max Ophuls understood how privileged he had been to be given access to the so-called Pat Line, the escape system based in Marseille, created by Captain Ian Garrow and controlled, after Garrow's betrayal and capture, by the pseudonymous "Commander Pat O'Leary", a Belgian doctor whose real name was Albert-Marie Guérisse. This line, operated by the DF Section of the British Special Operations Executive, was primarily set up and maintained for the rescue of British airmen and intelligence personnel marooned behind enemy lines, and in spite of the constant dangers of treachery and capture it had a spectacular record, smuggling over six hundred fighters back to safety. However, in the light of the growing tensions between Général de Gaulle and both Churchill and Roosevelt, it was most unusual for the services of the Line to be made available to a nonmilitary individual just because de Gaulle wanted him to join the Forces Françaises Libres at their Carlton Gardens headquarters. The reason for so exceptional an arrangement was the recent arrival at the FFL HQ of the wife of the général's new aide-de-camp, Mme François Charles-Roux, née Fanny Zarifi, whose namesake and aunt Fanny Vlasto Rodocanachi and her husband Dr George Rodocanachi had allowed their Marseille apartment to be used as the Pat Line's headquarters and local safe house. Max Ophuls, travelling down bumpy minor roads in the back of a produce truck under a mountain of beets, knew nothing of such arcana. He was wondering whether the rat-run would fail because the bumping and banging and the weight of the beet sacks broke his goddamn back. The one thing that never crossed his mind was that he was about to meet the extraordinary woman who would become his only wife.

Her name was the Grey Rat. Her real name was Margaret "Peggy" Rhodes but when she was introduced to Max in George and Fanny Rodocanachi's sitting room by her fellow Englishwoman Elisabeth Haden-Guest, it was her celebrated nickname that was used—a name the

Germans had given her on account of her elusiveness. "Niccolò the master forger," Haden-Guest said playfully, "meet the rat the ratcatchers can't catch." Max Ophuls was astonished by the air of relaxation and enjoyment, even of hilarity, that prevailed in the Rodocanachis' embattled apartment, and quickly saw that the orchestrator of the evening's good time was the Grey Rat herself. That the Rat was beautiful was obvious enough, even though she did her best to hide it. Her shock of fair hair looked like it hadn't been washed for a month and stuck out behind her head like a bottle brush. She wore a loose-fitting man's checked shirt which hadn't seen an iron in days and which she buttoned all the way up to the neck. The cuffs, too, were buttoned. Below the shirt were baggy corduroy pants and canvas shoes. She looked like a vagrant, Max thought, a buttoned-up hobo who had somehow strayed into the secret passages of the war. And yet her eyes were immense dark lakes and her body, furtively perceptible under all that camouflage, was long and lean. Above all she possessed so much exuberant energy that the room seemed too small to hold her.

"You are lucky you are going with her," Fanny Rodocanachi told Max. "When the fighting starts she's like five men." The Grey Rat roared with laughter. "God, Fanny darling, you really know how to recommend a girl to a fellow," she guffawed. "What do you say, Niccolò? Are you ready to crawl through the Spanish border thornbushes all alone with a girl who has killed a man with her bare hands?"

She was twenty-four years old, almost ten years younger than Max, and had already been married once, to a Marseillais businessman named Maurice Liota, who was tortured and killed by the Gestapo a year after their wedding for refusing to reveal her whereabouts, and whom she described to Max Ophuls before, during and after their own marriage as "the love of my life". She had escaped capture on skis, and by driving a car so fast and skilfully that the airplane chasing her couldn't stop her. Once she jumped from a moving train. Once in Toulouse she was detained in prison but she impersonated an innocent Provençal housewife so convincingly that after four days the Germans set her free and never knew that they had actually had the Grey Rat in their hands. "I hate war," she said to Max at that first meeting in the Marseille safe apartment, "but here it is, eh? So I'm not bally well planning to wave my hanky at the departing men and then stay home and knit them balaclavas."

The run was successful: terrifying, with close shaves so bizarre as to feel almost fictional, but they made it. Barcelona, Madrid, London. In the eyes of the *passeurs* on both sides of the border, beneath their studied neutrality of expression, Max sometimes thought he detected a strange combination of resentment and contempt. *You're going and we can't* alternated with *You're running and we're not.* He was too distracted to mind; because by the time they arrived at RAF Northolt in a British military aircraft, Maximilian Ophuls had fallen in love. Northolt was wrapped as always in the icy wind of the London winter; nor did it avoid the cliché of sleety rain. François Charles-Roux had been sent to meet hobbling Max, and a nameless intelligence officer was waiting for the Grey Rat. The two refugees stood bundled up on the tarmac in the frozen drizzle and the Grey Rat tried to say goodbye, but before they went their separate ways Max asked if he could see her again. This reduced her to confusion, and unleashed an astonishing routine of foot shuffling and deep blushing and hand-wringing and small sharp manic laughs punctuating bursts of staccato speech. "Ha! Ha! Well, I've absolutely no idea! Why you'd ever want to! But, ahem! Aha! If that is you're really, I mean! Serious, you know? One doesn't wish to! Hahaha! Impose! Not that it would be a bally imposition I suppose? Eh, eh, haha? Since you're doing the asking in the first place! Since you're, ah, kindly enough, oh *blow* I'm so pathetic at this! Oh, help, mother, all right." Then, moving towards him to peck him awkwardly on the cheek, she stepped hard on his foot.

Their first date, at the Lyons Corner House in Piccadilly, was a catastrophe. Margaret was a mess, red-eyed, runny-nosed and unable to restrain her tears. The Pat Line had been betrayed. A man they had trusted, Paul Cole, whose real name was Sergeant Harold Cole, and who used the alias of Delobel, turned out to be a fraudster and double agent and pointed the finger at everyone in the Marseille group. Fanny Vlasto and Elisabeth Haden-Guest escaped, but "Pat O'Leary"—Guérisse—was seized by the Gestapo and sent to Dachau. Astonishingly, he would survive torture and live to see a better day and to grow old in the new Europe which he had done so much to free. Dr George Rodocanachi was not so fortunate. He died in Buchenwald a few months after his capture.

"I'm going back in, you know," the Grey Rat said, blowing her nose fiercely. "I'm going back in just as soon as I can force them to let me." Max wanted to beg her to stay, but remained silent, and held her hands instead. Three months later she was allowed to return. The tide of the war had turned, and Maximilian Ophuls's life had changed direction, too, flowing powerfully towards this beautiful, gawky, fearless, sexually unawakened woman—and, in addition, away from France and towards America, because of the unexpected but powerful dislike, bordering on hostility, shown towards him by Général Charles de Gaulle.

London that winter was a cratered heart. The gashes of the Blitz were everywhere, the severed streets, the halved houses, the gaps, the lack, the lack. There weren't many cars on the road. Yet people went about their business matter-of-factly, as if nothing had happened, as if they weren't going to be spending the night on a tube station platform without so much as a change of clothes, as if their evacuated children's welfare wasn't preying on their minds. Carlton Gardens was relatively unscathed. Charles-Roux brought Max to meet the général. De Gaulle stood at a window in a wood-panelled office, in profile, like a cartoon of himself, and greeted Max without turning. "So: Danjon's young genius," he said. "Let me tell you this, monsieur. I do not question the judgement of my friend the vice-chancellor. Your accomplishments and talents are no doubt remarkable. However the propositions in your theses are for the most part untenable. Some sort of European association, very well. It will be necessary to forget what has happened and make friends with Germany. That, yes. Everything else you propose is barbaric rubbish which will deliver us, bound and gagged, into the power of the Americans, which is to say a new captivity following immediately upon an old one. This I shall never permit." Max remained silent. De Gaulle also ceased to speak. After a moment Charles-Roux touched Max's elbow and steered him from the room. As they left, de Gaulle, still positioned at the window with his hands clasped behind his back, was heard to remark, "Ah, when they know what broken bits of matchsticks I had to use to make France free!"

"You must understand that Roosevelt has been treating him like dirt," Charles-Roux said outside the général's door. "And Churchill also, he shows insufficient respect. There are many, even in the French diplomatic corps, who have advised against becoming too close to the FFL. Roosevelt would get rid of the général if he could. He favours, for example, Giraud." Max had few dealings with de Gaulle after that day. He was put to work in the propaganda section, writing messages to be dropped into France, translating German texts, marking time, waiting for the evenings, and the Rat.

Porchester Terrace, Bayswater, stripped by the requirements of the weapons industry of its traditional gates and railings, like all the denuded streets of London, hid its nakedness in the winter fog. Max was living in the basement of a house owned by Fanny Rodocanachi's brother Michel Vlasto. A large segment of the staircase had been destroyed by a phosphorus bomb and the house smelled strongly of burning. To go up and down it was necessary to hug the wall. Life everywhere had holes in it, was a book with pages ripped out, crumpled up, tossed away. "Newer min', eh," said Vlasto's Indian housekeeper, Mrs Shanti Dickens, an ample woman who affected a huge beret, baggy green overcoat and lacy boots. Mrs Dickens was a person of such great appetite that she chewed up the language itself. "Nobody being 'urt, 'at is the mai' thing, hisn't it." She pointed at a bucket of sand. "One isstanding on ewery flower. Baycement, ground flower, first flower, all. Case ow need." Mrs Dickens was able to recite from memory the crime reports in the Sunday rags. "'E chopp' 'er up, sir, just to 'magine," she'd say with relish. "Wery wery hawful, sir, hisn't it. Maybe 'e is heatin' 'er for 'is tea."

The Rat came to visit him whenever she could, struggling through the blackout and green fog, being careful to keep her torch pointed downwards. On the evenings when she didn't show up Max sat alone in his greatcoat by a single-bar electric heater, cursing fate. The depression that was always waiting in the corners of his brain surged into the centre of the room, using cold weather and loneliness as its fuel. Treason was the currency of the times. The Americans despised the Free French because they believed the organization to be penetrated by Vichy traitors, and the British responded by infiltrating Carlton Gardens with British informers as well. George Mathieu, Paul Cole. Your friends became your assassins. If you trusted too much, too easily, you died. Yet what kind of life was possible without trust, how could there be any depth or joy in human relations without it? "This is the damage we will all carry over into the future," Max thought. Distrust, the expectation of deceit: these were the craters in every heart.

"If we live through this, Ratty, I'll never betray you," he swore aloud in his lonely room. But he did, of course. He didn't kill her but he spent his life sticking the knives of his infidelities in her heart. And then came Boonyi Kaul.

The difficult truth was that Margaret "Peggy" Rhodes was a lousy lover. Her heart wasn't in it. She had been shaped by resistance and had no concept of the joys of yielding. Maximilian Ophuls tried carefully, and without appearing didactic, to school her, and for short periods she seemed willing to learn, but she didn't have the patience for it, she just wanted it over with so they could talk, and snuggle, and behave in the nude exactly like fully dressed people: not as lovers, but as friends. She had always had a "low libido", she confessed. She insisted, however, that she loved him. Holding him tightly under the tartan blankets of that basement winter, she swore that she had never been so happy, and that as a result she was newly afraid to die. She also told him she was barren. "I mean, does that make a difference? Is it all off? Because with a lot of chaps that would be it, you know? No possibility of sprogs, whole bally thing goes to the bally dogs. Ha! Aha! Hahaha!" He answered, surprising himself, that it did not matter. "Okay, jolly D," she said. "Change the subject? You don't mind? Fellow who met me at Northolt, remember him? MI9 johnny? Wants a word with you. I mean I'm just the messenger. No problem either way. But I could set it up."

The meeting with the intelligence officer, whose name was Neave, took place a week later in the Metropole Hotel on Northumberland Avenue. "I was rescued by the Pat Line myself, you know," the Englishman said by way of introduction. "So we're graduates of the same school, so to speak." Max Ophuls was thinking how warm it was in the Metropole, and that one might be prepared to do almost anything to be as warm as this. Would he have turned down the proposal Neave delivered that day if the deed had been done in a cold, draughty room? Was he as shallow as that? ". . . In short, we want you on board," Neave was finishing. "But that does mean you have to jump ship. Big decision, I know. You probably need to think about it. Go ahead. Take five minutes. Take ten." The moment he heard the proposition Max Ophuls knew he would not turn it down. The British, speaking with American knowledge and backing, *wanted him on board.* His way of thinking was *just the ticket,* and the world community was falling into line, even if the crusty big-nosed général wasn't. The Germans were going to lose the war. The future was going to be built in New Hampshire over three weeks in July at a place called Bretton Woods. Delegates from, probably, forty-odd nations would assemble with their "boffins", their "eggheads", their "dreamers", to shape the postwar recovery of Europe and to address the problems of unstable exchange rates and protectionist trade policies. Maximilian Ophuls was a *key piece of the puzzle.* There was a university chair in it for him, Columbia, most probably, and an Oxbridge fellowship. "Hands across the sea," Neave said. "We see you as one of the main chaps. You don't have to be affiliated to a national delegation. We need you to chair working parties, do the deep work, give us structures that will stand."

The future was being born and he was being asked to be its midwife. Instead of the weakness of Paris, the effete house of cards of old Europe, he would build the iron-and-steel skyscraper of the next big thing. "I don't need time," he said. "Count me in." He felt as if he had received, and accepted, a proposal of marriage from an unexpected but infinitely desirable suitor, and knew that France, the bride chosen for him by parentage and blood, France with whom a marriage had been arranged on the day of his birth, might never forgive him for leaving her at the altar. Certainly Charles de Gaulle would not. That night, huddled with Peggy Rhodes beneath the covers of his bed on the slightly sloping floor of the Porchester Terrace basement flat, he made a marriage proposal of his own. "Will you marry me, Ratty?" To which she replied, "Ooh. Ooh. Ooh. Ooh, yes, Moley, I will."

He met Neave once again, in the early 1980s, by which time Max Ophuls had rejoined the secret world while the former intelligence officer had become a member of Parliament and a close confidant of Prime Minister Thatcher. They had a drink on the terrace of the Palace of Westminster and talked about old times. Soon after their talk Airey Neave was blown to pieces by an IRA "tilt-bomb" while driving out of the House of Commons car park. There was no end to treachery. Survive one plot and the next one would get you. The cycle of violence had not been broken. Perhaps it was endemic to the human race, a manifestation of the life cycle. Perhaps violence showed us what we meant, or, at least, perhaps it was simply what we did.

In April 1944, Max Ophuls's newly-wed wife the Grey Rat was parachuted into the Auvergne. Her mission was to locate bands of maquis and lead them to the ammunition and arms that were being dropped by the RAF every other day. Then she was to help organize them for the armed uprising that was to coincide with the Normandy landings. As part of this process of preparation she led a Resistance raid against the Gestapo headquarters in Montluçon and also attacked a German gun factory. Then it was the sixth of June, it was D-Day, H-Hour, M-Minute, and she stayed on the ground to fight alongside the MUR, whose longed-for time had finally come. When Maximilian Ophuls left for the Bretton Woods conference at the end of June, he had no way of knowing if the Rat was alive or dead. As he had feared, the FFL had been instructed by its leader to treat him as a pariah, an almost-traitor. His disloyalty would never be forgiven. No information would reach him from that quarter. In the end it was Mrs Shanti Dickens who came through, by telephone. "Sir! Sir! Mr Max, hisn'it? Yes, sir! Wery good! Letter, Mr Max, from Mrs Max! I hopen it, sir? Yes, sir! Hokay! Mrs Max is bein' fine, sir! She is lovin' you, sir! Hurray! She is askin' sir, where the fuck you gone? Hokay? Wery good, sir! Hurray!"

On August 26, the day after the liberation of Paris, de Gaulle marched down the Champs-Élysées with representatives of the Free French movement as well as members of the Resistance. One Englishwoman marched with the French that day. And on August 27, Mrs Max, Margaret Rhodes, the Grey Rat, flew to New York and the Ophulses began their American married life.

Nearly twenty-one years later, on the night before she left with her husband for New Delhi, Mrs Margaret Rhodes Ophuls dreamed that after the long barren decades she would finally become pregnant and have a child in India. The baby was beautiful and furry with a long, curling tail but she was unable to love it and when she put it to her breast it bit her nipple painfully. It was a girl baby and even though her friends were horrified to see her cradling a black rattess she didn't care. She had once been a rat herself but she had turned into a human being eventually, hadn't she, these days she washed her hair and wore smart clothes and hardly ever twitched her nose or crawled through garbage or did anything rodentlike at all, and no doubt it would be the same with her baby girl, her Ratetta. And she was a mother now and so if she simply behaved as if she did love Ratetta then the love would probably begin to flow, there was just some sort of temporary blockage. Some mothers had trouble lactating, didn't they, the milk didn't want to come down, and she was having the same kind of trouble with love. After all she was in her middle forties and the baby had come to her late in life so a few unusual problems were to be expected. It was nothing serious. *Ratetta, sweet Ratetta,* she sang in her dream, *who could be better than you?*

She didn't tell her husband about the vision. By this time she and Ambassador Maximilian Ophuls pretty much led separate lives. However, a public façade was maintained. Max's memoir had made their wartime love story public property, had it not, and the book had remained on the bestseller lists for two and a half years, so how could they not continue to be the thing that had given them their shot at immortality? For they were, and had been for two decades, "Ratty and Moley", the golden couple whose New York kiss at the mighty battle's end had become for a generation an image, *the* iconic image of love conquering all, of the slaying of monsters and the blessings of fate, of the triumph of virtue over evil and the victory of the best in human nature over the worst. "If we tried to break up—ha! Hoho!—we'd probably—wouldn't we?—be lynched," she once said to him, concealing heartbreak beneath staccato stoicism. "Lucky, really, that I don't—heh-heh-heh!—actually *believe* in *bally divorce.*"

So the fiction of undying romance was kept up, impeccably by her, extremely peccably by him. She kept tabs, however. She was a wealthy woman nowadays. Since the deaths of her parents she had come into possession of impressive tranches of prime Hampshire farmland as well as substantial port wineries on the Douro. This gave her the wherewithal to finance her investigations, on the rare occasions that her old contacts in the shadow world came up empty-handed. Consequently she knew the name of every woman her husband had seduced, every adoring college postgrad, every assistant willing to be researched, every wanton uptown society beauty and downtown party slut, all the personal two-way simultaneous translators at his international conferences, every East End summer whore he'd fucked in their South Fork home perched on the forested heights left behind by retreating glaciers, the uplands of the terminal moraine. In most cases she had also acquired their home addresses and unlisted telephone numbers. She had never contacted any of these women but she told herself she liked to have the information, that she preferred to know. This was a self-deceiving lie. The women's names twisted in her like knives, their street addresses, apartment numbers, zip codes and phone numbers burned holes in her memory like little phosphorus bombs.

Yet she found it difficult to blame only Max. As the war retreated into the past so had her erotic urges. Her interest in such matters, always perfunctory and intermittent, seemed to wither on the vine. "Let the poor man get it elsewhere if he has to," she told herself grimly, "as long as he doesn't rub my bally nose in it. Then I can get on with my reading and gardening and not be bothered with all that sticky palaver." In this way she blinded herself to her real feelings so effectively that when misery assailed her, as it periodically did, causing her to burst into hot tears without warning and to suffer from inexplicable attacks of the shakes, she couldn't work out what she was so damned unhappy about. On the plane to India with the great man by her side she allowed herself to think, "Dash it, it is a pretty terrific love story, ours. Not conventional, I grant you; but then, what is conventional when you really look at it? Lift the lid of any life and there's strangeness, bubbling away; behind every quiet domestic front door lurk the idiosyncratic and the weird. Normality, that's the myth. Human beings aren't normal. We're an odd lot, that's the honest truth: off-kilter, rum. But we get by. Look, here we are, Max and I, flying high, and still holding hands after twenty years. Not so shabby, really. Not too bad at all." Then she closed her eyes and there was the vision again, the midnight rat standing up on its hind legs, begging for love, calling her *mother* in its high Ratetta voice. In India, she decided, she was going to have a great deal to do with orphans. Yes: the motherless children of India would discover that they had a good friend in her. Maybe that was the meaning of the dream.

"They liked Galbraith," Lyndon Johnson was rumoured to have told Dean Rusk, "so go ahead and send them another liberal professor, but don't let this one go native on us." When Secretary Rusk called Maximilian Ophuls in the immediate aftermath of the 1965 Indo-Pakistani war and offered him the Indian embassy, Max realized that he had been waiting for the call, waiting without knowing he was waiting, and that India, which he had never visited, might prove to be, if not his destiny, then at least the destination to which the mazy journey of his life had been leading all along. "We need you to go right away," Rusk said. "Those Indian gentlemen need a good old American spanking and it's our belief you're just the man to hand it to 'em." In his classic enquiry *Why the Poor Are Poor* Max Ophuls had used India, China and Brazil as economic case studies, and in the book's much-discussed last chapter had proposed a means by which these "sleeping giants" might awake. This was perhaps the first time a major Western economist had seriously analysed what came to be known as "South-South collaboration", and Max, putting down the telephone that humid Manhattan evening—it was late September but the summer wouldn't end—wondered aloud why an academic who had published a theoretical model of how Third World economies might flourish by learning to bypass the U.S. dollar should be chosen to represent the United States in one such southern land. His wife the Rat knew the answer to that. "Glamour, dear, glamour. Ha! Don't you get it, you dope? Everyone loves a star."

America didn't know what to do about India. Johnson liked the dictator of Pakistan, Field Marshal Mohammed Ayub Khan, so much that he was even willing to turn a blind eye to Pakistan's growing intimacy with China. "A wife can understand a Saturday night fling by her husband, so long as she's the wife," he told Ayub in Washington. Ayub laughed. Of course America was the wife, how could the president doubt it? Then he went home and forged even closer ties with China. Rusk, meanwhile, was openly hostile to Indian interests. This was the period in which the devaluation of the Indian rupee and the national food crisis had put India into the humiliating position of being dependent on American supplies. Yet these supplies were slow in coming, and B. K. Nehru, India's ambassador to the United States, had to confront Rusk about it: "Why are you trying to starve us out?" The answer was equally blunt: because India was receiving arms from the Soviet Union. Before Max left for New Delhi, he visited Rusk at Foggy Bottom and found himself on the receiving end of an extended anti-Indian tirade, in which Rusk not only opposed the Indian line on Kashmir but also criticized the annexations of Hyderabad and Goa, and the vocal support of several Indian leaders for the government of North Vietnam. "Professor Ophuls, we are at war with that gentleman, Ho Chi Minh, and you will be so good as to make plain to the Indian authorities that our enemy's friend can only be our foe." This was why Max Ophuls told Margaret, after the Radhakrishnan hand-holding incident, that his sudden popularity would probably prove short-lived. "If I dance to Rusk's tune," he said, "they'll start throwing things at us soon enough."

When he expressed a desire to go immediately to Kashmir, the Indian home minister Gulzarilal Nanda objected strongly: the security concerns were too great, his safety could not be guaranteed. Then for the first time in his life Max Ophuls exercised the power of the United States of America. "The nature of overwhelming might," he would later write in *The Man of Power,* "is such that the powerful man does not need to allude to his power. The fact of it is present in everyone's consciousness. Thus power does its work by stealth, and the powerful can subsequently deny that their strength was ever used at all." Within hours, Nanda was overruled by Prime Minister Shastri's office, and the visit to Kashmir was green-lit.

Five days later Ambassador Maximilian Ophuls, in fur earmuffs, greatcoat, bulletproof vest and hard hat, was standing on what was then called the ceasefire line, and would later come to be known as the Line of Control. His whole life suddenly seemed absurd. The Belle Époque Strasbourg mansion, the cottage in Gergovie, the Porchester Terrace basement, the economic summit in New Hampshire, the eleventh-floor apartment on Riverside Drive, and even Roosevelt House, the sprawling, recently completed ambassador's residence built by the half-praised, half-derided Edward Durrell Stone in the Chanakyapuri diplomatic enclave of the Indian capital . . . all these faded away. For a long moment Max slipped loose of all his different selves, the brilliant young economist, lawyer and student of international relations, the master forger of the Resistance, the ace pilot, the Jewish survivor, the genius of Bretton Woods, the bestselling author, and the American ambassador cocooned in the house of power. He stood alone and as if unclothed, dwarfed by the high Himalayas and stripped bare of comprehension by the scale of the crisis made flesh, the two frozen armies facing each other across the explosive borderline. Then his history reasserted itself and he climbed back into its familiar garments—in particular the history of his hometown, and the whiplash movements of the Franco-German frontier across its people's lives. He had come a long way but perhaps not so very far. Could any two places have been more different, he asked himself; could any two places have been more the same? Human nature, the great constant, surely persisted in spite of all surface differences. One snaking frontier had made him what he was, he found himself thinking. Had he come here, to another such unstable twilight zone, in order to be unmade?

The Indian foreign minister Swaran Singh touched his arm. "It's long enough," he said. "It really is not safe to stand still here for very long."

For the rest of his life Max Ophuls would remember that instant during which the shape of the conflict in Kashmir had seemed too great and alien for his Western mind to understand, and the sense of urgent need with which he had drawn his own experience around him, like a shawl. Had he been trying to understand, or to blind himself to his failure to do so? Did the mind discover likeness in the unlike in order to clarify the world, or to obscure the impossibility of such clarification? He didn't know the answer. But it was one hell of a question.

He had begun to look for allies in Washington and had found a few: the national security adviser, McGeorge Bundy, his eventual successor, Walt Whitman Rostow, and the man who would follow Max to New Delhi after the scandal, Chester Bowles. Bundy learned that the Ayub-China relationship was "significantly closer" than either would admit, and advised Johnson that India, the "largest and potentially most powerful non-Communist Asian nation", was "the biggest prize in Asia", and that on account of the United States' handing seven hundred million dollars in military aid to Pakistan, that prize was in danger of being lost. The tail was wagging the dog. Rostow agreed. "India is more important than Pakistan." And Bowles argued that America's unwillingness to arm India had pushed the late Jawaharlal Nehru, and now Lal Bahadur Shastri, into the Russians' arms. "Only when it became clear that we were not prepared to give India this assistance, did India turn to the Soviet Union as its major source of military equipment." Johnson remained reluctant to favour India. "We ought to get out of military aid to both India and Pakistan," he replied. However, Max Ophuls's Washington contacts charged him to discuss urgently, "on the front burner", what India wanted most: to purchase American supersonic fighter jets in significant numbers and on advantageous terms. Sitting on carpets and cushions in the Dachigam hunting lodge, laughing and drinking in the intermissions between the acts of the play being performed by the bhands of Pachigam, Ambassador Maximilian Ophuls, "the Flying Jew", the man who had flown the Bugatti Racer to safety, murmured to the Indian Foreign Ministry delegation about the various ways in which it might be possible to structure a deal for the high-speed jets. Then Boonyi Kaul Noman came out to dance and Max realized that his Indian destiny would have little to do with politics, diplomacy or arms sales, and everything to do with the far more ancient imperatives of desire.

Just as Anarkali dancing her sorceress's dance in the Sheesh Mahal, the hall of mirrors at the Mughal court, had captured Prince Salim's heart, just as Madhubala dancing in the hit movie had bewitched millions of gaping men, so Boonyi in the hunting lodge at Dachigam understood that her dance was changing her life, that what was being born in the eyes of the moonstruck American ambassador was nothing less than her own future. By the time he got to his feet and applauded loudly and long, she knew that he would find a way to bring her to him, and all that was left for her to do was to make a single choice, a single act of will, yes or no. Then her eyes met his and blazed their answer and the point of no return was passed. Yes, the future would come for her, a messenger descending from the heavens to inform a mere mortal of the decision of the gods. She needed only to wait and see what form the messenger would take. She put the palms of her hands together, touched her fingertips to her chin, gazed at and then bowed her head before the man of power, and had the feeling as she left his presence that she wasn't leaving the stage but making an entrance on the greatest stage she had ever been allowed to walk upon, that her performance was not ending but beginning, and that it would not end until her life ran out of days. It would be up to her to ensure that her story had a better ending than the court dancer's. Anarkali's punishment for the temerity of loving a royal personage was to be bricked up in a wall. Boonyi had seen the movie, in which the filmmakers had found a way of allowing the heroine to live: Emperor Akbar, relenting, has a tunnel constructed under her tomb to allow Anarkali to escape into exile with her mother. A lifetime's exile wasn't much better than death, Boonyi thought. It was the same as being bricked up, only in a larger grave. But times had changed. Maybe in the second half of the twentieth century it was permissible for a dancing girl to bag herself a prince.

The embassy aide Edgar Wood, floppy-haired, tall, pale and skinny, with a large, permanent zit on his right cheek to hint at his ridiculous youth, and the feeble shadow of a Zapata moustache to confirm it, was a former graduate student of international relations at Columbia who had followed Max to India at the ambassador's special insistence. The reason for this was not Wood's brilliance or industry (though he was indeed smart and a quick learner, known at Columbia as Eager Wood, a nickname he brought with him into the embassy). No, the reason Wood was indispensable was that he would do anything the ambassador needed done and keep his mouth shut about it. It wasn't easy to find the perfect set-up man, the loyal go-between, the faultless fixer, but without such a person it was impossible for a man in the public eye to lead the kind of life that Max Ophuls's nature compelled him to lead. He had his own nickname for Wood; in his eyes the kid was not so much an "Eager", more of a "Beaver"; but of course he never told him so. The first time he had broached the subject of his assignations with women and his need for a discreet assistant, Beaver Wood volunteered immediately. "Just one question, sir," he asked Max. "Do you have a bad back?" Max was puzzled. No, he answered, his back was fine. Wood bobbed his head in approval and apparent relief. "Excellent," he said. "Because too much sex and a bad back is what got the president assassinated."

This was strange, Max thought, and also evidence that Wood was a more interesting fellow than his raw young looks had yet found a way of revealing. "The truss, sir," Wood explained. "Kennedy's back was bad to begin with, but it got so much worse because of all the screwing around that he had to wear the truss all the time. He was wearing it in Dallas and that's why he didn't fall over after the first shot hit him. He was wounded and lurched over and the truss just sat him up again, boing, and then the second bullet blew off the back of his head. You see what I'm saying, Professor, maybe if he'd had less sex, he maybe wouldn't have been wearing the truss, and then no boing, he'd just have fallen flat after being wounded; the first bullet wasn't fatal, remember, and he wouldn't have been as they say *available* for the second shot, and Johnson wouldn't be president. There's a moral in there somewhere, I guess, but as you don't have a bad back, Professor, it doesn't apply to you."

In the hunting lodge at Dachigam, Max Ophuls reclining on carpets and cushions leaned backward, away from the Indian foreign minister, to whisper to Edgar Wood. "Get her details," he said. Wood replied: "Sir, she's allegedly buried in Lahore, Pakistan, and her real name was either Nadira Begum or Sharf-un-Nissa. Prince Salim gave her the love-name of Anarkali, meaning 'pomegranate bud'. Sir." Max frowned. "Not the damn character, Wood. Not the damn apocryphal historical figure." Wood grinned. "I'm on it, sir. I was just messing with you." Max tolerated such cheekiness. It was a small price to pay for the services Wood so uncomplainingly, even enthusiastically rendered. He turned back to Swaran Singh, a soft-spoken man of simple habits whose charm and erudition were as great as Max's own, and whom Max had begun to like very much. Swaran wanted to offer his own reaction to the dance piece. "You see, Akbar was remarkably tolerant of Hinduism," he said. "Indeed his own wife Jodhabai, Salim's mother, remained a practising Hindu throughout their marriage. Interesting that class difference was where he drew the line. Suggests that as a people social order matters more to us than religious belief. Just like the English, eh? No wonder we hit it off so well." Max laughed obligingly. "By the way," added Swaran Singh, who was known for his strict moral rectitude but was also a shrewd man who knew the effectiveness of a shock tactic, "did you by any chance notice that young woman's breasts?" He let out a loud guffaw, which Max, for the sake of Indo-American relations, felt the need to emulate. "National treasures," he replied seriously, using much self-control to conceal his deeper feelings, but fearing that Swaran had noted the powerful involuntary reaction he had gone fishing for. "Integral parts of India," he added, for good measure. This set Swaran Singh off again. "Ambassador," the foreign minister chuckled, "I can see that with you as our guide, the new India will become more pro-West than ever before."

When Peggy Ophuls, alone in the New York apartment, had answered her telephone and heard from one of her informants that Edgar Wood was slated for transfer to India her heart pounded and she threw the tall glass of Pellegrino she was holding as hard as she could in the general direction of *ZOOMMM!!!!,* the widescreen Lichtenstein portrait of her husband flying the Bugatti Racer which she had commissioned as a gift of love and which hung, when it was not being lent to this or that major gallery, on one long living-room wall in their capacious Riverside Drive home. Such was her agitation that the glass missed the large painting entirely and shattered on the white wall to the right of the unprotected canvas. She left the pieces where they fell, clenched both fists and controlled herself. Better the pimp you know, she told herself angrily. If Wood had been left behind in America her husband would certainly have found another little helper, and for a time Margaret wouldn't have known who was setting up the action without which Max Ophuls apparently couldn't live, and which she herself was, by this time, emphatically unwilling to provide. Neither Max nor Edgar had any idea that she knew all about them—that she knew *everything*—that she knew where all the bodies were—not buried—ha! aha!—what was the right word—yes! *laid,* that she knew *in detail* where all his damned damned damned bodies were well and truly laid, that she had made it her business to, that she was in a position to, that one of these days by God she would, that any woman in her situation—and she had killed a man once!—had a right to, to. To *take her dashed revenge.*

The seduction of Boonyi Kaul Noman—or, more accurately, the seduction of Max Ophuls by Boonyi—took time. Even for a man of Edgar Wood's unusual aptitudes it was not easy to arrange a private meeting between the American ambassador and a married Kashmiri dancing girl. At the end of the Dachigam hunting lodge festivities Wood voiced the ambassador's desire to thank personally all those who had given him such a delightful evening, and out they came in a crowd, the poets and santoor players, the actors and cooks. Max moved among them with an interpreter and the genuineness of his interest and concern touched everyone he spoke to. At one point, casually, as if it were not the point of the entire exercise, he turned to Boonyi and congratulated her on her artistry. "A talent like yours," he said, "must surely seek to advance and develop itself." The interpreter translated, and Boonyi, her eyes modestly downcast, felt a breeze on her cheek, as if a door were opening and the air of the outside world were being allowed to enter. She told herself, Patience is everything now. You must just fold your hands in your lap and wait for what will be.

"Ask her name," Max Ophuls ordered the interpreter. "Boonyi," the fellow answered. "She tells that it is her preferred, how to say it, her optioned name. Actually her given name is Bhoomi, the earth, but her friends are calling her by this Boonyi cognomen which, sir, is the beloved tree of Kashmir." "I see," said Max, "a name for outsiders and a pet name for her friends. Ask her then, Bhoomi the earth or Boonyi the beloved tree—as a dancer, in her career as a dancer, what is it she wants?" There was nothing personal in his voice or manner, no hint of impropriety. Her reply was similarly courteous, freighted with nothing, a neutral politeness. "Boonyi says first that she is Boonyi," the interpreter translated, "and second that to please you is joy enough." Max Ophuls saw Swaran Singh looking across the crowded room with a faint smile on his face, the most innocent of smiles, a gentle smile, quite devoid of guile.

Max moved away from Boonyi and didn't look in her direction again all evening. However, he spoke at length to Abdullah Noman, asking carefully about economic conditions in the valley, learning about the decline of the fortunes of the bhand pather, expressing a fascination with their ancient hand-me-down skills which he did not have to fake. Soon enough, Abdullah took the bait, as Max had known he would. "He, Pachigam headman, sir, is saying it would be lifetime honour for him if one day you will grace his village," the interpreter said. "It will be lifetime privilege for him to afford you full performances of traditional and modern plays and if interest is in you, also you may see how techniques et cetera are refined. Cooking too is there, wazwaan cooks are coming tonight from that place only." Here Edgar Wood intervened, all haste and business. "The ambassador's schedule does not presently permit . . ." Max patted his eager young aide on the arm. "Edgar, Edgar, we're just chatting," he said. "Who knows? Could be that some day even the American ambassador may have a moment to spare."

After so successfully choreographed an encounter, Max Ophuls returned to Delhi, to the cool, sprawling New Formalist palazzo of decorated modernism encased in a mosaic grillwork of white stone where he now lived. He walked by its fountain-lined reflecting pool, and, like Boonyi Noman, waited. Edgar Wood quietly arranged for him to receive daily private lessons in Hindi and Kashmiri. The ambassador's wife, meanwhile, was mostly absent from the ambassadorial residence. Transformed into her new persona of Peggy-Mata, mother of the motherless, she had embarked on a nonstop nationwide tour of Indian orphanages, and would occasionally send Max a note saying things like *These children are so beautiful I just absolutely want to scoop a few of them up and bring them home.* Her success in raising funds in America and Europe to improve conditions at orphanages all over India increased the couple's popularity. "Perhaps we should regard Peggy-Mata as the real U.S. ambassador," one newspaper editorial suggested, "and Mr Ophuls as her charming and personable consort." Next to the editorial was a large photograph of Peggy Ophuls standing beside a handsome young Catholic priest, Father Ambrose, and surrounded by smiling young girls from his orphanage, the Holy Love of India Evangalactic Girls' Orphanage for Disabled & Destitute Street Girls in Mehrauli. "The dying in Calcutta have Mother Teresa," Father Ambrose was reported to have said, "but for the living we have Peggy-Mata right here."

Meanwhile the Ophuls marriage continued to decay. Six months after the ambassador's first visit to Kashmir, the thing that Peggy Rhodes Ophuls had most dreaded had happened. Instead of playing the field and bedding every woman who succumbed to his famous charm, her bastard husband had become fixated on one particular girl, a nobody, a nothing, damn him. When the spring came he had visited the village of the travelling players who had by all accounts put on quite a show, drama, comedy, high-wire stunts and of course the dancing, and soon afterwards Max had decreed that a banquet be given "for Indian friends" at Roosevelt House, which by the by was the residence not only of the lecherous U.S. ambassador but of the ambassador's wretched wife as well, he probably came up with the idea just so that he could bring the hussy down to New Delhi on the pretext of providing after-dinner entertainment—after-dinner entertainment indeed!—the scheme had that young so-and-so Wood's fingerprints all over it, and the worst of it, the worst of the worst, was that he, her husband, the ambassador—the man she still loved, in her way, in the only way she knew, it didn't give him what he needed but that didn't mean it wasn't love—her Max had made her, Peggy, come home from her orphanage inspections to act as hostess, to sit in her own home and watch that girl dance for him, did he think she was blind, she didn't need any spies to see what that girl was doing, the effrontery of her hips, the recklessness of her eyes, it was as if they were naked and making love right there in front of Peggy, in front of everyone, the humiliation of it, she had seen a good deal of human cruelty in her life, they both had, so she wasn't going to lose perspective, this wasn't as bad as that, but still it was pretty goddamned cruel, pretty goddamned impossible to take.

They had come all this way together, the Rat and her Mole, they had survived so much, only to be shipwrecked at last on the rock of a gold-digging Kashmiri beauty. If the liaison lasted, Peggy Ophuls would of course have to leave him, after all this time and the expenditure of so much love and tolerance she would have to turn back into Margaret Rhodes and somehow live without him for the rest of her life. "Pumpkin time, Cinders," she told herself. The magic spell was about to break, her gown would once again be an ashy rag, her footmen would turn back into mice, the beautiful fiction of her marriage would finally have to yield to the unpalatable facts. The glass slipper didn't fit her any more. It was on another woman's foot.

The government of India was GOI. The government of Pakistan was GOP. In the aftermath of the Tashkent Peace Conference (TPC) between the two countries, during the period of partial political vacuum created by the fatal heart attack of the Indian prime minister Lal Bahadur Shastri (LBS) on the day following the signature of the Tashkent Declaration (TD), Max Ophuls launched a major new American initiative. In this interregnum, a bitter stalemate between the potentates of the Congress Party ended when the kingmakers Kumaraswami Kamaraj (KK) and Morarji Desai (MD) elevated Indira Priyadarshini Gandhi (IPG) to the premiership in the mistaken belief that she would be their helpless puppet. During this period of savage intraparty warfare only President Sarvepalli Radhakrishnan rose above the political storm. His national stature and his air of a philosopher-saint gave him unusual influence over all government matters, even though the authors of the Indian constitution had clearly intended the president's role to be largely ceremonial. Max's close friendship with this revered figure (PSK) provided the opening for the so-called Ophuls Plan.

The ambassador's idea was that if he could persuade both governments to work together on multilateral projects (GOI/GOP-MP) they could start getting used to interdependence instead of conflict. Mastering the language of unpronounceable acronyms which was the true lingua franca of the subcontinent's political class, he proposed a fuel exchange programme, or FEP: Pakistan would export its gas (PG) to India and India would send coal (IC) to Pakistan. He further proposed that the two nations cooperate over hydroelectric and irrigation projects (HAIP) in the Ganges-Brahmaputra-Tista river system (GBTRS or, colloquially, GABTRIS). He spoke to the Indian government minister for planning and social work (GOIMPSW or MINPLASOC), Asoka Mehta, and assured him of World Bank support. He encouraged his old pal the minister for foreign affairs, GOIMFA Swaran Singh, to send out a feeler to his GOP counterpart concerning the possibility of back-channel arms limitation talks (BALT). Indira Gandhi was settling in as GOIPM, a.k.a. MADAM, and Max urged her to move down the path of reconciliation. The result of all his cajoling and bullying was the briefly celebrated Islamabad Joint Statement, the so-called IJOSTAT or GOIGOPJS(ISL)66. Max received personal messages of congratulations from both POTUS and UNSGUT. Of late, America had been infected by a Western strain of the South Asian disease of acronymial initialitis. JFK, RFK, MLK, and POTUS of course was LBJ and UNSGUT was the secretary-general of the United Nations, U Thant.

The ugliness of the bureaucratic terminology, its aggressive uninterest in euphony, marked it out as power-speech. Power had no need for prettification, no need to make things easy. By showing its contempt for verbal felicity it revealed itself as itself, naked and unadorned. The iron fist took off the velvet glove.

Euphoria over the Islamabad accords proved short-lived. The estranged nations' common fondness for alphabet soup did not mean they had developed a taste for peace. MADAM summoned Max to tell him of her anger at the cancellation of all joint projects. The military backchannel proposals had been for territorial adjustments along the ceasefire line; India might compensate Pakistan for lost strategic areas. Or, if this were not acceptable to Pakistan, India had suggested it might agree to accept guarantees of more adequate controls by the U.N. Mrs Gandhi told Max the actual numbers of the war dead on both sides. They were much higher than the published figures. "We can't go on letting our young men perish like this," she said. "And the Pakistanis agree, you know. The generals are furious with Zulfy"—GOPMFA Zulfikar Ali Bhutto—"for leading them into a battle over a stretch of icy wasteland. *Quelques arpents de neige,* isn't it." In spite of the two nations' common concerns, there would be no effective moves towards greater cross-border understanding. Two powerful men combined to sabotage the Ophuls Plan. The old Congress grandee Vengalil Krishnan Krishna Menon—the great left-wing orator and wit who had once, at the Security Council, filibustered for eight hours without a prepared text on the subject of India's inalienable right to have and hold Kashmir; who called himself a "tea-totaller" because although he consumed no alcohol he drank a total of thirty-six cups of tea a day, and consequently spoke more rapidly than any man in India; whose rudeness was legendary; and who was considered an enemy by Indira Gandhi even though he had been her father's friend—had worked assiduously to sabotage the détente. He had found a willing ally in home minister Gulzarilal Nanda, who had been caretaker prime minister twice, for a few days each, first after Jawaharlal Nehru's death and again after Shastri's, whose resentment of those who got the job for real was bitter and absolute, and whose nose was still out of joint because Shastri had overruled him about the wisdom of letting Max Ophuls visit the war zone in Kashmir. Together Nanda and Krishna Menon worked hard to build opposition to Ophuls inside the Indian cabinet and parliament, while simultaneously bolstering the Indian army's military control over the Kashmir valley. At that early stage in her career Mrs Gandhi was obliged to confess that she had allowed herself to be outmanoeuvred. "You also, Mr Ophuls," she said. "GOIMHA Nanda and VKKM have foxed you too. Honestly! What a schmuck." SCHMUCK? wondered Max. Ah . . . Sabotage of Cooperative . . . what? . . . Harmony-Motivated Undertakings Concerning Kashmir? The prime minister of India stroked his arm gently. "It's not an acronym," she said.

Boonyi left Pachigam without her husband, because the Americans had only asked Abdullah Noman for a dance act. She had been commanded to give her Anarkali again, to dazzle the capital's grandees on a specially constructed stage in the residence's central atrium, below a pyramidal lantern. Himal and Gonwati were with her, to dance behind and beside her, content with their supporting roles, happy to shine a little in her reflected light. Habib Joo the old dance teacher was going, too, and a trio of musicians. "Pachigam sending a troupe to New Delhi, to the American embassy," Abdullah Noman said happily at the bus stop, embracing each of them. "What honour you bring on us all."

Shalimar the clown had come to see her off. When the bus arrived, making its usual devil-squawk of a racket and daubed with warnings to motorists and pedestrians alike, Noman climbed onto the roof with her bedroll and made sure everything was safely tied down. When Boonyi said good-bye to him she knew it was an ending. He understood nothing, did not foresee the breaking of his heart. He loved her too much to suspect her of having a traitorous soul. But he was just a clown, and his love led nowhere, would change nothing, would not take her where it was her destiny to go. As she went up through the door of the bus she looked back and saw Shalimar the clown standing with her damaged friend Zoon Misri, a vague drifting presence, half-human, half-phantom, whose place at his side was like a portent of the damage that she, Boonyi, would shortly be inflicting on him. She gave him her best, brightest smile and he lit up in return, as always. This was how she would remember him, his beauty illumined by love. Then the bus set off with a jerk and a rush, and turned a corner, and he was gone, and she began to prepare for what was about to happen. *What do you want,* the ambassador had asked her. She knew what he wanted. He wanted what men want. But to have an answer to his question was important. To know exactly what she wanted and what she was prepared to offer in return.

When he came to her she was ready. Edgar Wood, that peculiar young man, had arranged everything perfectly. The dancing girls were allocated comfortable rooms in the Roosevelt House guest wing, and Wood was careful to seek Mrs Ophuls's approval of the arrangements. Mrs Ophuls's private suite was at the far end of the building—she and the ambassador preferred not to share a bedroom—and Beaver Wood had handpicked the Marines guarding the route between the distinguished couple's quarters, and also the Marines stationed in the corridor outside the dancing girls' rooms. (After his arrival in New Delhi the Beaver had made it his first business to establish which members of the embassy security detail he could rely on, the ones who understood that their absolute loyalty lay to the ambassador and not to their Midwestern parents' conservative moral values or even to God.) It was embassy policy, Wood informed the young women, that in order to ensure their safety the residence's corridors would be off-limits until breakfast time, even for themselves. Himal and Gonwati made no objection, particularly as their rooms were filled with bolts of fabric, bottles of perfume and necklaces and wrist-cuffs made of antique silver, and with wicker baskets overflowing with good things to eat and drink. With cries of delight they rushed towards their gifts. Meanwhile Habib Joo and his trio of male musicians were taken to a suite of rooms at the Ashoka, where they made the acquaintance of minibars for the first time in their lives and decided contentedly that their religion made a special blind-eye exception for expenses-paid nights away from home in deluxe five-star hotels.

In her room at Roosevelt House, Boonyi examined no sari, smelled no perfume, ate no bonbon. Still wearing the clothes of Anarkali, the tight high scarlet bodice that revealed the slenderness of her midriff and the muscled flatness of her belly, the wide, much-pleated dancer's skirt in emerald green silk edged in gold braid, the white tights below to preserve her modesty when the skirt fanned and flared outwards as she whirled, and the costume jewelry, the "ruby" pendant around her neck, the "golden" nose-ring, the braids of fake pearls in her hair, she sat perfectly still on the edge of her bed, staying "in character", acting the part of the great courtesan waiting for the heir to the Mughal throne. With her hands folded in her lap she waited, without complaint. It was three o'clock in the morning before she heard a single, quiet knock on her door.

He had prepared a declaration in newly learned Kashmiri but she put a finger across his lips. How handsome he was, how much his eyes had seen, how much his body knew. "I can speak some little English," she said—not for nothing was she the daughter of Pyarelal Kaul!—and laughed as his whole body relaxed in surprised relief. She had prepared a speech, too, labouring over it in her racing mind as she lay sleepless during the small hours beside her unknowing husband. This was her stage and it was time for her soliloquy. "Please, I want to be a great dancer," she told him. "So I want a great teacher. Also, I want please to be educated to high standard. And I want a good place to live—please—so that I am not ashamed to receive you there. Finally," and now her voice trembled, "because I will give up much for this, please, sir, I want to hear from your own lips that you will keep me safe."

He was both moved and amused. "I will be guided by you in this," he replied, gravely. "*Meh haav tae sae wath.* Please show me the way." Whereupon for an hour they hammered out the treaty of their affiliation as if it were a back-channel negotiation or an international arms deal, each recognizing a need in the other that complemented their own. Max Ophuls was actually aroused by the young woman's naked pragmatism. Perhaps her notable openness concerning her ambition foreshadowed an equal openness in lovemaking. He looked forward to discovering if this were so. The negotiation was also pleasing in itself. The details of the "Understanding," as they both elected to call it—though Max privately preferred the term BKN/MO/JSA(C), which more fully summarized the joint statement of accord (classified) between Boonyi Kaul Noman and himself—were quickly agreed. Just as mutual self-interest was the only real guarantee of a durable accord between nations, so Boonyi's perception that this liaison was her best chance of furthering her own purposes constituted a reliable guarantee of her future seriousness and discretion. That the most delicate clause in the unwritten contract proved not to be an obstacle provided Max with a further necessary guarantee. "And for your part, if I do as you require?" he asked her: the question she had known he would ask, and to which, in her thoughts, her answer had been given, refined and given again a thousand and one times. She looked him in the eyes. "In that case I will do anything you want, whenever you want it," she replied in immaculate English. "My body will be yours to command and it will be my joy to obey."

Thus all Max's significant requirements were in place: not only discretion and seriousness but also complete docility, absolute compliance, maximum attentiveness, exceptional eagerness to please and unlimited access, all fueled by the girl's determination to better herself, to make the leap from the village to the world, to give herself the future she believed she deserved. The clown of a husband was a problem, but she insisted that Max need not concern himself with this aspect of things as it was something she could easily take care of. Everything was acceptable. Edgar Wood, whose forte was anticipation, had already found the apartment, at Type-1 Number-22 Southeast Hira Bagh, two pink rooms with harsh blue-white neon strip-lights and no balcony located in a sage-green concrete bunker of an apartment block in a low-rent residential "colony" to the south of the city centre. The rooms were on the floor above the purple-faced Odissi dance guru Jayababu—Pandit Jayanta Mudgal—who would be paid well to teach the girl everything he knew and to be deaf and blind to everything he should not know. Max and Boonyi actually shook hands on the deal. At the age of fifty-five Ambassador Ophuls was being offered a garden of earthly delights. There was, however, a strangeness. In spite of the cynicism of the Understanding, he felt something that had been asleep for a long time and should not have been awakened begin to stir within himself. Desire was to be expected, for he had rarely been in the presence of so beautiful a woman. But the worm stirring in him lay deeper than desire.

"Don't do this," he warned himself. "To fall in love would break the treaty—nothing can come of it but trouble." But the secret creature within him stretched and yawned, climbed out of its almost-forgotten cellar and rose towards the light. He began to smile a foolish smile whenever he thought of her, to visit her more often than was wise, and to lavish gifts on her. She wanted treasures from the U.S. diplomats' store: American cheese in a tin, the new ridged American potato chips that looked like miniature ploughed fields, 45 rpm recordings celebrating the joys of surfing and driving fast motorcars, and above all candy bars. Chocolates and sweets, which would be her downfall, entered her life in quantity for the first time. She also craved the women's fashions of 1966, not the boring Jackie Kennedy pillbox-hat-and-pearls styles but the looks in the magazines she devoured, the Pocahontas headbands, the swirling orange-print shift dresses, the fringed leather jackets, the Mondrian squares of Saint Laurent, the hoop dresses, the space-age catsuits, the miniskirts, the vinyl, the gloves. She only wore these things in the privacy of the love nest, dressing up eagerly for her lover, giggling at her own daring, and allowing him to undress her as he pleased, to take his time, or to rip the clothes roughly off her body and leave them in shreds on the floor. Edgar Wood, given the task of acquiring and later dispensing these gifts in such a way as to avoid suspicion falling on the ambassador, fulfilled his duties with a growing hostility which Boonyi regally ignored. He got his revenge by insisting on being present to watch her take the daily contraceptive pills that had been Understood to be essential to the deal.

As a result of Max's unexpected romantic infatuation—and also because Boonyi was every bit as attentive as promised—he failed to sense what she had silently been telling him from the beginning, what she assumed he knew to be a part of their hard-nosed agreement: *Don't ask for my heart, because I am tearing it out and breaking it into little bits and throwing it away so I will be heartless but you will not know it because I will be the perfect counterfeit of a loving woman and you will receive from me a perfect forgery of love.*

So there were two unspoken clauses in the Understanding, one regarding the giving of love and the other concerning the withholding of it, codicils that were sharply at odds with each other and impossible to reconcile. The result was, as Max had foreseen, trouble; the biggest Indo-American diplomatic rumpus in history. But for a time the master forger was deceived by the forgery he had bought, both deceived and satisfied, as content to possess it as an art collector who discovers a masterpiece concealed in a mound of garbage, as happy to keep it hidden from view as a collector who can't resist buying what he knows to be stolen property. And that was how it came about that a faithless wife from the village of the bhand pather began to influence, to complicate and even to shape, American diplomatic activity regarding the vexed matter of Kashmir.

Pachigam was a trap, she told herself every night, but the Muskadoon still scurried through her dreams, its cold swift mountain music singing in her ears. She was a girl from the mountains and the climate of the plains affected her badly. When it was summer in Delhi the air conditioners were invariably incapacitated by "load-shedding" power cuts at the hottest times of day. The heat was like a hammer, like a stone. Crushed beneath it, she collapsed onto her illicit bed of shame and thought of Chandanwari, of Manasbal and Shishnag, of flower-carpeted Gulmarg and the eternal snows above, of cool glaciers and bubbling springs and the high ice-temples of the gods. She heard the soft splash of a heart-shaped oar in the water of a mirror lake, the rustle of chinar leaves, the boatmen's songs and the soft beating of wings, thrushes' wings, mynah wings, the wings of bluetits and hoopoes, and the top-knotted bulbuls that looked like young girls who had put up their hair. When she closed her eyes she invariably saw her father, her husband, her companions, her appointed place on earth. Not her new lover but her old, lost life. *My old life like a prison,* she told herself savagely, but her heart called her a fool. She had it all upside down and backward, her heart scolded her. What she thought of as her former imprisonment had been freedom, while this so-called liberation was no more than a gilded cage.

She thought of Shalimar the clown and was horrified again by the ease with which she had abandoned him. When she left Pachigam none of her closest people guessed what she was doing, the dolts. None of them tried to save her from herself, and how could she forgive them for that? What idiots they all were! Her husband was super-idiot number one and her father was super-idiot number two and everyone else was pretty close behind. Even after Himal and Gonwati returned to Pachigam without her and the bad talk began, even then Shalimar the clown sent her trusting letters, letters haunted by the phantom of their murdered love. *I reach out to you and touch you without touching you as on the riverbank in the old days. I know you are following your dream but that dream will always bring you back to me. If the Amrikan is of assistance well and good. People always talk lies but I know your heart is true. I sit with folded hands and await your loving return.* She lay perspiring on her bed, held captive by the chains of her enslaving solitude, and tore the letters into smaller and smaller pieces. They were letters that humiliated both their author and their recipient, letters that had no business existing, that should never have been sent. Such thoughts should never have come into being, and would not have, were it not for the enfeebled mind of that man without honour whom it was her shame to have espoused.

The paper scraps fell from her enervated summer hand and floated like snowflakes to the bedroom floor, and indeed the messages they bore were as irrelevant to her new life as snow. What kind of husband was he anyway, this clown? Was he storming the capital in his wrath like a Muslim conqueror of old, a Tughlaq or Khilji at least if not a Mughal, or, like Lord Ram, was he at least sending the monkey-god Hanuman to find her before he launched his lethal attack on her abductor, the American Ravan? No, he was mooning over her picture and weeping into the waters of the stupid Muskadoon like an impotent goof, accepting his fate like a true Kashmiri coward, content to be trampled over by anyone who felt like doing a bit of trampling, a wrong-headed duffer who quarrelled with his brother Anees who at least had the guts to take matters into his own hands and blow up a few useless things. He was behaving like the performing dog he was, a creature who imitated life to make people laugh but who had not the slightest understanding of how a man should live.

On the night she first lay with him, she remembered, he had menaced her lovingly, swearing to pursue her and take her life, hers and her children's, if she ever did what she had just so callously done. What empty words men spoke when they had had their way with a woman. He was a weakling, a strutting turkey-cock, a fool. In his place she would have hunted herself down and murdered herself in a gutter, like a dog, so that the shame of it would outlive her.

The letters stopped. But still every night in her dreams he came to her, walking the high wire, jumping rope in the sky, bouncing on air as if it were a trampoline, playing leapfrog with his brothers along the high thin line, pretending to slip on an invisible banana skin, windmilling his arms, saving himself, regaining his balance, then slipping on a second imaginary banana skin and falling in a skilfully chaotic tumble all the way to the ground, a finale that always brought the house down. In her dreams she smiled at his genius but when she woke the smile withered and died.

In short, she could not get her cuckolded husband out of her mind, and because it was impossible to talk to her American lover about anything important she spoke heatedly of "Kashmir" instead. Whenever she said "Kashmir" she secretly meant her husband, and this ruse allowed her to declare her love for the man she had betrayed to the man with whom she had committed the act of treason. More and more often she spoke of her love for this encoded "Kashmir", arousing no suspicion, even when her pronouns occasionally slipped, so that she referred to his mountains, his valleys, his gardens, his flowing streams, his flowers, his stags, his fish. Her American lover was obviously too stupid to crack the code, and attributed the pronoun slippage to her incomplete command of the language. However he, the ambassador, took careful note of her passion, and was plainly moved when she was at her angriest, when she castigated "Kashmir" for his cowardice, for his passivity in the face of the horrible crimes committed against him. "These crimes," he asked, reclining on her pillows, caressing her naked back, kissing her exposed hip, pinching her nipple, "these would be actions of the Indian armed forces you're talking about?" At that moment she decided that the term "Indian armed forces" would secretly refer to the ambassador himself, she would use the Indian presence in the valley as a surrogate for the American occupation of her body, so, "Yes, that's it," she cried, "the 'Indian armed forces,' raping and pillaging. How can you not know it? How can you not comprehend the humiliation of it, the shame of having your boots march all over my private fields?" Again, those telltale slips of the tongue. Your boots, my fields. Again, distracted by her inflamed beauty, he paid no attention to the errors. "Yes, dearest," he said in a muffled voice from between her thighs, "I believe I do begin to understand, but would it be possible to table the subject for the moment?"

Time passed. Max Ophuls knew that Boonyi Noman did not love him but at first he shut the knowledge away, blinding himself to its consequences, because she had taken up temporary residence in a tender corner of his heart. He knew she hid a great deal of herself from him, exposing only her body, like a true courtesan, like any common whore, but he agreed with himself to forget this, deceiving himself into believing that she reciprocated what he was pleased to call his love. And he allowed her diatribes on the "occupation" of "Kashmir" to affect his thinking, never suspecting that she was secretly railing against himself and against the ineffectual husband who had failed to come to her rescue. He began to object, in private session and in public speeches, to the militarization of the Kashmir valley, and when the word *oppressors* passed his lips for the first time the bubble of his popularity finally burst.

Newspaper editorials lambasted him. Here, they said, here beneath all the phoney Indiaphile posturing, was just another cheap "cigarette" (this was a slang term meaning a Pak-American, an American with Pakistani sympathies, a play on the name of the Pak-American Tobacco Company), just another uncomprehending gringo. America was trampling over southeast Asia, Vietnamese children's bodies were burning with unquenchable napalm fire, and yet the American ambassador had the gall to speak of oppression. "America should put its own house in order," thundered India's editorial writers, "and stop telling us how to take care of our own land." It was at this point that Edgar Wood, correctly identifying the source of the ambassador's problems, decided that Boonyi Noman had to go.

Observe him, this unctuous rodent, this Eager Beaver Wood, this invisible, scurrying oiler of wheels, this subterranean enabler of the visible, this lizard person, this snake at the mountain's root! A pimp of this ilk, a pander of this water would seem to be ill equipped for the burdensome work of moral disapproval. It is not easy to look down on others when one's own position lacks elevation. Yet the feat was achieved by the ever-resourceful and duplicitous Wood, who proceeded entirely by inversions. The child of a Bostonian prelate (and therefore a Brahmin of sorts himself), he had turned away from religion at an early age. Having rejected religious observance, he nevertheless continued to harbour a secret love of sanctimony and pomp. Being covertly pompous and sanctimonious, he affected humility and open-minded tolerance. Being humble, he concealed within himself an overweening pride. Being prideful, he offered himself to Max Ophuls as a selfless devotee, an effacer of his own needs, a do-everything, see-nothing man without qualities, a servitor, a low footstool for his high master's shoe. Thus, though low-natured, he was still able to consider himself high-minded. See him now, coursing through the streets of the Indian capital in a little phut-phut scooter-rickshaw, his white kurta flapping in the wind. Behold the simple *chappals* on his feet. See him arrive at his residential quarters, and note, if you please, the Indian artworks and memorabilia therein, the Madhubani painting, the Warli tribal art, the miniatures of the Kashmiri and Company schools. Is this not the very picture of a Westerner gone native? Yet this same Wood was privately convinced of the innate superiority of the

West, and filled with a shadowy contempt for the nation whose style he sought so assiduously to ape. He was tormented, we may grant him that. Such tergiversations of the soul, such twists in the psyche, such tortuous contradictions between the apparent and the actual, would certainly be painful, we may concede, to endure.

Such a coiled and doubled man-serpent would have been too formidable an adversary for a heavily compromised and largely defenceless young woman in any case, but the truth was that she made his task much easier than he expected; and so, finally, did Max. Things in Delhi had not gone as Boonyi Kaul Noman would have wished. Pink, in her two small lonely rooms, rapidly became the colour of her isolation and self-loathing. The blue-white of the neon strip-lighting became the colour of judgement, a harsh contemptuous glare that erased shadows and left her no place to hide. And as for the sage-green colour of her dance guru's apartment walls, well, that became the colour of her failure. The Odissi master Pandit Mudgal had been scornful of her from the first. He was the guru of Sonal Karnaa and Kumkum Segal! He had taught Alarmel Mansingh! He was the master of Kiran Qunango! No man had done more than he to popularize the Odissi dance form! Where would they all be without him—Aloka Panigrahi, Sanjukta Sarukkai, Protima Mahapatra, Madhavi Mohanty? And now in his mottled old age came this raw, lazy village girl, this kept woman, this nothing. She was a rich American's toy, and he despised her for that; somewhat he despised himself for taking the Yankee dollars and becoming party to the arrangement, and this, too, he held against her. The lessons had gone badly from the start; nor had there been much subsequent improvement. At length Pandit Mudgal, a thickset man with the physiognomy—and all the sensuality—of an outsized eggplant, told her, "Yes, madam, sex appeal you have, that we can all see. You move and men watch you. That is only one thing. Great mastery requires a great soul and your soul, madam, is damned." She fled weeping from his sight and the next day the ambassador sent Edgar Wood to tell Mudgal that his salary would be increased—doubled!—if he persevered. Like Charles Foster Kane trying to make a singer out of his discordant wife, Max Ophuls tried to buy what could not be bought, and failed. Jayababu, once long, lean and beautiful and now a dark brinjal of a man, an ill-tempered aubergine, refused the cash.

"I am a man for a challenge," he told Edgar Wood. "But this girl is not for me. Hers is not the high calling, but the low."

Max's attention began to wander after that, though for a long time he refused to acknowledge the change in himself. He stayed away from Boonyi for longer periods. Once or twice he dined privately with his wife. Peggy Ophuls was annoyed with herself for feeling so pleased. She was legendary for her toughness but with him she was always weak. How easily she came back to him, how pathetically she opened her arms and let him slink shamefacedly home! He murmured something about the old days, about the Pat Line or the Lyons Corner House, and at once floods of repressed emotion surged through her body. He did his imitation of the vocal style of Mrs Shanti Dickens of Porchester Terrace as she relished the day's crime reports—*"Wery wery hawful, sir, hisn't it? Maybe 'e is heatin' 'er for 'is tea!"*—and tears of laughter stood in the Grey Rat's eyes. This time had been the hardest of all for her. She had lost him for so long that she had feared she would never get him back. But here he was, coming round to face her again. This was what they had, she told herself, this inevitability. They were built to last. She raised a glass to him and a smile trembled at the corners of her mouth. I am the most deluded woman in the world, she thought. But look at him, here he is. My man.

None of Max Ophuls's amours ever lasted very long before he came to India. Boonyi had been different. This was "love", and the nature of love was—was it not?—to endure. Or was that just one of the mistakes people made about love, Max got to wondering. Was he clothing an essentially savage, irrational thing in the garb of civilization, dolling it up in the dress shirt of endurance, the silk trousers of constancy, the frock coat of solicitude and the top hat of selflessness? Like Tarzan the ape man when he came to London or New York: the natural rendered unnatural. But under all the fancy apparel the untameable, unkind reality still remained, a feral thing more gorilla-like than human. Something having less to do with sweetness and tenderness and caring and more to do with spoor and territory and grooming and domination and sex. Something provisional, no matter what sort of treaties you acceded to, signed marriage contracts or private statements of accord.

When he began to speak in this way the matador Edgar Wood understood that the bull was tiring, and sent in the picadors, or, to be precise, the picadoras. The beauties he aimed at Max were carefully selected from the upper echelons of Delhi and Bombay society to make Boonyi look bad. They were wealthy, cultured, accomplished, extraordinary women. They circled him from a distance, then moved closer in. The lances of their flirtatious regard, their graceful motion, their touch, speared him time and time again. He fell to his knees. He was almost ready for the sword.

So perhaps it was her failure to be exceptional as well as beautiful that damned Boonyi, or perhaps it was just the passage of time. Shut away in her pink shame, sometimes for days on end (for the ambassador was an increasingly busy man), with only the opprobrium of her dance master for company, she slid downwards towards ruin, slowly at first and then with gathering speed. The excess of Delhi deranged her, its surfeit of muchness, its fecal odours, its hellish noise, its anonymity, its uncaring crowd of the desperate fighting to survive. She became addicted to chewing tobacco, keeping a little cud of it nestled between her lower molars and her cheek. To pass the empty time she frequently fell ill in a languid, faux-consumptive way, and (more truthfully) suffered often from stress, depression, hypertension, stomach trouble and all the other hysteric ailments, and so as the slow months passed she began to learn about medication, about the capacity of tablets and capsules and potions to make the world seem other than it was, faster, slower, more exciting, calmer, happier, more peaceful, kinder, wilder, better. Pandit Mudgal's thirteen-year-old *hamal,* the household boy whom the dance teacher periodically bedded in an offhand, seigneurial manner, led Boonyi deeper into the psychotropical jungle, teaching her about *afim:* opium. After that she curled herself into the metamorphic smoke whenever she could, and dreamed thickly of lost joy while time, cruelly, continued to pass.

But her narcotic of choice turned out to be food. At a certain point early in the second year of her liberated captivity, she began, with great seriousness and a capacity for excess learned from the devil-city itself, to eat. If her world would not expand, her body could. She took to gluttony with the same bottomless enthusiasm she had once had for sex, diverting the immense force of her erotic requirements from her bed to her table. She ate seven times a day, guzzling down a proper breakfast, then a midmorning plate, then a full luncheon, then a midafternoon array of sweet delicacies, then a hearty dinner, then a second dinner at bedtime, and finally a fridge-raiding gobble in the small hours before dawn. Yes, she was a whore, she admitted to herself with a twist of the heart, but she would at least be an extremely well-fed one.

Of all this her keeper Edgar Wood was fully aware, and in all of it he was wholly complicit. If she was setting out down the road to self-destruction (he reasoned), who was he to prevent her? It saved him the difficulty of steering her down exactly such a path. Without a word to his master he brought her the chewing tobacco that was ruining her smile, filled her little bathroom cabinet with pills to pop, clouded her mind with opium, and above all arranged for food to be cooked and delivered, food by the basketful, the trolleyful, delivered by unmarked car or by a dependable tiffin-runner pushing a laden two-wheeled wooden cart. All this he did with a sober grace that entirely deceived her. She had never trusted him until now, but his immaculate courtesy and her growing list of addictions forged a kind of trust, or at least pushed her to set the issue of his trustworthiness to one side. Pragmatism ruled; he was the only one who could satisfy her now. In a sense, he had become her lover, supplanting the ambassador. He was the one who gave her what she needed.

Edgar Wood himself was far too proper to make any such suggestion. He was simply there to be of assistance, he assured Boonyi. Nothing was too good for the woman the ambassador had chosen to love. She had only to ask. And ask she did. It was as if the nostalgic memory of the Kashmiri "super-wazwaan", the Banquet of Sixty Courses Maximum, had possessed her and driven her insane. Once she understood that Edgar was prepared to satisfy her every whim she grew increasingly promiscuous and peremptory in her gourmandizing. She sent for Kashmiri food, of course, but also for the tandoori and Mughlai cuisines of north India, the *boti kabab*s, the *murgh makhani,* and for the fish dishes of the Malabar coast, for the *masala dosa*s of Madras and the fabled early pumpkins of the coast of Coromandel, for the hot pickle curries of Hyderabad, for *kulfi* and *barfi* and *pista-ki-lauz,* and for sweet Bengali *sandesh.* Her appetite had grown to subcontinental size. It crossed all frontiers of language and custom. She was vegetarian and nonvegetarian, fish- and meat-eating, Hindu, Christian and Muslim, a democratic, secularist omnivore.

Elsewhere in the world it was the summer of love.

Inevitably her beauty dimmed. Her hair lost its lustre, her skin coarsened, her teeth rotted, her body odour soured, and her bulk—ah! her bulk—increased steadily, week by week, day by day, almost hour by hour. Her head rattled with pills, her lungs were full of poppies. Soon the pretence of lessons was dropped. The general education she had requested as part of her deal with the ambassador had ceased long ago; she had always been too lazy to be a good student, even in Pachigam. Now the dancing also fell away. Pandit Mudgal stayed downstairs with his young hamal, and Boonyi lived above him in a perpetual daze, with her head in a chemical spin and her belly full of food. Edgar Wood, her candyman, allowed himself to wonder idly if her astonishingly self-destructive behaviour might be a deliberate suicide attempt, but quite frankly he wasn't interested enough in her interior life to pursue the thought. What interested him more was the durability of the ambassador's feeling for her. Max went on visiting her for a considerable time after she had passed what Edgar Wood privately called the point of revoltingness. It must be like sleeping not only on but with a stinking foam mattress, he thought with a fastidious shudder: *yeuchh.* According to Mudgal's boy, a voyeuristic youth whom Wood was paying for information, the ambassador liked the Kashmiri woman's use during lovemaking of her teeth and clawlike nails. Like many others, Edgar Wood had read Max Ophuls's unusually frank account of his wartime exploits. How strange, he thought, that the famous anti-Nazi should still be aroused by his memory of the sexual preferences of the fascist Ursula Brandt, the Panther, whom he had fucked for the Cause. How very strange that a bloated Kashmiri woman should close that sexual circle, so that he went on needing her services long after she had ceased to be attractive. In the end, however, the break was made; the ambassador stopped visiting Boonyi. "It's impossible," he told Edgar Wood. "See that she is taken care of, the poor wretch. What a wreck she has made of herself."

When the man of power withdraws his protection from a concubine, she becomes like a child abandoned in wolf-infested hills. Mowgli's adoption by the Seeonee pack is untypical; this is not the way such stories usually develop. Boonyi Noman, prostrate on her groaning bed, gasping beneath the weight of her own body, saw Edgar Wood enter her quarters like a predator, without the civility of a knock or a word of greeting and with murder in his eyes, and understood that the crisis was upon her. It was time to tell him her secret.

Edgar Wood heard the news of her pregnancy and accepted that he had been outwitted by a master. He had come to terminate the Understanding, to give Boonyi a final cash payment, a ticket to oblivion and a warning of the dangers of future indiscretion, and he came to her in an ugly way because it was an ugly duty he had to perform, because the man whose ugly deed this was didn't have the decency to come here himself. But before he could deliver his message of ugliness she played her trump. He had brought her a contraceptive pill every day without fail and had watched her place it in her mouth, take a gulp of water and swallow, but plainly she had fooled him, she had tongued the pills to one side, concealing them beneath those ever-present wads of chewing tobacco, and now she was carrying the ambassador's child, and she was many months pregnant. She had grown so obese that the pregnancy had been invisible, it lay hidden somewhere inside her fat, and it was too late to think about an abortion, she was too far advanced and the risks were too great. "Congratulations," said Edgar Wood. "We underestimated you." "I want to see him," Boonyi answered. "Tell him to come at once."

In one version of the story of the dancing girl Anarkali, the Emperor Akbar himself spoke to the young beauty and persuaded her that Prince Salim's love affair with her must end, that she must trick him into believing she no longer loved him so that he could go away from her and return to the path of destiny that would lead him eventually to the throne; and, just as in *La Traviata,* just like Violetta giving up Alfredo after the visit from his father Germont, she agreed. But Boonyi was no longer Anarkali, she had lost her beauty and could no longer dance, and the ambassador was nobody's son but the man of power himself. And Anarkali didn't get pregnant. Stories were stories and real life was real life, naked, ugly, and finally impossible to cosmeticize in the greasepaint of a tale. Max Ophuls came to Boonyi's pink bedroom that night. He stood before her bed in the dark, leaning forward slightly and clutching at his straw hat's brim with both his trembling hands. The sight of her ballooning, cetacean body still had the power to shock him. What lay within it, what was growing daily in her womb, was even more of a shock. His child was taking shape in there. It would be his firstborn child. "What do you want," he asked in a low voice, while dark thoughts and wild emotions rioted in his inner squares and streets.

"I want to tell you what I think of you," she said.

Her English had improved and he had learned her language too. At their closest they had sometimes forgotten which language they were speaking; the two tongues blurred into one. As they drifted apart so did their speech. Now she spoke her own language and he spoke his. Each understood the other well enough. He had known there would be abuse and there was abuse. There were empty threats and accusations of betrayal. All this he comprehended. Look at me, she was saying. I am your handiwork made flesh. You took beauty and created hideousness, and out of this monstrosity your child will be born. Look at me. I am the meaning of your deeds. I am the meaning of your so-called love, your destructive, selfish, wanton love. Look at me. Your love looks just like hatred. I never spoke of love, she was saying. I was honest and you have turned me into your lie. This is not me. This is not me. This is you.

And then came another, older line of attack. I should have known, she was saying. I should have known better than to lie with a Jew. The Jews are our enemy and I should have known.

The past reared up. Briefly he saw again the army of the Jewish fallen. He set the memory aside. The wheel had turned. In this moment of his story he was not the victim. In this moment she, not he, had the right to claim kinship with the lost. At least I never spoke of love, she was saying. I kept my love for my husband though my body served you, Jew. Look what you have made of the body I gave you. But my heart is still my own.

"You never loved me, then," he said, hanging his head, when she had finished. He sounded ridiculously false and hypocritical even to himself. She was laughing at him, viciously. Does a rat love the snake that gobbles it up, she was asking. He winced at the sharpness of her tongue, at the violence welling up in her. "You will be well looked after. Everything you need," he said, and turned to go. In the doorway he paused. "I once loved a Rat," he said. "Maybe you were the snake that ate her."

The scandal broke a week later. A baby changed things. A pregnancy could not be winked at. Max Ophuls never found out who leaked the information to the papers—Boonyi herself, or the aubergine dancing master downstairs, or his young catamite, or one of the group of drivers and security guards handpicked for their alleged discretion by Edgar Wood, or even Wood himself, Wood washing his hands after many years of his master's grubby work—but within days of Max's last meeting with Boonyi, every journalist in the city had the story.

It was not the biggest story of the period, but it fed naturally into those stories. The working committee of the national conference of Jammu and Kashmir had unanimously passed a resolution calling for a permanent merger of the state with India. Indira Gandhi had asked for and been given powers to outlaw groups that questioned Indian sovereignty over the valley. A Kashmiri girl ruined and destroyed by a powerful American gave the Indian government an opportunity to look like it would stand up and defend Kashmiris against marauders of all types—to defend the honour of Kashmir as stoutly as it would defend that of any other integral part of India. Nothing less than Max's head on a plate would do. His friend Sarvepalli Radhakrishnan had retired from the presidency; the new president, Zakir Hussain, was making angry statements in private about the godless American's exploitation of an innocent Hindu girl. Nobody had said the words *sexual assault* yet but Max knew they could not be far from people's lips. He was no longer the well-beloved lover of India, but her heartless ravisher. And Indira Gandhi was out for blood.

The Vietnam War was at its height and so was American unpopularity in Asia. Draft cards were burned in Central Park and Martin Luther King led a protest march to the United Nations and in India the goddamn American ambassador was apparently fucking the local peasantry. So war-torn America turned on Max as well, his alleged oppression of Boonyi becoming a sort of allegory of Vietnam. Norman Mailer wrote about Boonyi and Max as if she were the countryside near Saigon and he was Operation Cedar Falls. Joan Baez made up a song about them. These interventions were not sympathetic to Max Ophuls. It was as if his previous selves were erased overnight—the Resistance hero, the bestselling author, the economic genius, the famous lover of his equally heroic wife, and the Flying Jew—and standing in their place was this Bluebeard-like ogre, this sexual predator who was fit for nothing but gelding. Tarring and feathering were too good for the likes of him. Che Guevara was killed around then, and that was just about the only thing that happened that wasn't laid at Max's door.

Back then there were no "media sieges" in the modern sense. All-India Radio sent a radio reporter to stand uncertainly outside the sage-green apartment building at Type-1 Number-22 Southeast Hira Bagh, holding out his microphone as if it were a begging bowl. Doordarshan, in those days the only television channel, sent a cameraman and sound recordist. The text of what they were permitted to say in commentary would no doubt be handed down later from the prime minister's office, so there was no need to send a journalist. There was a man from the PTI news agency and two or three other men from the print media. They saw Odissi dancing divas come and go, and Jayababu's boy running errands. The anonymous occupants of other apartments in the same building had seen nothing, knew nothing, shied away from the cameras and microphones as if from danger, and fled. Just once the great Jayababu himself sallied forth to scold the press for making too much noise and disturbing his dance class, whereupon the abashed reporters at once commenced to speak in whispers. Of the principal actors in the drama there was no sign. At mealtimes the watchers dispersed to seek refreshment, and they soon lost interest in staying at their posts. Delhi in winter was cold as a ghost and in the mornings and evenings the fog came down and pushed its clammy hands through your skin and froze your bones. There was no need for anyone to stay. The news was being constructed elsewhere. The American ambassador was being withdrawn in disgrace. The U.S. embassy was the place to be. Hira Bagh was just a gossipy footnote. In the winter mist it looked like a phantom world.

One fog-white night, at about three o'clock in the morning, long after the gentlemen of the press had departed, a hooded figure arrived at Boonyi's pink apartment. When the pregnant woman beached on her bed like a stranded sea-monster heard the key turning in her front door she assumed it was Edgar Wood making his nocturnal food run. These days he only visited her in the middle of the night, arriving out of breath, burdened by huge amounts of edibles. She had no sympathy for him. He was a necessary side effect of a sick life, like vomit. "I'm hungry," she called out. "You're late." He came into the bedroom wincing as if he were a schoolboy in a bully's armlock, a child whose ear was being twisted by a disciplinarian aunt. The hooded figure followed him into the room, unveiled herself, and looked Boonyi over with a brisk, nannyish sympathy. "Oh, dear me," she said. "Dear me, what a dreadful . . . ha! Can you believe it, my dear, I almost envied—haha!—oh, leave it.—But there's this. I almost forgave him. Can you believe *that*?—Extraordinary.—But I almost did, in spite of everything. In spite, my dear, of you.—But look at you. No discipline. We can't have this.—Hmm.—Edgar, you vile sticky creature, have you made the arrangements?—Well, of course you have, it's what you do.—It's what he does, dear. Yes, you loathe him too, of course you do, everyone does.—Harrumph.—We're going to get you away from here, my dear.—You'll be needing care. We'll see you through.—Oh, I see. You misunderstand me.—No, my husband did not send me here. He has left the country. He has left the diplomatic service. However, let me be plain, he has not left me. It is I who have left him.—You follow?—Hmm?—Left him after everything and in spite of everything and at the end of it all.—Oh, let it go.—The point is to get you somewhere else. No more prying eyes and a spot of good medical care.—Hmm?—How far gone are you? Seven months?—More? Eight? Aha. Eight. Good. Won't be long, then. Oh, get on with it, Edgar, for Christ's sake.—Edgar's been sacked too, dear, I thought you'd like to know. I'll make sure this little shit never works for his country again, I promise you that.—Tonight's your last hurrah, isn't it, Edgar? Outlived your blasted usefulness, I'd say.—Poor Edgar. What will you do?—Ha!—No, on reflection, I don't think we're going to worry about you, are we, dear?—No.—Well then, Edgar: where's the bally van?"

"Around the corner." Thus Edgar Wood through gritted teeth. "But I warned you she might be too big to fit through the door." Margaret Rhodes Ophuls whirled to face him, shriveling him in the dragon-fire of her gaze. "Quite right, Edgar," she said, sweetly. "So you did. Run along then, and fetch the bloody sledgehammer."

Boonyi gave birth to a baby daughter in a clean, simple bedroom in Father Joseph Ambrose's Holy Love of India Evangalactic Girls' Orphanage for Disabled & Destitute Street Girls, located at 77-A, Ward-5, Mehrauli, an institution that had benefited greatly from the ex-ambassador's wife's fund-raising skills and personal largesse. In spite of everyone at the Evangalactic Orphanage's affection and admiration for Peggy-Mata, the new resident she had foisted on them was not initially popular. Every detail of Boonyi's story somehow became common knowledge at the orphanage almost at once. There were girls at the Evangalactic who had been rescued from the whorehouses of Old Delhi at the age of nine, and these children gathered outside Boonyi's door and conversed in loud, impolite voices about the fallen rich man's tart who had actually chosen the demeaning life from which they had managed to escape. There were girls who looked like giant spiders because of spinal problems that obliged them to walk on all fours, and they joined the former child prostitutes to jeer at this new type of cripple, who had rendered herself almost immobile through sheer gluttony. There were country girls who had fled to the big city from the dirty old men to whom they had been betrothed—or, rather, sold into betrothal—and these girls, too, added to the crowd at Boonyi's door to express their disbelief that a woman should leave a good man who had truly loved her.

Things were on the brink of getting out of hand, until Father Ambrose, nudged by Peggy Ophuls, addressed the girls and shamed them into something like compassion. "The holy love of India brought all of you to the harbour of this safe place," Father Ambrose, a young but charismatic Catholic priest who had grown up in a Keralan fishing village and was accordingly fond of maritime metaphors, rebuked his charges. "God's love cast out its nets for you upon the filthy seas in which you swam. God caught up your souls from the black water and revealed your shining light. Show me, then, that you, too, can be fishers of the spirit. Cast out the nets of your compassion and bring back to a safe place this new soul crying out for your love."

After Father Ambrose's little speech Peggy Ophuls was able to find a few willing helpers, not only a doctor and a midwife but also girls to cook for Boonyi, and to wash her and oil her and comb her tangled hair. Mrs Ophuls made no attempt to limit the damaged woman's food intake. "Let's have the child out safely," she told Father Ambrose and the orphans (who muttered sullenly, but made no objection). "Then we can think about the mother."

In due course the baby was born. Boonyi, cradling her daughter, named her Kashmira. "Do you hear me?" she whispered into the little girl's ear. "Your name is Kashmira Noman, and I'm going to take you home."

This was when Peggy Ophuls's face hardened and she revealed her darker purpose, unveiling the secret she had kept hidden until this moment beneath the cloak of her apparently boundless altruism. "Young lady," she said, "it's time to face facts. You want to go home, you say?" Yes, replied Boonyi, it is the only thing I now want in the world. "Hmm," said Peggy Ophuls. "Home to that husband of yours in Pachigam. The one who never came for you. The one who stopped writing. The clown." Boonyi's eyes filled with tears. "Yes, my dear, I make it my business to know—Ha! I see!—That's the chap you're going back to with another man's baby in your arms?—Mmm?—And you imagine that's the chap who will give this little girl his name—*Kashmira Noman*—and take her for his own, and then it's off into the sunset for a spot of happily ever after?" The tears were streaming down Boonyi's face. "That's a non-starter, my dear," said Peggy Ophuls unsentimentally, moving in for the kill. "*Noman,* indeed!—That's not her name. And what did you say? *Kashmira?* No, no, darling. That can't be her future." Something new in the tone of her voice made Boonyi dry her tears.

"Tell you what, though," added Peggy Ophuls, as if the idea had just occurred to her. "Here's a bit of a plan.—Are you listening? You'd do well to listen." Boonyi was paying attention now. "It's winter," said Peggy Ophuls. "The road over the Pir Panjal is closed. No way into the valley by land.—No matter.—I can give you what you want. I can get an aircraft to fly you in. You're probably more than one seat wide. That can be taken into account.—You don't have to worry about nursing the child. I have a wet nurse standing by.—You can probably travel in, what, a week? Let's say a week. I can have a comfortable vehicle waiting for you at the other end to drive you back to Pachigam in style. How does that sound?—Hmm?—Sounds good, I expect. Ha! Of course it does."

Boonyi's tears had dried. "Please, I do not understand," she said at last. "What is the need for a wet nurse?" As the words left her lips she saw the answer to the question in her benefactress's eyes.

"Do you know the tale of Rumplestiltskin?" asked Peggy Ophuls, dreamily. "No, of course you don't.—Well, in brief.—Once upon a time there was a miller's daughter who was told by one of those whimsical fairy-tale kings, *If you have not spun this straw into gold by tomorrow morning, you must die.*—You know the type of fellow I mean, dear.—They'll screw you or chop off your head, those killer princes, love and death being the same sort of thing to them. They'll screw you *and* chop off your head. They'll screw you *while your head is being chopped off.* . . . —Sorry. As I was saying.—In the middle of the night, while she sat helpless and weeping, locked away in a castle tower, there was a knock at the door, and in came a little manikin, who asked, *What will you give me if I do it for you?* And he did it, you know, three nights running he spun the straw into gold, and the miller's daughter lived, and of course she married the whimsical king, and had a child. Silly woman! To marry the man who would have killed her as easily as blinking.—Well!—Scheherazade married her murderous Shahryar, too.—Can't beat women for stupidity, what?—Take me, for example. I married my whimsical prince as well, the murderer of my love.—But you know all about him, of course, I'm so sorry.—So, where was I.—Yes. In conclusion.—One night the little manikin came back. *You know what I came for,* he said. Rumplestiltskin was his name."

They were alone in the room; alone with their desperate needs. The silence was terrible: a dark, hopeless hush of inevitability. But the look on Margaret Rhodes Ophuls's face was worse, at once savage and happy. "*Ophuls,*" said Peggy-Mata. "That's her father's name. And *India*'s a nice name, a name containing, as it does, the truth. The question of origins is one of the two great questions. *India Ophuls* is an answer. To the second great question, the question of ethics, she'll have to find answers of her own."

"No," said Boonyi, shouting. "I won't do it." Peggy Ophuls put a hand on the young mother's head. "You get what you want," she said. "You live, and go home. But there are two of us here, my dear.—Don't you see?—Two of us to satisfy. Yes. You know, the night before I came to India I dreamed I would not leave without a child to call my own. I dreamed I was holding a little baby girl and singing her a song I'd made up specially.—And then all this time with all these children I've wondered when my child would come.—You understand, I'm sure.—One wants the world to be what it is not.—One clings to hope. Then finally one faces up.—Let's look at the world as it is, shall we?—I can't have a baby. That's clear. More than one reason now. Biology and divorce.—And you?—You can't keep this little girl. She will drag you down and she will be the death of you and that will be the death of her.—You follow?—Whereas with me she can live like a queen."

"No," said Boonyi, dully, hugging her daughter. "No, no, no."

"I'm so glad," said Peggy Ophuls. "Hmm?—Yes. Really!—Couldn't be more delighted. I knew you'd be sensible once it was all properly explained." As she left the room she was humming the dream-song to herself. *Ratetta, sweet Ratetta,* she sang, *who could be better than you?*

Here is ex-ambassador Maximilian Ophuls, falling, for the time being, out of history. Here he is in disgrace, plunging down through the turbulent waters of 1968, past the Prague Spring and the Magical Mystery Tour and the Tet Offensive and the Paris événements *and the My Lai massacre and the dead bodies of Dr King and Bobby Kennedy, past Grosvenor Square and Baader-Meinhof and Mrs Robinson and O. J. Simpson and Nixon. The swollen ocean of events, mighty and heartless, closes over Max as it always does over losers. Here is drowned Max, the invisible man. Underground Max, trapped in a subterranean Edgar Wood world, a world of the disregarded, of lizard people and snake people, of busted hustlers and discarded lovers and lost leaders and dashed hopes. Here is Max wandering among the high heaps of the bodies of the rejected, the mountain ranges of defeat. But even in this, his newfound invisibility, he is ahead of his time, because in this occult soil the seeds of the future are being planted, and the time of the invisible world will come, the time of the altered dialectic, the time of the dialectic gone underground, when anonymous spectral armies will fight in secret over the fate of the earth. A good man is never discarded for long. A use is always found*

for such a man. Invisible Max will find a new use. He will be one of the makers of this new age, too, until old age at last rings down the curtain, and Death comes to his door in the form of a handsome man, a Mercader, an Udham Singh, Death asking him, in the name of the woman they once both loved, for work.

Shalimar the Clown

The air was full of frozen particles of itself. Each breath she took scraped at her windpipe before melting, but to Boonyi standing on the Elasticnagar military airstrip the inhaled sharpness was the sweet sting of home. "O icy beauty," she lamented silently, "how could I ever have left you?" She shivered, and the shiver was the feeling of her self returning to herself. Since the day she left, her mother had not visited her in her dreams. "Even a ghost is more sensible than I," she thought, almost wanting to lie down on the tarmac and go to sleep then and there to renew her acquaintance with Pamposh. "My mother, too, is waiting for me at home." The chartered Fokker Friendship, named *Yamuna* after the great river, had been granted special permission to land here, away from prying eyes. Peggy-Mata had many friends. Boonyi had boarded the plane in a discreet corner of the general aviation sector at Palam, partially sedated to calm her hysteria, but as the small plane flew north the emptiness in her arms began to feel like an intolerable burden. The weight of her missing child, the cradled void, was too much to bear. Yet it had to be borne.

The plane reached the Pir Panjal and went into an upward spiral to gain height; then, without warning, it dropped two thousand feet down a hole in the air, and she cried out in terror. Twice it spiralled upwards, twice it fell, twice she shrieked. The Pir Panjal was the gateway to the valley and Boonyi felt as if the gate had been locked against her. The weight of the absent girl had grown so great that the plane could not carry it over the peaks. The mountains were pushing her back, telling her to take her mighty burden and begone. But they would not succeed. She had abandoned her baby so that she could go home and she would not permit the mountains to stand in her way. On the plane's third attempt she summoned all her remaining will and let the phantom baby go. There was no baby, she told herself. She had no baby daughter. She was returning home to her husband and there was no leaden void being carried in her cradling arms. She felt the weight in her lap lessen, felt the aircraft rise. She threw away her lost baby and forced the plane up and over. This time the spiral did not end in a fall and the mountains passed beneath the belly of the little plane, wrapped in a storm. Then the valley rolled out below her wearing its winter ermine. As the plane descended towards Elasticnagar she thought she saw Pachigam, and all the villagers were standing in the main street, looking up at the plane and cheering.

The *Yamuna* had no meal service and the small packed lunch that had been among Peggy Ophuls's farewell gifts was long gone. There was no cabinet of pharmaceuticals aboard and her supplier was gone as well. She felt hungry and crazy. There was no tobacco to chew. She had a craving for offal. There was a scream in her blood. Mighty invisible forces were pulling at her. The shadow planets were at war. Of course the villagers had not been cheering her homecoming. That was a delusion. She was vulnerable to delusions of all kinds, she knew that. Her dependencies were chastising her. She did not know if she could live without the things she needed, the bottled and the cooked. She did not know if she could live without her little girl. When she thought this, the weight crashed back into her lap and the plane's trajectory sagged downwards sharply. She closed her eyes and willed her child away. There was no Kashmira. There was only Kashmir.

"Madam, please to sit." A young soldier with a tumble-tongued Southern name and a smile full of big innocent teeth was waiting for her outside the small wooden arrivals building, seated behind the steering wheel of an army Jeep. Boonyi was wearing the dark phiran and blue head scarf that Peggy Ophuls had given her the day before. The *shahtush* shawl was folded away in her bag. She did not wish to seem ostentatious. She had asked that a kangri of hot coals be ready for her and the driver had it waiting. As she felt the familiar heat against her skin her spirits rose. The world was regaining its ordained shape. Her southern adventure was fading away. Perhaps it had never happened. Perhaps her innocence was still unstained. No, it had happened, but perhaps, at least, the stains would wash out easily, leaving no permanent mark. Boonyi Kaul was back. She had exchanged her baby for a phiran, a head scarf, a shawl, a packed lunch, a Fokker Friendship flight and a Jeep ride. When she thought this, the earth's gravitational force suddenly increased and she was unable to move. She gritted her teeth. *There is no Kashmira.* "Help me," she said, and with her hand in the driver's she hauled herself painfully into the Jeep's passenger seat. The driver was courteous and spoke to her as if she were a visiting dignitary but she was not delusional enough to think of herself in that way.

She had no plan except to beg for mercy. She would go to her village, leaving behind the world of VIP treatment to which she had briefly had access, and she would throw her bloated self at her husband's feet in the snow. At her husband's feet and at his parents' feet and at her own father's feet as well and she would beg until they raised her up and kissed her, until the world went back to being what it had been and the only remaining mark of her transgression was the imprint of her prostrate body in the omnipresent whiteness, a shadow-self which would be obliterated soon enough, by the next snowfall or by a sudden thaw. How could they not take her back when she had sacrificed her own daughter just to have a chance of being accepted? When she thought this, the immense weight, the growing weight of the lost child, thudded into her at once, and the Jeep lurched to the left and stalled. The driver frowned in puzzlement, stared at her briefly, apologized and restarted the car. Boonyi repeated her magic mantra to herself, over and over, *There is no Kashmira, there is only Kashmir.* The Jeep started up and moved forward.

The army was everywhere. She had been allowed to use military facilities so that she could slip out of one sphere of the world into another, so that she could leave behind the public and return to the private. There was reason to doubt whether such slippage was possible any more. As she drove out through the gates of Elasticnagar and was caressed by the shadows of the poplars and chinars lining the road that would take her through Gargamal and Grangussia to Pachigam, she remembered an argument between Anees Noman and his brothers that began when her bomb-making brother-in-law started insisting over dinner that the boundary, the *ceasefire line,* between private life and the public arena no longer existed. "Everything is politics now," he said. "The old comfortable days are gone." His brothers began to tease him. "How about soup?" asked Hameed the firstborn twin. "Is your mother's chicken broth politicized too?" And his secondborn brother Mahmood added, thoughtfully, "There is also the question of hair. The two of us are big hairy bastards who ought to shave twice a day, but you, Anees, are as smooth as a girl and the razor hardly needs to touch your cheek. So is hairiness conservative or radical? What do the revolutionaries say?"

"You'll see," Anees yelled, pounding the dinner table, falling into his brothers' trap and sounding ridiculous, "One day even beards will be the subject of ideological disputes." Hameed Noman twisted his lips judiciously. "Okay, okay," he conceded. "Fair enough. But they better leave my chicken soup alone."

Boonyi on the highway home saw Abdullah Noman's house in her mind's eye, illuminated by memory's golden glow. The patriarch sat at the head of the family table, lips pursed, staring into the distance with an amused twinkle in his eye, pretending to have higher things on his mind while his sons jostled and squabbled and lazy-eyed Firdaus banged a plate of food down in front of him as if challenging him to a duel. Yellow flame flickered in iron lanterns, and drums and santoors and pipes were stacked in a corner near a rack of regal costumery and a hook from which half a dozen painted masks hung down. The twins' loud knockabout act went on as usual and Anees of the dolorous countenance was irritated by it. This irritation, too, was customary. The family was eternal and would not, must not change, and by returning to it she would put it all back the way it had been, she would even heal the quarrel between Anees and her husband Shalimar the clown, and at Firdaus's table they would enjoy the happy ending of such meals together, blessed by the boundless gastronomic largesse of the sarpanch's wife.

As they neared Pachigam it began to snow. "Set me down at the bus stop," she told the driver. "Weather is inclement, madam," he replied. "Better to drop you at your homestead." But she was adamant. The bus stop was the place from which she had departed this life and it was at the bus stop that she would return to it. "Okay, madam," the driver said doubtfully. "Will I wait until they come for you?" But she did not want to be seen with an army man. It was snowing heavily as they turned the last corner. This was the bus stop. There was no sign but that didn't matter. Here was the produce store where her father and the sarpanch sold fruit from their orchards. It was boarded up against the blizzard. "Please, madam," the driver said. "I am fearful for your good health." She still knew how to look at a greenhorn with a hardy village woman's contempt. "The cold is warmth to us," she said. "The snow to me is like a hot shower would be to you. No cause for your concern."

So she was standing by herself in the snowstorm when the villagers first saw her, standing still at the bus stop with snow on her shoulders and snowdrifts pushing up against her legs. The sight of a dead woman who had somehow materialised at the edge of town with her bedroll and bag beside her brought the whole village out of doors, snow or no snow. Everyone was mesmerised by the sight of this stationary corpse that looked as if it had done nothing in the afterlife but eat. It looked like a snow-woman such as a child might build, a snow-woman with the body of the deceased Boonyi inside it. Nobody spoke to the snow-woman. It could be bad luck to speak to a ghost. But the whole village also knew that somebody would have to do some talking sooner or later, because Boonyi didn't know she was dead.

She saw them all through the snowstorm, circling her like crows, keeping their distance. She called out but nobody called back. One by one they approached her—Himal, Gonwati and Shivshankar Sharga, Big Man Misri, Habib Joo—and one by one they receded. Then the principal actors made their entrance, snow crusting their eyebrows and beards. Hameed and Mahmood Noman came arm in arm, giggling peculiarly, as if she had done something odd by returning, something that wasn't really funny. And this was Firdaus Noman, her mother's friend, Firdaus stretching out a hand towards her, then dropping it and running away. Boonyi thought she understood. She was being punished. She was being judged in dumb show and ritually ostracized. But surely they could not go on this way, not in this blizzard? Surely someone would take her in and scold her and give her a hug and something hot to drink?

When her sweet father came hopping awkwardly through the snow she was sure the spell would break. But he stopped six feet away and wept, the tears freezing on his cheeks. She was his only child. He had loved her more than his own life, until she died. If he did not speak now her dead gaze would curse him. A rejected child can place the evil eye upon the parent who spurns her, even after death. In a low voice, a voice she could barely hear over the whistling wind, he murmured superstitious words: *nazaré-bad-door.* Evil eye, begone. Then, slowly, as if struggling against chains, his feet took small steps away from her, and the snow clouded her sight, and he was gone. In his place, finally, was her husband, Noman Noman, who was Shalimar the clown. What was that look on his face? She had never seen such a look before. Humbly she told herself that it was the look she deserved, in which hatred and contempt mingled with grief and hurt and a terrible, broken love. And something else, something she didn't understand. His father the sarpanch was with him, holding him by the arm. His father who held them all in the palm of his hand. Abdullah Noman seemed to be restraining his son, pulling him away from her. And there too was her own father again, putting himself between her husband and herself. Why would he do that. Shalimar the clown was holding something in his fist. Maybe it was a knife, held in the assassin's grip, the reversed blade concealed up the sleeve of his chugha with the haft clenched in his hand. Maybe she would die here beneath her husband's blade. She was ready to die. She fell to her knees in the snow, arms outspread, and waited.

Zoon Misri the carpenter's daughter knelt down beside her. Zoon's olive-skinned Egyptian beauty seemed to belong to another place and time, a hot dry world of deserts and snakes in fig baskets and huge lions with the heads of kings. In happier times she had accentuated her exotic looks with dramatically upturned kohl-lines at the corners of her eyes, but since the assault of the Gegroo brothers she wore no embellishments.

She had grown thinner; her vivid eyes were two burning lamps set in a face of polished bone. "A lot of people around these parts think of me as a living ghost," she said distantly, not looking at Boonyi. "Those people think that when a thing happens to a woman like the thing that happened to me, the woman should go quietly into the trees and hang herself." She smiled faintly. "I didn't do that." Boonyi's spirits lifted slightly. Her friend was with her. Loyalty still existed in the world, even for a traitor such as herself. By her deeds, by sorrowful repentance and right action, she would earn the loyalty of the others again. Zoon's friendship was all the start she needed. She stretched out a hand. Zoon made a tiny negative movement of the head. "It's because I have been treated like this that I can speak," she said. "The living dead can speak to each other, can't they? Otherwise it wouldn't be fair." Now for the first time she looked Boonyi in the eye. "They killed you," she said. "After what you did. They said you were dead to them and they announced your death and they made us all swear an oath. They went to the authorities and filled out a form and got it signed and stamped and so you are dead, and you cannot return. You have been mourned properly for forty days with all correct religious and social observances and so of course you cannot just pop up again. You are a dead person. Your life has been ended. It's official." Zoon was controlling the muscles of her face, and her voice, as well, was strictly disciplined. "Who killed me," Boonyi asked. "Tell me their names." Zoon's silence went on so long that Boonyi thought she was refusing to answer. Then the carpenter's daughter said, "Your husband. Your husband's father. Your husband's mother. And." Boonyi's voice shook as she implored her friend to go on. "Who else?" she pleaded. "You're saying there was someone else."

Zoon turned her face away. "And your father," she replied.

It was snowing harder than ever and the cold was tightening its grip on her body, even through her protective layers of fat, and in spite of the kangri of hot coals nestled against her belly. The storm enclosed her and Zoon; the rest of Pachigam was a white cloud. Boonyi got to her feet to think about this new situation, about the business of being dead. "Can a dead person get shelter from a blizzard," she wondered aloud. "Or is it required that she freeze to death. Can a dead person get something to eat and drink, or must a dead person die all over again, of hunger and thirst.

I'm not even asking right now if a dead person can be brought back to life. I'm just thinking, if the dead speak, does anyone hear them, or do their words fall on deaf ears. Does anyone comfort the dead if they weep, or forgive them if they repent. Are the dead to be condemned for all time or can they be redeemed. But maybe these questions are too big to be answered in a snowstorm. I must be smaller in my demands. So it comes down to this for now. Can a dead person lie down in the warmth or must she find a spade and dig her own grave."

"Try not to be bitter," Zoon said. "Try to understand the grief that killed you. As for your question, my father says you can haunt his woodshed for the night."

The woodshed was weatherproof, at least, and in spite of her demise the Misris made her as comfortable as possible, softening the discomforts of the outbuilding with rugs and blankets. They hung an oil lantern from a nail. The storm abated as darkness fell and Boonyi retreated into her temporary world of wood to face her first night as a dead woman, or, to be precise, as a woman who knew she was no more, because as it turned out her life had actually been terminated for well over a year. The dead have no rights, she knew, and so everything that had formerly belonged to her, from her mother's jewelry to her husband's hand, was no longer in her charge. And there was possibly some danger also. She had heard stories of people being declared dead before, and when these deceased entities tried to return to life and reclaim their assets they were sometimes murdered all over again, in ways that ended all arguments over their status. But those other members of the fellowship of the living dead, the *mritak,* were killed by the greed of their relatives. Her own death was nobody's fault but her own.

In the small hours of night she suddenly heard a familiar voice. Her father was leaning against the outside wall of the woodshed, wrapped up in as many warm garments as he could find, for he was a man who suffered the cold badly. Pandit Pyarelal Kaul addressed the woodshed familiarly, as if it were a living person, or at least a member of the living dead. "Let us speak of the Ocean of Love," Pandit Pyarelal Kaul said to the woodshed through chattering teeth. "That is to say the *Anurag Sagar,* the great work of the poet K-K-K-Kabir." Even in the wretchedness of her death Boonyi entombed within the woodshed could not repress a smile.

"One of the big figures in the *Anurag Sagar* is Kal," her father told the woodshed. "Kal, whose name means yesterday and tomorrow, which is to say, T-T-T-Time. Kal was one of the sixteen sons of Sat Purush whose name means Positive Power, and after his fall he became the father of Brahma, Vishnu and Shiva. This does not mean that our world is born of evil. Kal is a lapsarian figure but he is neither evil nor g-good. Yet it is true that he insists on an eye for an eye and that the demands he makes of us limit us and prevent us from reaching what we have it in ourselves to be."

Her heart leapt for joy and the flame of her lantern burned more brightly because both flame and heart knew that this was Boonyi's father's way of returning to her, of returning her to him. His next sentence, however, allowed the darkness to close in once more. "According to Kabir," the pandit told the woodshed, "only the *m-m-m-mritak,* the Living Dead One, can rid himself of Kal's pain. What does this mean? Some say it should be read thus: only the brave can achieve the Beloved. But another reading is, only the living dead are f-f-f-free of Time."

Hear, O saints, the nature of mritak. I have been away longer than I thought, she told herself. My father the man of reason, my matter-of-fact father, has given in to his mystical streak, his shadow planet, and become some sort of sadhu. The scholarly learning to which the pandit had always added an edge of irony, dispensing his versions of the ancient ideas with a mischievous little smile, was now, it seemed, being offered up without any distancing devices at all. The highest of human aspirations, Pandit Pyarelal Kaul sang to the woodshed, was to live in the world and yet not live in it. To extinguish the fire burning in the mind and live the holy life of total detachment. "The Living Dead One serves the S-S-S-Satguru. The Living Dead One manifests love within her; and by receiving love her life spirit is set free." Boonyi heard the example of the earth. "The earth hurts no one. Be like that. The earth hates no one. Be like that as well." She heard the example of the sugarcane and the candy. "The sugarcane is cut up and crushed and boiled to make the j-j-j-jaggery. The jaggery is boiled to make the raw sugar. The sugar burns to make rock candy. And from rock candy, sugar candy comes, and everyone likes that. In the same way the Living Dead One bears her sufferings and crosses the Ocean of Life t-t-t-towards joy." She understood that her father was teaching her how she must now live; she hated the teaching and anger flared up in her. But she fought it back. He was right, just as Zoon had been right. She had to let go of anger and achieve humility. She had to let go of everything and be as nothing. It was not the love of God she sought, but the love of a particular man; however, by adopting the abnegatory posture of the disciple before the Divine, by erasing herself, she might also erase her crime and make herself what her husband could once again love.

Only a brave soul can do it. The Living Dead Person must control the senses, said the pandit to the shed. She controls the organ of seeing and understands "beautiful" and "ugly" as the same. She controls the organ of hearing and can bear bad words as well as good. She controls the organ of taste and ceases to know the difference between tasty and tasteless things. She does not get excited even if she is brought the Five Nectars. She does not refuse food without salt, and lovingly accepts whatever is served her. The nose, too, she controls. Smells pleasant and unpleasant are as one to her.

"Also controlled is the organ of lust." Pandit Pyarelal Kaul was particularly firm on this point, as if making sure that the woodshed understood that its sinful yearnings must cease. "The g-g-g-god of lust is a robber. Lust is a mighty, dangerous, pain-giving, negative power. The lustful woman is the mine of Kal. The Living Dead One has enlightened herself with the lamp of knowledge. She has drunk the nectar of the Name and merged into the Elementless. When she has done this, lust will be f-f-f-finished." At first she tried to find his true message in the words themselves. At a certain point, however, she began to hear the words beneath the words. The age of reason was over, he was telling her, as was the age of love. The irrational was coming into its own. Strategies of survival might be required. She remembered what he had said when he saw her standing at the bus stop covered in snow. *Nazarébaddoor.* She had mistakenly thought he was averting the evil eye when in fact he had been giving her advice, telling her where to go. The old Gujar prophetess had retreated from the world before she, Boonyi, had been born, and had cursed the future with her last speech. *What's coming is so terrible that no prophet will have the words.* Years later the Gegroo brothers would immure themselves in a mosque for fear of the wrath of Big Man Misri; but

Nazarébaddoor had shut herself away because she feared Kal, the passage of Time itself. She had seated herself cross-legged in the *samadhi* position and simply ceased to be. When the villagers finally plucked up the courage to look inside the hut her body had acquired the fragility of a withered leaf and the breeze from the doorway blew it away like dust. Now it was Boonyi's turn. A dead person who wished to overcome Kal would do well to follow the prophetess's path. And there was another precedent, which Boonyi the former dancing girl did not fail to recall. Anarkali, too, had been immured for indulging a forbidden lust. And the trapdoor and the escape passage that set her free? That was just in the movies. In real life there were no such easy escapes.

Go up the mountain and die properly. If that was her father's message to her then she had no choice but to obey. He was no longer outside the woodshed. The snowstorm had stopped and she was alone. She was a fat cow but she would haul herself up that hill to the prophetess's hut and wait for death to come. There was no end to the list of the things she craved and could no longer have. Food, pills, tobacco, love, peace. She would do without them all. The impossible weight of her absent daughter knocked her flat. As if all the logs in the woodshed had rolled down onto her body. She lay smashed and gasping on the floor. She felt the moorings of her sanity loosen and welcomed the comforting madness. A beautiful day began.

When she emerged from the woodshed she stood knee-deep in whiteness. The wooded hill hung over her like a threat. The meadow of Khelmarg was up there, with its memories of love. And in another direction, in the heart of the evergreen forest, was Nazarébaddoor, the dead awaiting the dead. Each step was an achievement. She was carrying her bedroll and her bag. Her feet her knees her hips all screamed their protests. The snow pushed back against her forward thrusts. Still she went on her slow, thudding way. More than once she fell against the drifts, and getting back to her feet was not easy. Her clothes were wet. She could not feel her toes. Stones hidden beneath the snow cut her feet and buried pine needles stabbed at her. Still she leaned into the slope and forced her legs to move. Speed was unimportant. Motion was all.

She saw Zoon watching her from a distance. The carpenter's daughter stayed about fifty feet away, and never said a word; but she came all the way up the hill with Boonyi. Sometimes she leapt ahead and then stood waiting like a sentinel, an arm upraised to indicate the easiest path. Their eyes never met, but Boonyi, glad of the help, followed her old friend's lead. Her thoughts had lost coherence, which was a mercy. It would have been impossible to climb the mountain with Kashmira's great weight on her back, but her daughter had been mislaid for the moment, somewhere in the jumble of her mother's mind. Boonyi scooped up handfuls of snow and thrust them greedily in her mouth to slake her thirst.

Halfway up the mountain she found a brown paper parcel in her path. Inside it was the miracle of food: a thick circle of unleavened *lavas* bread, a quantity of dum aloo in a little tin container, and two pieces of chicken in another such tin. She wolfed it all down, asking no questions. Then up the hill she went again, the heat of the sun punishing her from above, the cold of the snow from below. Her breath came in long wheezing gulps. The forest circled her, whirling about her and about. She was stumbling now, staggering, not even sure if she was going up or down the wooded slope. Faster and faster the trees spun around her, and then unconsciousness came, like a gift. When she awoke she was propped up against the doorway of a Gujar hut.

In the days that followed her hold on her sanity weakened further, so that it seemed to her that she was the one who was alive and everyone else was dead. The interior of Nazarébaddoor's hut had been cleaned and swept, as if a ghostly presence had known she was coming, and a new mat had been laid on the floor. A fire had been laid and lit and there was dry wood stacked by the side of the fireplace. A pot of bubbling stew, lotus stems in gravy, simmered over the fire, covered by a cheap aluminum plate. There was water in an earthen *surahi* in a corner. The roof of moss and turf was in bad shape, and water from the melting snow kept dripping through, but she would wake at night to hear the scurrying footfalls of ghosts running over the roof like mice, and in the morning there was new turf in place of the old, and there were no more drips. She cried out for her mother. *"Maej."* Her mother Pamposh, nicknamed for the walnut kernel, had come back from the dead to take care of her newly dead child.

When she poked her head out of the hut she thought she saw shadows moving among the trees and she remembered her father's lesson about Haput the black bear, Suh the leopard, Shal the jackal and Potsolov the fox. These creatures were dangerous and maybe they were closing in on her to kill her but they could not be blamed because they were true to their natures. *Only Man wears masks. Only Man is a disappointment to himself. Only by ceasing to need the things of the world and relieving oneself of the needs of the body* and so on. Her body ached with hunger and other needs and her head was not entirely her own but for some reason she was not afraid. For some reason she described the shapes in the trees to herself as guardians. For some reason there was always fresh water in the surahi when she awoke and food left at the door or, once she felt well enough to take short walks, on the fire. For some reason she had not been abandoned. One could not expect to jump back into paradise from hell, she told herself. A purgative period in a middle place was required. Slowly the addictions would leave her body and her mind would begin to clear. In the meantime she had her mother by her side. The snow melted and she went out as far as Khelmarg and the wildflowers were coming out. She picked bunches of *krats,* which could be eaten as a vegetable and was good for the eyes, and *shahtar,* which produced a sweetly cooling effect when mixed with the whey that was left in a pot at her door. On the slopes of the mountain she found the shrub *kava dach,* which helped to purify her blood, and she ate, too, the fruit and leaves of the *wan palak* or goosefoot. The white flowers of the shepherd's purse or *kralamond* were everywhere. She picked it and ate it raw. She gathered *phakazur,* fennel, and daphne, which was *gandalun.* As she ate the blue-flowered *won-hand* chicory and lay down in fields of *maidan-hand* dandelion she felt her life and her mind returning. The flowers of Kashmir had saved her. In her father's orchards the almond trees would be blooming. Spring had come.

After he learned of her infidelity with the American Shalimar the clown sharpened his favourite knife and headed south with murder on his mind. Fortunately the bus in which he had left Pachigam broke down under a small bridge at Lower Munda near the source of the Jhelum at

Verinag. His brothers Hameed and Mahmood, dispatched by their father, caught up with him at the depot, where he was waiting impatiently for the next available carrier. "Thought you could run away from us, eh, little *boyi,*" cried Hameed, the louder and more boisterous of the twins. "No chance. We're double trouble, us." Troop transport vehicles were refuelling all around them and a group of cheroot-smoking soldiers stared idly, and then not so idly—the words *double trouble* had not been well chosen—at the three quarrelling brothers. The army was jumpy. Two nationalist leaders, Amanullah Khan and Maqbool Butt, had formed an armed group called the Jammu and Kashmir National Liberation Front and had crossed the ceasefire line from what they called Azad Kashmir into the Indian sector to launch a number of surprise raids on army positions and personnel. These three argumentative young men could easily be NLF recruits spoiling for a fight. Mahmood Noman, always the more cautious of the twins, said quickly to Shalimar the clown: "If those bastards find that dagger you're carrying, *boyi,* we're all going to jail for good." This was the sentence that saved Boonyi Noman's life. Shalimar the clown burst into loud, fake laughter and his brothers joined in, slapping each other on the back. The soldiers relaxed. Later that afternoon all three Nomans were on a bus back home.

Firdaus Noman looked into the eyes of her betrayed and cuckolded son Shalimar the clown when his brothers brought him back, and was so horrified that she resolved to give up quarrelling forever. Her famous battles with her illustrious husband over the nature of the universe, the traditions of Kashmir and each other's bad habits had entertained the village for years, but now Firdaus saw the consequence of her fractious disposition. "Look at him," she whispered to Abdullah. "He has an anger in him that would end the world if it could."

The sarpanch was in a distracted state of mind. His health had begun to deteriorate. He had started feeling the first twinges of the pain in his hands that would eventually cripple them, leaving them frozen into useless claw-shapes that made it hard for him to eat or hold tools or wash his own behind. As the pain grew so did his feelings of discontentedness. He felt caught in between things, between the past and the future, the home and the world. His own needs were in conflict. Some days he longed for the applause of an audience and regretted the slow decline in the fortunes of the bhand pather thanks to which such gratification was harder and harder to come by, while at other times he yearned for a quiet life, sitting smoking a pipe by a golden fire. Even greater was the conflict between his personal requirements and the needs of others. Maybe he should give up his position as village headman. Maybe one could only be selfless for so long, and after that it was time for a little selfishness. He could not go on forever holding everyone in his hands. His hands were hurting. The future was dark and his light had begun to dim. He needed a little gentleness.

"Treat him gently," Abdullah told Firdaus absently, thinking mostly about himself. "Maybe your love can put out the flame."

But Shalimar the clown withdrew into himself, barely speaking for days at a time except during rehearsals in the practice glade. Everyone in the acting troupe noticed that his style of performance had changed. He was as dynamically physical a comedian as ever, but there was a new ferocity in him that could easily frighten people instead of making them laugh. One day he proposed that the scene in the Anarkali play in which the dancing girl was grabbed by the soldiers who had come to take her to be bricked up in her wall might be sharpened if the soldiers came on in American army uniform and Anarkali donned the flattened straw cone of a Vietnamese peasant woman. The American seizure of Anarkali-as-Vietnam would, he argued, immediately be understood by their audience as a metaphor for the Indian army's stifling presence in Kashmir, which they were forbidden to depict. One army would stand in for another and the moment would give their piece an added contemporary edge. Himal Sharga had stepped into Boonyi's old role and didn't like the idea. "I know I'm not a great dancer," she said petulantly, "but you don't have to turn my big drama scene into some kind of silly stunt just because you have a reason for hating Americans." Shalimar the clown rounded on her so savagely that for a moment the gathered players thought he was going to strike her down. Then he suddenly deflated, turned away and went to squat dejectedly in a corner. "Yes, bad idea," he muttered. "Forget it. I'm not thinking straight just now." Himal was the prettier of Shivshankar Sharga the village baritone's two daughters. She went over to Shalimar the clown and put her hand on his shoulder. "Just try seeing straight instead," she said. "Don't look for what's not here, but look at what there is."

After the rehearsal Himal's sister Gonwati warned her, with the bitter almond of spite souring her words, that her cause was hopeless. "When you stand next to Boonyi you completely disappear," she said, gravely malicious behind the thick lenses of her spectacles. "Just the way I vanish when I'm standing next to you. And in his mind you'll always be standing next to her, a little shorter, a little uglier, with a nose that's a little too long, a chin that's a little too weak and a figure that's too small where it should be big and too big where it should be small." Himal grabbed her sister's long dark plait high up, near her head, and pulled. "Stop being a jealous bitch, four-eyes," she said sweetly, "and just help me catch him like a good *ben* should."

Gonwati accepted the rebuke and put aside her own hopes in the family cause. The Sharga sisters set about plotting the capture of Shalimar the clown's broken heart. Gonwati asked him the name of his favourite dish. He said he had always been partial to a good gushtaba. Himal at once set to work with a will, pounding the gushtaba meat to soften it, and when she offered him the results as a gift "to cheer you up" he immediately popped a meatball in his mouth. A few seconds later the expression on his face told her the bad news, and she confessed that she was famous in her family as the worst cook they had ever known. Next, Gonwati suggested to Shalimar the clown that Himal could replace Boonyi in the tightrope routine they had developed, and which he could not perform without a female aide. Shalimar the clown agreed to teach Himal to walk the wire, but after a few lessons, when the wire was still just a foot off the ground, she confessed that she had always suffered dreadfully from vertigo, and that if she ever stepped out across the air even her desire to please him would not prevent her from falling to her death. The third strategy was more direct. Gonwati told Shalimar the clown that her sister had recently been unlucky in love herself, that a bounder from the village of Shirmal whose name she would not deign to speak had toyed with her affections and then spurned her. "The two of you should comfort each other," she proposed. "Only you can know how she suffers, and only she can come close to grasping the scale of your terrible grief." Shalimar the clown allowed himself to be prevailed upon and accompanied Himal on a moonlit walk by the waters of the Muskadoon. But under the double influence of the moonlight and his beauty poor Himal lost her head and confessed that the Shirmali rascal didn't exist, that he, Shalimar the clown, had always been the man she loved, there was nobody else but him for her in the whole of Kashmir. After this third catastrophe Shalimar the clown kept his distance from the Sharga sisters who continued, nevertheless, to hope.

The idea of declaring Boonyi dead was Gonwati Sharga's brainwave. Gonwati's bespectacled features gave her a look of studious virtue that concealed her sneaky chess-player's nature. "He'll never forget that woman while she's alive," her sister said mournfully after the disaster of the moonlit walk. "God, sometimes I wish she was dead." Gonwati answered, without at first understanding what she was saying, "Hold tight, *ben.* Wishes can come true." In the next few days her purpose revealed itself to her, and then she set about making other people believe they had had the idea all by themselves. Over a family dinner she quoted her sister's sentiment back at her. "If that Boonyi was dead instead of just in Delhi with her American," she said, "then perhaps poor Shalimar could start up his life again." Her father Shivshankar Sharga snorted a deep baritone snort. "In Delhi with an American," he said, thumping the table with his fist, "is what I call as good as dead." Gonwati turned large myopic eyes upon Shivshankar. "You're in the panchayat," she said. "So couldn't you make that official?"

Before the next panchayat meeting Shivshankar sounded out Habib Joo the dancing master on the subject of declaring Boonyi deceased. "She is dead to me," he answered, and then confessed to a guilty sense of responsibility for her misdeed. "It is the skill I taught her that she used to betray us all." That was two out of five. Together they approached Big Man Misri. "I don't know," the carpenter said doubtfully. "Zoon loved her, after all." Shivshankar Sharga found himself arguing the case vehemently. "Don't you want to make it difficult for men to run off with our girls?" he demanded. "After what happened in your household, I'd have thought you'd be the first to go along with our plan." That was three out of five; which left the two fathers, Pyarelal and Abdullah, to persuade. "The sarpanch is so soft-hearted he will be a hard nut to crack," said

Gonwati when her father reported progress a few evenings later. "Trust me, it is Boonyi's own daddy who will agree."

The reason for Gonwati's confidence was her newly forged intimacy with Pandit Pyarelal Kaul. For many months after his daughter's flight south the pandit had been lost in contemplation. His inattention to his duties as head waza of Pachigam had become so noticeable that the junior wazas finally asked him, gently, to stay home on wazwaan days until he felt better. Pyarelal inclined his head and left the world of cookpots and banquets behind. He had loved food all his life but it now seemed like an irrelevance. Alone at home, he prepared as little as possible, ate perfunctorily what was necessary for life, and took no pleasure in it. He meditated for eleven hours every day. The external world had become too painful to be bearable. His daughter's disappearance felt like his wife's second death. Not even the beauty of Kashmir could assuage the agony of a loss that was not only physical but moral. Her absence was bad enough but her immorality was worse. It made her a stranger to him. He felt himself crumbling, as if he were an old building whose foundations had rotted away. He felt a tide tugging at him and knew he was in danger of drowning. Meditating, he could make the sphere of feeling recede and reach out for succor toward the light of philosophy. At some point in his meditations he thought of Kabir.

People said that Kabir had been the child of a virgin birth, circa 1440, but Pyarelal was not interested in such flummery. What was known was that Kabir was raised by Muslim weavers and the only word he knew how to write was *Rama.* This also was relatively uninteresting. The interesting thing was Kabir's concept of two souls, the personal soul or life-soul, *jivatma,* and the divine over-soul, *paramatma.* Salvation was to be gained by bringing these two souls into a state of union. The interesting thing was to let go of the personal and be absorbed into the divine. And if this was a form of death in life, that was merely an external perception. The internal perception of such an achievement would be ecstatic joy.

One day Pyarelal emerged from his meditations to see a young woman sitting on a rock by the Muskadoon and for a confused instant he thought Boonyi had returned. When he realized that it was Gonwati Sharga the singer's daughter he fought down his disappointment and went out to keep her company. "Panditji," she said after a time, "I used to see Boonyi and Shalimar the clown sitting here and forgive me, panditji, but I was a little jealous. I also wanted to hear your brilliant words. I also wished to benefit from your wisdom. Yet I was not your daughter and had to accept my lot." Pandit Pyarelal Kaul was deeply moved. He hadn't known! He had sometimes felt his own daughter was merely humouring him when she sat with her beau and listened to his ramblings. But this girl actually wanted to learn! Gonwati's confession put a smile on Pandit Pyarelal Kaul's face for the first time in months. In the following weeks the girl came to sit at his feet as often as she could and such was the seriousness and sympathy of her attention that he unburdened himself of many of his most private thoughts. Finally she rose from her rock by the river, went over to take Pyarelal's hand in her own, and offered her own version of her sister's advice to Shalimar the clown.

"Don't blame yourself for what's dead," she said, "but thank God for what's alive."

Abdullah Noman could not stand against the *mritak* plan if Boonyi's own father was in favour of it. "Are you sure?" he asked Pyarelal at the next panchayat meeting. They were drinking pink salty tea in the upstairs meeting room at the Noman house. Pyarelal's cup began to rattle against its saucer as he pronounced the sentence of death. "For eleven hours a day," the pandit told his old friend, "I have contemplated the topic of living in the world while also not living in it. Much has become clear to me regarding the meaning of this riddle. Bhoomi my child has chosen the path of death in life. Once she has so chosen I must not cling to her. I choose to let her go. And then," he added, "there is also the question of bringing your enraged son under control."

"They killed you," Zoon Misri told Boonyi in the snowstorm. "They killed you because they loved you and you were gone."

There was a deserted stretch of the Muskadoon just past Pachigam where the river was shielded by foliage from prying eyes. In childhood summers the four inseparable girls, the Sharga sisters, Zoon Misri and Boonyi Kaul, would rush there after school, throw off their garments and dive in. The bite of the water was exciting, even arousing. They screamed and laughed as the river god's cold hands caressed their skin. Then they dried themselves by rolling on the grassy banks and rubbed their hair between the palms of their hands and didn't go home until the evidence of their transgression had dried off. And on winter evenings the four fast friends, along with the rest of the village children, would crowd for warmth into the panchayat chamber upstairs from the Nomans' kitchen and the adults would tell them stories. Abdullah Noman's memory was a library of tales, fabulous and inexhaustible, and whenever he finished one the children would scream for more. The women of the village would take turns to tell them family anecdotes. Every family in Pachigam had its store of such narratives, and because all the stories of all the families were told to all the children it was as though everyone belonged to everyone else. That was the magic circle which had been broken forever when Boonyi ran away to Delhi to become the American ambassador's whore.

On the day she returned to Pachigam, obese, crippled by addictions, covered in snow, her old friends Himal and Gonwati circled her in the blizzard and the emotions they felt did not include any trace of their childhood love. If Gonwati Sharga felt any guilt about the cold-blooded machinations that had led to Boonyi's killing, she suppressed it beneath her anger. "How dare she come back here," she hissed at her sister, "after all the harm she's caused?" But Himal was filled with happiness at the changes in Boonyi's appearance, the advantages of which greatly outweighed the outrage of a dead woman's return to life. "Just look at her," she whispered to Gonwati. "How can he love her now?"

The terrible truth, however, was that Himal Sharga's failure to seduce Shalimar the clown had nothing whatsoever to do with his continuing feelings of love for his treacherous wife. The truth was that Shalimar the clown had stopped loving Boonyi the instant he learned of her infidelity, stopped dead like an unplugged automaton, and the immense crater left behind by the destruction of that love had at once been filled by a sea of bile-yellow hatred. The truth was that even though he had been brought home from Lower Munda by his brothers he had sworn an oath on the bus that he would kill her if she ever returned to Pachigam, he would cut off her lying head, and if she had any bastard offspring with that sex-crazed American he would show them no mercy, he would cut off their heads as well. The main reason Pyarelal Kaul had supported the idea of his daughter's death by official decree, and Abdullah Noman had gone along with the plan, was that the bureaucratic killing of Boonyi was the only way of holding back Shalimar the clown from committing a horrible crime. The two fathers worked hard to persuade the abandoned husband that there was no need to think about decapitation when a person was already deceased. Shalimar had been doubtful about the *mritak* plan at first. "If we all agree to lie," he had argued, "then how are we better than her?" Abdullah and Pyarelal argued with him without sleeping for three days and two nights and when all three of them were dying with exhaustion the two fathers managed to persuade Shalimar the clown to accept the compromise, made him swear that he accepted it as a full settlement of his legitimate grievance, but in his secret heart he knew that the day would come when his two oaths would come into conflict, his two shadow planets, the dragon's-head Rahu-oath that obliged him to murder her and the dragon's-tail Ketu-oath that obliged him to let her live on, to the degree that dead people can and sometimes do, and he was unable to foretell which of the two promises he would break.

To lay a trap for himself as well as Boonyi he went on writing letters to her, those same letters which had angered her and led her to despise him for his weakness, letters whose purpose was to fool her into believing that he was ready to forgive and forget, and whose deeper purpose was to bring matters to a head, to bring her back and to force him to choose between his oaths, so that he could find out what sort of a man he really was. And then there she was at the bus stop in a blizzard, coated in adipose tissue and covered in snow, and without stopping to think he ran towards her with his knife in his hand, but the two fathers blocked his way, grabbing him by the dragon's tail and reminding him of his vow. They circled her in the thickly falling snow, and Pyarelal Kaul told Shalimar the clown, "If you try to break your word you will have to kill me on the way to her," and Abdullah Noman confirmed, "You will have to kill me as well." This was when Shalimar the clown solved the riddle of the two oaths. "In the first place," he said, "the oath I made to the two of you was my personal promise to you, and so I will respect it as long as even one of you is alive. But the oath I made to myself was a personal promise as well, and when you are both dead you will no longer be able to hold me back. And in the second place," he concluded, turning to go without so much as a nod in the direction of his dead wife, "keep the whore out of my sight." The snow kept falling, thickly falling, upon all the living and the dead.

The spring was an illusion of renewal. Flowers blossomed, baby calves and goats were born and eggs burst open in their nests, but the innocence of the past did not return. Boonyi Kaul Noman never went back to live in Pachigam. For the rest of her life she inhabited that hut on the pine-forested hill where a prophetess had once decided that the future was too horrible to contemplate and had waited cross-legged for death. She slowly became competent in practical matters, but her hold on reality grew correspondingly more erratic, as though something inside her refused to grasp that the world in which she was getting to be so self-sufficient would never turn back into the one she wanted, the one in which she could fold her husband's love around herself while also wrapping him up in hers. Her phantom mother was now her perpetual companion, and as Pamposh's ghost did not age the two dead women became more and more like sisters. When Pyarelal Kaul visited his daughter to warn her against visiting the village because it was all he and Abdullah could do to hold back Shalimar the clown when she was out of sight, and it was impossible to guarantee her safety if she came down to Pachigam, she replied with the gaiety of madness, "I'm fine here with Pamposh. Nobody can lay a finger on me while she is by my side. You should stay with us. Neither of us ladies is allowed in the village, it seems, but the three of us could have a high old time up here by ourselves."

Faced with the derangement of his beloved daughter, Pandit Pyarelal Kaul entered into a darkness of his own. He climbed the mountain every day to care for her needs and listen to her ramblings and was not able to tell her of the disillusion that had taken hold of his own optimism and squeezed it almost to death. The love of Boonyi and Shalimar the clown had been defended by the whole of Pachigam, had been worth defending, as a symbol of the victory of the human over the inhuman, and the dreadful ending of that love made Pyarelal question, for the first time in his life, the idea that human beings were essentially good, that if men could be helped to strip away imperfections their ideal selves would stand revealed, shining in the light, for all to see. He was even questioning the anticommunalist principles embodied in the notion of *Kashmiriyat,* and beginning to wonder if discord were not a more powerful principle than harmony. Communal violence everywhere was an intimate crime. When it burst out one was not murdered by strangers. It was your neighbours, the people with whom you had shared the high and low points of life, the people whose children your own children had been playing with just yesterday. These were the people in whom the fire of hatred would suddenly light up, who would hammer on your door in the middle of the night with burning torches in their hands.

Maybe *Kashmiriyat* was an illusion. Maybe all those children learning one another's stories in the panchayat room in winter, all those children becoming a single family, were an illusion. Maybe the tolerant reign of good king Zain-ul-abidin should be seen—as some pandits were beginning to see it—as an aberration, not a symbol of unity. Maybe tyranny, forced conversions, temple-smashing, iconoclasm, persecution and genocide were the norms and peaceful coexistence was an illusion. He had begun to receive political circulars to this effect from various pandit organizations. They told a tale of abuse that went back many hundreds of years. *Sikander the iconoclast crushed Hindus the most.* The crimes of the fourteenth century needed to be avenged in the twentieth. *Saifuddin crossed all limits of cruelty.* Saifuddin was the prime minister under Sikander's son, Alishah. *Out of the fear of conversion Brahmins jumped into the fire. Many Brahmins hanged themselves to death, some consumed poison and others drowned themselves. Innumerable Brahmins jumped to death from the mountains. The state was filled with hatred. The supporters of the king did not stop even a single person from committing suicide.* And so on, all the way up to the present day. Maybe peace was his opium pipedream, in which case he was as much of an addict in his own way as his poor daughter, and he, too, needed to go through a painful cure.

He forced such forebodings to the back of his mind and nursed his daughter. The delirium of her withdrawal symptoms worsened, and for long periods she shook convulsively and sweated ice and her mouth was full of needles and her hungers felt like wild beasts that would gobble her up if they weren't given what they really wanted. Then slowly the crisis passed, until she was no longer at the mercy of the chemicals she could no longer have; and her tobacco habit, too, was broken. During the hallucinatory period of her helplessness she knew that the guardians in the trees were taking care of her. Gradually they emerged from the shadows, and in her groggy condition she imagined her mother Pamposh leading them to her, her daring, independent mother who did not judge people for giving in to their sexual urges. Pamposh's ghost was at least as substantial to her daughter as the others who visited her, and although she recognized among her angels her own father above all, and Firdaus Noman and Zoon and Big Man Misri as well, it made her happy to believe that her beloved mother was actually running the show.

Pyarelal blamed himself for her obesity. "Poor girl inherited my physique and not her slim mother's," he chastised himself inwardly. "Even as a child she was buxom. No wonder Shalimar the clown fell for her when she was still a child. Food was my weakness and this, too, I passed on to her." But his body had changed as a result of his new ascetic's régime, and her body changed as well. Her beauty returned slowly, as her physical health improved. The months lengthened into years and the fat fell away—nobody around here was going to help her eat seven meals a day!—and she looked like herself again. Some damage remained. She suffered from backaches. Black veins stood out on her legs and in some places the skin hung off her more loosely than it should have. The tobacco's discoloration of her teeth never entirely faded, even though she was assiduous in the use of the neem sticks with which her father kept her supplied. She intuited, from occasional spells of arrhythmia, that her heart had been damaged, too. Never mind, she told herself. It was not her destiny to grow old. It was her destiny to live among ghosts as a half-ghost until she learned how to cross the line. She said this aloud once and her father burst into tears.

Her self-sufficiency was hard won. The food addiction was as painful to break as the chemical dependencies, but in the end her attitude to all things edible became less rapacious. For a long time her father and the other friendly villagers continued to provide her with essential supplies, and she learned how to supplement them. She began to grow her own vegetables. One day she found a pair of young goats tethered to a post outside the hut. She learned how to raise them and as time passed her flock grew. It became possible for her to sell goats' milk, and other things. Her father carried a metal milk-churn down the hill to the store every day, and tomatoes in season. This was a small rehabilitation. People accepted the idea of paying real money to buy things from the dead. Her days were filled with physical labour and as long as she was using her body the madness was held at bay. Her body strengthened. Muscles made their appearance in her buttocks, arms and legs. Her shoulders hardened and her belly flattened out. This third-phase Boonyi was beautiful in a new way, the bruised, life-hardened, imperfect way of an adult woman. It was her reason that had been bruised most deeply and at night those bruises still hurt. At night, when the day's work was done, when it was time for the mind to take over from the body, her thoughts ran wild. Some summer nights, she was sure, Shalimar the clown prowled in the trees around the hut. On those nights she deliberately went outdoors and took off all her clothes, challenging him to love her or kill her. She could do this because everybody knew she was mad. Her mother Pamposh came out with her and they danced naked in the moon like wolves. Let a man try to approach them! Let him only dare! They would rip him to shreds with their fangs.

She was right; Shalimar the clown did sometimes climb the hill, knife in hand, and watch her from behind a tree. It comforted him to know she was there, that when he was released from his oath she would be right there to kill, defenceless, just as his life had been defenceless when she ruined it, defenceless and vulnerable just as his heart had once been, defenceless and vulnerable and fragile just like his shattered capacity for trust. Dance, my wife, he told her silently. I will dance with you again one day, for one last time.

Shalimar the clown decided he had to murder the American ambassador at some point not long after the end of the Bangladesh war, around the time that the Pachigam bhands went north to perform near the ceasefire line which had just turned into the Line of Control; that India and Pakistan signed the agreement at Simla which promised that the status of Kashmir would be decided bilaterally at a future date; that the Indian military tightened its choke hold on the valley—because tomorrow was for politicians and dreamers but the army controlled today—and stepped up the toughness of its approach to the majority population; and that Bombur Yambarzal's wife bought the first television in the locality and set it up in a tent in the middle of Shirmal. Ever since the commencement of television transmissions at the beginning of the 1960s the panchayat of Pachigam had taken the view that as the new medium was destroying their traditional way of life by eroding the audience for live drama, the one-eyed monster should be banned from their village. The waza of Shirmal, however, was swept along by the entrepreneurial spirit of his bride, the red-haired widow Hasina "Harud" Karim, a woman with a strong desire for self-improvement and two secretive sons, Hashim and Hatim, who had learned the electrician's trade in Srinagar and were keen to bring the village into the modern age. "Give everyone a free show for a couple of months," Hasina Karim urged her new husband, "and after that you can start charging for tickets and nobody will argue about the cost."

To finance the purchase of the black-and-white set she sold some pieces of wedding jewelry from her first marriage. Her sons, who, like her, were of a practical cast of mind, made no objection. "You can't watch soap operas on a necklace," Hashim the elder pointed out reasonably. The two brothers were not close to Bombur Yambarzal but not opposed to their mother's new husband either. "If we know you are not lonely then it liberates us to follow our own paths, about which it's better that you don't know too much," Hatim the younger explained. He was a tall young fellow but his mother reached up and ruffled his hair affectionately as if he were a toddler. "I taught my boys good sense," she said proudly to Bombur Yambarzal. "See how well they calculate life's odds?"

Once the Yambarzals' TV soirées got going in Shirmal, evening life changed, even in Pachigam, whose residents proved perfectly willing to set aside the long history of difficulties with their neighbours in order to be able to watch comedy shows, music and song recitals, and exotically choreographed "item numbers" from the Bombay movies. In Pachigam as well as Shirmal it became possible to talk about any forbidden subject you cared to raise, at top volume, in the open street, without fear of reprisals; you could advocate blasphemy, sedition or revolution, you could confess to murder, arson or rape, and no attention would be paid to what you said, because the streets were deserted—almost the entire population of both villages was packed into Bombur the waza's bulging tent to watch the damn-fool programmes on "Harud" Yambarzal's shining, loquacious screen. Abdullah Noman and Pyarelal Kaul were among the few who refused to go, Abdullah for reasons of principle and Pyarelal on account of the bitter, deepening depression that had spread outwards from his physical person to affect his immediate surroundings, hanging in the enclosed air of his empty home like a bad smell. Some days it would shrivel the riverbank flowers as he walked by. Some mornings it would curdle his milk supply.

Firdaus was itching to see the new marvel but ever since Boonyi's return she had been working mightily to change her behaviour and avoid quarrelling with Abdullah, no matter how great the provocation. So after the labours of the day were over she remained grumpily but uncomplainingly at home. After a few days, however, Abdullah couldn't bear the nightly pressure of her silent frustration any more. "Damn it, woman," he expostulated, burbling the water violently in his hubble-bubble pipe, "if you want to walk a mile and a half to sell your soul to the devil, I don't want to stand in your way." Firdaus leapt to her feet and put on her outdoor clothes. "What you mean to say," she told Abdullah with majestic self-control, "is, 'Dear wife, after all your hard work, you deserve to go off and have a little fun, even if I am such an old curmudgeon that I've forgotten what fun is.' " Abdullah gave her a hard look. "Exactly," he agreed in a new, cold voice, and turned his face away.

All the way over to Shirmal, Firdaus was thinking about that new voice and its shocking coldness. She had given this man her life because of his gentle manner and his air of caring for everyone's well-being. She hadn't minded, or had taught herself not to mind, that he had never pampered her, never remembered her birthday, never brought her a bunch of wildflowers plucked by his own hand. She had learned to accept the solitude of her marital bed, had resigned herself to a lifetime of sleeping beside a man whose most prolonged and enthusiastic sexual performance had been less than two minutes in duration. She had admired his concern for their children and for the community whose shepherd he was, and had ignored or at least tried to understand his corresponding lack of interest in the needs and desires of his wife. But something had changed in him since the claw disease began to cripple his hands; his compassion for others had diminished as his self-pity increased. True, he had restrained Shalimar the clown from committing a vile crime; but perhaps that was a last twitch of the dying personality of the old Abdullah, the Abdullah whose gifts were tolerance, moral rectitude and great personal warmth, in whose place this new, crippled Abdullah seemed to be showing up more and more often. In a cold country no woman should live with a cold man, she told herself as she arrived in Shirmal, and her amazement at having considered the possibility of leaving her husband was so great that she failed to pay attention to the miracle of the television broadcast which she had walked all this way to witness, until the news bulletin began.

The evening news bulletin, the least interesting programme of the night because of the deadening and often fictionalizing effect of heavy government censorship, usually emptied the tent. People went outside to smoke beedis, joke and gossip. Although men and women sat together inside the Yambarzal auditorium as equal members of the great national television audience, they separated when they emerged, and stood in separate groups. But Firdaus Noman joined neither group; she was a first-timer and remained in her place. An Indian Airlines Fokker Friendship called *Ganga* after the great river had been hijacked by Pak-backed terrorists, two cousins called Qureshi, who had absconded across the border to Pakistan. The cousins Qureshi had allowed the passengers to leave, then blown up the plane and surrendered to the Pak authorities who had gone through the pretence of jailing them but had refused to entertain Indian requests for extradition. It was manifestly plain that the archterrorist Maqbool Butt who now based himself in Pakistan with the full connivance and collusion of the Pak leadership was behind the exploit. Zulfikar Ali Bhutto had visited the terrorists in Lahore, described them as freedom fighters, and declared that their "heroic action" was a sign that no power on earth could stop the Kashmiri struggle. He further promised that his party would contact the Kashmiri National Liberation Front to offer its cooperation and assistance, which would also be given to the hijackers themselves. Thus the Pak régime's entanglement with terrorism was proved for all the world to see. After some sort of show trial, the report conjectured, the bounders would doubtless be released as heroes. However, the Indian government's resolve would never weaken. The state of Jammu and Kashmir was an integral part, et cetera et cetera, the end. When the audience charged back into the tent at the end of the news Firdaus stood up and told them about the hijacking, whereupon an extraordinary thing happened. Members of the minority community unanimously condemned the treacherous Qureshi cousins and their leader Maqbool Butt's desire to destabilize the situation in Kashmir, while members of the majority cheered the hijackers loudly and drowned out the angry Hindus' protests. There was no trace of a Shirmal-Pachigam divide, no distinction between male and female opinion, only this deep communal rift. The Muslim majority eyed their Hindu pandit opponents with a sudden distrust that crept uncomfortably close to open hostility. Yet a few minutes earlier they had been smoking and gossiping together outside the tent. It was suddenly oppressive to be there in that ugly crowd. Wordlessly, as if some sort of vote had been taken, every member of the pandit community rose up and left the tent. Firdaus remembered Nazarébaddoor's last prophecy—"what's coming is so terrible that no prophet will have the words to foretell it"—and her appetite for further TV entertainment disappeared.

The Shirmal-Pachigam road was a humble country lane, rutted and dusty, running along a *bund* or embankment a few feet higher than the fields on either side; and it was lined with poplar trees. Shalimar the clown was waiting for Firdaus near the midway point of her journey home. He had not been in the television tent; in fact, he had been away for several weeks, because the bhands of Pachigam had been hired by the state government's cultural authorities to provide entertainment in one of the world's least entertained areas, the villages and army bases to the immediate south of the de facto border drawn through the broken heart of Kashmir. Abdullah, nursing his damaged hands, had told his talented son to take charge of the troupe. "You'll have to do it eventually," the sarpanch had said in a clipped voice stripped of all emotion, "so you may as well start up right now in that godforsaken part of the world in front of our brutalized countryfolk and those Indian soldiers for whom I can't find the words without using language I do not care to employ in front of my children." Abdullah's politics were changing like the rest of him. These days he was disillusioned with the Indian government, which kept putting his namesake, the leader Sheikh Abdullah, in jail, then doing secret deals with him, then reinstalling him in power on the condition that he supported the union with India, then getting irritated all over again when he started talking about autonomy in spite of everything. "Kashmir for the Kashmiris, and everybody else, kindly get out," Abdullah Noman said, echoing his hero. "Because if we get protected by this army for much longer we're going to be ruined for good."

It was a moonless night and Shalimar the clown was wearing dark clothes and had been lying low in the fields and he jumped up in front of Firdaus like a poplar coming to life and scared her. "I've been asleep," he said. She understood at once that her son wasn't speaking literally but was telling her that he'd arrived at a turning point in his life, which was why she didn't interrupt him even though he was on fire, speaking to her in the foulmouthed language his father had refused to use, the speech of a man who has started dreaming of death. A cold wind was slicing through her heart. "I've been wasting my time," Shalimar the clown continued. "All I ever learned how to do is walk across a rope and fall over like an idiot and make a few bored people laugh. All that is becoming useless and not just because of the stupid television. I've been looking at bad things for so long that I'd stopped seeing them, but I'm not sleeping now and I see how it is: the real bad dream starts when you wake up, the men in tanks who hide their faces so that we don't know their names and the women torturers who are worse than the men and the people made of barbed wire and the people made of electricity whose hands would fry your balls if they grabbed them and the people made of bullets and the people made of lies and they are all here to do something important, namely to fuck us until we're dead. And now that I've woken up there is something important I need to do also and I don't know how to go about it. I need you to tell me how to get in touch with Anees."

Their dark phirans flapped in the night wind like shrouds. "Be glad you're not a mother in these times," she answered him. "Because if you were you would be happy that your two quarrelling sons were about to be reunited but at the same time you would be filled with the fear that both children would probably end up dead, and the conflict of that happiness and that terror would be too much to bear."

"Be glad you're not a man," he retorted. "Because once we stop being asleep we can see that there are only enemies for us in this world, the enemies pretending to defend us who stand before us made of guns and khaki and greed and death, and behind them the enemies pretending to rescue us in the name of our own God except that they're made of death and greed as well, and behind them the enemies who live among us bearing ungodly names, who seduce us and then betray us, enemies for whom death is too lenient a punishment, and behind them the enemies we never see, the ones who pull the strings of our lives. That last enemy, the invisible enemy in the invisible room in the foreign country far away:

that's the one I want to face, and if I have to work my way through all the others to get to him then that is what I'll do."

Firdaus wanted to beg and plead, to ask him to forget about the monsters in his waking dream, to set aside thoughts of the vanished American, and to forgive his wife and take her back and be happy with life's blessings, such as they were. But that would make her an enemy too and she didn't want that. So she agreed to do what Shalimar the clown required, and the next evening after working all day in the fruit orchards she walked to Shirmal again and this time when the news bulletin began she got up and followed Hasina Yambarzal outside, tugging at her shawl to indicate that she wanted a private word. At first, when Firdaus told the waza's wife what she wanted, Hasina feigned bewilderment, but Firdaus raised the palm of her right hand to indicate that the time for subterfuge was past. "Harud, excuse me," she said, "but stop, please, your bullshit. I don't know you as well as I should, but I already know you better than your husband does, who is too besotted with love to see you straight. I recognize the pain in your eyes because I have the same pain in mine. So tell your sons the secretive electricians that when next they run into my son the wood-whittler, my boy who was always so clever with his hands, they should mention that his brother wants to be friends with him again." The other women were gathered around a brazier of hot coals and began to throw curious glances in their direction, so they started laughing and giggling as if they were sharing risqué confidences about their husbands the waza and the sarpanch. Hasina Yambarzal's eyes were not laughing, however. "The resistance isn't a social club," she giggled, putting her hands over her mouth and widening those calculating eyes as if she had just been told something really awful. "I'm not a fool, madam," chuckled Firdaus severely. "And Anees will surely understand what I mean." One of her eyes was lazy but the brightness in it was unmistakably energetic. Hasina shut up fast, nodded and went back into the tent to watch TV.

The next morning Firdaus demanded that Abdullah accompany her into the saffron field where, many years earlier, she had disported herself with the young Pamposh Kaul. Here, far from imprudent ears, she told her husband that an evil demon had gotten into their son Shalimar the clown up there in the frozen north, near the Line of Control. "He just wants to kill everyone now," she told Abdullah Noman. "His wife, okay, that was a problem before, but now it's also the philandering ambassador, and the whole army, and I don't know who else. So either a djinni has taken him over or else it has been hiding inside him all this time, as if he was a bottle waiting for someone to uncork him, and either that's what Boonyi did when she came back from the American or something happened to him when he was far from home. *Hai-hai,*" she wailed. "What did my son ever do wrong, to be captured by the devil?"

"That's not a devil talking, it's his manhood," Abdullah Noman told her, without tenderness. "He's still young enough to have the idea that he can change history, whereas I am getting accustomed to the idea of being useless, and a man who feels useless stops feeling like a man. So if he is fired up by the possibility of being useful, don't put out that flame. Maybe killing bastards is what the times require. Maybe if my hands still worked I would strangle a few myself."

Discord had entered Pachigam, never to depart. Abdullah Noman did not tell his wife that relations between himself and Shalimar the clown were at a low ebb, partly because the sarpanch hadn't liked the look of eagerness in his son's eyes when the opportunity to replace his father as leader of the bhands had presented itself, but mostly because of the creepy feeling that Shalimar the clown was waiting for Abdullah and Pyarelal Kaul to die, so that he could be released from his oath. These days the two sexagenarians didn't speak much. Abdullah had started mentioning the word *azadi,* but to Pyarelal the word didn't mean freedom but something more like danger, and it made a difficulty between the two old friends. They did their work and thought their thoughts and came together for panchayat meetings, after which Pyarelal went back to his home at the far end of the village and stayed there staring at the burning pinecones in the fire. But Abdullah Noman knew that the pandit had the same problem as himself with the watchful stare of Shalimar the clown; it was like being watched by a vulture or a carrion crow. It was like being watched by Death himself. So if Shalimar the clown wanted to go off into the mountains with Anees and the liberation front fighters, maybe that wasn't such a bad thing on the whole, let the fellow go and do what he had to do, even if the liberation front was still a bunch of comedians trying to find out how to live up to their name.

Two weeks later, Shalimar the clown went to Shirmal to watch television and during the news-bulletin cigarette break he stood by a coal brazier with his back to the secretive electricians and got the instructions he had been waiting for. Hatim and Hashim pretended to be talking to each other about the beauties of the high pine meadow of Tragbal, located at twelve and a half thousand feet above sea level and looking down on the Wular Lake, and agreeing that it would be at its loveliest soon after midnight tomorrow. Shalimar the clown walked away from them without commenting, and went into Bombur Yambarzal's tent to join in the furious argument that had broken out in there on account of Hasina Yambarzal's announcement that from now on an admission fee would be charged, a small fee, the merest token, because life was not a charity, after all. People should respect what the Yambarzals were doing for them, and the tickets would be a sign of that respect. After she said this people began shouting in a way that didn't sound respectful at all, whereupon that incisive and pragmatic lady bent down, picked up the electric cable and broke the connection. That shut everyone up at once, as if she had pulled out their plugs as well, and her very sensible sons came in with brass bowls and went around the audience gathering low-denomination coins. Shalimar the clown paid up, but when the soap opera returned to the screen he left without watching what happened to the weeping heroine in the clutches of her wicked uncle. He was all done with weeping heroines. He was going to the Wular Lake to enter the world of men.

Shalimar the clown left Pachigam the next morning carrying nothing but the clothes he stood up in and the knife in his waistband and was not seen again in the village for fifteen years. Above the shining shield of the Wular Lake and just below the Tragbal field he met his future on a hillside strewn with boulders. His future took the shape of a pair of men with woollen hats pulled low over their eyes and scarves wrapped around the lower parts of their faces. One of these men was whittling a wooden bird. Another was Bombur Yambarzal's stepson, Hashim Karim. There was a third man standing behind a rock, and that was the man who mattered. "You wished to see your brother," the man behind the rock said.

"Your brother is here." Anees's knife went on whittling wood without pausing. "This would be touching," said the man behind the rock, "if we were in the business of being touched. Or maybe it would be funny, if we were in the laughing business. Why don't you tell me what I'm doing here listening to a crummy play-actor who wants to play an action hero for real, and maybe a martyr as well." Shalimar the clown remained calm. "I need to learn a new trade," he said. "And you're going to need people with those skills as time goes by." The man behind the rock thought about this. "What I hear," he said, "is that you've been talking big to anyone who'll listen about all the people you intend to wipe out, including the former American ambassador. That sounds like clown behaviour to me." Shalimar's face tightened. "For now and until freedom comes I'll kill anyone you want me to," he said, "but yes, one of these days I want the American ambassador at my mercy."

There was a grunt from behind the rock. "And I want to be the king of England," the invisible man said. Then there was a long silence. "Okay," said the man behind the rock. A longer silence followed. Shalimar the clown turned to his brother, who shook his head. "In some minutes," said Anees Noman, "it will be our turn to leave." "Am I coming with you?" asked Shalimar the clown. His brother's whittling knife paused for one brief beat.

"Yes," he said. "You're coming."

Before they left that hillside Shalimar the clown went behind a boulder to relieve himself. Only after the hot stream died away did he look down and see the enormous snake, the king cobra, lying coiled under the rock, an inch away from the puddle. During his exploits with the liberation front he often thought about that sleeping serpent, which reminded him of his mother Firdaus's superstitions. "Snake luck," he said one day to his brother as they crouched behind a rock near Tangmarg waiting for an army troop convoy to pass over the mines they had laid in the steeply ascending road. "I must have snake luck on my side. It's a good sign." Anees Noman's habitual melancholy was deepened by this excavated memory of a mother he feared he might never see again, but he disguised his sadness and twisted his face into a rueful smile. "Anyway," Shalimar the clown whispered further, "it's what we do. I mean, pissing on a snake. If that snake had woken up that night, I'd be a dead man now. But this snake, the one we keep pissing on, it's awake all right, awake and wet and mad."

Anees chewed the end of a beedi gloomily. "Just aim for its mother-fucking eyes," he said. His vocabulary had been coarsened by the years. "If you piss hard enough maybe you'll drill a hole in its sisterfucking head."

In those days before the crazies got into the act the liberation front was reasonably popular and *azadi* was the universal cry. Freedom! A tiny valley of no more than five million souls, landlocked, preindustrial, resource rich but cash poor, perched thousands of feet up in the mountains like a tasty green sweetmeat caught in a giant's teeth, wanted to be free. Its inhabitants had come to the conclusion that they didn't much like India and didn't care for the sound of Pakistan. So: freedom! Freedom to be meat-eating Brahmins or saint-worshipping Muslims, to make pilgrimages to the ice-lingam high in the unmelting snows or to bow down before the prophet's hair in a lakeside mosque, to listen to the santoor and drink salty tea, to dream of Alexander's army and to choose never to see an army again, to make honey and carve walnut into animal and boat shapes and to watch the mountains push their way, inch by inch, century by century, further up into the sky. Freedom to choose folly over greatness but to be nobody's fools. *Azadi!* Paradise wanted to be free.

"But free isn't free of charge," Anees Noman told his brother in his sad-sack way. "The only paradise that's free that way is a fairy-tale place full of dead people. Here among the living, free costs money. Collections must be made." Though he didn't know it, he sounded exactly like Hasina Yambarzal announcing to the villagers of Shirmal and Pachigam that they needed to start paying to watch TV.

The first phase of Shalimar the clown's initiation into the world of the liberation front involved him in the group's fund-raising activities. The first principle of this work was that operatives working in the financial field could not be sent back to their own localities, because fund-raising was sometimes no joke and such humourlessness never went down well with one's own folks. The second principle was that as it was a well-established fact that the poor were more generous than the rich it was proper to be more so to speak persuasive when dealing with the rich. It was not necessary to spell out the precise nature of such persuasion. Each operative could be trusted to devise the tactics best suited to the situation. Shalimar the clown, a member of his brother's financial team, a man newly awakened to rage and ready for extreme measures, prepared himself to threaten, slash and burn.

However, Abdullah and Firdaus Noman had raised their sons to be courteous at all times, and even though Shalimar the clown had been possessed by a devil his brother Anees had not. When they arrived, at twilight, at a large lakeside mansion at the edge of Srinagar whose gloomy look perfectly matched Anees's own, the lady of the house, a certain Mrs Ghani, informed them that her husband the affluent landowner was not at home; whereupon Anees decided it would be improper for half-a-dozen armed men to enter a decent lady's home when the man of the house was absent, and announced that he and his colleagues would wait for her husband Mr Ataullah Ghani outside. They waited for four hours, hunkered down outside the servants' entrance with their rifles rolled up inside scarves, and Mrs Ghani sent out hot tea and snacks. At length Shalimar the clown insubordinately expressed his anxiety. "The level of risk is unacceptable," he said. "The lady could have telephoned the security forces many times by now." Anees Noman stopped whittling wood into owl shapes and raised an admonitory finger. "If it is our time to die, then we shall die," he replied. "But we will die as men of culture, not barbarians." Shalimar the clown subsided into sullen silence, fingering the edge of his blade inside the folds of his cloak. One of the hardest things about becoming a freedom fighter was having to accept his brother's seniority in the organization.

After four and a half hours Mr Ghani returned and came out to smoke a pensive cigarette with the financial committee on the back stoop. "This house," he said, "belonged to my late paternal Ghani-uncle, the well-known Andha Sahib, the blind philanthropist who lived to the great age of one hundred and one, God be praised, and died only three years back. Perhaps you have heard about him? His personal life was a great tragedy, a poor reward for all his generosity, because he lost his beloved daughter, his only child, who moved to Pakistan and then died there in '65 in consequence of Indian aerial bombing during that foolish war. Before Andha Sahib this was the residence of other eminent members of my family for a hundred and one years more. There is a collection of European paintings of quality. There is a picture of Diana the Huntress that is particularly fine. If you care to see it I will gladly conduct a tour. Also naturally there is my wife and there are my daughters. I thank you for respecting the sanctity of the house and the honour of my womenfolk. To express my gratitude, and in the blessed memory of Naseem Ghani, the child of this house and my personal cousin whom the Indian air force bombed to death in her own kitchen in Rawalpindi on September 22, 1965, I will assure you of the following sum, to be paid at quarterly intervals."

The sum named was large enough to make it difficult for the liberation fighters to continue to look impassive. There were muffled gasps behind their woollen hoods. Afterwards, as they retreated into the shadows, Shalimar the clown looked shamefaced about his earlier fears, but Anees Noman had the grace not to rub it in. "Srinagar isn't like back home," he said. "It takes time to acquire local knowledge. Where the backing is, where it isn't, where it needs a little encouragement of the type you're itching to provide. You'll get the hang of it soon enough."

It was not possible to go home. A system of billets was in operation. The brothers Noman were assigned a series of temporary lodgings with families who sometimes welcomed them, at other times had to be coerced into housing such potentially dangerous guests and treated them with a mixture of anger and fear, barely speaking to them except when absolutely necessary, locking up their marriageable daughters, and sending the younger children to live elsewhere until the peril had passed. Anees and Shalimar the clown stayed with a friendly family working in the trout hatcheries of Harwan, and with passionate supporters in the Srinagar silk industry; in a hostile household of pony-wallahs and farmhands near the famous spring of Bawan, sacred to Vishnu, with its holy tank bursting with hungry fish, and in an even more threatening encampment of limestone miners near the Manasbal quarry, a billet they abandoned after a single night because they both dreamed the same dream, a nightmare of being killed in their sleep, of having their skulls crushed by angry men with rocks in their fists. They slept for a season in an attic room in the home of a terrified truck driver's family in Bijbehara near the tourist village of Pahalgam. This was the neighbourhood in which the spy Gopinath Razdan had been murdered some years earlier, after leaking the news of Boonyi's liaison with Shalimar the clown. It was therefore a region of which the Nomans had some prior knowledge. Shalimar the clown felt oddly homesick here. The fast-flowing Liddar reminded him of the smaller Muskadoon, and the lovely mountain meadow of Baisaran above Pahalgam, where Razdan had actually been killed, called to mind flower-carpeted Khelmarg, where his great and lethal love had been consummated. The devil inside him was aroused by the memory of his faithless wife, and murder again filled all his thoughts.

Another summer the brothers stayed among kindly people, the Hanji and Manji tribal boatmen who rowed and punted their craft down the myriad waterways of the valley, gathering *singhare,* water chestnuts, on the Wular Lake, or working market gardens on Lake Dal, or fishing, or dredging for driftwood in the rivers. When a boatman ferried passengers on his craft the brothers Noman sat huddled up at the back of the vessel with their faces wrapped up in shawls. At other times, on the big boats, they pitched in and worked as hard as their hosts. Poling a boat carrying seven thousand pounds of grain from lake to lake was a hard day's work. By night, after so effortful a day, the brothers gathered with the boating families at the kitchen end of one of the giant covered boats with its barrel-thatched roof and ate meals of highly spiced fish and lotus root. The boatman with whom they stayed longest was the unofficial patriarch of the Hanji tribe, Ahmed Hanji, who not only resembled an Old Testament prophet but believed that his people were the descendants of Noah, and that their boats were the pygmy children of the ark. "Boat's the best place to be right now," he philosophized. "Another flood's coming, and God knows how many of us will be drowned this time." "That's the trouble with this damn country of ours," Anees Noman muttered to his brother when they lay down to sleep that night. "Everyone's a prophet."

All the men in the liberation front were afraid almost all the time. There were not enough of them, the security forces were hunting them down, and in every village there were stories of families shot to death on suspicion of having harboured insurrectionists, stories that made it harder to recruit new members or to gain the support and assistance of the frightened and downtrodden population. *Azadi!* The word sounded like a fantasy, a children's fable. Even the freedom fighters sometimes failed to believe in the future. How could the future begin when the present had such a stranglehold on everyone and everything? They feared betrayal, capture, torture, their own cowardice, the fabled insanity of the new officer in charge of all internal security in the Kashmir sector, General Hammirdev Kachhwaha, failure and death. They feared the killing of their loved ones in reprisal for their few successes, a bridge bombed, an army convoy hit, a notorious security officer laid low. They feared, almost above all things, the winter, when their high-ground encampments became unusable, when the Aru route over the mountains became impassable, when their access to arms and combat supplies dwindled, when there was nothing to do but wait to be arrested, to sit shivering in loveless garrets and dream of the unattainable: women, power and wealth. When Maqbool Butt himself was arrested and jailed, morale hit an all-time low. Butt's old associate Amanullah Khan ended up in exile in England.

The resistance changed its name and became the JKLF, four initials instead of five, "Jammu and Kashmir Liberation Front" without the "National," but it made no difference. The Kashmiris of England, in Birmingham and Manchester and London, could dream on about freedom. The Kashmiris of Kashmir were shivering, leaderless and very close to defeat.

In the old stories, love made possible a kind of spiritual contact between lovers long separated by necessity or chance. In the days before telecommunications, true love itself was enough. A woman left at home would close her eyes and the power of her need would enable her to see her man on his ocean ship battling pirates with cutlass and pistol, her man in the battle's fray with his sword and shield, standing victorious among the corpses on some foreign field, her man crossing a distant desert whose sands were on fire, her man amid mountain peaks, drinking the driven snow. So long as he lived she would follow his journey, she would know the day-by-day of it, the hour-by-hour, would feel his elation and his grief, would fight temptation with him and with him rejoice in the beauty of the world; and if he died a spear of love would fly back across the world to pierce her waiting, omniscient heart. It would be the same for him. In the midst of the desert's fire he would feel her cool hand on his cheek and in the heat of battle she would murmur words of love into his ear: *live, live.* And more: he would know her dailiness too, her moods, her illnesses, her labours, her loneliness, her thoughts. The bond of their communion would never break. That was what the stories said about love. That was what human beings knew love to be.

When Boonyi Kaul and Shalimar the clown first fell in love they didn't need to read books to find out what it was. They could see each other with their eyes closed, touch each other without making physical contact, hear each other's endearments even when no word was spoken aloud, and each would always know what the other was doing and feeling, even when they were at opposite ends of Pachigam, or dancing or cooking or acting away from each other in distant no-account towns. A channel of communication had been opened then, and though their love had died the channel was still functioning, held open now by a kind of anti-love, a force fuelled by strong emotions that were love's dark opposites: her fear, his wrath, their belief that their story was not over, that they were each other's destiny, and that they both knew how it would end. At night in his appointed city garret, or on a straw bed in a stinking country barn, or aboard a lurching boat wedged in between sacks of grain, Shalimar the clown went looking for Boonyi in his mind, he prowled through the night and found her, and at once the fires of his rage flared up and kept him warm. He nursed this heat, the hot coals of his fury, as if in a kangri next to his skin, and even when the fight for freedom was at its lowest ebb this dark flame kept his will strong, because his own goals were personal as well as national, and would not be denied. Sooner or later two deaths would release him from his vow and make possible a third. Sooner or later he would find his way to the American ambassador as well and his honour would be avenged. What happened after that was unimportant. Honour ranked above everything else, above the sacred vows of matrimony, above the divine injunction against cold-blooded murder, above decency, above culture, above life itself.

There you are, he greeted her every night. *You can't get away from me.*

But he couldn't get away from her either. He spoke to her silently as if she were lying by his side, as if his knife were at her throat and he were confessing his secrets to her before she took them to her grave, he told her everything, about the finance committee, the billeting, the impotence, the fear. It turned out that hatred and love were not so very far apart. The levels of intimacy were the same. People heard him murmuring in the dark, his fellow fighters heard him and so did his hosts, but the words couldn't be made out, and nobody cared anyway, because all the other fighters were murmuring too, talking to their mothers or daughters or wives and listening to their replies. The murderous rage of Shalimar the clown, his possession by the devil, burned fiercely in him and carried him forward, but in the murmurous night it was just one of many stories, one small particular untold tale in a crowd of such tales, one minuscule portion of the unwritten history of Kashmir.

He said: *Don't leave that hut, the place of your exile, or you will release me from my oath and I will return, I will certainly know and I will certainly return.*

She said: *I'll stay here and wait and I know you will return.*

He said: *This terrible time, this in-between time in which we have all been dying of doing nothing, is coming to an end. I am going over the mountains. Here I am, in the mountains. I am taking the Tragbal Pass. Above me stands Nanga Parbat the mighty peak that veils its face in storm clouds and spits lightning at all who dare to pass it by. On the far side of the mountains is freedom, the part of Kashmir that is free. Gilgit, Hunza, Baltistan. Our lost places. I am going to see what Kashmir looks like when it's free, when its face is not veiled in tears.*

He said: *I quarrelled with Anees again. I spoke of our Pak allies and told him I would put my trust in them and in our common God and he called me a liar and a whore who wants to be fucked from both ends, from behind and in front at the same time. He has a filthy mouth these days. He is against Pakistan and doesn't want to talk about religion. He laughed in my face when I spoke of my faith and told me I didn't know what faith was if I could be faithless to my own brother. I said there was a higher allegiance and he laughed in my face again and said maybe I could fool everyone else but I couldn't fool him that all of a sudden I had turned into some kind of fire-eater for God. He speaks like an old man. I don't care about the old ways any more. I want to drive the army bastards out and our enemy's enemy is our friend. He said no, our enemy's enemy is our enemy too. But he knows as well as I do that many of our comrades are going over the mountains. His own boss is leaving him and coming with me. He is with me now. I am in the mountains now. I left my brother behind but I am with my brothers. Anees and I parted on bad terms which I regret. He says he knows he will not live to be an old man but who wants to be old in hell. I am wearing dark green gumboots and inside them I have wrapped my legs in a woollen blanket torn in half. I am wearing everything warm I could find but there is no hot coal for my kangri. They gave me a polythene coat and pants to put over it all. Over the mountain there are training camps. Over the mountain there are comrades and weapons and money and political backing. Over the mountain I will find the rainbow's end.*

He said: *There are six of us climbing the paths. The invisible commander, Anees's boss, says he has no regrets. We have left Anees behind, left him to his outmoded ways, and are heading towards the future. The insurgency is divided; very well then, it is divided. We are throwing in our lot with the radicals over the mountains. The name of the invisible commander is Dar, but there are ten thousand Dars in Kashmir. He says his people were from Shirmal originally. I don't know any Dars in Shirmal. We all make ourselves up now, we don't have to be ourselves any more. He trained as a junior cook, he says, but he has been with the resistance almost from the beginning, almost from childhood. He learned invisibility early and now nobody sees him unless he chooses to let himself be seen. I see his bundled clothes pulled tightly around him, his goggles, the ice crusting his beard. His face is a mystery. He is younger than I am, he says. In the mountains people confide in one another. We whisper our secret lies. We may die at any minute, from the cold, from a bullet. From a frozen bullet. I call him Doorway, Dar-waza, put his name and his old job side by side and that's what they mean. I call him Naked Mountain because like Nanga Parbat he never shows his face. They say that on those rare days when the mountain unveils herself she is so beautiful that she blinds all who see her. Perhaps my Doorway-Darwaza, my Naked Mountain of a leader, is also an exceptionally handsome man, whose beauty blinds. At any rate he will be my door into the next place. Over the mountains I will be trained and my power will increase. I will meet men of power and draw power from them. I will learn the subtle arts of deception and deceit of which you are already a mistress and I will perfect the art of death. The time for love is past. We may die at any minute. The Indian troops know the routes we use and maybe they are lying in wait. We are going in dead of winter when only crazy people would go because maybe they will not be watching. It is too cold. It is impossible to cross the mountains. We are crossing the mountains. We are impossible. We are invisible and impossible and we are going over the mountains to be free.*

Boonyi talked to herself too, about mountain passes and danger and despair. Zoon Misri came up to visit her and heard her friend muttering about the return of the iron mullah and the survival of the rapist brothers, and began to tremble. The basket she had brought Boonyi as a gift, with home-baked breads and kababs wrapped in a cloth, fell from her hand. She ran all the way down the hill to Pyarelal's house by the stream. "The longer she stays up there in Nazarébaddoor's hut, the more she begins to sound like some kind of crazy Gujar prophetess herself," she wept. "Only she's turning into some sort of curse-giving Nazarébad, just the evil eye without the begone."

Pyarelal tried to console her. "People who spend a lot of time alone do begin to talk to themselves," he said. "It means nothing. She probably doesn't know she's doing it." Zoon went on sobbing. "No, she is crazy, she really is," she insisted, her tongue loosened by emotion. "She talks to Shalimar the clown as if he was sitting right beside her, talks to him about how he's going to kill her—as if it was some small unimportant thing, you know?—as if it was lovers' talk, can you imagine?—sweet nothings about death. Hai-hai! She asks where he's going to stab her first and how many times and what-all—how can a person ask such questions and react as if the answers excited her, as if excuse me ji they aroused her?—and now she's started saying worse things, things that will be the death not only of her but of me as well." What things are those, Pyarelal tried to ascertain, but Zoon just shook her head and wept. There were words she could not say, names she could not bring herself to speak. *The Gegroo brothers are alive and so is Bulbul Fakh.* That was the sentence which would end her life if spoken in Pachigam. As long as it only hung in the air in a madwoman's hillside hut it might be possible for Zoon Misri to survive. "I can't visit her any more," she told Pyarelal. "Don't ask me to say why. It's too dangerous for me up there, that's all."

Boonyi said: "They have crossed the Tragbal Pass. No Indian soldiers were lying in wait for them and they have safely crossed. Men have come to meet them and one of these men is Maulana Bulbul Fakh. The iron mullah has placed them under his protection. He lives in Gilgit and plots his triumphant return. The three Gegroos are with him. They were sealed up in the Shirmal mosque like Anarkali but there was a secret passage just like in *Mughal-e-Azam.* They escaped into the woods and went over the mountains and waited for their time."

Pyarelal asked her: "How do you know these things?" It was winter, so they were huddled round the fire in her hut. The goats were in the barn he had helped her build. He heard the clanking of the small brass bells around their necks. His daughter was in a condition not unlike a trance. She was at once there in the hut and somewhere else as well. She could hear what he was saying but she was also listening elsewhere. She said: "My husband tells me. He has crossed the mountains to meet the iron mullah. The iron mullah says that the question of religion can only be answered by looking at the condition of the world. When the world is in disarray then God does not send a religion of love. At such times he sends a martial religion, he asks that we sing battle hymns and crush the infidel. The iron mullah says that at the root of religion is this desire, the desire to crush the infidel. This is the fundamental urge. When the infidel has been crushed there may be time for love, although in the iron mullah's opinion this is of secondary importance. Religion demands austerity and self-denial, says Bulbul Fakh. It has little time for the softnesses of pleasure or the weaknesses of love. God should be loved but that is a manly love, a love of action, not a girlish affliction of the heart. The iron mullah preaches to many hundreds of men from many parts of the world. They are preparing for war."

Pyarelal asked: "How does your husband tell you this?"

She answered: "He speaks to me as you speak. He is full of fire and death. When you and the sarpanch are no more he will come here for his honour."

"This then is a part of what he says," her father needed to know.

"This is the reason we are able to speak," she replied. "This is our bond that cannot be broken." She fell sideways and was unconscious. Pyarelal caught her and laid her gently down to sleep. "Then I will never die," he whispered to her sleeping body. "I will live forever and he will never be released from his oath."

This was not how things were supposed to go, according to the old story. In the old story Sita the pure was kidnapped and Ram fought a war to win her back. In the modern world everything had been turned upside down and inside out. Sita, or rather Boonyi in the Sita role, had freely chosen to run off with her American Ravan and willingly became his mistress and bore him a child; and Ram—the Muslim clown, Shalimar, misplaying the part of Ram—fought no war to rescue her. In the old story, Ravan had died rather than surrender Sita. In the contemporary bowdlerization of the tale, the American had turned away from Sita and allowed his queen to steal her daughter and send her home in shame. In the ancient tale, when Sita returned to Ayodhya after defending her chastity throughout her captive years, Ram had sent her back into forest exile because her long residence under Ravan's roof made that chastity suspect in the eyes of the common people. In Boonyi's story, she too had been exiled to the forest, but it was the people—her friend Zoon, her father, even her father-in-law—who had helped her and saved her life, deflecting her husband's vengeful knife, making him swear an oath; after which, and at the wrong time, her husband went off to war, and she knew that for him the battle was a form of waiting, that he would fight other enemies, slay other foes, until he was free to return and take her unfaithful life.

But it was something more than that. It was also a way of being with her. While he was away his thoughts returned to her and they could commune as they once had. And even if his thoughts were murderous this prolonged communion often felt, strongly felt to her, like love. All that remained between them was death, but the deferment of death was life. All that remained between them, perhaps, was hatred, but this yearning hatred-at-a-distance was surely also one of love's many faces, yes, its ugliest face. She began to entertain fantasies of earning his forgiveness and winning back his heart. In the great old book Sita had called upon the gods to defend her virtue, stepping into a fire and emerging from it unscathed; and she had asked the underworld to open so that she could depart from this world in which her innocence was not enough, and the gates of the underworld did open, and she went down into darkness. If she, Boonyi, set fire to herself no god would protect her. She would burn and the forest would burn with her. Accordingly, she lit no fire. Once in despair she did ask the gates of hell to open in the earth below her feet, but no cavity yawned. She was already in hell.

The iron mullah Maulana Bulbul Fakh was their appointed superior. His breath was still the sulfurous dragon-breath that had earned him his stinky name, *fakh,* and he still spoke in the old harsh way, as if human speech were painful to him, but he was taller than Shalimar the clown remembered, a giant over six feet tall, and also leaner and much more beautiful than in the old days in Shirmal. Was it possible that he had grown bigger and more attractive with the passing years? As for his being made of iron, there could no longer be any argument about that. There were places on his shins and shoulders where the knocks of a hard life had rubbed away the covering of skin and the dull metal beneath had become visible, battle hardened, indestructible. These proofs of his miraculous nature gave Bulbul Fakh great authority in the camps over the mountains. He carried a lump of rock salt at all times. "This is Pakistani salt," he told the liberation front commander and his men. "This we will bring to Kashmir when we set it free." He wrapped the salt in a green handkerchief and put it away in a bag. "The green is for our religion which makes all things possible. God willing," he said. "With the blessing of God," they replied.

The iron mullah led them to a "forward camp", known as FC-22, a front-line facility of the Markaz Dawar centre for worldwide Islamist-jihadist activities set up by Pak Inter-Services Intelligence. FC-22 in those early days was a shithole. There were few pukka buildings—the only sleeping accommodation was in filthy, patched-up tents—and not enough food or warmth. However, there were staggering quantities of weapons available, and there were ISI personnel on hand to offer training in the use of these weapons, including high-precision sniper-killer training. There were firing ranges with moving targets and instructors who would push the new recruits in the back or jog their elbows at the same time as ordering them to fire, and they had to learn not to miss, because hitting a moving target when they were off balance was what they were being taught. There were weekly seminars about, and real-time training exercises in, high-speed, guerrilla-style strike-and-withdraw operations across the Line of Control. There was a bomb factory and a course in fifth-column infiltration technique, and above all there was prayer.

The five daily prayers at the camp *maidan* were compulsory for all the fighters and the only book permitted at the site—training manuals excepted—was the Holy Qur'an. In between formal prayers there was much discussion of God by foreigners speaking in languages which Shalimar the clown did not understand, in which only the word for God stood out. Maulana Bulbul Fakh was his guide to weaponry and foreigners alike. But before he was ready to embark on the great work at hand his consciousness had to be altered. Shalimar the clown was asked to make certain revisions in his worldview. "It is not possible to shoot straight," Bulbul Fakh said bluntly, "if the way you see things is all screwed up."

Ideology was primary. The infidel, obsessed with possessions and wealth, did not grasp this, and believed that men were primarily motivated by social and material self-interest. This was the mistake of all infidels, and also their weakness, which made it possible for them to be defeated. The true warrior was not primarily motivated by worldly desires, but by what he believed to be true. Economics was not primary. Ideology was primary.

The iron mullah took upon himself the task of reeducating all newcomers. It was a part of his gift to the revolution, a part of God's work. Shalimar the clown sat on a boulder by a frozen mountain stream and listened to the iron mullah as once he had listened to Pandit Pyarelal Kaul while longing for the simple happiness of Boonyi's touch. But that happiness had proved to be an illusion, a deception, and Shalimar the clown's memory of being deceived made the iron mullah's lessons easier for him to accept.

Everything they thought they knew about the nature of reality, about how things worked and what things were, was wrong, the iron mullah said. That was the first thing for the true warrior to understand.—*Yes,*

Shalimar the clown thought, that's right, everything I thought I knew about her was a mistake.—The visible world, the world of space and time and sensation and perception in which they had believed themselves to be living, was a lie.—*Yes, that's so.*—Everything that seemed to be, was not.—*Yes.*—By crossing the mountains they had passed through a curtain and stood now on the threshold of the world of truth, which was invisible to most men.—*Thank God, thought Shalimar the clown. Truth. At last. Truth that endures. Truth that will never become a lie.*—In the world of truth, the iron mullah preached, there was no room for weakness, argument, or half measures. Before the power of truth, every knee must bow, and then truth will protect you. Truth will keep your soul safe in the palm of its mighty hand.—*In the palm of its hand.*—Only the truth can be your father now, but through the truth you will be fathers of history.—*Only the truth can be my father.*—Only the truth can be your mother now, but when the truth has won its victory all mothers will bless your names.—*Only the truth can be my mother.*—Only the truth can be your brother, but in the truth you will be a brother to all men.—*Only the truth can be my brother.*—Only the truth can be your wife.—*Only the truth can be my wife.*

Time itself was the servant of truth, the iron mullah told them. Years could pass in an instant, or a moment could be infinitely prolonged, if the truth were best served by doing so. Distance, too, was as nothing in the eye of truth. A journey of a thousand miles could be accomplished in a single day. And if time and distance could be moved and changed, if these great things were the malleable disciples of truth, then how much more easily moulded was the human self! If the so-called laws of the universe were illusions, if these fictions were no more than the fabric of the veil behind which truth was concealed, then human nature was an illusion also, and human desires and human intelligence, human character and human will, would all bow to truth's imperatives once the veil was removed. No man could face the naked truth, defy it and survive.

The new recruits listening to the iron mullah felt their old lives shrivel in the flame of his certainty. The invisible commander who called himself Dar from Shirmal even though there were no Dars in Shirmal leapt up suddenly and flung off his woollen balaclava-style hat, his polythene outer garments, his woollen waistcoast, his gumboots, the woollen blanket-strips wrapping his feet, his grey sleeveless V-neck woollen jumper, his long khaki-coloured woollen kurta and pyjamas, his socks and his underpants, and stood before Bulbul Fakh stripped and ready for action. "I have no name," he cried loudly, "except the name of truth. I have no face but the face you choose for me. I have no body but the one that will die for the truth. I have no soul but the soul that is God's." The iron mullah came to him and gently, as a father might, helped him to dress again. "This warrior," Bulbul Fakh tenderly announced when the man whom Shalimar the clown thought of as Naked Mountain was fully clothed once more, "has put off the garments of the lie and put on those of truth. He is ready for the war."

While the invisible commander was naked, Shalimar the clown had understood how young he was: probably only eighteen or nineteen years old, young enough to be prepared to erase himself in a cause, young enough to make himself a blank sheet upon which another man could write. For Shalimar the clown the total abnegation of the self was a more problematic requirement, a sticking place. He was, he wanted to be, a part of the holy war, but he also had private matters to attend to, personal oaths to fulfil. At night his wife's face filled his thoughts, her face and behind hers the face of the American. To let go of himself would be to let go of them as well; and he found that he could not order his heart to set his body free.

"The infidel believes in the immutability of the soul," said Bulbul Fakh. "But we believe that all living things can be transformed in the service of the truth. The infidel says that a man's character will decide his fate; we say that a man's fate will forge his character anew. The infidel holds that the picture of the world he draws is a picture we must all recognize. We say that his picture means nothing to us, for we live in a different world. The infidel speaks of universal truth. We know that the universe is an illusion and that truth lies beyond the illusion, where the infidel cannot see. The infidel believes the world is his. But we shall drive him from his redoubts and cast him into darkness and live in Paradise and rejoice as he plunges into the fire."

Shalimar the clown rose to his feet and tore off his garments. "Take me!" he cried. "Truth, I am ready for you!" He was a trained performer, a leading actor in the leading bhand pather troupe in the valley, and so of course he could make his gestures more convincing, and imbue his journey towards nakedness with more meaning, than any eighteen-year-old youth. He stripped off his shirt and shouted out his acquiescence—"I cleanse myself of everything except the struggle! Without the struggle I am nothing!"—he screamed his assent—"Take me or kill me now!"—and stripped off his undergarments. The passion of his avowals made an impression on the iron mullah. "We knew that those who chose to make the arduous winter journey over the Tragbal Pass must have been driven from within to do so," he said. "But in you the desire burns more fiercely than I had thought." He helped Shalimar the clown put his clothes back on, to dress himself in garments transformed by his shedding of them into the raiment of belonging. When he was fully clothed again Shalimar the clown prostrated himself at the feet of Bulbul Fakh, and almost believed his own performance, almost believed that he was no longer what he was and could indeed leave the past behind.

Later that day, however, he was accosted at the mess table by a little Far Eastern–looking guy with an almost absurdly innocent face, a man in his late thirties who looked ten years younger, who seemed to shine with some sort of crazy internal light, and who spoke enough broken Hindi to make himself understood. The little guy asked politely, "Okay? I sit? Okay?" Shalimar the clown shrugged and the little guy sat down. "Moro," he said, tapping his own chest. "Filipino Muslim. From Basilan, Mindanao. You can say this?" Shalimar the clown went along with it. "Basilan, Mindanao," he said. The little guy applauded. "Was fisherman there, son of fisherman," he said. "Janjalani, Abdurajak Abubakar. This also you can say?" "Janjalani," repeated Shalimar the clown. "Not fish long. Fish stink. Fish rot from head. Filipino state stink like rotten fish. Join Moro National Liberation Front," Janjalani said in his faltering Hindi. "But broken away. Join al-Islamic Tabligh, good movement. Cash from Saudi, also Pakistan. Send me to school West Asia. Which is, you say, Mideast." Shalimar the clown twisted his mouth to show he was impressed. "You're far from home," he suggested. "Study. Learn," said the little man. "Saudi Arab. Libya. Afghanistan. Study at the Base. You know the Base? Brother Ayman, brother Ramzi, Sheikh Usama. Learn many good thing. Field-strip rifle, I learn. Ambush I learn. Kidnap I also learn. Extortion, bombing, assassination. Fight Russian, kill Russian. Good education." He laughed heartily. "Education in person's character I have already. So I see through you, sir. I see through you like window. You are not man of God." Shalimar the clown's body tightened and he calculated the speed at which he could draw his knife and attack if an attack became necessary. "No, no, sir," the little man replied in mock alarm. "Peace, please. I here in observer capacity only. Noncombatant status. Ha! Ha! Full respect, please. Man of God in his place, fighter killer in his. Man of God inspire. Man of war do. Combination person of Bulbul Fakh style very rare. You not combination person I think. You act combination person to please iron Bulbul but really you a fighter killer. It is okay. I however am combination person like Bulbul, same same. Fighter, also *ustadz.* Preacher. It is my fate."

Everyone's story was a part of everyone else's. Shalimar the clown at forward camp 22 befriended the luminous little man who had fought with Afghans and al-Qaeda against the Soviet Union, who had accepted U.S. arms and backing but loathed the United States because American soldiers had historically backed the settlement of Catholics in Mindanao against the wishes of the local Muslims. The majority Muslim population of seven million people had been pushed into increasingly cramped and crowded living conditions to make room. Basilan, the small island to the southwest of the main Mindanao island, was a place of grinding poverty where gun law had begun to rule. The Christians controlled the economy and the Muslims were kept poor. "In seventies big war. One hun'red thou, hun'red twenty thou die. Then peace deal, then MNLF split, MNLF-MILF, then fight again. Hate Filipino government. Hate also U.S.A. U.S. secret ambassador comes to the Base to give weapons and support. I hold my fire but in my heart I want to kill this man." When Shalimar the clown heard the ambassador's name he sat bolt upright at the refectory table. "Abdurajak, my friend," he said, his voice trembling because of his discovery, "this man I also want to kill."

"Let me know if I can help," the Filipino revolutionary said.

Sometimes, now, she did not hear his voice for weeks, even months. In the night she reached out for him but found only a void. He had gone beyond her

reach and she could only wait for him to return, not knowing if she wanted him to return so that she could preserve her dream of a happy ending, or if she wished him dead because his death would set her free. But he always returned in the end, and when he did it seemed that in his life only a single night had passed, or at the very most two or three. Years of her life were vanishing but in the place from which he called to her, time ran at a different speed, the space around him took a different shape. She did not know how to tell him everything that was happening in Pachigam. There was no time. Increasingly, however, he wanted only to send her the message of himself, of the fire that continued to burn in him, and the only question to which he needed an answer was the old, macabre one: Are they dead yet? But Abdullah Noman and Pyarelal Kaul were alive, though their years, too, were rushing by during his weeks. In his time, he wouldn't have long to wait.

The Russians were in Afghanistan and consequently many Afghans had fled to Pakistan, and were even to be found at forward camp number 22 in the "free"—Azad—sector of Kashmir. In spite of the enormous numbers of refugees occupying huge, town-sized camps in the Pak northwest, the Afghans were not poor. There were extensive opium fields in the vicinity of the camps and the refugee chieftains bought their way into the poppy business, using the gold and jewelry they had brought across the border for capital and backing it up with menaces and guns. Once they had gained control of the poppy fields they instituted a system of double-cropping so that they could produce heroin as well as opium. The income from the heroin was large enough to pay off the Pak authorities and to pay for the costs of the refugee camps as well. The authorities turned a blind eye to what was going on in the poppy fields because it prevented the refugees from becoming a burden on the state and besides there were the payoffs, which were generous.

The Afghans had freedom fighters of their own, and the United States decided to support these fighters against its own great enemy, which had occupied their country. U.S. operatives in the field—CIA, Counter-Terrorism and Special Units personnel—took to referring to these fighters as the Muj, which sounded mysterious and exciting and concealed the fact that the word *mujahid* meant the same thing as the word *jihadi*, "holy warrior". Weapons, blankets and cash poured into northern Pakistan, and some of this aid did reach the Muj. Much of it ended up in the arms bazaars of the wild frontier zone, and a percentage of it reached Azad Kashmir. After a while the fighters gathering in Pakistani-controlled Kashmir started calling themselves the Kashmiri Muj. The ISI provided them with powerful long-range missiles which had been intended for the Afghan front, but had unfortunately been diverted along the way. Other high-quality arms also began to appear at FC-22: automatic grenade launchers of Soviet and Chinese origin, rocket pods with solar-powered timing devices that made possible delayed-firing rocket barrages, 60-mm mortars. At a certain point Stinger missiles, SAMs, were also made available to the "Kashmiri Muj". Weapons training took up much of every day. The chief instructor was an Afghan war buddy of Janjalani the Filipino's, a black-turbanned warrior from Kandahar who called himself simply Talib, meaning "the student". The word for knowledge was *taleem.* Those who acquired knowledge were scholars: *taliban.* Talib the student was a mullah of a sort, or, at least, had been trained at a religious school, a madrasa. Like the iron mullah Bulbul Fakh, however, he never mentioned the name of his seminary. Talib the Afghan had lost an eye in battle and wore a black patch. As a result he had been temporarily withdrawn from the front line, but he was determined to return to combat duties as soon as possible. "In the meanwhile," he said, "God's work can be done here also."

Talib the Afghan's one eye bored through Shalimar the clown and seemed to read his thoughts, to see the pretence there as Janjalani had, the untold, forbidden secret. Janjalani understood his reasons but Shalimar the clown feared Talib would not. He felt like a fraud and feared exposure constantly. He had not surrendered his self as he had been required to do, had hidden it deep beneath a performance of abnegation, the greatest performance he had ever given. He had his own goals in life and would not give them up. *I am ready to kill but I am not ready to stop being myself,* he repeated many times in his heart. *I will kill readily but I will not give myself up.* But his goals did not officially exist, not in this dangerous place. "You were an actor," Talib the Afghan said scornfully in bad, heavily accented Urdu. "God spits on actors. God spits on dancing and singing. Maybe you are acting now. Maybe you are a traitor and a spy. You are fortunate I am not the one in charge of this camp. I would immediately order the execution of all entertainers. God spits on entertainment. I would also order the execution of dentists, professors, sportsmen and whores. God spits on intellectualism and licentiousness and games. If you hold the rocket launcher like that it will break your shoulder. This is the way to do it."

Shalimar the clown thought at first that he understood one-eyed Talib's rage, thought it was the anger of the wounded warrior deprived of war, of the doer forced to be a teacher. Later he revised his opinion. Talib's rage was not a side effect. It was his reason for being. An age of fury was dawning and only the enraged could shape it. Talib the Afghan had become his wrath. He was a student, a scholar of rage. Of all other learning he was contemptuous but he was wise in the ways of anger. It had burned through him and now it was all that remained: the rage, and his attachment to Zahir, the boy he had brought with him from Kandahar, his protégé, disciple and lover. A warrior of Kandahar, like some ancient Greek, would take such a boy for a time, make a man of him and let him go. Zahir the Boy slept in Talib's tent and looked after his weapons and attended to his normal, nocturnal needs. But this was not homosexuality. This was manliness. Talib the Afghan was in favour of executing homosexuals, those unnatural effeminates upon whom God expectorated most violently of all.

Shalimar the clown forged a friendship of sorts with Zahir, who often seemed lonely and scared, and whose need to confide was great. Zahir spoke of Kandahar, of parents and friends, of his closed, destroyed school, of his love of kite flying and horses, and of what he had seen of blood and terrifying death. It was from Zahir the Boy that Shalimar received, by the merest chance, news of the man he wanted to kill more than any other man on earth. "The Americans bring us weapons to kill the Russians," Zahir said. "Thus even the infidel can be made to do the work of God. They send their important people to deal with us and think of us as allies. It is amusing." Ambassador Max Ophuls, who these days was supporting terror activities while calling himself an ambassador for counterterrorism, had been in charge of liaison with Talib the Afghan's branch of the Muj. A tiger leapt up inside Shalimar the clown whenever he heard that name, and caging it again was hard. Talib's one eye would have seen that leap and suspected it at once, but Zahir the Boy was too wrapped up in the past to see what was going on under his nose.

Our lives touch again, Shalimar said silently to the ambassador. *Maybe the gun I'm holding was brought to this region by you. Maybe one day it will point at you and fire.* But he knew he did not want to shoot the ambassador. His weapon of choice had always been the knife.

He was ready for battle. Winter was dissolving into spring and the mountain pathways were becoming passable. The forward bases were filling up with men. FC-22 was bursting at the seams with men with the snarling, spittle-flecked manner of attack dogs straining to be unleashed. New groups were appearing every day, or so it seemed: Harakats, Lashkars, Hizbs of this or that, martyrdom or faith or glory. The word was that Amanullah Khan had come to Pakistan from England to assume command of the JKLF. Shalimar the clown went through his daily routine, the fitness regimen, the commando training, the weapons work, and wondered what it would be like to kill a man. Then the iron mullah asked him if he would like to go abroad.

The weight of her lost daughter still hit her almost every day, and as the daughter grew older in the other world to which Boonyi had surrendered her the weight increased. Now when Boonyi thought about Kashmira it was like being crushed beneath a house. It was as though the earth's gravitational force increased and dragged her down and shackled her. The pressure on her chest was so great that her lungs could barely function. If you're going to kill me, my husband, she thought, come home and do it soon, or else my daughter, whose name I don't know, whose face I can't see, will beat you to the punch. But her husband did not come to her for a long time. When at last he did come, there were strange words in his messages, the names of places of whose existence she was only dimly aware: Tajikistan, Algeria, Egypt, Palestine. When she heard these names she knew only that the old Shalimar was dead. In his place, bearing his name, was this new creature, bathed in strangeness, and all that was left of Shalimar the clown was a murderous desire. She gave up her dream of a happy ending and waited for his return.

And all of a sudden he was forty years old, battle hardened, and no longer needed to ask himself what murder might be like. On a street corner outside a car park in North Africa an agent of the FIS had paid a cigarette vendor a few dinars to leave his tray behind and disappear for an hour. Then he had been brought forward, Shalimar the clown clean shaven and wearing Western clothes, and a bearded man wearing a *khamis* robe and smelling heavily of musk put the strap of the vending tray around his neck and left a pistol on it wrapped in a white cloth and then disappeared. Shalimar the clown felt strangely potent, he felt like Superman, because they had stuck a needle in his arm and injected an off-white liquid into it. He had no language in common with the people for whom he was carrying out the hit, but one-eyed Talib had sent Zahir the Boy with him to be his translator and aide. Talib said that Zahir the Boy spoke excellent Arabic and it was time he became a man. They had shown Shalimar the clown a picture of a man and brought him here in a windowless van and injected him and left him on the street with the gun. In the van Zahir the Boy had translated what the bearded man said. The man he was going to kill was a godless man, a writer against God, who spoke French and had sold his soul to the West. That was all he needed to know. He should not need to ask questions. It was a simple job.

Shalimar the clown stood on the street corner surrounded by Arabic and when men came up for cigarettes Zahir the Boy did the work and Shalimar the clown grinned stupidly and pointed at his ears and open mouth, meaning *I'm deaf and dumb, I can't talk to you, I have no idea what you're saying.* Then the man in the photograph appeared, wearing blue-tinted sunglasses and an open white shirt and cream slacks and carrying a folded newspaper in his left hand. The man walked quickly towards the car park and Shalimar the clown took off the vending tray, picked up the cloth with the pistol inside and followed him. He was holding the cloth in his left hand and didn't take the gun out because he wanted to know what it would feel like when he placed the blade of his knife against the man's skin, when he pushed the sharp and glistening horizon of the knife against the frontier of the skin, violating the sovereignty of another human soul, moving in beyond taboo, towards the blood. What it would feel like when he slashed the bastard's throat in half so that his head lolled back and sideways off his neck and the blood gushed upwards like a tree. What it would feel like when the blood poured over him and he stepped away from the corpse, the useless twitching thing, the piece of fly-blown meat. Zahir came running and the windowless van came round a corner fast and the man who smelled of musk pulled him inside and slammed the door and the van drove away quickly while the man who smelled of musk shouted at him for a long, long time. Zahir the Boy said, "He says you are insane. The gun had a silencer fitted and would have been quick and clean. You disobeyed orders and he should kill you for this." But Shalimar the clown was not killed. Zahir the Boy translated what the man who smelled of musk said after he had calmed down. "For a man like you, a complete fucking crazy asshole, there will always be plenty of work."

So he knew the answer to his question and had learned something about himself that he had not known before. The years passed and indeed there was plenty of work. He became a person of value and consequence, as assassins are. Also, his secret purpose was achieved. He had passports in five names and had learned good Arabic, ordinary French and bad English, and had opened routes for himself, routes in the real world, the invisible world, that would take him where he needed to go when the time for the ambassador came. He remembered his father teaching him to walk the tightrope, and realized that travelling the secret routes of the invisible world was exactly the same. The routes were gathered air. Once you had learned to use them you felt as if you were flying, as if the illusory world in which most people lived was vanishing and you were flying across the skies without even needing to get on board a plane.

FC-22 was different when he returned: larger, more solidly constructed. It no longer looked like a bandits' hideout. Many wooden houses had been built, and Nissen huts erected. Talib the Afghan had returned to active military service and Zahir the Boy was also long gone. Maulana Bulbul Fakh was there, however, and welcomed Shalimar the clown with the words, "You're just in time. The uprising is near." He had been away too long. Sheikh Abdullah, the Lion of Kashmir, had been dead for five years. There had been India-Pakistan clashes on the Siachen

Glacier, twenty thousand feet above sea level. But it was the just-concluded polls that changed everything. This was the year 1987, and the Indian government had held state elections in Kashmir. Farooq Abdullah, the Sheikh's son, was the government's preferred choice. The opposition party, the Muslim United Front, named as its candidate one Mohammad Yousuf Shah, described by General Hammirdev Kachhwaha as the state's "most wanted militant". Unofficially, as the results came in, it became plain that the wrong man was winning. So the election was rigged. MUF supporters and electoral agents were seized and tortured. Mohammad Yousuf Shah went underground, and as Syed Salahuddin became the chief of the militant group Hizb-ul-Mujaheddin. His closest aides, the so-called HAJY group (Abdul *H*amid Shaikh, *A*shfaq Majid Wani, *J*aved Ahmed Mir and Mohammad *Y*asin Malik), crossed the mountains and joined the JKLF. Thousands of previously law-abiding young men took up arms and joined the militants, disillusioned by the electoral process. Pakistan was generous. There were AK-47s for everyone.

Abdurajak Janjalani had gone home and started up a new group of his own, the "Sword Bearers," or Abu Sayyaf faction. He had often talked about doing this, and more than once tried to recruit Shalimar the clown to help him. "Brothers from everywhere gathering," he had said. "You see. It will be triumph for our international." Seeing that Shalimar the clown had other things on his mind, Janjalani had not pressed him, but had assured him that there would always be a place for him in the struggle. "If you want to come to Basilan," he said, "this person, call him. All fixed very quick and well. Brother Ramzi coming. There are so-much funds." The name on the piece of paper meant nothing to Shalimar the clown but when the Sword Bearers hit the news fast with a campaign of bombings and kidnappings for ransom, the world's visible and invisible networks began to buzz and various names did begin to crop up, such as Mohammed Jamal Khalifa, a cousin of Sheikh Usama's who ran a large number of Islamic charities in the southern Philippines and was spoken of as a major financier of the new group. President Qadhafi of Libya condemned Abu Sayyaf but Libyan charities in the southern Philippines also came under suspicion as possible channels for Libyan state cash. Likewise, the names of certain prominent Malaysian figures began to occur in the same sentence as the words *Abu Sayyaf.* The name and telephone number on Shalimar the clown's piece of paper were both Malaysian, but neither ever appeared in the press. Of course the piece of paper had existed for less than an hour. Shalimar the clown had fixed the name and the number in his head and burned the paper as soon as the work of memorization was done.

The Gegroo brothers had gone, too. The secular nationalist ideas of the JKLF militants had never been to their liking, and Talib the instructor had steered them (before he also left) in the direction of the most "Afghan" of the newer groups, the Lashkar-e-Pak or Army of the Pure. The LeP had moral as well as political aims. A month before Shalimar the clown's return to FC-22, the Gegroos had taken part in an LeP raid on the village of Hast in Jammu & Kashmir Rajouri district. LeP posters had appeared in the village ordering all Muslim women to don the burqa and adhere to the dress and behavioural principles laid down by the Taliban in Afghanistan. Kashmiri women were mostly unaccustomed to the veil and ignored the posters. On the night in question the LeP group, including the Gegroos, took reprisals. They entered the home of Mohammed Sadiq and killed his twenty-year-old daughter, Nosen Kausar. In the home of Khalid Ahmed they beheaded twenty-two-year-old Tahira Parveen. In the home of Mohammed Rafiq they killed young Shehnaaz Akhtar. And they beheaded forty-three-year-old Jan Begam in her own home.

In the months that followed the LeP grew bolder and moved its activities into Srinagar itself. Women teachers were doused with acid for failing to adhere to the Islamic dress code. Threats were made and deadlines issued and many Kashmiri women put on, for the first time, the shroud their mothers and grandmothers had always proudly refused. Then, in the summer of 1987, the LeP posters appeared in Shirmal. Men and women were not to sit together and watch television any more. That was a licentious and obscene practice. Hindus were not to sit among Muslims. And of course all women must instantly put on the veil. Hasina Yambarzal was outraged. "Tear all those posters down and announce business as usual," she ordered her sons. "I don't intend to watch my TV programmes through a hole in a one-woman tent, nor do I plan to be liberated into a different kind of jail."

The last performance ever given by the bhands of Pachigam took place early the next year, at the start of the tourist season, on the day the national insurrection began. Abdullah Noman at the great age of seventy-six brought his troupe of players to an auditorium in Srinagar to perform for the valley's Indian and foreign visitors, on whom the economy depended. His great stars were gone. There was no Boonyi to dance her Anarkali and devastate audiences with her beauty, no Shalimar to clown with dizzying skill on a high wire without a net, and he himself found it extremely painful to draw and brandish a kingly sword with his ageing, crippled hands. The youngsters of today had other interests and had to be coerced into performing. The sullen woodenness of these younger actors was an insult to the ancient art. Abdullah mourned inwardly as he watched them at rehearsal. They were broken bits of matchstick pretending to be mighty trees. Who will watch such clumsy rubbish? he wondered sadly. They will pelt us with fruit and two veg and boo us off the stage.

He apologized in advance to his septuagenarian friend and

longtime ally, the retired Sikh cultural administrator and celebrated horticulturalist Sardar Harbans Singh, who had supported the bhand pather throughout his career and, in retirement, had persuaded his young successors—who were as impatient with the old crafts as the youth of Pachigam—to give the old stagers the occasional break. "After tonight, Sardarji," Abdullah Noman told the elegant old gent, "the organizers will probably want to give us not breaks but broken heads." "Don't worry about it, old man," Harbans replied dryly. "The tourists have been fleeing the valley in droves this past week, and most of them never showed up in the first place anyway. It's a catastrophe, a shipwreck, and I'm afraid it's your job to provide the entertainment while we go down with all hands."

Firdaus had not come to Srinagar with the company. Abdullah knew she was unhappy, because she had started muttering about snake omens. When his wife started seeing snake-shapes in the clouds, in the branches of trees, in water, it invariably meant she was brooding about the miseries of life. Recently she claimed that actual snakes had been coming into the village, that she saw them wherever she went, in animal feeding barns and fruit orchards and produce stalls and homes. They had not started biting yet, no snake-deaths of livestock or human beings had been reported, but they were gathering, Firdaus said, like an army of invasion they were massing ranks and unless something was done about it they would attack at a moment of their choosing and that would be that. Once upon a time Abdullah Noman would have roared his disbelief and the village would have gathered delightedly outside his house to listen to the quarrel, but Abdullah didn't roar any more, even though he knew she would prefer it if he did. He had retreated into himself, old age and disappointment had pushed him into a cold place and he didn't know how to get out of it. He saw his wife looking at him sometimes, fixing him with an unhappy questioning stare that asked *where did you go, what happened to the man I loved,* and he wanted to shout out to her, *I'm still in here, save me, I'm trapped inside myself,* but there was a coating of ice around him and the words couldn't get through.

"If the show goes as badly as I fear," he told her stiffly, "then I'm going to stop. To hell with it! I don't plan to spend my last years being humiliated in public in shows I wouldn't pay to see myself." Pachigam was much poorer than either of them could remember. Theatrical bookings were few and far between and since Pandit Pyarelal Kaul's withdrawal from the position of vasta waza, chief cook, the reputation of Pachigam's wazwaan had declined. Firdaus replied to her husband's announcement with a few stiff words of her own. "So, if we're going to be even harder up than we are now," she said, "then it's just as well I never developed any fancy ideas about living in style." Abdullah knew she was complaining about his behaviour, his failure to make her feel loved, but the words that would soften her heart stuck in his throat and he left for Srinagar saying, with a curt nod, "Quite so. The poor should never succumb to the dream of a comfortable life."

The bus bringing the actors and musicians to Srinagar could not get to the depot on account of the crowds gathering in the city streets under the nervous eyes of the army and police. The bhands had to get out, carry their props and walk. There were already more than four hundred thousand people clogging up the roads. Abdullah Noman asked the bus driver what was going on. "It's a funeral," he replied. "They have come to mourn the death of our Kashmir."

The curtain rose on the story of the good king Zain-ul-abidin, and Abdullah walked out onto the stage with a raised sword in one hand and a spear in the other, clenching the weapons tightly, ignoring the spears of pain shooting down his hands. He was leading by example for the last time in his life, sending a message to his bored, mutinous troupe. *If I can rise above my pain then you can rise above your indifference.* But the auditorium was three-quarters empty, and the few tourists who were sitting out there weren't really listening to him, because through the walls of the theatre came the muffled sound of the start of the uprising, the crowd of one million persons marching through the streets carrying flaming torches above their heads and bellowing *Azadi!* Sardar Harbans Singh was sitting with his son Yuvraj, a strikingly handsome young man whose modernizing inclinations were trumpeted by his shaven face and lack of a Sikh turban, in the middle of the otherwise empty seventh row. With the sense of a man plunging from a high pinnacle to his death Abdullah Noman fixed his old comrade with his fiercest, most glittering stare and launched into the play with all the power he had left. For the next hour, in the silent tomb of the auditorium, the bhands of Pachigam told a story which nobody wanted to hear. Several members of the audience got up and left during the show. In the intermission Sardar Harbans Singh's son Yuvraj, a businessman who in spite of the worsening political situation was successfully exporting Kashmiri papier-mâché boxes, carved wooden tables, numdah rugs and embroidered shawls to the rest of India and to Western buyers as well, who supported him "as an act of ridiculous optimism, considering that the region is on the verge of going insane," warned Abdullah Noman that things might get out of hand in the street and demonstrators might even burst into the theatre. "You're holding a sword and a spear," Yuvraj Singh reminded Abdullah. "If they do get inside here, a word of advice? Never mind about the play. Throw the props down and run." He himself would have to miss the second act, he apologized. "The situation, you understand," he explained, vaguely. "One has one's proper duties to discharge."

In the hollow vacuum of the empty theatre Abdullah Noman saw his troupe of disaffected youngsters give the performances of their young lives, as if they had suddenly understood a secret which nobody had explained to them before. The pounding drumbeats of the demonstration echoed around them, the chanting of the demonstrators was like a chorus crying doom, the menace of the ever-growing crowd crackled around the empty seats like an electric charge. Still the bhands of Pachigam went on with their show, dancing, singing, clowning, telling their tale of old-time tolerance and hope. At one point Abdullah Noman succumbed to the illusion that their voices, their instruments had become inaudible, that, even though they were declaiming their lines and singing their songs and playing their music with a passion they had not been able to muster for a long time, there was complete silence in the theatre, the few scattered spectators sat mutely watching a dumb show, while outside in the streets the noise was already immense and grew louder by the instant, and now a second group of noises was superimposed on the first, the noises of troop transports, Jeeps and tanks, of booted feet marching in step, of loaded weapons being readied and finally of gunshots, rifle shots as well as automatic fire. The chanting turned into screaming, the drumbeats turned into thunder, the march turned into a stampede, and as the auditorium began to shake the tale of King Zain-ul-abidin silently reached its happy ending and the actors joined hands and took their bow, but even though Sardar Harbans Singh, the only person left in the audience, applauded as heartily as he could in the circumstances, his clapping hands didn't make any sound at all.

For a time it was impossible to return home. Forty demonstrators had been killed. The situation in the streets was highly unstable, there were roadblocks and troops and armoured vehicles everywhere, and public transport was not a priority. The bhands of Pachigam blockaded themselves inside the theatre and waited. Sardar Harbans Singh refused to stay with them. "I'm going to sleep in my own bed, chaps," he declared. "The wife would be most suspicious if I don't. Besides which, I have my garden to attend to." Harbans's walled garden villa was one of the secret wonders of the city, and was believed by some to have been placed under an enchantment by a *pari* from Pari Mahal, a magic spell which protected it and all who dwelt there from coming to harm. But Harbans didn't seem to need the assistance of fairies. He managed to find his way back to the old-town residence on foot in spite of the wildness of the city. Harbans was an intrepid old fox, knew all the city's byways and back alleys, and came back every day without fail, immaculately turned out in *achkan* jacket and trousers, his silver beard and moustache trimmed and pomaded, to bring the company food and essential supplies. He was sometimes escorted by his son, but more often came alone, on account of Yuvraj's unspecified "duties", which turned out to involve the hiring and management of a private security force to protect his business premises and warehouses against looters and firebombers. Sardar Harbans Singh shook his head sadly. "My son is a person of high ideals and noble beliefs," he told Abdullah, "who is obliged by the times to deal with guttersnipes and bounders, mercenary hooligans whom he hires to save our goods from other hooligans, and whom he then has to watch like a hawk in case they do the bad hats' dirty work themselves. Poor fellow never sleeps, but never complains. He does the needful. As we all must." Sardar Harbans Singh carried a silver-headed walnut swordstick and walked briskly through the unsafe streets, pooh-poohing the risk to himself. "I'm an old man," he said. "Who would trouble to do anything to me when Father Time is doing such a dashed good job already?" Abdullah shook his head wonderingly. "You can know a man for fifty years," he said, "and still not know what he's capable of." Harbans shrugged in self-deprecation. "You never know the answer to the questions of life until you're asked," he said.

The bus service to Pachigam started running again five days after these events. When Abdullah Noman arrived at his front door Firdaus could not prevent herself from weeping copiously for joy. Abdullah fell to his knees in the doorway and asked for her forgiveness. "If you can still love me," he said, "then please help me find the courage to face the coming storm." She raised him up and kissed him. "You are the only great man I have ever known," she said, "and I will be proud to stand beside you and beat back death, the devil, the Indian army or whatever other trouble's on its way."

Bombur Yambarzal had done a brave thing once, when he faced down the rabble-rousing iron mullah Maulana Bulbul Fakh at the door of the Shirmal mosque, but now that life was asking difficult questions again in his great old age, his fear for the safety of his beloved wife led him astray. He was no longer the big-bellied vasta waza of yore. The years had withered him, palsied his hands, dotted him with liver spots and put cataracts in his eyes, and he cut a skinny, unimpressive figure as he wondered with some trepidation whether he would live to see the dawn of his eightieth year. This enfeebled Bombur expressed the view that the Lashkar-e-Pak would look more favourably on Shirmal and be less likely to attempt any "funny business" if people responded to the radicals' poster campaign in a spirit of compromise, not confrontation. "We should agree to at least one thing they propose, Harud," he said, "or we'll be the ones who look unreasonable and hard line."

Hasina Yambarzal, that powerfully built lady whom age had not weakened in the slightest and who continued to henna her hair in order to justify the rubicund nickname "Harud', was preparing the television tent for the evening's viewing. "What do you suggest?" she said in an uncompromising voice. "I told you my views about the burqa and if you try to stop the women coming in here there will be hell to pay." The waza of Shirmal accepted her argument. "In that case," he said, "can't we just just tell our Hindu brothers and sisters that in response to the LeP intervention, and having regard to the gravity of the regional situation, and having weighed the available options, and only for the time being, and in this dangerous climate, and until things blow over, and for their own good as well as ours, and purely as a precautionary measure, and without meaning anything bad by it, and taking everything into consideration, and in spite of our deep reluctance, and with a heavy heart, and while fully appreciating their very understandable feelings of disappointment, and hoping earnestly for better days to come soon, and with the intention of reversing the decision at the earliest feasible opportunity, it might be better for all concerned if." He stopped talking because he could not say the final words aloud. Hasina Yambarzal nodded judiciously. "There are a few pandit families over in Pachigam who won't like it, of course," she said, "but here in Shirmal there's no need for anyone to get upset."

When news reached Pachigam that the television tent was now for viewing by Muslims only, Firdaus could not restrain herself. "That Hasina, excuse me if I mention," she told Abdullah, "people say she's a very pragmatical lady but I'd put it another way. In my opinion she'd sleep with the devil if it was in her business interest to do so, and she's got that dope Bombur so twisted up that he'd think it was his good idea."

Two nights later the Yambarzal tent was full of Muslim-only TV watchers enjoying an episode of a fantasy serial in which the legendary prince of Yemen Hatim Tai, during his quest to solve the mysterious riddles posed by the evil Dajjal, found himself in the land of Kopatopa on the occasion of their new year celebrations. The Kopatopan phrase meaning "happy new year"—*tingi mingi took took*—so delighted the enthralled viewers that most of them leapt to their feet and started bowing to one another and repeating it over and over again: "Tingi mingi took took! Tingi mingi took took!" They were so busy wishing one another a happy Kopatopan new year that they didn't instantly notice that some person or persons had set fire to the tent.

It was fortunate indeed that nobody was burned to death in the blaze. After a period of screaming, panic, jostling, terror, trampling, anger, running, bewilderment, crawling, cowardice, tears and heroism, in short all the usual phenomena that may be observed whenever and wherever people find themselves trapped in a burning tent, the congregation of the faithful all escaped, in better or worse condition, suffering from burns or not suffering from them, wheezing and gasping on account of the effects of smoke inhalation, or else by good luck neither gasping nor wheezing, bruised or not bruised, lying around on the ground some distance from the now-incandescent tent, or else (and more usefully) fetching water to ensure that the fire, which had by that time taken hold of the tent too powerfully to be extinguished before it had consumed its prey, at least did not spread to the rest of the village, but burned itself out on the spot.

As a result everybody missed the scene in which Hatim Tai met the immortal princess Nazarébaddoor whose touch could turn away not only the evil eye but also death itself. At the precise instant when Nazarébaddoor attempted to kiss Prince Hatim—he valiantly refused her advances, reminding her that he loved another "more than his very life"—the television set of the Yambarzal family exploded loudly and died, taking with it a major source of the family's income, but, as against that, a significant cause of communal discord as well.

The next morning the three Gegroo brothers, Aurangzeb, Alauddin and Abulkalam, rode back into Shirmal on small mountain ponies, bristling with guns and festooned in cartridge belts. It was a beautiful spring day. Early moisture glistened on the corrugated metal roofs of the little wooden houses and flowers sprouted by every doorstep. The loveliness of the day only served to heighten the ugliness of the black circle of charred grass and earth that marked the spot where the fire had consumed the Yambarzals' place and means of entertainment, and the Gegroos halted by the still-smoking spot and fired pistols into the air. Such villagers as were able to do so came out of their homes and saw three phantoms from their past, older, but still giggling and unshaven. Their old home was still standing, locked up and empty like a ghost house, but the brothers didn't appear to care. They had just stopped by to say hello on behalf of their present employers, the LeP. "Did you do this to us?" Hasina Yambarzal demanded. They giggled at that. "If the LeP had laid the fire," screamed Aurangzeb Gegroo at the top of his thin voice, "then every soul in that tent would have met his or her maker by now." This was either true or not true. It was getting to be a characteristic of the times that people never knew who had hit them or why.

Alauddin Gegroo rode right up to Hasina Yambarzal, dismounted and shrieked into her face. "Don't you know, you stupid disobedient woman flaunting before me the shamelessness of your uncovered features, that it's only on account of us that the Lashkar hasn't punished you people yet? Don't you know that we've been protecting our own home village from the Lashkar's holy wrath? Why don't you wretched ignorant people understand who your real friends are?" But an alternative explanation was that it was only on account of the Gegroo brothers' desire for vengeance that the LeP had taken the risk of sending a team as far afield as Shirmal. However, this was plainly not the time for a debate.

Abulkalam Gegroo completed his brother's harangue at some length, baring a set of decayed teeth in an exaggerated snarl that marked him out as the very worst kind of weak man, the type who might very well kill you to prove his strength. "You are the same damn-fool villagers who sent away the great Maulana Bulbul Fakh. The same damn-fool villagers that won't observe the simplest Islamic decencies as politely requested and who nevertheless expect to be protected from the consequences of your refusal. The same damn-fool villagers who thought we were dust, us, the worthless Gegroo brothers whom you were ready to starve to death in a mosque, whose lives weren't worth two paisas to you, the pathetic Gegroos who couldn't count on their own people to save them from the murderous Hindus—the same people who are only alive today because those same Gegroo brothers keep interceding for them. Arré, how stupid can even stupid people be? Because even these useless dead Gegroos whom you were prepared to throw away like the corpses of dead dogs can work out that the people who burned your tent must be the same people you threw out of it, your Hindu brothers and sisters, whom you love so much you feel bad about what you did to them even though you didn't give a damn about what you thought you did to us, and you still don't get it, you don't see that the Hindus who set the fire, your pandit pals, would have been happy to see the whole lot of you laid out in the street here, burned to a crisp like so many overcooked sikh kababs."

"He's right," said Hashim Karim suddenly, taking his mother by surprise.

"He probably is correct," his brother Hatim agreed. "That Big Man Misri loved watching TV, and he was always a big man for revenge."

A carpenter could always find work in Kashmir in the spring, when wooden houses and fences all over the valley needed attention, so Big Man Misri was one of the few citizens of Pachigam to be immune from the general economic depression. He travelled the country roads on a little motor scooter with his sack of tools on his back and often, when he passed a secluded little grove of trees that stood just out of sight of his home village around a bend in the Muskadoon, he parked the scooter, concealed himself in the trees, set down his tool sack and danced.

Big Man had always been of the view that his terpsichorean skills had been too harshly judged by the Pachigam bhands, and that he could leap as high and twirl as effectively as the next man. Abdullah Noman had told him kindly but firmly that the world was not yet ready for a jumping giant, and so Big Man Misri was obliged to practise his art in secret, without hope of an audience, for love alone, and often with his eyes closed, so that he could imagine the rapt faces of the audience he would never be allowed to have. On the last day of his life he was leaping and pirouetting in his army surplus boots when he heard the sound of insincere applause. Opening his eyes, he saw that he was surrounded by the three heavily armed Gegroo brothers on their mountain ponies, and understood that his time had come. There was a knife tucked into each of his boots and so he went down on one knee and begged to be spared in the most pitiful and cowardly voice he could produce, which amused the brothers mightily, as he knew it would. I could have been an actor as well as a dancer, he mused fleetingly, and in the same instant, when the Gegroos were shaking with laughter instead of concentrating on their victim, he reached for both his knives and threw them. Abulkalam Gegroo was hit in the throat and Alauddin Gegroo in the left eye and they fell from their mounts without making any further contribution to events. Aurangzeb Gegroo, distracted by the calamity that had befallen his brothers, delayed his reaction almost long enough to allow the charging carpenter to seize him. Big Man Misri the private dancer made the biggest leap of his life, his hands outstretched towards Aurangzeb Gegroo, but the eldest and only surviving sibling came to his senses just in time and fired both his AK-47s into the soaring Big Man at point-blank range. Big Man Misri was already dead by the time his body hit

Aurangzeb, knocking him backward off his pony and breaking his puny neck.

That same night, after the dead body of Big Man Misri was discovered lying on top of Aurangzeb Gegroo as if they were lovers who had made a death pact, with the other two dead Gegroos by their side, Zoon Misri climbed up the hill to the edge of the Khelmarg meadow and hanged herself from a majestic spreading chinar, the only tree of its kind to have taken root and survived at this height, among the evergreens. She was discovered by Boonyi Noman, who understood at once the meaning of this eloquent, final message from her beloved friend. The horror was upon them now and would not be denied.

General Hammirdev Suryavans Kachhwaha realized, as he thought about his approaching fifty-ninth birthday, that the reason he had never married was that for almost thirty years Kashmir had been his wife. For more than half his life he had been wedded to this ungrateful, shrewish mountain state where disloyalty was a badge of honour and insubordination a way of life. It had been a cold marriage. Now things were coming to a head. He wanted to be done with her once and for all. He wanted to tame the shrew. Then he wanted a divorce.

The coming battle against the insurgency, reflected General Hammirdev Suryavans Kachhwaha, would be a conflict that lacked all nobility. The true soldier wanted a noble war, sought out such nobility as might be available. This struggle was a dirty bare-knuckle fight against dirty gutter rats and there was nothing in it to exalt the martial soul. It was not General Kachhwaha's way to fight dirty but when one faced terrorists any attempt to stay clean was doomed to ignoble defeat. It was not his way to take off his gloves but there was a time and a place for gloves and Kashmir was not a boxing ring and the Marquess of Queensberry's rules did not apply. This was what he had been saying to the political echelon. He had informed the political echelon that if he were allowed to take his gloves off, if his boys were allowed to stop pussyfooting and namby-pambying and mollycoddling and pitter-pattering around, if they were allowed to crack down on the miscreants by whatever means necessary, then he could clean up this mess, no problem, he could crush the insurgency's testicles in his fist until it wept blood through the corners of its eyes.

For many years the political echelon had been reluctant. For too long it had said yes and no at the same time. But now at last there was movement. The character of the political echelon had changed. Its new belief system was supported by prominent members of the intellectual tier and the economic stratum and held that the introduction of Islam in the classical period had been uniformly deleterious, a cultural calamity, and that centuries-overdue corrections needed to be made. Heavyweight figures in the intellectual tier spoke of a new awakening of the suppressed cultural energy of the Hindu masses. Prominent inhabitants of the economic stratum invested massively in this glistening new zero-tolerance world. The political echelon responded positively to such encouragement. The introduction of President's Rule provided security personnel with unrestricted powers. The amended code of criminal procedure immunized all public servants, soldiers included, against prosecution for deeds performed in the line of duty. The definition of such deeds was broad and included destruction of private property, torture, rape and murder.

The political echelon's decision to declare Kashmir a "disturbed area" was also greatly appreciated. In a disturbed area, search warrants were not required, arrest warrants ditto, and shoot-to-kill treatment of suspects was acceptable. Suspects who remained alive could be arrested and detained for two years, during which period it would not be necessary to charge them or to set a date for their trial. For more dangerous suspects the political echelon permitted more severe responses. Persons who committed the ultimate crime of challenging the territorial integrity of India or in the opinion of the armed forces attempted to disrupt same could be jailed for five years. Interrogation of such suspects would take place behind closed doors and confessions extracted by force during these secret interrogations would be admissible as evidence provided the interrogating officer had reason to believe the statement was being made voluntarily. Confessions made after the suspect was beaten or hung by the feet, or after he had experienced electricity or the crushing of his hands or feet, would be considered as being voluntary. The burden of proof would be shifted and it would be for these persons to prove the falsehood of the automatic presumption of guilt. If they failed so to do the death penalty could be applied.

In the dark General Kachhwaha experienced a smooth, ovoid feeling of satisfaction, even vindication. His own old theory, which proposed the essentially sneaky and subversive nature of the Kashmiri Muslim population in toto, and which in bygone times he had reluctantly set aside, was one whose time had come. The political echelon had sent word. *Every Muslim in Kashmir should be considered a militant. The bullet was the only solution.* Until the militants were wiped out normality could not return to the valley. General Kachhwaha smiled. Those were instructions he could follow.

He had moved on from Elasticnagar to Army Corps Headquarters at Badami Bagh, Srinagar. In spite of its name this was no fragrant almond garden but a centre of naked power. General Kachhwaha on his arrival at the giant base had immediately given orders for the replication of his old suite of rooms in Elasticnagar and soon sat once more in darkness, at the centre of the web. There was nothing he needed to witness in person any more. He knew everything and forgot nothing. He went nowhere and was everywhere. He sat in darkness and saw the valley, every cranny of it, bathed in garish light. He felt the bloat of memory expanding his body, he was all swollen up, stuffed full of the babel of the unforgotten, and the confusion of his senses grew ever more extreme. The idea of violence had a velvet softness now. One took off one's gloves and smelled the sweet fragrance of necessity. Bullets entered flesh like music, the pounding of clubs was the rhythm of life, and then there was the sexual dimension to consider, the demoralization of the population through the violation of its women. In that dimension every colour was bright and tasted good. He closed his eyes and averted his head. What must be, must be.

The insurgency was pathetic. It fought against itself. Half of it was fighting for that old fairy tale, Kashmir for the Kashmiris, while the other half wanted Pakistan, and to be a part of the Islamist terror international. The insurrectionists would kill each other while he watched. But he would kill them too, to hurry things along. He didn't care what they wanted. He wanted them dead. In the darkness, while he waited, he had refined and perfected the philosophy and methodology of the coming crackdown. The philosophy of crackdown was, *fuck the enemy in the crack.* The methodology of crackdown could be expressed technically as cordon-and-search. Curfews would be imposed and soldiers would go house to house. It could also be expressed colloquially as, *and then fuck them in the crack again.* Town by town, hamlet by hamlet, every part of the valley would be visited by his wrath, by men who had taken their gloves off, his warriors, his storm troopers, his fists. He would see how much these people loved their insurgency then, when they had the Indian army fucking them in the crack.

He knew everything and forgot nothing. He read the reports and closed his eyes and ate with relish the scenes he conjured up, drawing nourishment from the details. Village Z came under crackdown and the headmaster of the school was picked up, a bastard by the name of A. He stood accused of being a militant. He dared to lie and deny it, saying he was not a militant but a headmaster. He was asked to identify which of his pupils were militants and this man, this self-avowed headmaster, had the nerve to claim not only that he did not know about his own students but also that he didn't know any militants at all. But every Kashmiri was a militant as had been laid down by the political echelon and so this liar was lying and needed to be assisted towards the truth. He was beaten, obviously. Then his beard was set on fire. Then electricity was offered to his eyes, his genitals and his tongue. Afterwards he claimed to have been blinded in one eye, which was an obvious lie, an attempt to blame the investigators for a previously existing condition. He had no pride and begged the men to stop. He repeated his lie, that he was just a schoolteacher, which offended them. To assist him they took him to a small stream containing dirty water and broken glass. The liar was pushed into the stream and kept there for five hours. The men walked over him with their boots, applying his head to the rocks in the water. He lost consciousness to avoid questioning, so when he woke up they chastised him again. In the end it was deemed correct to let him go. He was warned that the next time he would be killed. He ran away screaming, *I swear I'm not a militant. I'm a schoolteacher.* These people were beyond saving. There was no hope for them.

The town of Y came under crackdown and a middle-aged man by the name of B was picked up along with his sixteen-year-old son, C. The door to his home, a suspected terrorist rat's nest, was kicked down. To show him that the matter was serious his father's Qur'an was thrown to the floor and muddy boots were applied to it. There would be no more special treatment for Muslims. That had to be understood. His daughter was ordered into the back room from which she crawled out of a window and escaped, which was unfortunate but proved that this was a high-value family of rat terrorists. The sixteen-year-old was formally accused of terrorism. He had the cheek to deny. Again he was accused and again denied. And a third time, ditto. He said he was a student and such subterfuge inflamed the sentiments of the men. He was taken outside and rifle butts were applied to his person. The father, B, tried to intervene and he also required vigorous physical attention. When the terrorist youth, C, lost consciousness he was put in the back of a truck and taken away for his own benefit, for medical assistance. At a later time the middle-aged man, B, claimed that his son had been located in a ditch unclothed and with a bullet in his back. This was not the doing of the men. Probably after he had received medical attention and was allowed to go home he encountered terrorists of a rival faction and they attended to him.

The village of X, high up near the snow line and the Line of Control, came under crackdown because militants often crossed the border in its vicinity and so it was plain that the villagers harboured them, gave them beds to rest in and food to eat. Reports had been received of the presence in the locality of the so-called iron mullah, Maulana Bulbul Fakh, whom General Kachhwaha had once made the mistake of tolerating, back in the old days of tolerant weakness. Those days were gone, as the notorious priest and his gang of desperadoes would discover soon enough, as their henchpersons in X had already learned—the malevolent youth D, who would trouble the security forces no further, the dotards E (gender m.) and F (gender f.) whose house had been demolished to punish them, and the women G, H and I, upon whom the virile wrath of the Indian forces had been potently unleashed. The bayonetting of the womb of the pregnant woman J was a scurrilous allegation, however: pure fiction. None of the personnel on duty that day had carried bayonets; only automatic weapons, grenades, knives. The enemies of the state would stop at nothing to slander its military protectors. This would no longer inhibit the security forces from doing the needful. The manifestation of the protectors' virile wrath against the female population was an important psychological tool. It discouraged the menfolk from carrying out the subversive acts which it was in their nature to perform. Consequently, the danger to the security forces diminished. These were strategic and tactical matters and should not be discussed emotionally.

It was just the beginning. Things would move faster now. He was no longer Tortoise Colonel. He was the Hammer of Kashmir.

That dark summer after the Misris perished the fruit in Pandit Pyarelal Kaul's apple orchards was bitter and inedible, but the peaches of Firdaus Noman were as succulent as usual. The saffron in Pyarelal's saffron field was paler and less potent, but the honey in Abdullah's beehives was sweeter than ever before. These matters were difficult to understand; but when Pyarelal heard on the radio that the well-known pandit leader Tika Lal Taploo had been gunned down the nature of the portents became plain. "In the time of Sikandar But-Shikan, Sikander the Iconoclast," he told his daughter at her Gujar hut in the woods, "Muslim attacks on Kashmiri Hindus were described as the falling of locust swarms upon the helpless paddy crops. I am afraid that what is beginning now will make Sikandar's time look peaceful by comparison." In the weeks that followed his prophecy came true and he told Boonyi, "Now that everything I have stood for is in ruins I am ready to die, but I will live on to protect your life from the insanity of your husband, even though neither one of us has anything left to live for." The radical cadres of the Jamaat-i-Islami party had new words for "pandit": *mukhbir, kafir.* Meaning spy, infidel. "So we are slandered as fifth-columnists now," Pyarelal mourned. "That means the assault cannot be far away."

In the aftermath of the Muslim insurgency against Indian rule another pandit was murdered in Tangmarg. Posters appeared on the road leading from Srinagar to Pachigam demanding that all pandits vacate their property and leave Kashmir. The first Hindus to respond to the poster campaign were the gods, who began to disappear. The famous black stone statue of Maha-Kali was one of twenty deities who vacated their home in Hari Parbat Fort and vanished forever. A priceless deity from the ninth century fled the Lok Bhavan in Anantnag and was never seen again. The Shiva-lingam of the Dewan temple also mysteriously departed. These exits were timely, because soon after they occurred the firebombings began. The Shaivite temple complex at Handwara, near the famous shrine of Kheer Bhawani, was gutted by a blaze. Pyarelal sat beside Boonyi and buried his face in his hands. "Our story is finished," he told her. "It is no longer the story of our lives, but the story of a plague year during which we have the misfortune to be around to grow buboes in our armpits and die unclean and stenchy deaths. We are no longer protagonists, only agonists." A few days later in Anantnag district there began a week-long orgy of unprovoked violence against pandit residential and commercial property, temples, and the physical persons of pandit families. Many of them fled. The exodus of the pandits of Kashmir had begun.

Firdaus Noman came to see Pyarelal at his house to assure him that Pachigam's Muslims would protect their Hindu brethren. "My wise and gentle friend," she said, "never fear; we will take care of our own. The killing of Big Man Misri and Zoon's suicide was bad enough, and we won't let it happen again. You are too precious to lose." Pyarelal shook his head. "It is out of our hands," he said. "Our natures are no longer the critical factors in our fates. When the killers come, will it matter if we lived well or badly? Will the choices we made affect our destiny? Will they spare the kind and gentle among us and take only the selfish and dishonest? It would be absurd to think so. Massacres aren't finicky. I may be precious or I may be valueless, but it doesn't signify either way." He kept the radio close to his ear at all times. As the bitter apples fell from their trees and rotted on the ground Pyarelal remained indoors, cross-legged, with the transistor held up against his head, listening to the BBC. Loot, plunder, arson, mayhem, murder, exodus: these words recurred, day after day, and a phrase from another part of the world that had flown many thousands of miles to find a new home in Kashmir.

"Ethnic cleansing."

"Kill one, scare ten. Kill one, scare ten." Hindu community houses, temples, private homes and whole neighbourhoods were being destroyed. Pyarelal repeated, like a prayer, the names of the places struck by calamity. "Trakroo, Uma Nagri, Kupwara. Sangrampora, Wandhama, Nadimarg. Trakroo, Uma Nagri, Kupwara. Sangrampora, Wandhama, Nadimarg. Trakroo, Uma Nagri, Kupwara. Sangrampora, Wandhama, Nadimarg." These names had to be remembered. Forgetting would be a crime against those who suffered "whole-hog" burning of their neighbourhoods, or seizure of their property, or death, preceded by such violences as could not be imagined or described. *Kill one, scare ten,* the Muslim mobs chanted, and ten were, indeed, scared. More than ten. Three hundred and fifty thousand pandits, almost the entire pandit population of Kashmir, fled from their homes and headed south to the refugee camps where they would rot, like bitter fallen apples, like the unloved, undead dead they had become. In the so-called Bangladeshi Markets in the Iqbal Park-Hazuri Bagh area of Srinagar the things looted from temples and homes were being openly bought and sold. The shoppers hummed the most popular song of the times as they bought their pretty pieces of Hindu Kashmir, a song by the well-beloved Mehjoor: "I will give my life and soul for India, but my heart is with Pakistan."

There were six hundred thousand Indian troops in Kashmir but the pogrom of the pandits was not prevented, why was that. Three and a half lakhs of human beings arrived in Jammu as displaced persons and for many months the government did not provide shelters or relief or even register their names, why was that. When the government finally built camps it only allowed for six thousand families to remain in the state, dispersing the others around the country where they would be invisible and impotent, why was that. The camps at Purkhoo, Muthi, Mishriwallah, Nagrota were built on the banks and beds of nullahas, dry seasonal waterways, and when the water came the camps were flooded, why was that. The ministers of the government made speeches about ethnic cleansing but the civil servants wrote one another memos saying that the pandits were simply internal migrants whose displacement had been self-imposed, why was that. The tents provided for the refugees to live in were often uninspected and leaking and the monsoon rains came through, why was that. When the one-room tenements called ORTs were built to replace the tents they too leaked profusely, why was that.

There was one bathroom per three hundred persons in many camps why was that and the medical dispensaries lacked basic first-aid materials why was that and thousands of the displaced died because of inadequate food and shelter why was that maybe five thousand deaths because of intense heat and humidity because of snake bites and gastroenteritis and dengue fever and stress diabetes and kidney ailments and tuberculosis and psychoneurosis and there was not a single health survey conducted by the government why was that and the pandits of Kashmir were left to rot in their slum camps, to rot while the army and the insurgency fought over the bloodied and broken valley, to dream of return, to die while dreaming of return, to die after the dream of return died so that they could not even die dreaming of it, why was that why was that why was that why was that why was that.

She knew where he was. He was in the north with the iron mullah at the Line of Control. He was part of the elite "iron commando". She knew what he was doing. He was killing people. He was killing time. He was killing everyone he could find to kill so that he could tolerate the time that had to pass until he could kill her. She blamed herself for their deaths. Come and get it over with, she told him. Come: I release you from your restraints. Never mind what you promised my father and the sarpanch. My father is right, there is no longer any reason for any of us to live. Come and do what you have to do, what you need to do in a place so deep it causes you pain. I have nothing but you and my father, his love and your hatred, and his love is ruined now, his capacity for it is damaged, his picture of the world has been broken and when a man does not have a picture of the world he goes a little mad, which is how my father is. He says the end of the world is coming because his apples are too bitter to eat. He says there is an earthquake trembling in the earth and he has started believing in the snake stories of the sarpanch's wife, he has started believing the snakes will awake, out of their disgust for humankind they will come forth and kill us all and the valley will have peace, snake peace, the peace it is beyond human beings to make. He says the earth is sodden with blood and will give way and no house can stand upon it. He says the mountains will thrust up all around us, they will push higher

into the sky and the valley will be gone and that is what should happen to it, we don't deserve such beauty, we were the guardians of beauty and we could not do our work. I say we are what we are and we do what we do and I am beyond pride in myself I am just a thing that lives and breathes and if I stopped breathing or living it would make no difference except to him, except, in spite of everything, and for a few more moments, to him. Come if you want. I'm waiting. I no longer care.

He said: *Everything I do prepares me for you and for him. Every blow I strike, strikes you or him. The people leading us up here are fighting for God or for Pakistan but I am killing because it is what I have become. I have become death.*

He said: *I'll be there soon enough.*

The situation as it stood had developed new characteristics that lent themselves to advantageous exploitation by the armed forces. General Hammirdev Suryavans Kachhwaha closed his eyes and let the pictures flow. Already the army had made contact with renegade militants around the country and when extrajudicial activity was required these renegades could be used to kill other militants. After the executions the renegade militants would be given the use of uniforms and would bring the corpses to this or that house belonging to this or that individual and place the corpses in the said location with guns in their hands. The renegades would then depart and be relieved of their uniforms while the armed forces attacked the house, blew it to bits and murdered the dead militants all over again for public consumption. If the householder and his family objected they could be charged with harbouring dangerous militants and the consequences of such charges would be dire. The householder, knowing this, was unlikely to squawk.

There was beauty in such schemes, elegance and beauty. General Kachhwaha was discussing with himself whether or not the renegade militants might be used against other categories of person, such as journalists and human rights activists. The deniability of such operations was a big plus. The possibilities should be explored.

The battle against the weaklings of the JKLF would be won soon enough. General Kachhwaha despised the fundamentalists, the jihadis, the Hizb, but he despised the secular nationalists more. What sort of God was secular nationalism? People would not die for that for very long. Already the crackdown was having an effect. Soon the two leading JKLF factions would sue for peace. The HAJY group's Yasin Malik would crack, and so would Amanullah Khan himself. The back channels would open and the deals would be done. This month, next month, this year, next year. It didn't matter. He could wait. He could tighten his grip on the testicles of the insurgency and let it come to him. Word was reaching him from over the mountains, floating over the ice caps and fluttering down into his ear, that Pak Inter-Services Intelligence felt the same way about the JKLF as he did. ISI funding to the JKLF was being reduced and the Hizb was getting the cash instead. The Hizb was strong, maybe ten thousand strong, and he could respect that. He could despise them and respect them simultaneously. No difficulty there.

Intergroup rivalries played into his hands. Already there had been a case of a JKLF area commander murdered by the Hizb. Once the JKLF was done with, the jihadis would turn against one another. He would see to that. The Lashkar of this and the Harkat of that. He would see to them all right. Also the feared "iron commando" of Maulana Bulbul Fakh. Soon he would have the bastards in his sights.

Anees Noman had taken over leadership of his roving JKLF militant group after the departure across the mountains of the invisible commander Dar. His heroes were Guevara the Cuban and the FSLN of Nicaragua and he liked to cultivate the Latino guerrilla look. When the group was on an operation he affected a beret, Western combat fatigues and black boots, and wanted to be known as Comandante Zero after a famous Sandinista fighter, but his soldiers, who were less solemnly respectful of him than he would have wished, called him Baby Che. In the period after the start of the insurgency his mine-laying skills had led to some notable successes against military convoys and the reputation of the Baby Che group grew. Word of its existence reached the ear of General Kachhwaha in Badami Bagh, and though the identity of Baby Che was uncertain the military authorities had had their suspicions for some time. More than once, however, the proposal to put Pachigam under crackdown so that its subversive associations could be properly explored had been vetoed by the civilian authority. An army attack on the folk arts of Kashmir, on its theatrical and gastronomic traditions, was exactly the kind of story that made headlines. Even in retirement Sardar Harbans Singh was standing up for his old friend the sarpanch of Pachigam. Even in his claw-fingered old age Abdullah Noman could still claim to be protecting his village, just as he always had.

There was no work, however. There was no money. The Noman family's peaches and honey were distributed free of charge among the villagers. Pachigam was a lucky village, with its fertile fields and animal herds, but everyone knew that great hardship was just around the corner. If the crisis continued, a statewide famine was a real possibility. "We'll face the famine if it comes," Firdaus Noman told her husband. "Right now I'm so sick of honey and peaches I might even prefer to starve." Her sons Hameed and Mahmood agreed. "Anyway," Hameed said cheerfully, "maybe we won't live long enough to reach the point of starvation." Mahmood nodded. "What a stroke of luck! We can choose from so many different ways to die."

Firdaus Noman awoke one night with her husband snoring by her side and another man's hand over her mouth. When she recognized the shaggy, beret-wearing figure of the son she had not seen for many years she allowed herself to weep, and when he made as if to remove the precautionary hand from her lips she seized it and covered it in kisses. "Don't wake him up right now," she told Anees, looking across at Abdullah. "I want you to myself for a while. And what do you think you look like with that hair? Before you meet your father you'd better start looking like his son, not a wild man from the woods." She led him to the kitchen, sat him down on a stool and cut his hair. Anees didn't object, didn't tell her it was dangerous for him to stay too long, didn't hurry her up or insist she wake his brothers or his father. He sat on the wooden stool, closed his eyes and leaned back against her, feeling her body move slowly against his back as the dark curls fell from his head. "Do you remember, *maej*," he said, "when I was the saddest clown in Pachigam, and people actually cheered up when I left the stage?" She made a small dismissive noise with her lips. "You were the most profound of my children," she said proudly. "I used to worry that you would go so deep inside yourself that you might just vanish completely. But look at you: here you are."

When the men of the house were awake the family held a kitchen-table council of war. "Because Big Man Misri did us all a favour and rid the world of those worthless Gegroos before he died, the Lashkar-e-Pak now has Pachigam in its sights much more than Shirmal," Anees said quietly. "This is bad. Even without the Gegroos those crazy LeP bastards have maybe forty or fifty soldiers in the area and there is no question that they will pick their moment and attack." Firdaus Noman shook her head. "How can a woman's face be the enemy of Islam?" she asked angrily. Anees took her hands in his. "For these idiots it's all about sex, *maej,* excuse me. They think it is a scientific fact that a woman's hair emits rays that arouse men to deeds of sexual depravity. They think that if a woman's bare legs rub together, even under a floor-length robe, the friction of her thighs will generate sexual heat which will be transmitted through her eyes into the eyes of men and will inflame them in an unholy way." Firdaus spread her hands in a gesture of resignation. "So, because men are animals, according to them, women must pay. This is an old story. Tell me something else." Anees nodded in his grave, unsmiling way. "That's why I'm here," he said. "My unit has decided that we will defend Pachigam and Shirmal too, if need be. Don't worry. We have a hundred good guys and can get some friends to assist. But you must be prepared. Hide weapons in every house but don't try to fight them when they first come. Be patient and take whatever insults they hand out. When we start the battle, then and then only you can help us beat the living shit out of them, excuse me, *maej.* Soldier's talk." Firdaus thumped the table, softly. "Little boy," she said, "you won't know what the living shit looks like until you've seen me at work."

The Lashkar-e-Pak came to Pachigam on horseback three weeks later, in broad daylight, not expecting any resistance. The leader, a black-turbanned Afghan homicidal maniac aged fifteen, ordered everyone into the street and announced that since the women of Pachigam were too shameless to conceal themselves as Islam required they should take off their clothes completely so that the world could see what whores they really were. A great murmur arose from the villagers but Firdaus Noman stepped forward, took off her phiran and began to undress. Taking their cue from her, the other women and girls of the village also started to strip. A silence fell. The LeP fighters were unable to take their eyes off the women, who were stripping slowly, seductively, moving their bodies rhythmically, with their eyes closed. "Help me, God," one of the LeP's foreign fighters moaned in Arabic, writhing on his horse, "These blue-eyed she-devils are stealing away my soul." The fifteen-year-old homicidal maniac pointed his Kalashnikov at Firdaus Noman. "If I kill you now," he said nastily, "no man in the whole Muslim world will say I was unjustified." At that moment a small red hole appeared in his forehead and the back of his head blew off. The Baby Che group was getting to be known for the marksmanship of its snipers as well as for its land mines and it had a reputation to protect.

The battle for Pachigam didn't last long. Anees's men had been well positioned and were eager for the fight. The LeP militants were encircled and outnumbered and, in a few minutes, also dead. Firdaus Noman and the other women put their clothes back on. Firdaus spoke sadly to the dead body of the fifteen-year-old Lashkar commander. "You discovered that women are dangerous, my boy," she said. "Too bad you didn't get a chance to become a man and discover we're also good to love."

The extermination of the LeP group of radicals failed to reassure some of the villagers. The old dancing master Habib Joo had passed away peacefully in his bed some years earlier, but his grown-up sons and daughter, all in their twenties now, sober, quiet young people who had inherited their father's love of the dance, still lived in the village. The eldest son, Ahmed Joo, came to inform Abdullah Noman that his younger brother Sulaiman, his sister Razia and he had all decided to go south with the pandit refugees. "How long can Anees protect us?" he said, and went on, "We don't think it's a good idea to be Jewish when the Islamists come to town again." Abdullah knew that the Joo children were gifted dancers like their father, they were the future of the Pachigam bhands except that the Pachigam bhands didn't seem to have a future. He didn't try to stop them. The next day the village's dance troupe was further impoverished when the Sharga girls came to say that they, too, were leaving. Himal and Gonwati had been terrified by the stories of the attacks on pandit families and had forced their father the great old baritone to go with them. "This is no time for songs," Shivshankar Sharga said, "and, anyway, my singing days are done."

Sad to say, the Joos and Shargas were not saved by their decision to flee. The crowded bus in which they were heading south met with an accident at the foot of the mountains not far from the Banihal Pass. The driver, terrified of being stopped by anyone, security forces or militants, had been charging onwards as fast as possible. He screeched around a certain bend only to discover that one of the huge piles of garbage that were accumulating everywhere in the valley on account of the breakdown of the sanitation system had toppled forward across the road. Frantically, he took evasive action, but the bus ended up on its side in a roadside ditch. The driver and most of the passengers were seriously injured and one of the older passengers, the noted singer Shivshankar Sharga, was dead.

There followed a long topsy-turvy wait in the crashed bus. The air was full of petrol fumes. Everyone who could scream or cry was doing so. (Himal was screaming, while Gonwati wept.) Others, less vocally capable, contented themselves with moans (the Joo siblings fell into this category), while still others (e.g. the deceased baritone) were unable to make any sound at all. Eventually the emergency services showed up and the injured passengers were hospitalized in a nearby medical facility. The emergency room was dirty. The sheets in it were badly stained. Rusty red marks ran down the walls. There were few beds and the mattresses on the floor were filthy and torn. The passengers were placed on the beds, on the mattresses, on the floor and along the corridor outside. One single doctor, an exhausted young man with a thin moustache and a numbed expression on his face, addressed the crash victims, who continued to scream (Himal), weep (Gonwati) and moan (Ahmed, Sulaiman, Razia Joo) while he spoke. "It is my onerous obligation before proceeding," the young doctor said, "to offer you our obsequious apologies and to seek from you an obligatory clarification. This is odious but indispensable current routine. Heartfelt apology is primarily offered for understaffing.

Many pandit personnel have decamped and policy does not permit replacement. Many ambulance drivers also are being accosted by security forces and are being extremely chastised and therefore no longer are reporting for duty. Apology is secondarily offered for shortages of supplies. Asthma medication is unavailable. Treatment for diabetics is unavailable. Oxygen tanks are unavailable. Owing to load shedding certain medicaments are not refrigerated and condition of said medicaments is dubious. Replacements, however, are unavailable. Apology is additionally offered for failure of all X-ray machines, sterilization devices and such equipment as is designed to analyse blood. Apology is further extended owing to supply of blood not tested for HIV. Ultimate apology is regarding presence of meningitis epidemic in this facility, and for impossibility of quarantining same. Guidance at this time is sought from your good selves. Under circumstances as sorrowfully outlined above you will kindly and severally confirm or de-confirm your wish to be admitted to or de-admitted from this facility so that treatment is able to proceed or de-proceed. Have no doubt, ladies and gentlemen, that if you trust in us we will make our best effort."

Alas! Not one of the Pachigam contingent of five dancers survived, succumbing to an undetected internal hemorrhage (Himal), an untreated and subsequently gangrenous broken leg (Gonwati), horrific and eventually fatal convulsions brought on by being injected with bad medicines (Ahmed and Razia Joo) and, in the case of Sulaiman Joo, acute viral meningitis caught from a seven-year-old girl who happened to be dying in the bed next to him. There were no relatives on hand to collect the bodies and no facility existed for returning the five dancers to their home village and they were burned on the municipal pyre, even the three Jews.

Their characters were not their destinies.

In early 1991, before the spring thaw, Pandit Pyarelal Kaul felt his life detaching itself from his body in a series of small, painless, inaudible pops. Well, that was all right, he thought, he had nobody to teach any more except himself, and even to himself he no longer had any knowledge to impart. He spent much time in his small library in those final days, alone with his old books. These books, his true treasure, would also be lost when his time came. He ran his fingers along the worn spines of the treasure vaults on the shelves and pulled out the English romantics. *Now more than ever seems it rich to die, to cease upon the midnight with no pain.* Ah! Poor Keats. Only the very young could imagine that death was a proper response to beauty. We in Kashmir have heard the Bulbul too, he apostrophized the great poet across space and time, and he may prove to be the death of us all.

He closed his eyes and pictured his Kashmir. He conjured up its crystal lakes, Shishnag, Wular, Nagin, Dal; its trees, the walnut, the poplar, the chinar, the apple, the peach; its mighty peaks, Nanga Parbat, Rakaposhi, Harmukh. *The pandits Sanskritized the Himalayas.* He saw the boats like little fingers tracing lines in the surface of the waters and the flowers too numberless to name, ablaze with bright perfume. He saw the beauty of the golden children, the beauty of the green- and blue-eyed women, the beauty of the blue- and green-eyed men. He stood atop Mount Shankaracharya which the Muslims called Takht-e-Sulaiman and spoke aloud the famous old verse concerning the earthly paradise. *It is this, it is this, it is this.* Spread out below him like a feast he saw gentleness and time and love. He considered getting out his bicycle and setting forth into the valley, bicycling until he fell, on and on into the beauty. *O! Those days of peace when we all were in love and the rain was in our hands wherever we went.* No, he would not ride out into Kashmir, did not want to see her scarred face, the lines of burning oil drums across the roads, the wrecked vehicles, the smoke of explosions, the broken houses, the broken people, the tanks, the anger and fear in every eye. *Everyone carries his address in his pocket so that at least his body will reach home.*

"Ya Kashmir!" he cried out. "Hai-hai! Ya Kashmir!"

He would not see his daughter again, his only child, whose life he had saved by making an exile of her, transforming her into a tribal wild woman. What a strange tale hers had been. He did not know her fully any more, could not grasp her thoughts. She had turned within herself and was communing with death. As, now, was he. Bhoomi Kaul, Boonyi

Noman. He could protect her no longer. He sent her a word of loving farewell and felt a breeze lift it up and carry it away to her enchanted wood.

He wondered if he would live to see the blossom on his apple trees, and felt an answering pop inside himself. Ah, so it would not be long now. It began to snow lightly, the last flakes to fall before the spring. He put on his wedding finery, the clothes he had worn long ago when he married his beloved Pamposh, and which he had kept all this time wrapped in tissue paper in a trunk. As a bridegroom he went outdoors and the snowflakes caressed his grizzled cheeks. His mind was alert, he was ambulatory and nobody was waiting for him with a club. He had his body and his mind and it seemed he was to be spared a brutal end. That at least was kind. He went into his blighted apple orchard, seated himself cross-legged beneath a tree, closed his eyes, heard the verses of the Rig-Veda fill the world with beauty and ceased upon the midnight with no pain.

Anees Noman was captured alive, though suffering from gunshot wounds in the right leg and shoulder, after an encounter with security forces in the southwestern village of Siot, where he had holed up with twenty militant fighters aged between fifteen and nineteen above a food store called Ahdoo's whose owner called in the troops because the youngsters drank all his cans of condensed milk, a decision he regretted after the army wrecked his shop with grenades that blew out the whole front wall of the small two-storey wooden building, and several hundred rounds of automatic fire from an armoured vehicle parked at point-blank range which destroyed all the produce that had managed to survive the grenade blast. "Look what your greed has done," old man Ahdoo complained to the corpses of the militants as they were dragged out of his upstairs room, adding, in an explanation to the world in general, "They drank my imported goods. Goods from foreign! Then what was I to do?"

Several of the dead boys had been involved in the defence of Pachigam against the LeP, and they saved Anees's life too by coming between him and the grenade blast and bullets. It would have been better if they had let him die in Siot, however, because then he would not have met his end in the secret torture chambers of Badami Bagh, those rooms which had never existed, did not exist and would never exist, and from which nobody ever heard a scream, no matter how loud it was.

On the wall of the room somebody had written two words in black crayon. They were the last words Anees would ever read.

Everybody talks.

After the capture of Anees Noman, the son of the sarpanch of Pachigam, the decision makers of Badami Bagh knew that it was no longer possible for Sardar Harbans Singh or any other high-ranking bleeding-heart string-puller to protect the traitorous sisterfuckers of that village of so-called traditional actors and cooks. General Kachhwaha himself signed the document of authorization and the cordon-and-search crackdown teams moved out on the double. The sheltered status of the bhand village had been a long-standing annoyance to jawans and ranking officers alike. The crackdown on Pachigam would therefore be particularly satisfying, and the gloves, of course, would be off.

The army officer who brought Anees Noman's body back to his mother's house, the detachment in charge, did not offer his name or his condolences. The corpse was tossed onto the doorstep, wrapped in a bloodied grey blanket, and the front door was smashed down. Firdaus was dragged out by her grey hair and pushed so that she stumbled over her dead son. A single cry escaped her lips, but after that, in spite of everything she saw on his body, she remained silent, until she stood up and looked the incharge in the eye. "Where are his hands?" she asked. His hands that were so deft, that had whittled and shaped so much. "Give me back his hands."

Anees's father knelt proudly by his son, placed his twisted hands together and began to recite verses. The incharge was unimpressed. "Why is your woman making noise about hands," he said to Abdullah, "when your hands don't even know how to pray?" He made a gesture and two soldiers grabbed the sarpanch's hands and pushed them against the floor. "Hands, is it," the incharge said. "Before going any further let's straighten these two out right here."

What was that cry? Was it a man, a woman, an angel or a god who keened thus, who howled just so? Could any human voice make such a desolate noise?

There was the earth and there were the planets. The earth was not a planet. The planets were the grabbers. They were called this because they could seize hold of the earth and bend its destiny to their will. The earth was never of their kind. The earth was the subject. The earth was the grabbee.

Pachigam was the earth, the grabbee, helpless, and powerful uncaring planets stooped low, extended their celestial and merciless tentacles and grabbed.

Who lit that fire? Who burned that orchard? Who shot those brothers who laughed their whole lives long? Who killed the sarpanch? Who broke his hands? Who broke his arms? Who broke his ancient neck? Who shackled those men? Who made those men disappear? Who shot those boys? Who shot those girls? Who smashed that house? Who smashed *that* house? Who smashed *that* house? Who killed that youth? Who clubbed that grandmother? Who knifed that aunt? Who broke that old man's nose? Who broke that young girl's heart? Who killed that lover? Who shot his fiancée? Who burned the costumes? Who broke the swords? Who burned the library? Who burned the saffron field? Who slaughtered the animals? Who burned the beehives? Who poisoned the paddies? Who killed the children? Who whipped the parents? Who raped that lazy-eyed woman? Who raped that grey-haired lazy-eyed woman as she screamed about snake vengeance? Who raped that woman again? Who raped that woman again? Who raped that woman again? Who raped that dead woman? Who raped that dead woman again?

The village of Pachigam still exists on the official maps of Kashmir, due south of Srinagar and west of Shirmal near the Anantnag road. In such public records as are still available for inspection its population is given as three hundred and fifty, and in a few guides for the benefit of visitors there are passing references to the bhand pather, a dying folk art, and to the dwindling number of dedicated troupes that seek to preserve it. This official existence, this paper self is its only memorial, for where Pachigam once stood by the blithe Muskadoon, where its little street ran along from the pandit's house to the sarpanch's, where Abdullah roared and Boonyi danced and Shivshankar sang and Shalimar the clown walked the tightrope as if treading upon air, nothing resembling a human habitation remains. What happened that day in Pachigam need not be set down here in full detail, because brutality is brutality and excess is excess and that's all there is to it. There are things that must be looked at indirectly because they would blind you if you looked them in the face, like the fire of the sun. So, to repeat: there was no Pachigam any more. Pachigam was destroyed. Imagine it for yourself.

Second attempt: The village of Pachigam still existed on maps of Kashmir, but that day it ceased to exist anywhere else, except in memory.

Third and final attempt: The beautiful village of Pachigam still exists.

The increased use of *fidayeen,* suicide bombers, by the group led by Maulana Bulbul Fakh and also by other insurgents, Hizb-ul-this, Lashkar-e-the-other, Jaish-e-whatever-you-want, was a new annoyance, thought General Hammirdev Kachhwaha hunkered down in the dark, but it was also an indication that purely military activities, even of the so-called iron commando, had been judged to lack sufficient teeth, and that a second, decisive phase had begun. The milquetoasts of secular nationalism had had their day, and as the months passed looked more and more like sidelined irrelevances. "Kashmir for the Kashmiris" was no longer an option. Only the big boys were left standing, and so it was to be Kashmir for the Indians or Kashmir for the Pakistanis whose proxies the terror organizations were. Things had clarified and the creation of clarity was after all the universal goal of military activity. General Kachhwaha liked this simpler, clearer world. Now, he told himself, it's either us or them, and we are the stronger, and will inevitably prevail.

He had to concede that the suicide missions had had

successes. Here they all were in his memory. July 13 last year, attack on Border Security Force camp at Bandipora, deputy inspector general and four personnel killed. August 6, one major and two junior commissioned officers slain at Natnoos army camp. August 7, colonel and three personnel done to death at Trehgam army camp. September 3, in a daring raid on the perimeter area of Army Corps HQ Badami Bagh itself, ten personnel murdered including a public relations officer (no loss, in General Kachhwaha's unexpressed private view). And so it went on, pinprick after pinprick. December 2, Army HQ, Baramulla, one JCO lost. December 13, Civil Lines, Srinagar, five personnel. December 15, army camp, Rafiabad, many injuries, no fatalities. January 7, meteorological centre, Srinagar, attacked. Four personnel lost. January 10, car bomb in Srinagar. February 14, unmanned pony used to carry an IED (improvised explosive device) into security force camp at Lapri, district Udhampur. General Kachhwaha could admire initiative when he saw it. However, the enemy's losses during these encounters were also heavy. They had been hit hard. The iron commando had been shot full of holes. Hence the new tactic. They accepted some small loss of life in order to inflict large wounds. February 19 saw the first fidayeen attack on Badami Bagh. Two personnel killed. Three weeks later, a second suicide bomb attack on HQ, four army personnel dead.

There were those who claimed that the terrorists, inspired by fidayeen activities, were gaining momentum, that the war was being lost. There were calls for General Kachhwaha to be replaced. Fidayeen bombed the police control room in Srinagar (eight personnel killed). Fidayeen attacked Wazir Bagh base in Srinagar (four killed). Fidayeen attacked Lassipora army base, district Kupwara (six). And alongside this, there was a non-fidayeen ambush at Morha Chatru, Rajouri district (which claimed fifteen lives), a patrol party ambushed at Gorikund, Udhampur (five lives), an attack on Shahlal base, Kupwara (five), on Poonch police station (seven). IEDs were placed under military buses at Hangalpua (eight) and Khooni Nallah (five). Very well, General Kachhwaha grudgingly conceded, the list was long. Fidayeen attacks at Handwara, twice. The annual Amarnath pilgrimage attacked, nine pilgrims killed. More Hindus dead at Raghunath temple in Jammu courtesy of two fidayeen bombers. Fidayeen attacked a bus stand in Poonch, and the deputy superintendent of police was killed. A three-man fidayeen squad stormed the army camp at village Bangti on Tanda Road, Akhnoor, Jammu: eight dead, including a brigadier, and four top generals injured. Then, at last, there were some successes to report. Baby Che, the notorious militant Anees Noman, was dead. A fidayeen attack on a security force camp in Poonch was foiled; two foreign mercenaries were slain. A daring and highly dangerous fidayeen attack on the chief minister's residence on Maulana Azad Road, Srinagar, was thwarted; both terrorists were killed. The tide was turning. The political echelon must appreciate this. The situation was being stabilized. Approximately one hundred alleged insurgents and their alleged associates were being shot dead every day. The point was to have the will to succeed. If fifty thousand deaths were required there would be fifty thousand deaths. The battle would not be lost while the will was there and he, General Kachhwaha, was the embodiment of that will. Therefore the battle was not being lost. It was being won.

News of the razing of Pachigam spread quickly. The Hammer of Kashmir had made an example of this village and his strong-arm tactics had been effective in their way. People were even more scared of harbouring militants than before. The few survivors of the crackdown action, some oldsters, some children, a few farmhands and shepherds who had managed to hide in the wooded hills behind the village, made their way to the neighbouring village of Shirmal where they were shown such kindnesses as the Shirmalis could afford in that time of empty pockets and open mouths. The old resentments between Pachigam and Shirmal were forgotten as if they had never been. Bombur Yambarzal and his wife Hasina a.k.a. Harud personally ensured that the refugees were fed and housed for the time being. The ruins of Pachigam were still smoldering. "First let things cool down," Harud Yambarzal told the terrified, heartbroken Pachigamis, "and then we'll see about rebuilding your homes." She was trying to sound as reassuring as she could but was inwardly panic-stricken. In the privacy of the Yambarzal home she hit both her sons across their faces with an open hand and said that unless they broke all their connections with militant groups immediately she personally would cut off their noses while they slept. "If you think I will allow what happened to Pachigam to befall this village," she hissed at them, "then, boys, you don't know your mother. I raised you to be sensible and practical fellows. This is when you repay the debt of childhood and do as you are told." She was a formidable lady and her sons the secretive electricians mumbled okay, okay, and skulked out the back way to smoke beedis and wait for the ringing in their ears to stop. By that time there was a shortage of young men in the villages of Kashmir. They had gone underground in Srinagar, which was still safer than the villages, or underground to join the militants, or underground into the army's counterinsurgency fifth columns, or underground across the Line of Control to join the Pakistani ISI's jihadi groups or just underground into their graves. Hasina Yambarzal had held on to her boys by sheer force of personality. She wanted them where she could see them: overground, at home.

Seven nights after the crackdown on Pachigam, to Hasina Yambarzal's horror, Maulana Bulbul Fakh entered Shirmal in the first of three Jeeps, accompanied by Shalimar the clown and twenty more riders from the terrifying iron commando. Soon the Yambarzal home was besieged by armed men. The iron mullah came inside with a few of his aides, one of whom was the only surviving son of the deceased sarpanch of Pachigam. Even Bombur Yambarzal, a man whose sense of self-importance made him a bad observer of others, noticed the change in Shalimar the clown and later that night, in bed with his wife, he asked her about it. "Tragedy has struck that man so hard it's not surprising he looks like he would cut your throat if you snapped your fingers at the wrong time, eh, Harud," he said softly, afraid to raise his voice in case anyone was listening outside. Hasina Yambarzal shook her head slowly. "The tragedy is a new wound, and you can see its pain, that's for sure," she answered in a voice as low as her husband's. "But I also saw in his eyes the thing you're talking about, and I'm telling you that assassin's look has been there for a long time. That's not the look of a man shocked by his family's death, but the expression of a man accustomed to killing. God alone knows where he's been or what he's become, to come back wearing a face like that."

"Our bereaved brother needs to visit his parents' graves," Bulbul Fakh had said without preamble. "For tonight therefore I require your assistance in the matter of accommodation and food for the animals and men." Bombur Yambarzal shook in his shoes and temporarily lost the power of speech because he was sure that the iron mullah had not forgotten the day he had defied him so many years ago, and so it was Hasina who said, "We'll do what we can but it won't be easy because we already have the homeless from Pachigam to feed and find roofs for." She proposed, however, that the abandoned Gegroo house be opened for the fighters' use, and the iron mullah agreed. Bulbul Fakh stationed himself in that dusty old ruin with half of his fighters on guard and Bombur personally served them a simple meal of vegetables, lentils and bread. The other fighters ate quickly and then dispersed into the shadows around Shirmal to keep watch.

Shalimar the clown borrowed a pony and rode off alone in the direction of Pachigam without a word to anyone.

"Poor fellow," Bombur Yambarzal said as he watched him go. Nobody replied. Hasina Yambarzal had noted some time earlier that her two sons were nowhere to be seen, which meant that the instructions she had issued the moment she saw the fighters of the iron commando ride into town were being followed. The thing to do now was for everyone to get indoors. "Come to bed," she said to Bombur, and he knew better than to argue with her when she used that particular voice.

In the small hours of the night General Hammirdev Kachhwaha's forces, informed of the situation by Hasina Yambarzal's emissaries, Hashim and Hatim Karim (who were highly commended for their patriotism and immediately inducted into places of honour in the anti-insurgency militia), launched a major assault on Shirmal. "First the Hizb-ul-Mujaheddin started betraying the JKLF," General Kachhwaha reflected, "and now the people have started betraying the Hizb. The situation has many satisfactory aspects." The sanitary cordon around the Shirmal area was established so stealthily and swiftly that none of the iron-commando fighters managed to escape. As the noose tightened the sentries in the woods fell back toward the Gegroo house and there made their last stand. When the army tanks rumbled into Shirmal there was no indiscriminate destruction of the type so recently suffered by Pachigam. Co-operation had its rewards, and in any case, thanks to Hasina Yambarzal, the rats were already neatly in their trap. After a brief but overwhelming period of grenade explosions and artillery fire the Gegroo house had ceased to exist and nobody inside it remained alive. The bodies of the iron-commando fighters were brought out. Inside the garments of Maulana Bulbul Fakh no human body was discovered. However, a substantial quantity of disassembled machine parts was found, pulverized beyond hope of repair.

General Hammirdev Suryavans Kachhwaha lying in bed in his darkened quarters at Army HQ, Badami Bagh, slipped contentedly towards sleep. He had been awakened by a phone call informing him of the successful eradication of at least twenty iron-commando fighters and the presumed death of their leader, the jihadi fanatic known as Maulana Bulbul Fakh. General Kachhwaha replaced the receiver, sighed gently and closed his eyes. The women of Jodhpur appeared before him, spreading their arms to welcome him. Soon his long northern marriage would be over. Soon he would return in triumph to that land of hot colours and fiery women and at the age of sixty would be restored to vigorous youth by a beauty whose attentions he had earned, whose sweet attentions he so fully deserved. The beauty approached him, beckoning. Her arm slipped around his shoulder, supple as a snake, and like a snake her leg coiled around his. Then like a third snake her other arm and like a fourth snake her other leg until she was slithering all over him, hanging around his body, licking at his ear with her forked tongues, her many forked tongues, the tongues at the ends of her arms and legs. She had as many arms and legs as a goddess, and multilimbed and irresistible she coiled and tightened around him and, finally, with all the power she possessed, she bit.

The accidental death by king cobra snakebite of General H. S. Kachhwaha was announced at Badami Bagh the next morning and he was buried with full honours in the military cemetery on the base. The details of the accident were not made public but in spite of the authorities' best efforts it wasn't long before everyone knew about the writhing swarm of snakes that had somehow penetrated the innermost sanctum of military power in Kashmir, the snakes whose numbers multiplied in the retelling until there were dozens of them, fifty, a hundred and one. It was said, and soon came to be commonly believed, that the snakes had burrowed their way beneath all the army's defences—and these were giant snakes, remember, the most poisonous snakes imaginable, snakes arriving after a long subterranean journey from their secret lairs at the roots of the Himalayas!—to avenge the wrongs against Kashmir, and, people told one another, when General Kachhwaha's body was discovered it looked like he had been attacked by a swarm of hornets, so many and so vicious were the bites. It was not widely known, however, that as she died Firdaus Noman of Pachigam had called down a snake curse upon the army's head; accordingly, this macabre detail was not a part of the story that did the rounds.

She knew he was coming, could feel his proximity, and prepared for his arrival. She killed the last kid goat, skinned it, dressed it with her choicest herbs and prepared a meal. She bathed in the mountain stream that ran through the meadow of Khelmarg and braided her hair with flowers. She was almost forty-four years old, her hands were rough with toil, she had two broken teeth, but her body was smooth. Her body told the story of her life. The obesity of her insane time was gone but had left its wounds, the broken veins, a looseness in the skin. She wanted him to see her story, to read the book of her nakedness, before he did what he had come to do.

She wanted him to know she loved him. She wanted to remind him of the hours by the Muskadoon, of what had happened in Khelmarg, of the village's bold defence of their love. If she showed him her body he would see it all there, just as he would see the marks of another man's hands, the marks that would force him to commit murder. She wanted him to see it all, her fall, and her survival of the fall. Her years of exile were written on her body and he should know their tale. She wanted him to know that at the end of the story of her body she loved him still, or again, or still. She wore no clothes, stirred the pot of food on the low fire and waited.

He came on foot, holding a knife. There was a horse's whinny somewhere but he did not ride. There was no moon. She stepped out of her hut to greet him.

Do you want to eat first? she asked, pushing a strand of hair away from her face. If you want to eat, there's food.

He said nothing. He was reading the story of her skin.

Everyone is dead, she said, my father's dead, and yours, and I think maybe you're dead too, so why should I want to live?

He said nothing.

Get on with it, she said. Oh God, be done with it, please.

He moved towards her. He was reading her body. He held it in his hands.

Now, she commanded him. Now.

He was on his way down the pine-forested hill with tears in his eyes when he heard the explosions in Shirmal and guessed the rest. That simplified things, in a way. He had been the iron mullah's right-hand man and communications chief but the two men no longer saw eye to eye. Shalimar the clown had never liked the use of fidayeen suicides, which struck him as an unmanly way of making war, but Bulbul Fakh was increasingly convinced of the tactic's value and was rapidly moving from military raids of the iron-commando type towards fidayeen recruiting and training activities. The business of finding young boys and even young girls who were ready to blow themselves up felt demeaning to Shalimar the clown, who had therefore decided to make his break with the iron mullah as soon as he could think of a way of doing so that wouldn't lead to his execution for desertion. The explosions in Shirmal solved that problem. There was nothing left for him in Kashmir and now that the last obstacle had been removed it was time for him to make his run.

He got off the little mountain pony he had borrowed from Bombur Yambarzal, wiped his face and fished in his backpack for the satphone. It was always risky to use satellite telephone communications because satchat was often monitored by the enemy, but he had no choice. He was too far from the northern passes over the mountains and the southern end of the Line of Control was heavily militarized and hard to cross. There were crossing places if you knew where to look, but even though he had a good idea of where to head for it would be a difficult trick to pull off on his own. He needed what would once, in another war, in another time, have been called a *passeur.*

The first phone call set that up. The second was a gamble. But the Malaysian intermediary's phone number was a real number, and was answered by a voice that spoke and understood Arabic, and the codes he had been given seemed to mean something, the message he needed to send was accepted for transmission, and an instruction was given in return. But nothing could be done until he crossed the Line of Control. As things turned out, however, that wasn't his biggest problem. The *passeur* showed up and did his work on the Indian side of the LoC and the fighter he thought of as the doorway, the militant known as Dar, whom he called Naked Mountain, was waiting for him across the line with a group of hoodlums who didn't seem pleased to see him. "I'm sorry," Naked Mountain said in Kashmiri, "but you know how it goes." This was Shalimar the clown's last human contact with his old life. He was blindfolded and taken for debriefing in a windowless room where he was tied to a chair and invited to explain how it was that he alone had survived the massacre at Shirmal, and to give his intelligence interlocutors one good reason why he should not be thought of as a dirty traitorous bastard and shot within the hour. Blindfolded, not knowing the name of his interrogator, he spoke the coded phrase he had been given on the satphone and there was a long silence in the room. Then the interrogator left and after several hours another man entered. "Okay, it checks out," the second man said. "You're a lucky bastard, you know that? Our plan was to cut off your balls and stuff them between your teeth but it seems you have friends in high places, and if the *ustadz* wants you alongside him then that, my friend, is exactly where you will go."

After that the real world ceased to exist for Shalimar the clown. He entered the phantom world of the run. In the phantom world there were business suits and commercial aircraft, and he was passed from hand to hand like a package. At one point he was in Kuala Lumpur but that was just an airport and a hotel room and then an airport again. At the far end of the phantom run there were place-names that meant next to nothing: Zamboanga, Lamitan, Maluso, Isabela. There were several boats. Around the main Basilan island there were sixty-one smaller islands and on one of these, a part of the Pilas group, he emerged from the phantom world in a palm-thatched stilt-house in a village smelling of tuna and sardines, and was greeted by a familiar face. "So, godless man," the *ustadz* said in his bad, cheerful Hindi, "as you see I am back to fisherman again, but also—right? right?—one pretty good fisher of men."

Abdurajak Janjalani had wealthy backers but his Abu Sayyaf group was in its infancy. There were less than six hundred fighters in all. "So, my friend, we need good fighter killer like you." The plan was simple. "Everywhere in Basilan and western Mindanao we ambush Christians, we bomb Christians, we burn Christian business, we kidnap Christian tourists for ransom, we execute Christian soldiers, and then we ambush them some more. In between we show you good time. Land of plenty! Plenty fish, plenty rubber, plenty corn, plenty palm oil, plenty pepper, plenty coconut, plenty women, plenty music, plenty Christians to take it all and leave nothing for plenty Muslim. Plenty language. Want to learn? Chavacano, sort of Spanish. Also Yakan, Tausug, Samal, Cebuano, Tagalog. Forget it, never mind. Now we bring our new language. In our language few words are needed. Ambush, bomb, kidnap, ransom, execute. No more mister nice guy! We are the Bearers of the Sword." They were eating mackerel and rice in the fisherman's hut. The *ustadz* leaned in close. "I know you, my friend. I remember your quest. But how will you find your quarry? He knows the secret world, and the world, also, is large." Shalimar the clown shrugged. "Maybe he will find me," he said. "Maybe God will bring him to me for justice." Janjalani laughed merrily. "Godless fighter killer, you are funny man." His voice dropped. "Fight with me one year. What else is there for you? We will try to find him. Who knows? The world is full of ears. Maybe we are fortunate."

Exactly one year later—one year to the day!—they were in Latuan, to the east of Isabela, and had just finished burning a rubber plantation called Timothy da Cruz Filipinas. Against an apocalyptic backdrop of flame Abdurajak Janjalani turned to him wearing a red and white Palestinian keffiyeh and the sudden glory of his big smile. "Wonderful news! My friend! I keep my word." Shalimar the clown took the envelope the *ustadz* was holding out. "The ambassador, no?" Janjalani grinned. "His picture, his name, his home address. Now we will send you on your mission. Look inside, look inside! Los Angeles, my friend! Hollywood and Vine! Malibu Colony! Beverly Hills 90210! We will send you to become big big movie star and soon to be kissing American girls on TV and driving fancy motorcars and making stupid thank-you speech at Oscars! I am man of my word, don't you agree?"

Shalimar the clown looked at the envelope. "How did you do this?" he asked. Janjalani shrugged. "Like I say. Maybe we got lucky. Filipinos are everywhere, with eyes to see and ears to hear." A thought struck Shalimar the clown. "How long have you known? You've known all along, haven't you?" Ustadz Abdurajak Janjalani pretended to look remorseful. "My friend! Fighter killer! Please forgive. I needed you for one year. Thank you! This was the deal. And now I send you where you need to go. Thank you! Our stories touched. Okay. It's enough. This is my good-bye gift."

And after another plunge into the phantom world, after boats, cars and planes, after a Canadian border crossing by helicopter shuttle from Vancouver to Seattle and a coach ride south, after a strange assignation at the IHOP on Sunset and Highland with his local contact, a middle-aged Filipino gentleman sporting slicked-down hair and a silk smoking jacket, after a night's sleep in a downtown flophouse across the street from the Million Dollar Hotel, he stood in his business suit outside high gates on Mulholland Drive and spoke open-sesame words into an entry-phone. I am for Ambassador Max and my name is Shalimar the clown. No, sir, not tradesman. Sir, I am not understanding. You please to inform Ambassador Max, sir, wait on sir, sir, please, sir. And on the second day, again, the speech to the unnamed voice, the hostile, aloof, dismissive voice, the voice of security, taking no risks, considering the worst-case scenario, taking steps. On the third day there were dogs on the other side of the gate. Sir, he said, no dogs, please. I am known to Ambassador Max. No trouble, sir, please. Only please to inform Excellency and I will wait on his pleasure.

He slept in the rough grasses below the road's rim, keeping out of sight of the cruising patrol cars. He was trained in many things. He could have caught the dogs by their jaws and ripped their heads in half. He could have faced the security voice and shown it some tricks, could have forced it to roll over like a dog and play dead like a dog. It was a dog's voice and its owner could be killed like a dog. But he controlled himself, was humble, supplicant, mild. When the ambassador's Bentley came out through the gates on the fourth day Shalimar the clown rose into view. Security guards raised their weapons but he had a woollen Kashmiri hat in his hands, his head was bowed and his demeanour was worshipful and sad. The window of the car came down and there was the target, Ambassador Max, old now but still the man he wanted, his prey. One's prey can be hunted in many ways. Some of these are stealthy. Who are you, the ambassador was saying, why do you keep coming here. Sir, he said, my name is Shalimar the clown and once in Kashmir you met my wife. She danced for you. *Anarkali.* Yes, sir, Shalimar. Yes, sir, Boonyi, my wife. No, sir, I don't want trouble. What's done is done. No, sir, unfortunately she is deceased. Yes, sir. Some while back. Sad, yes, sir, very sad. Life is short and full of sorrow. Yes, sir, thank you for asking. I am happy to be here in land of frees home of braves. Only I am in need of employment. This, for her sake, sir, I ask. Sir, if you are able, for love. God bless you, sir. I will not disappoint.

Come tomorrow, the ambassador said. We'll talk then. He bowed his head and backed off. On the fifth day he buzzed again. I am for Ambassador Max and my name is Shalimar the clown.

The gates opened.

He was more than a driver. He was a valet, a body servant, the ambassador's shadow-self. There were no limits to his willingness to serve. He wanted to draw the ambassador close, as close as a lover. He wanted to know his true face, his strengths and weaknesses, his secret dreams. To know as intimately as possible the life he planned to terminate with maximum brutality. There was no hurry. There was time.

He knew the ambassador had a wife, from whom he was estranged. He knew there was a daughter who had been raised by the wife but now lived in Los Angeles also. Mr Khadaffy Andang, the odd-looking Filipino gentleman, was a connection of the *ustadz*'s connections, a long-term sleeper planted in California by the operatives of the Base, and had been activated by the Sheikh at the *ustadz*'s request, to assist Shalimar the clown. By chance, or divine intervention, the sleeper resided in the same apartment building as the Ophuls girl. He talked to her at the laundry machines and his gentle courteous old-world manner put her at her ease. This was how the information about the ambassador had come to light. This was the way of the world. Sometimes your heart's desire hung from the highest branch of the highest tree and you could never climb high enough to reach it. Or else you just waited patiently and it fell into your lap.

The ambassador kept no framed photographs of his family on his desk. That was his preference, to be low key in family matters. Then it was his daughter's birthday and the ambassador sent him up to her apartment with flowers. When he saw her, when those green eyes speared him, he began to tremble. The flowers shook in his hands and she took them quickly from him, looking amused. In the elevator he couldn't take his eyes off her until she saw him staring and then he dragged his gaze away and forced himself to look down at the floor. She spoke to him. His heart pounded. The voice was incredible. It was the ambassador's voice on the surface but beneath the English words he could hear a voice he knew. He was from Kashmir, he said, answering her question. He made his English sound worse than it was, to prevent a conversation from beginning. He couldn't speak to her. He could barely speak. He wanted to reach out to her. He didn't know what he wanted. She let her hair down and there were tears in his eyes. He watched her drive away with her father and all he could think was, She's alive. He didn't know what he wanted. She was living in America now and by some miracle she was twenty-four years old again, mocking him with her emerald eyes, she was the same and not the same, but she was still alive.

He had warned Boonyi against leaving him. In Khelmarg long ago he promised her, "I'll never forgive you. I'll have my revenge. I'll kill you and if you have any children by another man I'll kill the children too." And here now was that child, the child she had concealed from him until the end, the child in whom the mother was reborn. How beautiful she was. He would love her if he still knew how to love. But he had forgotten the way. All he knew now was slaughter. *I'll kill the children too.*

Kashmira

What was justice, the old ladies chorused, the toothless old ladies from Croatia, Georgia, Uzbekistan, the widows in their dark cassocks swaying in slow unison with Olga Volga the house super naked at their head, grinding her hips, rotating her lumpy white body like a giant peeled potato, there was no justice, the women keened, your husbands died, your children abandoned you, your fathers were murdered, there was no justice but revenge.

After a while India Ophuls didn't even have to be asleep to see the dream, it came to her whenever she closed her eyes, whenever she sat stiff-backed in a Shaker chair in her little vestibule, waiting for whatever she was waiting for. When she saw the gossipy old ladies in the corridors now she immediately pictured them dressed in cassocks and when she ran into Olga Simeonovna she imagined her without her clothes on, which made an intimacy between them. The former Astrakhani sorceress had taken the grief-distracted younger woman under her wing, becoming her newest surrogate mother, tidying her apartment for her while she stared silently into space, and cooking her thick-gravied meat stews with dumplings and potatoes, or potato soup, or, when time was short, getting organic vegeburgers and Ore-Ida french fries out of the freezer. She was putting potatoes to work in other, more occult ways as well. The manhunt for Shalimar the assassin was coming up empty, infuriating Olga. "The LAPD, excuse me, they couldn't catch a cold in a Russian draft," she said contemptuously. "But by the power of potato magic we will haul in that asshole's ass."

In a distant part of her consciousness India knew that she was filling the hole in Olga Simeonovna's heart left behind by the two departed daughters whose names she never spoke, the twin sisters who had offended against their mother's moral code by posing for saucy pictures and developing an innuendo-rich blonde bombshell sister act to go with them, and who were probably languishing now in some Vegas flea pit or worse, some Howard Johnson hell of multiple ruinations, their noses ruined by drug habits, their mouths and breasts ruined by cheap plastic surgery gone wrong, their finances ruined by the managers slash husbands who ran off with such pathetic assets as they had managed to amass. They had dropped off the map, probably too ashamed to come home and face the mother who daily cursed their names but in whose ample bosom they might nevertheless find redemption, or, at least, themselves.

People were moving out of the building in a hurry, and some of the remaining tenants had suggested unkindly that India should be the one to move, that she was putting them all in danger by staying. Olga reacted to these suggestions with unconcealed maternal fury. "They say me it once, maybe, if they dare," she told India, bridling, "but, I swear, they don't gonna say me it twice." There was a large sign outside the apartment building advertising vacancies but blood takes time to wash away. The arrest, or, to use his preferred word, the word his lawyer used, the *surrender* of Mr Khadaffy Andang had spooked many residents already rendered fearful by the murder on their doorstep, the, to use a word that had appeared in the newspaper, *execution.* The word *sleeper* was frightening. "All that time I thought he was only waiting for his wife," Olga Simeonovna marvelled in her dark apartment with postcards of Roublev icons and travel agency posters of the Caspian Sea pinned to the wall, pouring India many cups of dark tea—the cups were glasses, really, glass receptacles held in beaten-metal frames—and sighing a deep, Caspian sigh. "Turns out he was a bad guy in spite of his silk dressing-gowns. Asleep, like Rip Van Winkle, but gone over to the Dark Side." Mr Khadaffy Andang had shouted up at India as she stood on her balcony and watched his last shuffling exit, his hands cuffed behind his back, the burly LAPD officers ungentle all around him, the street ablaze with the flashing lights of police cars and journalists' cameras, the air full of megaphoned orders and microphoned reports, *everybody go inside,* but she stayed on her balcony with her arms crossed over her heart, with her hands hugging her shoulders, not caring about the upturned snouts of the cameras in the street, looking at the police operation, the white vans of the information media with the uplink dishes on their roofs, the police snipers on the building across the road, the crime reporters filing copy, the pool photographers taking her picture; and because she was out there, floating above the event, feeling a little crazy, she heard what Mr Khadaffy Andang shouted out, twisting himself around and looking right at her just before a police officer put a hood over his head, *I don't buzz him in, Miss India,* he shouted. *Miss India, he want me to buzz him but I don't buzz.*

She guessed then that Mr Khadaffy Andang might have surrendered in part on her account, partly because he had chatted to her in the laundry room and she had listened to his tales of his homeland and he didn't want her blood on his hands, but probably also because he was just a silver-haired cuckolded old gent nowadays, a loser with a fondness for silk who might have agreed to be a sleeper years ago but who never expected to "awake", and he just wanted out of the sleeper business, because it scared him, too.

After that she accepted she was possibly in danger herself, just as the police officers had told her she was, she knew she should move out in spite of her obstinate desire to stick around here just to spite her cowardly neighbours, *Maybe a few weeks with a family member or friend,* the police officers suggested, *you could use the emotional support,* she was her father's only heir, the lawyers told her, all of it came to her, starting with the big house on Mulholland Drive, fully staffed, with all the latest high-security equipment and twenty-four-hour Jerome security, all the codes had already been changed, procedures reviewed, and personnel numbers would be augmented if she moved in, so Shalimar's inside knowledge of the property, of security configurations and staffing levels, wouldn't help him. But she wasn't ready to move back, to live up there on the skyway again, to step into her dead father's outsized shoes and sleep in his bed and go through the papers in his mahogany-panelled study, she wasn't ready for the smell of his cologne or the secrets in his safe, so she stayed on in her apartment and found herself thinking that if the killer showed up to finish the job she really didn't care, let him come, she might even welcome him in.

The world does not stop but cruelly continues, the widows chorused in the hallways. At a time of tragedy you wonder at it, the world's capacity for continuing. When our husbands left us we expected the planet to cease its spinning so we could all float off into space, we expected silence, respect, but the traffic doesn't care what the heart needs, the billboards don't care, things move right along. There's a new giant lady holding a golden beer bottle up near the Château. There's a new place a mile east, women dance on the bar while the smart kids howl with lust. Lust continues, sure it does, honey, power continues, bargains are struck, hands are shaken and arms are twisted, winners and losers continue, honey, dog walking continues, right on our block the dogs walk past the scene of the crime every morning, dogs don't care, they move on. The new horror movies open every Friday, business is business, and real-life horror continues too, here it is on TV, the unexplained sacrifice of goats at the Hollywood Bowl in the middle of the night, the discovery in the morning of maybe forty stinking carcasses and the blood, all that congealing blood, craziness continues, black magic continues, the darkness never ends. Clothes are on sale all around. Clothes go on, also goes on the hunger of the citizens and the relief of hunger. There is fine pizza to be had. Valet parking continues. The stars come out to play. A woman's father dies, she mourns alone. His death is already old news.

After her father died she sat on the Shaker chair in the vestibule of her apartment, for how long, an hour, a year, looking straight ahead, seeing nothing, while in the corridors and by the courtyard pool the old ladies gossiped and on the sidewalk the "guy community" of whom Olga Volga idly and not ill-naturedly complained came to scope out the scene of the crime, the guy gym rats, the guy girls in the haircut business, the guy Hispanic builders whose work a block away was never done, the guy Emperor of Ice Cream who woke the street up every morning when he reversed his van out of its parking bay, its tinkling ice-cream melodies turned up high like a mechanical dawn chorus or his empire's national anthem. The (straight) young man who wanted to marry India had climbed across onto her balcony from the apartment next door and hammered on her sliding glass doors but he was an irrelevance now, she was done with him, he didn't even have a name, and what did he think he was doing hammering like that out there, what was she supposed to do, *open up and put out?* but that was disgusting, this was no time for sex.

Where was justice? Shouldn't justice be done? Where were the forces of justice, where was the Justice League, why weren't superheroes swooping down out of the sky to bring her father's murderer to justice? But she didn't want the Justice League, really, those goody-goodies in their weird suits, she wanted the Revenge League, she wanted dark superheroes, hard men who wouldn't meekly hand the killer over to the authorities, who would gladly kill the bastard, who would shoot him down like a dog, or like wild dogs themselves tear him to bloody bits, who would take his life from him slowly and with pain. She wanted avenging angels, angels of death and damnation, to come to her aid. Blood called out for blood and she wanted the ancient Furies to descend shrieking from the sky and give her father's unquiet spirit peace. She didn't know what she wanted. She was full of thoughts of death.

We don't fully understand his motivation, Ms Ophuls, it looks political at this point, your father served his country in some hot zones, he swam for America through some pretty muddy water, yes ma'am, and the assassin's a pro, no doubt. Used to be the case that they didn't make war on women and children, it was kind of a code-of-honour thing, the target was the target and you got no points in heaven for killing kids or spouses. But things are rougher now, some of these guys aren't so squeamish any more, and in this case there's some stuff we don't understand yet, we have some blanks to fill in, so we've got to have a degree of concern, ma'am, we respect your feelings but we want to get you to a secure location.

Stern men offered her stiff-backed police-officer comfort and advice, some of them—*all* of them—secretly wanting to offer comfort of a more personal, informal kind: uniformed police officers and plainclothesmen from previously-unknown-to-her counterterrorist outfits, hunting for answers and issuing disgraceful interim warnings. *You owe it to the neighbourhood.* They were siding with the jumpy residents. This wasn't right. She was an innocent woman. She owed nobody anything and to suggest otherwise was ugly. It was, gentlemen, *unattractive.* She imagined the circling officers in oiled *Full Monty* undress, wearing police hats and studded leather posing pouches with their badges pinned on the front, imagined them swarming around her seated body, caressing her without touching her, and placing, against her unsurprised cheek, their cold, long-barreled guns. She imagined them in white tie and tails, soft-shoe shuffling—*gumshoe* shuffling—or tap-dancing with top hats and canes, imagined herself a ginger to their freds, being tossed lightly about from hand to manly hand. She imagined them as a second chorus to go with the cassocked gossips. Her thoughts were acting up, she couldn't help it. She was a little crazy right now.

After a further while—a week, or a decade—she picked up her golden bow and drove to Elysian Park and rained arrows on a target hour after hour. She opened the little wall-safe where she kept her firearms and drove the DeLorean, her father's absurd last gift to her, into the desert for a weekend at Saltzman's range. She taped her hands and booked ring time at Jimmy Fish, where the other boxers watched her with the deferential respect accorded to those wearing the numinous mantle of tragedy, with the religious adoration accorded to those who have had their picture on TV and in *People* magazine as well. They looked like the citizens of Mycenae scrutinizing their grief-maddened queen after her daughter had been sacrificed, Iphigenia offered to the gods by Agamemnon to summon up a wind to blow his fleet to Troy. She felt like Clytemnestra, cold, patient, capable of anything. She went back to her Wing Chun master to practise her close combat skills and he spoke appreciatively of the new venom of her forehand smash. (Her defensive weaknesses, however, continued to be a concern.) She couldn't sleep until she was physically exhausted and when she finally slept she dreamed of circling choruses. Her younger self was being reborn in her. She went out by herself at night looking for trouble and once, twice, had rough sex with strangers in anonymous rooms and came home with dried blood under her fingernails. She showered and went back to Elysian Park, to Santa Monica and Vine, to 29 Palms. Her arrows hissed into the heart of the target. Her handgun shooting, never of the highest quality, always a tad wild, grew a little more accurate. In Fish's boxing ring she ordered her instructor to glove up, to put down the pads he wore on his hands, the flat pads she was supposed to hit without being at risk of being hit back. That was bullshit, she told him. She wasn't showing up for exercise any more. She was showing up to fight.

She had been planning a documentary feature called *Camino Real,* the Discovery Channel had been this close to green-lighting it. The idea was to examine the contemporary life of California by following the trail of the first European land expedition, from San Diego to San Francisco, an expedition led by Captain Gaspar de Portola and Captain Fernando de Rivera y Moncada, whose diarist had been Fray Juan Crespi, the same Franciscan priest who named Santa Monica after the tears of St Augustine's mother, and who, for good measure, named L.A. as well. She hadn't thought of the historical angle as much more than a hook, she wasn't really interested in the twenty-one Franciscan missions established along the trail, because the now stuff was what she was after, the changing gang culture of the barrios, the trailer-park families in the shadow of the freeways, the swarming immigrant armies that fed the housing boom, the new pleasantvilles being built in the firetrap canyons to house the middle-class arrivistes, the less-pleasantvilles in the thick of the urban sprawl filling up with the Koreans, the Indians, the illegals; she wanted the dirty underbelly of paradise, the broken harp-strings, the cracked haloes, the narcotic bliss, the human bloat, the truth. Then her father died and she stopped working on the film and sat on her Shaker chair and got up and went out and shot arrows and bullets and worked the punchball and tangled with her martial arts teacher and fucked strangers once each and drew blood and came home to shower and what she kept thinking was where are the angels, where were they when he needed them, the truth being that there weren't any, no winged marvels keeping watch over the City of Angels. No guardian spirits to save her father. Where were the goddamned angels when he died.

The city's angels were far away, in another earthquake zone. They were Italian and had never seen the city. Along with the Virgin Mary they were painted on the altar wall of St Francis of Assisi's first, little church of La Porziuncola, *porciúncula* in Spanish, meaning the "very small plot of land". On Wednesday, August 2, 1769, the Portola expedition had reached the purlieus of what was now Elysian Park and made camp on Buena Vista Hill, and Fray Juan Crespi, struck by the beauty of the valley, named the river after St Francis's church, whose memory he carried with him like a cross. He was forty-eight years old and already bore within himself the worm of a slowly approaching death, but whenever the worm stirred in him the image of the angels of La Porziuncola acted as an antidote, pushing away morbidity and reminding him of the joyous and everlasting life to come. He named the Los Angeles River after the angels of Assisi and their holy mistress and twelve years later, when a new settlement was established here, it took its title from the river's full name, becoming El Pueblo de Nuestra Señora la Reina de los Angeles de Porciúncula, the Town of Our Lady the Queen of the Angels of the Very Small Plot of Land. But the City of Angels now stood on a Very Large Plot of Land Indeed, thought India Ophuls, and those who dwelt there needed mightier protectors than they had been given, A-list, A-team angels, angels familiar with the violence and disorder of giant cities, butt-kicking Angeleno angels, not the small-time, underpowered, effeminate, hello-birds-hello-sky, love-and-peace, sissy-Assisi kind.

The murder of Ambassador Maximilian Ophuls was being mourned worldwide. The French government officially lamented the fall of one of the last surviving heroes of the Resistance, and the French press glowingly retold the story of the flight of the Bugatti Racer. India's fragmenting, infighting leadership united to praise Max as a true friend of the country, committed to "an honourable Indo-Pak détente", and the scandal that had ended his ambassadorship was barely mentioned. There were tributes from the White House and from the U.S. intelligence community as well. As with the invisible man in the movie, death restored Max to something like full visibility, declassifying many details of his life;

the lengthy obituaries and effusive encomia revealed his long service to his country at the heart of the invisible world during his last, hidden career as a senior spook, in the Mideast, the Gulf, Central America, Africa and Afghanistan. Three years after the ignominious termination of his New Delhi posting he was deemed to have atoned for his sins, to have been cleansed by the temporary withdrawal of power, and he was offered a chance to serve in a new capacity. The post of U.S. counterterrorism chief, which Max agelessly went on to hold for longer than anyone else, under several different administrations, was of ambassadorial rank, but was never spoken of in public. The person who held the job could not be named, his movements were not mentioned in the newspapers; he slipped across the globe like a shadow, his presence detectable only by its influence on the actions of others. India Ophuls had believed herself to have grown close to her father in his last years but she learned, now, of another Max, about whom the Max she knew had never spoken, Max the occult servant of American geopolitical interest, *Your father served his country in some hot zones, he swam for America through some pretty muddy water,* Invisible Max, on whose invisible hands there might very well be, there almost certainly was, there had to be, didn't there, a quantity of the world's visible and invisible blood.

What then was justice? Was she, in mourning her butchered parent, crying out (she had not wept) for a guilty man? Was Shalimar the assassin in fact the hand of justice, the appointed executioner of some unseen high court, was his sword righteous, had justice been *done to Max,* had some sort of sentence been carried out in response to his unknown unlisted unseen crimes of power, because blood will have blood, an eye demands an eye, and how many eyes had her father covertly put out, by direct action or indirect, one, or a hundred, or ten thousand, or a hundred thousand, how many trophied corpses, like stags' heads, adorned his secret walls?

The words *right* and *wrong* began to crumble, to lose meaning, and it was as if Max were being murdered all over again, assassinated by the voices who were praising him, as if the Max she knew were being unmade and replaced by this other Max, this stranger, this clone-Max moving through the world's burning desert places, part arms dealer, part kingmaker, part terrorist himself, dealing in the future, which was the only currency that mattered more than the dollar. He had been a puissant speculator in that mightiest and least controllable of all currencies, had been both a manipulator and a benefactor, both a philanthropist and a dictator, both creator and destroyer, buying or stealing the future from those who no longer deserved to possess it, selling the future to those who would be most useful in it, smiling the false lethal smile of power at all the planet's future-greedy hordes, its murderous doctors, its paranoid holy warriors, its embattled high priests, its billionaire financiers, its insane dictators, its generals, its venal politicians, its thugs. He had been a dealer in the dangerous, hallucinogenic narcotic of the future, offering it at a price to his chosen addicts, the reptilian cohorts of the future which his country had chosen for itself and for others; Max, her unknown father, the invisible robotic servant of his adopted country's overweening amoral might.

Her telephones rang but she didn't answer them. Her buzzer buzzed but she didn't respond. Her friends were concerned, they left urgent expressions of concern on her voice mail, they shouted their concern from the street below her balcony, *Come on, India, let us in, you're scaring us here,* but she kept her defences up, her defences being Olga Volga and the pairs of police officers guarding her floor in two-hour shifts, *No visitors,* she told them, banishing her increasingly angry friends from her presence. Her beloved friend the high-powered executive headhunter, a gesticulating Italian woman with acute foot-in-mouth disease, sent her an e-mail expressing the general exasperation, *Okay, darling, so your dad is dead, okay, it's sad, I agree, it's horrible, no question about it, but what, are you going to kill us all as well, we're dying here with worry, how many deaths do you want on your conscience?* But even her closest intimates didn't feel real to her any more, not even her film producer friend who had only just survived a heart attack at the age of thirty-eight and who now, restored to health, had taken to recommending the quadruple-bypass operation enthusiastically to all his colleagues, not even her friend the personal trainer, presently unattached, whose eggs had made babies for four other women but who had no children of her own, not even her friend (and former lover) who managed a band whose name changed every day and who kept signing contracts with indie outfits that immediately went belly-up so that the band was getting an unfortunate reputation as a jinx, not even her friend who broke up with her husband because he got angry when she complained about his snoring, not even her friend who left his wife for a man of the same name, not even her geek friend who was losing his dot-com fortune, not even her broke friends who were always broke, not even her cameraman, her sound guy, her accountant, her lawyer, her therapist, these were stories she couldn't relate to right now, she was the only person who felt real to herself, apart from her dead father and the assassin, they were real, and when she was in the ring with her instructor Jimmy Fish he briefly felt real as well.

Fish was a stocky middle-aged man with thick bottle-black Italian hair, heavy in the gut, his face still handsome in a flat-nosed Marciano way, and he was pulling his punches, which didn't mean they didn't hurt. The first time he hit her, in the stomach, avoiding her breasts, she was badly shocked and a little scared, but she stayed calm, the ice didn't leave her veins, and moments later she connected with a pair of fast left jabs to the chin and had the satisfaction of seeing the anger flare up in his eyes, seeing him working to fight it down. He called a time-out. They were both breathing heavily. "Listen," he said. "You're a beautiful lady, you don't want me to damage anything you can't fix." She shrugged. "Seems to me," she said, "that you're the one who just got himself cluster-punched in the mouth by a woman." He shook his head mournfully, and spoke more slowly, like a parent. "You're not paying attention," he said. "I was a ranking light-heavy. You know this. I was *ranking.* I got in the ring with people you don't want to even imagine getting in the ring with, not even to hold up the card saying what round. You think you can take me? Lady, I'm a professional fighter. You follow? You're a Sunday driver. Don't make me hit you. Let me put the pads back on my hands and you can get yourself a great workout, tone that body you got there, that's like a national treasure. You work with what God gave you and stop dreaming. You think I'm fighting you here? Baby, you can't fight me. You fight me, you're dead. Pay attention now. This is serious. You're not in the family business. You're a civilian. You're Kay Corleone. You can't fight me."

She touched gloves with him and backed off, going into her crouch, shuffling, dancing. "I've got nothing to say to you," she said. "I don't come here to talk."

Her father's killer was her mother's husband. The investigation had uncovered this one immense, all-explaining, devastating thing. The crime, which had at first looked political, turned out to be a personal matter, insofar as anything was personal any more. The assassin was a professional, but the consequences of U.S. policy choices in South Asia, and their echoes in the labyrinthine chambers of the paranoiac jihadi mind, these and other related geopolitical variables receded from the analysis, could with a high percentage of probability be eliminated from the equation. The picture had simplified, becoming a familiar image: the cuckolded and now avenged husband, the disgraced and now very nearly decapitated philanderer, locked in a final embrace. The motive, too, turned out to be conventional. *Cherchez la femme.* India had learned the murderer's real name, which sounded more like an alias than his alias, and the reports confirmed his wife's name as well, her mother's name, which India knew already because she had found it in an old copy of the *Indian Express* preserved on microfiche at the British Museum's newspaper library in Colindale. Neither India's father nor the woman she lived with when she was a child had ever spoken that name: not once in a quarter-century. Her father had once accidentally referred to his lover by the name of her greatest role, Anarkali, and India, watching him as only children watch their parents, saw an expression cross his face that only crossed it when he thought about her mother, an expression in which his undimmed desire for the young dancing girl mingled with shame, nostalgia and something darker, a premonition of death, perhaps, an intuition of how this particular Anarkali's story would end. As for the woman who was not her mother, the woman she had lived with when she was a child, on the rare occasions when that woman was forced by India's questions to allude to the birth mother she used the term *paramour,* as in *your father's paramour,* and when irked by India's insistence she would say in a tone of finality, *We will not speak of her.* But now the wheel had turned and it was that woman's name which was never spoken, not by India, anyhow, whereas Bhoomi a.k.a. Boonyi Kaul Noman's name was travelling the world's airwaves on, for example, CNN.

The élite Special Forces officers, looking a little disgusted at the case's turn toward the ordinary, handed over responsibility for the investigation to Central Homicide, the regular, nonterrorist, crime-related-elimination guys, and two new detectives, Lieutenant Tony Geneva and Sergeant Elvis Hilliker, sad-eyed men with high mileage numbers on their clocks, came to inspect the murder scene, but they weren't interested in briefing India on the status of the search for the man she was now trying to think of as "Noman", maybe there was classified material which they were keeping to themselves but the only things they came out with were bland, ready-to-wear formulations like *the manhunt is intensifying, ma'am,* and snippets of useless facts, *He planned his day carefully, took a change of clothing along in the trunk, we found the soiled garments in there,* Lieutenant Geneva said, and Sergeant Hilliker added, *He abandoned the car just a few blocks east of here, on Oakwood near Crescent Heights, and if he's on foot in this town he's going to be hard to miss, plus if he tries to steal himself a ride we'll have him in our sights, so we'll get him, ma'am, don't doubt it, this isn't Indian country, it's ours.*

She understood their remarks to mean that they were under pressure from their senior officers and needed to sound effective. (When she innocently used the term *superiors* to describe their bosses at City Hall, they had plenty to say, they momentarily achieved something like volubility, *They're not our superiors, ma'am, senior officers is all they are,* Lieutenant Geneva rebuked her, and Sergeant Hilliker vehemently added, *Which doesn't make them our betters.* Everybody was sensitive nowadays. Everybody had a vocabulary to peddle. Words had become as painful as sticks and stones, or maybe skins had grown thinner. India blamed the ozone layer, apologized and changed the subject.) Max's death was a big story, and they had more than just the commissioner on their backs, the TV audience was impatient, too, it wanted the pictures right away, a shoot-out, preferably, or a car chase with helicoptered cameras, or at the very least a good, close-up look at the captured murderer, manacled, shaggy haired, and in orange or green or blue prison fatigues, pleading to be put to death by lethal injection or cyanide gas because he didn't deserve to live.

She had no way of knowing if an arrest was near because she wasn't fully in the information loop. But the truth—the impossible truth, the truth that proved to her she was more than a little crazy right now, the truth she couldn't share with anyone, and which consequently sealed her off from the people who loved her—the insane, segregating truth was that she knew things about the fugitive which the police did not, because she had begun to hear his voice inside her head. Or not exactly a voice but a disembodied nonverbal transmission, like a wild screech full of static and internal dissension, hatred and shame, repentance and threat, curses and tears; like a werewolf howling at the moon. She had not experienced anything like this before, and in spite of her occasional power of second sight she was made greatly afraid by this auditory manifestation, by her transformation into a medium for the living. She locked her apartment door and sat in darkness, doubting her own sanity, until she slowly came to terms with what was happening. The shouted, argumentative, out-of-control babble in her head was the cry of a deranged soul, a man in a state of elated horror, He might be a professional, she thought, but he's not reacting professionally this time, something about this hit has unhinged him, this wasn't done in cold blood. This was hot.

I am for Ambassador Max and my name is Shalimar the clown. The sentence with which the murderer had introduced himself and named his quarry, quoted by one of the Mulholland Drive security guards to the police, had somehow found its way into the papers, and she had been worrying away at it, trying to unlock its secrets. *Shalimar the clown.* What did that mean. He was her mother's husband. What was she to do with information of such power. Now she understood what he had been staring at in the elevator that first day, her birthday, he had been seeing in her what she herself could not see, what her survival instincts, her private defence mechanisms, had made her block out of her vision. He had found her mother in her and now that mother within was hearing his silent demented scream.

She went to her bedroom, stripped off her clothes and examined her body in the mirrored closet doors, kneeling on her bed, stretching, leaning, trying to see in her unclothed form what he had seen in her when she was fully attired, straining to look beyond the echoes of her father and find the woman she had never been able to see. Slowly her mother's face began to form in her mind's eye, blurry, out of focus, vague. It was something. A gift from a killer. He had taken her father but her mother was being given to her. She felt angry all of a sudden. In a rage she called out to him, naked, with her eyes closed, like a witch at a séance. Tell me about her, she cried. Tell me about my mother, who wanted to go back to you, who was ready to give me up, who would have left me for you if she hadn't died first. (This cruel fragment of knowledge had been imparted long ago by the woman who was not her mother, the woman who did not give her life but gave her her name, the name she did not like.) Tell me, she cried into the night, about my mother who loved you more than me. Then came a thought unbidden: *She's still alive. Maybe it wasn't true about her dying, and she's still alive.* Where is she, she asked the voice in her head. Is this what she wanted, to kill her lover, to allow her husband to regain his honour by murdering the man she left him for. Did she send you to do this. How she must hate me, to abandon me and then have my father killed. What is she like. Does she ask about me. Have you sent her photographs of me. Does she want to see me. Does she know my name. Is she still alive.

Her desire to understand the killer had been fighting against more vengeful longings. A part of her believed that the act of taking a life was never trivial, always profound, wanted to believe it even in an age of interminable slaughter, a primitive age in which hard-won ideas, the sovereignty of the individual, the sanctity of life, were dying beneath the piles of bodies, buried beneath the lies of warlords and priests, and this part wanted to know in full the why of it, not to excuse the deed but at least to comprehend, to know the other who had with such finality altered the condition of her self. For another, possibly larger part, the memory of her father subsiding in blood was all the knowledge that was required. What was justice? Was comprehension necessary before judgement could be made and sentence passed? Had Shalimar the clown understood the man he killed? And if he felt he had, would that make his actions defensible? Did understanding drag justice in its wake? No, she told herself, understanding and justice were unrelated things, like repentance and forgiveness. An understanding man could also be unjust. A woman might see her father's killer repent, truly repent, and still be unable to forgive.

He had no answers for her. He was inchoate, contradictory, storm clouded. He was a hunted animal living in a ravine, like a coyote, like a dog. He was starving and thirsty. He was venom and blood. Is my mother here too, she asked him, over and over again. Did you bring her with you, is she waiting for you somewhere, holed up in some cheap freeway motel, to celebrate my father's death. What do you do to celebrate your kills, do you drink yourself stupid, no, you wouldn't drink, or is it sex, is that how you release your brutal delight, or do you pray, you and my mother, will you both get down on your knees and bang your joyful foreheads against the floor. Where is she, take me to her, let me look her in the face. She has to look me in the face. She cut me loose and never looked back and she has to look me in the face. She's here, isn't she. She wouldn't miss this. She's here, in a neon motel, waiting. Did she ask you to cut off his head. Did she want him decapitated but he was too tough for you, he didn't give you that satisfaction. His head stayed on his shoulders and thwarted your obscene aims, your attack against humanity. Where is she. If she sent you she has to face me.

This isn't over. I'm still here. I have to be reckoned with. I will call you to account. Blood will have blood. Sooner or later I will have to be faced.

He had no answers for her. He faded, like a dream. The sudden silence in her head was like a theft. For a moment she could not breathe, and gasped asthmatically for air. Then she cried. She thrust her face into her pillow and wept the first tears she had shed since her father's death, wept for three hours and seventeen minutes without stopping and then fell into a deep sleep, from which she was only awakened fifteen and a quarter hours later by Olga Simeonovna, who had let herself into the apartment with her master key, accompanied by a spectre from the past. Massed choruses encircled her in her dreams, but the dreams were not frightening, they were entertaining, she watched them like movies and forgot them when she awoke. India Ophuls had no need for nightmares any more. The waking world was nightmarish enough.

The cassocked chorus of gossipy old women moved clockwise around her, keening softly, Ah, the orphaned princess, what will she do now, she's a little crazy, we think, she may have all the money in the world but it won't buy back what she lost, she's just human like the rest of us, she'll have to deal with that, she'll have to come down to earth; we fear she's planning to take a terrible revenge, but beware!, princess, beware!, this guy is a bad guy!, the worst!, and you're not even in the family business, you can't fight him, you're

Kay Corleone. Around the first circle, the chorus of the widows, she could see a second circle, moving widdershins, the flaccid unhappy torsos of sack-bellied police officers, the hard-bodied Chippendales élite had disappeared, leaving these middle-aged Tonys and Elvises behind, We're closing in, ma'am, they chanted, a definite sighting on Ventura Boulevard, his days are numbered, uh-huh, uh-huh, a hundred percent make in a computer store on Pico, he may run ma'am but he can't hide, reports of a vagrant in Nichols Canyon, reports of a vagrant near Woodrow Wilson, reports of a vagrant on Cielo Drive, uh-huh, uh-huh, it's just a matter of time. And again the cassocked women raised their voices, Justice would be meaningless without injustice, they first intoned, and then, secondly, Justice is strife. War makes us what we are. Even though she was asleep she recognized Heraclitus speaking through the widows' mouths—Heraclitus the Greek Buddha, the lost poet of broken wisdom, part philosopher, part fortune cookie, bubbling up from the days when she read such things, the days when she read, to add his two cents' worth. Now, around the Eastern crone and the sagging policemen, she perceived a third circle, an outer circle made up of her friends, who were moving clockwise, like the old women, and singing in electronic voice-mail voices a yearning beseeching song. Come back, her friends sang in tinny harmony, baby, come back. Her friends singing the old Equals hit, Oh won't you please! Come back. I'm on my knees! Come back. Baby come back.

Olga Simeonovna was shaking her. "Wake up," Olga Volga said. "And don't say you tell me no visitors, because this is different, okay? Here is good news. Here is your mother who has crossed an ocean and a continent to be beside her daughter when trouble comes. Wake up, India, please. Here your mother waits." Was this a part of the dream, she wondered. No, she was awake, the pounding in her chest could not be dreamed. Excitedly she turned towards Olga and saw the trousered, septuagenarian woman who stood behind her and a little to one side, her hair an unkempt grey haystack under which a rat might safely hide. The sucker punch of disappointment hit India hard. She turned away and pulled the comforter over her head, ignoring Olga the abandoned parent's frown of disapproval: Olga, for whom, in spite of all her abuse of her departed children, an embrace between a long-separated mother and daughter was a cherished fantasy. "Ha! A fine welcome, I must say," chided Margaret Rhodes. "You may not like it, my dear, but—ahah! hah!—it's true, your darling mother's in town."

Ratetta, sweet Ratetta. Peggy Rhodes had returned to England with a baby girl in her arms and a look on her face that made it impossible for anyone to ask after her husband or even to speak his discarded name. The adopted child was baptized India Rhodes and, as her mother's work with orphanages was well known, there was little need to explain her provenance. The Rumplestiltskin truth, that she had disposed of a husband and taken his love child in his place, was so strange that nobody suspected it. She had forced Max to swear to keep the secret, to relinquish all parental rights and responsibilities, and to stay away from mother and child alike. She was cleaning up his mess, she told him, and she didn't want him making things messy again. Hanging his head, ashamed, he did not argue. He tried to express his feelings. "Don't apologize, for God's sake," she said. "D'you imagine an apology can make up for what you did?" He was silenced. For seven years he vanished from her life.

The only other people who knew the facts were Father Joseph Ambrose, whose Evangalactic Orphanage depended for its financial well-being on Peggy Rhodes's largesse, and the pander Edgar Wood, who was tragically hit by a car in a Long Island country lane fifteen months after his return from New Delhi, and was killed outright. Peggy herself did not return to the United States. She bought a town house in Lower Belgrave Street, SW1, from a straitlaced English lady who was escaping the permissive society of late-sixties London and immigrating to Falangist Spain in search of a country with a little more discipline. In the years that followed the Grey Rat became a figure of fear in the street, snapping at noisy children playing on the pavement, complaining about the freshness of the produce at the greengrocers, calling the police when the noise from the Plumber's Arms, the pub across the road, became too loud, knocking on her neighbours' door to accuse them of blocking her drains by putting tampons down the toilet and refusing to accept their argument that their property did not share drainage facilities with hers.

She began to wear men's clothing: loose corduroy pants and white linen shirts. She hacked at her wiry hair and left it to do as it pleased. In the season she went to the grouse moors and shot copious numbers of birds. She smoked heavily, drank scotch and soda, became a single-digit-handicap golfer and developed a fondness for gambling, spending many evenings at the Clermont Club in Berkeley Square playing baccarat and chemin de fer. She knew that her divorce had damaged what was womanly in her but did nothing to mend what was broken. In spite of what she had done, the lengths she'd gone to in order to acquire a child, in spite of the strangeness of her actions, she became a careless, negligent mother, whose relationship with her adopted daughter was, at best, vague, who began to believe that she had made a terrible mistake, because whenever she looked at her adopted daughter she saw her own humiliation made flesh, she imagined Max and Boonyi making love and her husband's seed wriggling towards the ruthless, desperate egg. So India was handed over to a series of nannies (none of whom lasted long, for Peggy Rhodes had turned into an intolerant, choleric employer), and began to run wild.

By the age of seven the young girl was becoming a problem child, a savage, kickboxing playground scrapper who seemed, at times, like a creature possessed by demons, and a vicious biter, who caused at least one serious injury to a classmate at her exclusive Chelsea girls' primary school. On two occasions she came close to being expelled for "unacceptable behaviour". The first time expulsion was threatened, however, she immediately and somewhat alarmingly changed her ways completely, adopting, for the first time, the cool, restrained, disciplined persona that would become her preferred disguise throughout her life. She became solemn, nonviolent, still, and her transformation scared her classmates into something like reverence, gave her the electric charisma of a leader. The mask slipped only once, just before her seventh birthday, when she assaulted the school bully, a sadistic eleven-year-old thug named Helena Wardle, hitting her on the back of the head with a large grey stone. Helena was known to the staff as a girl whose behaviour was often brutish, and who had a habit of accusing her victims of bullying before they could accuse her, so when she ran to the school matron with a cut head, India, who claimed Helena had fallen and hurt herself accidentally, was given the benefit of the doubt, especially as her lie was verified by several of her classmates, who all disliked Helena Wardle as heartily as she did.

There was no denying her dark hair, her un-English complexion, the absence in her face of any trace of Peggy Rhodes's genes. Three days before her seventh birthday the troubled girl found out she was adopted, discovered it by plucking up her courage and asking, after her injured victim had started a playground whispering campaign. Peggy Rhodes had flushed angrily when challenged, but had given India an answer of sorts. *I'm very sorry,* the Grey Rat told her, *but, hmmm, hmmm, I don't know the name of the woman who bore you. Hang it! I believe she died shortly after you were born. The identity of the father is likewise not confirmed. You must—eh? hah!—stop asking these questions. I am your mother. I have been your mother since the first days of your life. You have no other mother or father, there's just me, I'm afraid, and I will not have these blasted questions.* So she was trapped inside a lie, far away from the truth, held captive in a fiction; and within her the turbulence grew, an unquiet spirit moved, like a giant coiled serpent stirring at the bottom of the sea.

The event that would shatter the cocoon of the lie in which she lived took place some months later, in November 1974, when there was a notorious, bloody murder on Lower Belgrave Street, in the house at number 46. An English aristocrat named Lord Lucan, estranged and living apart from his wife Veronica, entered the family home in the evening of November 7 wearing a hood, and, in the basement kitchen, murdered his children's nanny, Mrs Sandra Rivett, probably mistaking her, in the dark, for his wife. He went upstairs and in spite of the presence in the house of his three young children assaulted Lady Lucan violently, forcing three gloved fingers down her throat, then trying to strangle her, gouge out her eyes and bludgeon her on the head. She was a tiny woman, but she grabbed his testicles and squeezed, and when he crumpled in pain she escaped. She ran down the street and burst into the Plumber's Arms crying murder. Lord Lucan escaped, abandoning his car in the port town of Newhaven, and was never found. He left behind several notes to friends, many of them financial in content, and several large gambling debts.

John Bingham, "Lucky" Lucan, was the seventh earl. The third earl of Lucan had acquired his own bad reputation 120 years earlier. During the Crimean War, the third earl was the man responsible for ordering the catastrophic charge of the Light Brigade. This was during the battle of Balaclava. Curiously enough, the woollen hood worn by his murderous great-great-grandson was of the type known as a balaclava.

On the morning after these events a police officer rang the Rhodes household's doorbell and asked if anyone had heard anything unusual the previous night. India had been asleep, and Peggy Rhodes said she had heard nothing. When the story broke in the evening papers, and everyone knew about Lady Lucan's run to safety, India wondered how Peggy could have failed to notice something, considering that it was an unseasonably warm evening and their sitting-room windows had been opened wide; and, after all, the Plumber's Arms was right across the street. Later the police returned to ask Peggy if, as a fellow member of the high-roller Clermont Club, she had known Lord Lucan. "No," she said, "I knew him by sight, but he wasn't particularly a friend." India had heard her mother speak more than once about her "chums", Aspinall, Elwes and Lucky, yet now she was lying to the police, why was that. She afterwards learned that her mother wasn't the only liar in the story. One widely held view was that the upper class had closed ranks to protect one of their own behind an aristocratic version of *omertà,* the Sicilian code of silence. But India heard Peggy sobbing hard at night. *John, oh John.* She drew no conclusions. She was only seven years old. A few days later the police issued a statement criticizing Lucan's set for being unhelpful to the enquiry and pointing out that withholding information in a murder case was a criminal offence, even if the withholders were millionaires and aristocrats. But India had forgotten all about Lucky Lucan by then, because two days after the murder Peggy Rhodes had come to her in her bedroom at night, her eyes red-rimmed from weeping, and said, "There are things I must tell you, yes, yes. Hum! Ha! Things you ought to know."

You have a daddy. One month after the Grey Rat, in the grip of an unexplained emotion, gave her father a name, Maximilian Ophuls was standing at the door of the house in Lower Belgrave Street holding flowers and a stupid doll. "I don't play with dolls," India told him solemnly, revealing much about Peggy's attitude to parenting and taste in children's toys. "I like bows and arrows and slingshots and excaliburs and guns." Max looked back at her straight-faced and thrust the doll into her hands. "Here," he said. "Use her for target practice. It's no fun if you don't have a target." Then he picked her up and hugged her hard and she fell in love with him, just like everybody else. He sat her beside him in the back of a large silver car and told the driver to take them as fast as possible to a posh restaurant by the river. He was sixty-four years old and knew the words to the song, send me a postcard, drop me a line. Will you still need me, will you still feed me. "You're a very old daddy, aren't you," she asked him over ice cream. "Are you going to die soon?" He shook his head very seriously. "No, my plan is never to die," he said. "You will one day," she argued. "Maybe," he said, "maybe when I'm two hundred and sixty-four and too blind to see it coming. But until then, pah! I snap my fingers at Death, I thumb my nose at him, and then I bite my thumb."

She giggled. "So do I," she said, but she couldn't snap her fingers. "Anyway," she added, "I want to die when I'm two hundred and sixty-four as well."

By the end of the day he was nuzzling her neck and finding the birds hidden there and she was learning the words to "Alouette" and she was climbing up his shoulders and then somersaulting back and away. When he delivered her back to her mother he looked the Grey Rat in the eye and thanked her, and she knew he had stolen the girl from her, that from now on his daughter would no longer be hers. If I'm his daughter I should have his name, the girl said that night, and Peggy Rhodes didn't know how to refuse, and India Ophuls was born. What about my mummy, the girl said, tucked up in bed with a night-light sending stars whirling across her ceiling. I want to know about my mummy too. Is she really dead or is she hiding like Daddy was. Peggy Rhodes lost her temper. *That woman is dead to everyone now—all right? mmm?—but she was already, ah, ah, dead to me in life. She left her husband and tried to steal your daddy away and—pah!—had his baby and was ready to abandon it and where would you have been if I hadn't taken you in. She was going to leave you behind, hmm? hmm?, and go back where she came from and she didn't want the shame of a baby, didn't want the shame—d'you see?—of you. Then there were, ah, complications and she, hmph, died.* What did she die of? Where was she going back to? *I won't answer these questions.* But didn't she like me really? *It doesn't matter. She didn't choose you. I chose you.* But mummy, what was my mummy's name? *I'm your mummy.* No, mummy, my real mummy, I mean. *I'm your real mummy. Good night.*

Then Max disappeared from her life again. "I'm afraid he's like that, dear," the Grey Rat told her flatly, "I know he's your father but you must understand, ahmm, he's sort of the fly-by-night type," and when he finally did show up, twice a year, on her birthday and on Christmas morning, there were things he wasn't saying, things he wouldn't talk about, and it took her close to a decade to understand the hidden war between the woman she lived with and was growing to hate and the father she barely knew but loved with all her heart, she never understood him until he saved her life. Max never spoke against Peggy, and even when India beseeched him he never betrayed the secrets the Grey Rat did not want revealed, knowing that his ability to see his daughter at all depended on accepting the Grey Rat's ferocious terms, but for a long time India blamed him for his absences and silences, and her anger with him screwed her up even more than her dislike of the woman she lived with, because he was the lovable one, he was the one she wanted to see every day and laugh at and somersault off and drive with in fast cars and shoot BB pellets into dolls with and embrace and kiss and love. She didn't understand that the woman she lived with had banished Max again, had denied him all but the most perfunctory access to the increasingly truculent adopted daughter for whom she, Peggy, had such mixed feelings but who represented the bone of contention in her undying quarrel with Max, and who consequently had to be held on to even if her presence was a daily reminder of past shame.

"Yes, your mother is dead," he told India when she asked him. He had his own reasons for confirming his ex-wife's untruth. "Yes, it's just as Margaret said." Then he said no more.

These were the confusions inside which India Ophuls grew up in the 1970s. She held herself together for a few years, she went hungry for three hundred and sixty-three days of the year and made do with the two days of feasting, but as she neared thirteen she wore the stricken look of a storm-tossed ship heading towards jagged inescapable rocks. When puberty struck, she went dramatically off the rails. There followed a delinquent descent into hell. Hell seemed preferable to the overworld of lying mothers and absent fathers in which she was trapped, and from which, during her ruined adolescence, she consequently tried to escape down all the various self-destructive routes available to her. The downward spiral had been fast, and she had been lucky to survive the smash at the end of it. By the age of fifteen she had been a truant, a liar, a cheat, a dropout, a thief, a teenage runaway, a junkie and even, briefly, a tart plying for trade in the shadow of the giant gas cylinders behind King's Cross Station. Waking up in her L.A. bedroom to find the woman she loathed looking down at her with eager Olga by her side, she felt her repressed fifteenth year boiling back into her head, like the high tide churning through a breach in a vellard. She fought the memories down but they insisted on rising. She remembered a sweating, febrile room with stains on the walls and a stranger unzipping his pants. She remembered the drugs, the hallucinogens putting reason to sleep and bringing forth monsters, the hard brightness of white powder, the needle's deadly bliss, the white fedora of the Jamaican pimp. She remembered violence done to her and by her, she remembered retching, and shivering in the heat, and a face in the mirror so pale and blue it made her scream. She remembered slashing her wrists and swallowing pills. She remembered stomach pumps. She remembered a judge's harsh words for the woman whose name she would never use again, *You have been, madam, an abject failure as a parent,* and she remembered that it had been Max who saved her, Max who swooped down from the sky like an eagle and scooped her out of the gutter, who told the woman she loathed that he would no longer stand silently by, who asked the judge for judgement and prised that woman's clutching fingers off his child's wounded arms and spirited his daughter away to be healed, first at a Swiss clinic high up on what she would always think of as the Magic Mountain, and then by sunshine, palm trees and the cobalt blue of the Pacific. She imagined his last conversation with the woman she hated, *You had your chance with her but you'll never have another one,* she heard him saying, and saw in fancy's eye the bitter features of the Grey Rat contort like Rumplestiltskin's into a mask of defeat.

Take her then, she said.

Outside the realm of India's imagination, however, Max Ophuls went on refusing to criticize his former wife, perhaps because of his feelings of guilt about his old betrayal. Once or twice, in tones of sorrow, he spoke about the power of life's violent blows and slow agonies to divert a good person from his or her natural path, just as dynamite or erosion can—dramatically or gradually—change the course of a river, and in these speeches he might have been talking about Margaret, but he might also have been describing himself. And his secretiveness was a trait he shared with his ex-wife, they were both citizens of the underworld, they both had things to hide. But at least he understood about underworlds and followed India all the way down into her own private inferno and stayed by her side for months on end, until the dark god released her and let her follow him up into the light, and the Swiss doctors pronounced her well enough to reenter the overworld of ordinary life and he brought her down from the mountain in the back of a new Bentley driven by a new liveried chauffeur, cradling her in his arms as if she were the Ten Commandments, and restored her, if not to ordinary life, then to Los Angeles, at least.

The house on Mulholland Drive was sprawling, with staff quarters, stables, a tennis court, a guest cottage and a pool, and built in the Spanish Mission style, white walled, with barrel-tiled roofs and a bell tower that reminded her of Hitchcock's *Vertigo* and gave the place an inappropriately ecclesiastical air. She thought of Kim Novak falling from the tower of the San Juan Bautista Mission at the end of the movie and shuddered and refused her father's offer to take her up to the top of the tower to show her the carillon. For a while, when she first arrived in L.A., she stayed indoors, curled up in chairs and corners, grateful to be alive, but taking her time to make sure she was safe. She preferred to keep her feet on the ground and a roof over her head. The stone floors felt cool beneath her unshod feet and the stained glass in the living-room windows poured colours over her every day. Kim Novak had played an impostor, a woman called Judy, hired to impersonate a woman named Madeleine Elster whose husband had murdered her. There were days when India felt like an impostor too, when she felt as if she'd been hired by Max to impersonate a daughter who had died.

Max's study was a sombre anomaly in this house of colour and light: wood panelled, with heavy European couches and mahogany tables, its shelves lined with books printed long ago by Art & Aventure, a Belle

Époque movie set of a room designed to echo another long-lost room, his father's library in Strasbourg: more a memory than a place. He did not allow himself the open sentimentality of hanging his parents' pictures on the wall. The room itself was their portrait. He spent much of his day in this room, reading and remembering, and allowed his daughter the run of the rest of the big, empty old place. One day, rummaging through the closets in the guesthouse, she found a hatbox containing a short blond wig, a castoff of one of her father's long-forgotten lovers, and she backed away from it, terrified, as if it were a death sentence. There was something of James Stewart's slow grace in Max and when the shadows fell across his face in a certain way he scared her. He had to remind her that Jimmy Stewart hadn't been the murderer in *Vertigo,* he was the good guy. She had been a little crazy in those days too, clean but skittish, but he had waited her out. Which is not to say he was kindly. Kind, yes, in his way, good in a crisis, expecting no thanks for doing what he saw as his duty, but not kindly. When she brought up Kim Novak and the blond wig in the closet he did not restrain his tongue. "Be so good," he said at the conclusion of an eloquent tirade, "as to cease to cast yourself in fictions. Pinch yourself, or slap yourself across the face if that's what it takes, but understand, please, that you are nonfictional, and this is real life."

Then for a time she was sane and happy in the house on Mulholland Drive and surprised herself by becoming a proficient athlete and a brilliant student with a strong interest in history and biography and, more particularly, in fact-based films. After leaving high school she travelled alone to London to study the work of the British documentary film movement of the thirties and forties and—though she mentioned this to nobody—to do a little documentary research of her own. During these months she lived in a poorly lit but spacious and high-ceilinged room in furnished student digs near Coram's Fields and made no attempt to contact the Grey Rat. She never travelled south to Lower Belgrave Street but she did make her way up the Northern Line to Colindale, where she unearthed the frustratingly patchy newspaper records of the events surrounding her birth. She returned to Los Angeles and kept the trip to the newspaper library to herself but volubly informed her father of her newfound reverence for the British documentarists John Grierson and Jill

Craigie, and her determination to turn away from the dangers of the imagination and make a career in the world of the nonfictional, to make films that insisted, as he had insisted, on the absolute paramountcy of the truth. *This is real life.* In the late eighties she studied documentary filmmaking at the AFI Conservatory and graduated with flying colours and moved into her own apartment on Kings Road and was ready to make her father proud of her when his killer cheated her of the chance.

The woman had come to confess. She had carried a burden for a quarter of a century and it had weighed her down; after a lifetime of upright bearing she had entered a stooped old age. The burden, the years, the loneliness had made her body a question mark. She didn't matter any more, India thought, she had no power. She had come out of the house of power empty-handed, the flying bird-men had ripped her treasure out of her hands, and people were jeering at her in the street. Why had she come, it was not necessary to receive her condolences in person. She had come to assist the police with their inquiries, she said, sounding like a character from the days of black-and-white television. There aren't any policemen here, India said, so there's no one for you to assist.

The woman opened her purse and took out a photograph and tossed it down onto the bed. "The work it took to keep this out of the papers, hah! you have no idea." Then, talking rapidly, just to get it said, the confession of the lie. "She didn't die she gave you to me and went back to Kashmir I arranged a plane and a car I sent her where she wanted to go and I never heard of her again so she might as well have been dead but actually she didn't die." The name of the village, her mother's village. The village of the travelling players. The village of Shalimar the clown. "Are you listening to me?" No, India wasn't listening, she was hearing the words but the picture had all her attention. Her father was dead but her mother was coming back to life, except this wasn't her mother, this was another lie, her mother was a great dancer, she had seduced Max by dancing for him, so this swollen woman could not be her. She saw the tears fall onto the photograph and realized they were her own. "I'm sorry," the woman was saying. "Dreadful thing to have done, I suppose.

Hah! I'm sure you think so. But she chose to give you up and I chose to take you in. I'm your mother. Forgive me. I made your father lie as well. I'm your mother. Forgive me. She didn't die."

Repentance is for the sinner. Forgiveness is for the victim: who looked at the damp photograph, and did not, could not, forgive. Who was all intransigence, not knowing that a harder blow was yet to fall.

"Kashmira," the woman said, spinning on her heel, removing her hateful unwanted world-altering presence. "Kashmira Noman. That was your given name." She felt as if the weight of her body had suddenly doubled, as if she had suddenly become the woman in the photograph. Gravity dragged at her and she fell backward on the bed, gasping for air. She heard the bed frame groan, saw in the mirror the mattress yield and sag. Kashmira. The weight of the word was too much for her to bear. Kashmira. Her mother was calling to her from the far side of the globe. Her mother who didn't die. Kashmira, her mother called, come home. I'm coming, she called back. I'll be there as fast as I can.

"Today I forgive my daughters," Olga Volga announced, caressing India's hair while they both cried. "It don't matter no more what they done."

At San Quentin State Prison, a thirty-nine-year-old man named Robert Alton Harris was put to death in the gas chamber. Pellets of sodium cyanide wrapped in cheesecloth were lowered into a small vat of sulphuric acid and Harris began to gasp and twitch. After about four minutes he became still and his face turned blue. Three minutes later he coughed and his body convulsed. Eleven minutes after the execution began Warden Daniel Vazquez declared Harris dead and read out his last words: "You can be a king or a street sweeper, but everybody dances with the Grim Reaper." This was a line paraphrased from the Keanu Reeves movie *Bill & Ted's Bogus Journey.*

Everywhere was a mirror of everywhere else. Executions, police brutality, explosions, riots: Los Angeles was beginning to look like wartime Strasbourg; like Kashmir. Eight days after Harris's execution, when India Ophuls a.k.a. Kashmira Noman flew out of LAX, heading east, the jury returned its verdict in the trial of the four officers accused of the beating of Rodney King in the San Fernando Valley Foothill Police Division, a beating so savage that the amateur videotape of it looked, to many people, like something from Tiananmen Square or Soweto. When the King jury found the policemen not guilty, the city exploded, giving its verdict on the verdict by setting itself on fire, like a suicide bomber, like Jan Palach. Below India's rising aircraft drivers were being pulled from their cars and chased and beaten by men holding rocks. The motionless body of a man called Reginald Denny was being savagely beaten. A huge piece of cinder block was thrown at his head by a man who did a war dance of celebration and made a gang sign at the sky, taunting the news helicopters and airline passengers up there, maybe even taunting God. Stores were looted, cars were torched, there were fires everywhere, on, for example, Normandie, Florence, Crenshaw, Arlington, Figueroa, Olympic, Jefferson, Pico and Rodeo. What was burning? Everything. Auto repair shops, Launderlands, Korean eateries, limo services, Rite Aids, mini-marts and Denny's all over the city. L.A. was a flame-grilled Whopper that night. The lizard people were rising up from their subterranean redoubts; the sleeping dragon had woken. And India, flying east, was on fire also. There is no India, she thought. There is only Kashmira. There is only Kashmir.

She would not be India in India. She would be her mother's child. As Kashmira, then, Kashmira in a baseball cap and jeans, she walked into the Press Club in Delhi and with American daring asked the old India hands for guidance and help, and was warned that she might have trouble getting press accreditation to go up into the valley with a documentary film crew, or even without one. When these old hands patted her on the back and also on the derrière and counselled her not to even think of going up there, where things were worse than ever, the killings were at an all-time high and foreign backpackers were showing up headless on the hillsides and there was fury in the air, she exploded with rage herself. "Where do you imagine I've just come from," she bellowed, "fucking Disneyland?" The vehemence of her outburst made sure she had their attention, and a few hours later that hot night, sitting in a deck chair on the lawn of another exclusive club near the Lodi Gardens, she drank beer with the most senior member of the foreign press corps and, after establishing that she was speaking one hundred per cent off the record, told him her story. "This isn't journalism," the Englishman told her. "It's personal. Forget about the camera and sound equipment. You want to get in? We'll get you in. As to safety, however, it's at your own risk." Three days after this conversation took place she was in a Fokker Friendship bound for Srinagar with papers and introductions and phone numbers and a new name whose meaning she needed to learn. The need didn't feel like excitement. It felt like pain. As the plane crossed the Pir Panjal she felt as if she had passed through a magic portal, and all at once the pain intensified, it clutched at her heart and squeezed hard, and she wondered in sudden terror whether she had come to Kashmir to be reborn, or to die.

Sardar Harbans Singh passed away peacefully in a wicker rocking-chair in a Srinagar garden of spring flowers and honeybees with his favourite tartan rug across his knees and his beloved son, Yuvraj the exporter of handicrafts, by his side, and when he stopped breathing the bees stopped buzzing and the air silenced its whispers and Yuvraj understood that the story of the world he had known all his life was coming to an end, and that what followed would follow as it had to, but it would unquestionably be less graceful, less courteous and less civilized than what had gone. On that last evening Sardar Harbans Singh had been speaking with nostalgia about the glories of the so-called Khalsa Raj, the twenty-seven-year-long period of the nine Sikh governors of Kashmir that followed the conquest of the valley by Maharaja Ranjit Singh in 1819, during which, as he told his son, "all agriculture blossomed, all crafts flowered, all gurdwaras, temples and mosques were cared for, and everything in the garden was lovely, and even if people criticized Maharaja Ranjit Singh for falling prey to the charms of women, wine and Brahminical practices, what of it? These are not grave failings in a man. You, my son," he continued, changing tack, "may or may not know much about Brahminical practices or wine, but you had better find yourself a woman before too long. I don't care how full your warehouses are or how fat your bank balance is. A full *godown* and a bulging wallet do not excuse an empty bed."

These were his last words, and so, when a woman calling herself Kashmira presented herself at the house of mourning carrying a letter of introduction from his father's friend the famous English journalist, when she arrived on the ninth day after the cremation, when the complete reading of the Guru Granth Sahib was one day away from being finished, Yuvraj considered it as a sign from the Almighty and welcomed her like a member of the family, offering her the hospitality of his house, insisting upon her staying, even though it was a time of sadness, and allowing her to take part in the Bhog ceremony with which the rituals ended on the tenth day, to listen to the hymns of passing, to partake of the *karah parsad* and *langar,* and to watch him being presented with the turban that made him the new head of the family. Only when his relatives had dispersed, without wailing or lamentation, as was the preferred way among Sikhs, did he have the time to talk to her about the reason for her visit, and by this time he already knew the real answer, namely that she had come to his house so that he could fall in love. In short, she was his father's dying gift.

"You have come into our story at the end," he told her. "If my dear father were still with us he could answer all your questions. But maybe the truth is that, as he used to say, our human tragedy is that we are unable to comprehend our experience, it slips through our fingers, we can't hold on to it, and the more time passes, the harder it gets. Maybe too much time has passed for you and you will have to accept, I'm sorry to say it, that there are things about your experience you will never understand. My father said that the natural world gave us explanations to compensate for the meanings we could not grasp. The slant of the cold sunlight on a winter pine, the music of water, an oar cutting the lake and the flight of birds, the mountains' nobility, the silence of the silence. We are given life but must accept that it is unattainable and rejoice in what can be held in the eye, the memory, the mind. Such was his credo. I myself have spent my life in business pursuits, dirtying my hands with money, and only now that he is gone can I sit in his garden and listen to him talk. Only now that he has sadly departed but you have gladly come."

He described himself as a businessman but he had a poetic side to him. She asked him about his work and undammed a torrent of speech. When he told her about the handicrafts he bought and sold his voice was full of feeling. He spoke about the origins of the craft of numdah rug making in Central Asia, in Yarkand and Sinkiang, in the days of the old Silk Route, and the words *Samarkand* and *Tashkent* made his eyes shine with ancient glory, even though Tashkent and Samarkand, these days, were faded, down-at-heel dumps. Papier-mâché, too, had come to Kashmir from Samarkand. "A prince of Kashmir in the fifteenth century was put in prison there for many years and learned this craftwork in jail." Ah, the jails of Samarkand, said the sparkle in his eyes, where a man could learn such things! He told her about the two parts of the creative process, the *sakhtsazi* or manufacture, the soaking of waste paper, the drying of the pulp, the cutting of the shape, the layering with glue and gypsum, the pasting of layers of tissue paper, and then the *naqashi* or decorative phase, the painting and lacquering. "So many artists together make every piece, the final work is not one man's alone, it is the product of our whole culture, it is not only made in but in fact made by Kashmir."

When he described the weaving and embroidery of the shawls of Kashmir his voice dropped with awe. He compared them lyrically to Gobelin tapestries though he had never seen such things. He fell into technical language, *the decoration is formed by weft threads interlocked where the colours change,* and such was his boyish excitement at the weavers' skill that she, listening, was excited too. He told her about *sozni* embroidery techniques, which could be so skilful that the same motif would appear on both sides of the shawl in different colours, about satin-stitch and *ari* work and the hair of the ibex goat and the legendary *jamawar* shawls. By the time he was done, apologizing for boring her, she was already half in love.

But she had not come to Kashmir to fall in love. What then was this man doing, loving her? What, when his father was not two weeks dead, was that foolish expression doing on his face, his admittedly handsome face, that expression which needed no translation? And what was wrong with her, by the way, why was she lingering here in this strange garden that seemed immune to history, setting aside her quest and listening instead to the buzzing of these innocent bees, wandering between these hedges which no evil could penetrate, breathing this jasmine air unpolluted by the smell of cordite, and passing her days bathed in this stranger's worshipful regard, listening to his interminable accounts of handicraft manufacture and his recitals of poetry in his admittedly beautiful voice, and somehow insulated from the city's daily noises of marching feet, clenched-fist demands and the age's insoluble complaints? Feeling was rising in her also, it was necessary to concede this, and though it had been her habit not to surrender to feeling, to control herself, she understood that this feeling was strong. Perhaps it would prove stronger than her ability to resist it. Perhaps not. She was a woman from far away who had defended her heart for a long time. She did not know if she could satisfy his needs, did not see how she could, was amazed that she was even thinking about satisfying them. This was not her purpose. She felt shocked, even betrayed, by her emotions. Olga Simeonovna had warned her about the essentially sneaky nature of love. "It don't approach from where you're looking," she had said. "It will creep up from behind your left ear and hit you on the head like a rock."

At night he sang for her and his voice kept her trapped in his spell. He was enough his father's son to know something of the music of Kashmir and could play, albeit falteringly, the santoor. He sang the *muquam* ragas of the classical form known as Sufiana Kalam. He sang her the songs of Habba Khatoon, the legendary sixteenth-century poet-princess, who introduced *lol* or lyric love poetry to Kashmir, songs of the pain of her separation from her beloved Prince Yusuf Shah Chak, imprisoned by the Mughal emperor Akbar in faraway Bihar—"my garden has blossomed into colourful flowers, why are you away from me?"—and he apologized for not having a woman's voice. He sang the irregular-metre *bakhan* songs of the Pahari musical style. The music had its effect. For five days she stayed in the enchanted garden, soporific with unlooked-for pleasure. Then on the sixth day she awoke and shook herself and asked him for help. "Pachigam." She spoke the name as if it were a charm, an open-sesame that would roll back a boulder from the door of a treasure cave inside which her mother glistened and gleamed like hoarded gold. Pachigam, a place from a fable that needed to be made real. "Please," she said. And he, declining to mention the dangers of the country roads, agreed to take her, to drive her into fable, or at least into the past. "I do not know the situation in that village and to my shame cannot tell you what you want to know," he told her. "The village came under crackdown some time back. This was reported. It was my father who had contacts there. I regret I have not been sufficiently active in the culture area. I am a businessman." What did that mean, crackdown, she wanted to know. Was anyone, is anyone, what happened. He did not tell her how brutal an event a crackdown could be. "I don't know," he repeated wretchedly. "As to specifics I am regrettably unaware." But we will go and find out, won't we, she said. "Yes," he miserably assented. "We can go today."

She sat in his olive-green Toyota Qualis and when they drove out of the gates of his house, that tiny Shangri-La, that miraculous island of calm in the middle of a war zone, she gave him a sidelong look, half expecting him to wither and die, to age horribly before her eyes as immortals do when they leave their magical paradise. But he remained himself, his beauty and grace undimmed. He saw her looking at him and was vain enough to blush. "Your home, your garden, is so beautiful," she said quickly, seeking to disguise the light in her eyes: too late. His blush deepened. A man who blushed was irresistible, it could not be denied. "In my childhood, it was a heaven inside a heaven," he said. "But now Kashmir is no longer heavenly and I am not a gardener like my father. I fear the house and garden will not last, without." He stopped in midsentence. "Without what?" she teased him, guessing the unspoken words, but he blushed again and concentrated on the road ahead. *Without a woman's touch.*

Kashmir in spring, the leaves budding on the chinars, the swaying poplars, the blossom on the fruit trees, the cradling mountains circled all around. Even in its time of darkness it was still a place of light. How easy it was, at first, to avert the gaze from the burned-out houses, the tanks, the fear in every woman's eye, the different terror in the eyes of the men. But slowly the spell of Sardar Harbans Singh's garden wore off. Yuvraj's mood darkened also. "Tell me," she said. "I want to know." "It is hard to speak of such things," he said. *This is real life.* "I need to know," she said. Awkwardly, full of euphemisms at first and then more plainly, he told her about the two devils tormenting the valley. "The fanatics kill our gents and the army shames our ladies." He named certain towns, Badgam, Batmaloo, Chawalgam, where militants had murdered locals. Shootings, hangings, stabbings, decapitations, bombs. "This is their Islam. They want us to forget but we remember." Meanwhile the army used sexual assault to demoralize the population. In Kunan Poshpora, twenty-three women had been raped by soldiers at gunpoint. Systematic violation of young girls by entire Indian army units was becoming commonplace, the girls taken to army camps, naked, and strung up from trees, their breasts cut with knives. "I'm sorry," he said, apologizing for the ugliness of the world. His left hand shook on the steering wheel. She placed her right hand over it. It was the first time they had touched.

A stream ran beside the road. "It is called the Muskadoon," he said. "We are close to Pachigam." The world disappeared. There was only the stream, its babble like thunder in her ears. She felt as if she were drowning. "Are you okay?" he asked. "Not carsick, is it? Shall I stop for some time so you can rest?" Dumbly, she shook her head. They rounded a bend in the road.

It was as if giant burrowing creatures, ants or worms, had wriggled up from underground and built a colony of earthworks in a graveyard. The ruins of the old village were still visible, the charred foundations of the wooden houses, the blighted orchards, the broken street, and around and in between these ghosts new dwellings had sprung up, ramshackle hovels of sticks and earth and moss thrown together without any evidence of care or thought, mud igloos with blue smoke issuing through holes in the roofs, "the slovenly products of an inferior species," Yuvraj called them, sounding angry, "or of our own kind, regressing towards savagery." Torn rags hung over the doorways and there were sullen faces peering out, silent, unwelcoming. "Something has happened here that is not so good, I fear," Yuvraj cautiously said. "The original villagers are not these. I have seen the bhand pather players of Abdullah Noman and these are not they. New people are here. They do not want to talk because they have seized land that is not theirs and they fear to lose it."

They walked down to the Muskadoon watched by suspicious eyes. Nobody came forward to greet them or ask them questions or tell them to go away. They were being treated like phantoms, like entities that did not exist, who could be made to vanish by being ignored. There were smooth boulders by the riverside and they sat down several yards apart and looked at the rushing water without speaking. She could feel the fingers of his longing stretching towards her, and she understood again that she desired him also, she wondered what his hands would feel like on her body, she closed her eyes and felt his lips at the nape of her neck, felt his tongue moving there, but when she opened her eyes he was still sitting on his rock some yards away, looking at her, helpless with love.

At that moment he was hating his life, the entrepreneurial work to which he had dedicated himself and what that work had made him, his banal businessman self. He was not worthy of her, was nothing more than a seller of carved wooden houseboats and papier-mâché vases, a purveyor of shawls and rugs. The shades of the departed bhands tugged at him and he wanted to give up his merchant existence and spend the rest of his life playing the santoor and singing the songs of the valley to her in his garden where no harmful thing could enter. He wanted to declare himself but did not because he could see the shadow over her, the deepening fear to which she could not yet give a name. He yearned to comfort her but had no words. He longed to get down on his knees and beg for her heart but did not and cursed inwardly at the fate that filled him with inappropriate longings, but blessed it as he cursed. He was a good man who knew how to love, he wanted to say but could not. He would worship her always and shape his life to her whims but this was no time to say so. This was no time for love. She was in agony and he could not be sure she would accept him even if she were not. She was a woman from far away.

Her feelings were unable to rise to the surface, they were buried beneath her fear. She did not know about the shadow planets but she felt in the presence of dark forces. This was her mother's stream, she thought. By this water her mother danced. In those woodland glades her father's killer learned the art of the clown. She felt lost and far from home. On a rock a few yards away a stranger sat, dying absurdly of love.

Yuvraj suddenly thought about his father, Sardar Harbans Singh, who had in a way prophesied the coming of this woman, who had perhaps arranged it after passing through the fire of death, Harbans who had loved and husbanded the old traditions amidst whose ruins his son now sat, who had been a gardener of their beauty. Feelings of loss and frustration pulled Yuvraj upright and pushed harsh words out of him. "What's the point of sitting on here?" he burst out. "This place is finished. Places get smashed and then they are no longer the places they were. This is how things are." She got to her feet too, full of impotent frenzy, her hands clenching, the fear choking her. She glared at him angrily and he wilted, as if scorched. "I apologize," he said. "I am a clumsy fool and I have distressed you by my thoughtless words." He didn't need to explain. She saw the pain in his eyes and shook her head, forgiving him. Her own eyes were desperate for answers. It was necessary to find someone who would talk.

There were narcissi growing by the stream, visited by bees. Yuvraj Singh remembered a name his father had mentioned, the name of the celebrated vasta waza of Shirmal, master of the Banquet of Sixty Courses Maximum, who was named after the bumblebee, *bombur,* and the narcissus flower. "There was a man near here called Yambarzal," he said.

"So Boonyi had a daughter," Hasina Yambarzal said, and through the slit in her black burqa her eyes squinted hard at the young woman, this Kashmira from America with an Englishwoman's voice. "Yes, it's true," she decided. "You have the same look of wanting what you want and never mind if the whole world goes to hell as a result." Bombur Yambarzal, a decrepit, antique figure these days, added loudly from his smoker's stool in the corner, "Tell her her bastard grandfather wasn't content with his fields and orchards, he had to try to take away my livelihood as a cook. He was not fifteen per cent of my quality, but still he gave himself airs. One may call oneself a vasta waza but it doesn't change the facts. It doesn't matter now, of course, even he managed to die but here I am still sitting waiting for my turn."

The village of Shirmal, like most places in the valley, had been stricken by the twin diseases of poverty and fear, that double epidemic which was wiping out the old way of life. The decaying houses seemed actually to be built of poverty, the unrepaired rooftops of poverty, the unhinged windows of poverty, the broken steps of poverty, the empty kitchens of poverty and the joyless beds. The fear was revealed by the striking fact that the women—even Hasina Yambarzal—were all veiled now: Kashmiri women, who had scorned the veil all their lives. The large, gleaming vehicle parked outside the sarpanch's residence seemed like an invader from another world. Inside the house a veiled old lady who no longer had it in her to be angry at her fate offered such hospitality as she could to the son of Sardar Harbans Singh and the daughter of Boonyi Kaul Noman. Even though nothing was visible of her except her hands and eyes it was evident that she had been a formidable woman in her time and that some remnant of that power lingered on. In a corner behind her sat her withered, milky-eyed octogenarian husband smoking a hookah and filled with the gummy malice of old age. "I am sorry that you see us in this condition," Hasina Yambarzal said, offering her guests hot glasses of salty tea. "Once we were proud but now even that has been taken from us." The old fellow in the corner shouted out, "Are they still here? Why are you talking to them? Tell them to go so I can die in peace." The veiled woman did not apologize for her husband. "He is tired of life," she calmly explained, "and it is a part of the cruelty of death that it is taking our little children, also our men and women in their prime, and ignoring the pleas of the one person who begs every day for it to come."

After the events in Shirmal leading up to the death of the iron mullah Maulana Bulbul Fakh, other militants had come by night. They had entered the sarpanch's house and dragged him out of bed and conducted a trial on the spot, finding him, on behalf of his whole village, guilty of assisting the armed forces, betraying the faith and participating in the ungodly practice of cooking lavish banquets that encouraged gluttony, lasciviousness and vice. Bombur Yambarzal on his knees was sentenced to death in his own house and his wife was told that if the villagers did not cease their irreligious behaviour and adopt godly ways within one week the militants would return to carry out the sentence. At that moment Bombur Yambarzal, with a gun at his temple and a knife at his throat, lost the power of sight forever, literally blinded by terror. After that the women had no choice but to wear burqas. For nine months the veiled women of Shirmal pleaded with the militant commanders to spare Bombur's life. Finally his sentence was commuted to house arrest but he was told that if he ever again cooked the evil Banquet of Sixty Courses Maximum, or even the more modest but still disgusting Banquet of Thirty-Six Courses Minimum, they would cut off his head and cook it in a stew and the whole village would be forced to eat it for dinner.

"Tell her what she wants to know," blind Bombur muttered spitefully, surrounded by smoke. "Then see if she's happy she came."

On the morning after Maulana Bulbul Fakh and his men had been slaughtered in the old Gegroo house in Shirmal, Hasina Yambarzal had realized that Shalimar the clown had not returned, and the pony he had borrowed was also missing. If that boy escaped, she thought, then we'd better be prepared for him to come back someday and get even. She thought of his youthful clowning on the high rope, his extraordinary gravity-free quality, the way the rope seemed to dissolve and one experienced the illusion that the young monkey was actually walking on air. It was hard to put that young man into the same skin as the murderous warrior he had grown into. Twenty-four hours later the pony found its way back to Shirmal, hungry but unharmed. Shalimar the clown had disappeared; but that night Hasina Yambarzal had a dream that horrified her so profoundly that she woke up, dressed, wrapped herself in warm blankets and refused to tell her husband where she was going. "Don't ask," she warned him, "because I don't have words to describe what I'm going to find." When she arrived at the Gujar hut on the wooded hill, the home of Nazarébaddoor the prophetess which afterwards became the last redoubt of Boonyi Noman, she discovered that the putrescent, fly-blown reality of the world possessed a horrific force far in excess of any dream. None of us is perfect, she thought, but the ruler of the world is more cruel than any of us, and makes us pay too highly for our faults.

"My sons brought her down the hill," she told Boonyi's daughter. "We laid her in a decent grave."

She stood by her mother's grave and something got into her. Her mother's grave was carpeted in spring flowers: a simple grave in a simple graveyard at the end of the village near the place where the forest had reclaimed the iron mullah's vanished mosque. She knelt at her mother's graveside and felt the thing enter her, rapidly, decisively, as if it had been waiting below ground for her, knowing she would come. The thing had no name but it had a force and it made her capable of anything. She thought about the number of times her mother had died or been killed. She had heard the whole story now, a tale told by an old woman shrouded in black cloth about a younger woman sewn into a white shroud who lay below the ground. Her mother had left everything she knew and had gone in search of a future and though she had thought of it as an opening it had been a closing, the first little death after which came greater fatalities. The failure of her future and her surrender of her child and her return in disgrace had been deaths also. She saw her mother standing in a blizzard while the people among whom she had grown up treated her like a ghost. They had all killed her too, they had actually gone to the proper authorities and murdered her with signatures and seals. And meanwhile in another country the woman she would not name had killed her mother with a lie, killed her when she was still alive, and her father had joined in the lie so he was her killer too. Then in the hut on the hillside followed a long period of living death while death circled her waiting for its time and then death came in the guise of a clown. The man who killed her father had killed her mother too. The man who killed her father had been her mother's husband. He killed her mother too. The cold weight of the information lay like ice upon her heart and the thing got into her and made her capable of anything. She did not weep for her mother not then nor at any other time even though she had believed her mother to be dead when in fact she had been alive and then believed her mother to be alive when she was already dead and now, finally, she had had to accept that her dead mother was dead, dead for the last time, dead in such a way that nobody could kill her any more, Sleep, Mother, she thought by her mother's graveside, sleep and don't dream, because if the dead were to dream they could only dream of death and no matter how much they wanted to they would be unable to awake from the dream.

The day was drawing on and it would have been better to set off for the city while the light remained but she had things to see that needed to be seen, the meadow of Khelmarg where her mother made love to Shalimar the clown and the Gujar hut in the woods where he murdered her by cutting off her head. The woman in the burqa came with her to show her the way and the man who had fallen in love with her came too but they didn't exist, only the past existed, the past and the thing that got inside her chest, the thing that made her capable of whatever was necessary, of doing what had to be done. She did not know her mother but she learned her mother's places, her sites of love and death. The meadow glowed yellow in the long-shadowed late afternoon light. She saw her mother there, running and laughing with the man she loved, the man who loved her, she saw them tumble and kiss. To love was to risk your life, she thought. She glanced at the man who had driven her here, who evidently loved her although he had not yet had the courage to declare his love, and without meaning to she took a step back, away from him. Her mother had stepped towards love, defying convention, and it had cost her dearly. If she was wise she would learn the lesson of her mother's fate.

The hut in the woods was in ruins; the roof had fallen in, and before allowing her to enter Yuvraj beat at the overgrown floor with a stick, in case of snakes. In a rusted pot on a long-dead fire the smell of uneaten food somehow lingered. Where did he do it, she asked the woman in the burqa, who was unable to speak, unable to describe, for example, the half-eaten condition of the mutilated corpse. Dumbly, Hasina Yambarzal pointed. *Outside,* she said. *I found her there.* The grass grew thick and dark where Boonyi fell. Her daughter imagined it was nourished by her blood. She saw the downward slash of the knife and felt the weight of the body hitting the ground and all of a sudden the pull of gravity increased, her own weight dragged her down, her head grew dizzy and she briefly fainted, collapsing onto the spot where her mother had died. When she regained consciousness she was lying in Hasina's lap and Yuvraj was walking around her helplessly, flapping his hands, being a man. Light was failing on the hill and the people she was with took her by the arms and led her down. She was not capable of speech. She did not thank the woman in the burqa or look back in farewell as the car drove her away.

On the way back to the city the dangerous night closed in. Men with rifles and flashlights waved at them to stop at a checkpoint, men in uniform and not in uniform with woollen scarves wrapped around their heads, knotted under their chins. It was impossible to know if these men were members of the security forces or the militants, impossible to know which group would be more dangerous. It was necessary to stop. There were obstacles in the road: fences of metal and wood. There were lights shining in their faces and her companion was speaking firmly and fast. Then in spite of her shocked condition the thing inside her came out and stared at the men outside and what they saw in her eyes made them back away and remove the roadblocks and allow the Qualis to proceed. She was unstoppable now. She did not need to be here any more, the uses of the place had been exhausted. The man driving the car was trying to say something. He was trying to express sympathy or love, sympathy *and* love. She was not able to pay attention. She had awoken from the fantasy of love and happiness, had departed from the lotus-land dream of joy, and she needed to return home. Yes, this was a man who loved her, a man she might be able to love if love were a possibility for her which at present it was not. Something got into her at her mother's grave and it would not be denied.

The Qualis drove through Yuvraj's gate and this time the magic didn't work, the real world refused to be banished. She wasn't well. She was running a fever and a doctor was summoned. She was confined to bed in a cool shuttered room and stayed there for a week. In a four-poster bed made of walnut wood and shrouded in mosquito netting she sweated and shook and when she slept saw only horrors. Yuvraj sat by her bedside and placed cold compresses on her brow until she asked him to stop. When her health returned she got out of bed and packed her bags. "No, no," he begged, but she hardened her heart. "Attend to your business," she told him coldly, "because I have to attend to mine." He flinched slightly, nodded once and left her to her packing. When she was ready she stayed indoors until it was time to leave, refusing to set foot in the garden lest its soporific enchantments weakened her resolve. He was all injured nobility, stiff and monosyllabic. How second-rate men were, she told herself. Why would any woman yoke herself to a species of such pouting mediocrity? He couldn't even say plainly what was written all over his face. Instead, he flounced and sulked. It was men who went in for the behaviour they had the effrontery to call feminine, while women carried the world upon their backs. It was men who were the cowards and women who were the warriors. Let him hide behind his pots and rugs if he wanted! She had a battle to fight, and her war zone was on the far side of the world.

At the airport, however, he finally achieved courage and told her he loved her. She gritted her teeth. What was she supposed to do with his declaration, she asked him, it was too heavy, took up too much room, it was baggage she couldn't carry with her on the flight. He refused to be slapped down. "You can't escape me," he said. "I'll soon come for you. You can't hide from me." This was a false note. The image of an earlier, similarly blustering suitor, the American underwear model, popped into her head. *You'll never get me out of your mind,* he'd said. *You'll think of my name in bed, in the bathtub. You might as well marry me. It's inevitable. Face the facts.* But standing at the barrier at Srinagar airport she had no idea what the American's name had been, could barely remember his face, though his underwear had been memorable. Her self-possession strengthened its grip on her. She shook her head. This man, too, she would manage to forget. Love was a deception and a snare. The facts were that her life was elsewhere and that she wanted to return to it. "Look after that beautiful garden," she told the handicrafts entrepreneur, touched his cheek briefly with a vague, distracted hand and flew ten thousand miles away from the unstable dangers of his useless love.

Three days after she returned to Los Angeles the prime suspect in the murder of Ambassador Maximilian Ophuls was taken alive in the vicinity of Runyon Canyon. He had been living in the high wilderness areas up there, living like a beast, and was suffering from the effects of prolonged exposure, hunger and thirst. *Acting on information received we ran him to ground he was one sorry sonofabitch came pretty quiet seemed happy to give himself up,* Lieutenant Tony Geneva said on TV, into the thicket of thrusting microphones. The suspect had come down from the heights and broken cover to scavenge for food in a trash can in the dog park at the canyon's foot, and had been somewhat ignominiously captured while holding a red McDonald's carton and fishing for the few cold discarded fries it still contained. When Olga Simeonovna heard the news she took credit for the arrest. "Great is the power of the potato," she crowed to anyone who would listen. "Whoo! Looks like I don't lose my touch." The man in custody had been positively identified as Noman Sher Noman, a known associate of more than one terrorist group, also known as "Shalimar the clown".

When she heard the news Kashmira Ophuls found herself wrestling with a strange sense of disappointment. There was a thing inside her that had wanted to hunt him down itself. His voice, his chaotic voice, was absent from her head. Perhaps he was too weakened to be heard. Kashmir lingered in her, however, and his arrest in America, his disappearance beneath the alien cadences of American speech, created a turbulence in her that she did not at first identify as culture shock. She no longer saw this as an American story. It was a Kashmiri story. It was hers.

The news of the arrest of Shalimar the clown made the front page and gave the riot-battered Los Angeles Police Department some much-needed positive ink at a time of exceptional unpopularity. Police Chief Daryl Gates had left office, after initially refusing to do so. Lieutenant Michael Moulin, whose terrified and outnumbered officers had been withdrawn from the corner of Florence and Normandie when the troubles began, leaving the area in the hands of the rioters, also left the force. The damage to the city was estimated at over one billion dollars. The damage to the careers of Mayor Bradley and District Attorney Reiner was irreparable. At such a time the solid police work of Lieutenant Geneva and Sergeant Hilliker turned them into media heroes, good cops to set against the notorious Rodney King quartet, Sergeant Koon and Officers Powell, Briseno and Wind. Rodney King himself appeared on TV, calling for reconciliation. "Can we all get along?" he pleaded. Lieutenant Geneva and Sergeant Hilliker were interviewed on one of the last late-night shows hosted that May by Johnny Carson, and were asked by the host if the LAPD could ever regain the public's trust. "We sure can," Tony Geneva said, and Elvis Hilliker, smacking his right fist into his left palm, added, "And there's a bad guy in jail tonight who proves just exactly why."

Then for a moment there were Elvis and Tony T-shirts for sale on Melrose and at Venice Beach. One of the television networks announced plans for a movie about the manhunt, with the parts of Tony and Elvis to be played by Joe Mantegna and Dennis Franz. With astonishing speed Shalimar the clown had become a bit player in the story of the policing of Los Angeles, and Kashmira Ophuls, who was always Kashmira now, who was making everyone she knew use the name, Kashmira whose mother and father he had foully killed, grew steadily angrier. She had knelt by her mother's grave in Shirmal and something got into her there, something that mattered, but now the meaning of the great events of her life was being leached away, all the talk was of police corruption and rotten apples and good honest officers called Hilliker and Geneva. The world did not stop but cruelly continued. Max no longer signified in it, and nor did Boonyi Kaul. Tony and Elvis were the heroes of the hour and Shalimar the clown was their property, their villain. He was, you could say, their happy ending, their last big bust, the one that gave meaning to their lives, that took meaning from her life and handed it to them. Alone in her apartment bedroom Kashmira beat her fists against a wall. It felt, how did it feel, it felt obscene. I want to write to him, she thought. I want him to know I'm out here waiting. I want him to know he belongs to me.

I am going to tell you about my father, she wrote. You should know more about the man you killed, with whom you established so intimate a relationship, becoming the bringer of his death. He didn't have long to live but you couldn't wait, you were in a hurry for his blood. It was a grand life you took and you should know its grandeur. I am going to teach you what he taught me about entering the house of power, and what he was like when I was a small girl, how he put his lips against my neck and made bird noises, and I am going to tell you about his foolish obsession with the imaginary lizard people who, or so he thought, once lived below L.A. I am going to take you with him on a plane flight across France and into the Resistance which will be interesting for you I believe. I am sure you think of your violent deeds as having been done in the cause of some sort of liberation so you will be interested to know that he was a warrior too. I want you to know the songs he sang—*je te plumerai le cou!*—and the food he liked best, the sauerkraut with Riesling and the honeyed lamb of his Alsatian youth, and I want you to know how he saved his daughter's life and that his daughter loved him. I am going to write and write and write to you and my letters will be your conscience and they will torture you and make your life a living hell until if things go as they should it is brought to an end. Even if you do not read them, even if they are never given to you or, if they are, even if you rip the envelopes to shreds, they are still spears that will transfix your heart. My letters are curses they will shrivel your soul. My letters are threats they should frighten you and I will not stop writing them until you are dead and maybe after you die I will go on writing them to your spirit as it burns and they will torment you more agonizingly than the inferno. You will never see Kashmir again but Kashmira is here and now you will inhabit me, I will write a world around you and it will be a prison more dreadful than your prison, a cell more confined than yourself. The hardships I send you will make the hardships of your imprisonment seem like joys. My letters are poisoned arrows. Do you know the song of Habba Khatoon in which she sings about being pierced? Oh marksman my bosom is open to the darts you throw at me, she sang. These darts are piercing me, why are you cross with me. Now you are my target and I am your marksman however my arrows are not dipped in love but hatred. My letters are arrows of hate and they will strike you down.

I am your black Scheherazade, she wrote. I will write to you without missing a day without missing a night not to save my life but to take yours to wind around you the poisonous snakes of my words until their fangs stab your neck. Or I am Prince Shahryar and you are my helpless virgin bride. I will write to you and my voice will haunt your dreams. Every night I tell the story of your death. Can you hear me? Listen to my voice. Every day I will write to you. Every night for however many nights it takes I will whisper in your ear until the story's done. You can't get into my head any more. I'm in yours instead.

Shalimar the clown spent a year and a half in the Los Angeles County Men's Central Jail on Bauchet Street waiting for his trial to begin. He was segregated from other prisoners and housed in the jail's 7000 section where the high-profile inmates were kept. He wore ankle chains and was given his meals in his cell and permitted three one-hour exercise periods per week. In the early weeks of his confinement he was in a highly disturbed condition, often screaming out at night, complaining about a female demon who was occupying his head, jabbing hot shafts into his brain. He was placed on suicide watch and given a high dosage of the tranquillizer Xanax. He was asked if he would like to receive visits from a priest of the Islamic faith and he said that he would. A young imam from the USC mosque on Figueroa Street was provided and reported after his first visit that the prisoner had genuinely repented of his crime, stating that owing to his poor command of the English language he had misunderstood certain statements regarding the Kashmir issue made by Maximilian Ophuls on a television talk show and had been quite erroneously driven to assassinate a man he had mistakenly thought of as an enemy of Muslims. The killing was therefore the result of an unfortunate linguistic lapse and he was consequently consumed with remorse. On the young imam's second visit, however, the prisoner was in a heightened state of agitation in spite of the Xanax and seemed at times to be addressing an absent person, apparently female, in English which, while not by any means perfect, was nevertheless good enough to undermine his earlier assertions. When the young imam pointed this out the prisoner became menacing and had to be restrained. After that the imam declined to return and the prisoner refused to see another priest even though a qualified member of the Latino Muslim Association of Los Angeles, Francisco Mohammed, was occasionally at the Men's Central Jail to counsel other inmates and had indicated that he would be available if required.

The new district attorney, Gil Garcetti, who had replaced Ira Reiner after the riots, argued when Shalimar the clown's case came up before the Los Angeles County grand jury that the accused's statements to the Figueroa Street imam confirmed that he was a devious individual, a professional killer with many work-names and alter egos, whose protestations of remorse and repentance were not to be taken at face value. Shalimar the clown was duly indicted by the grand jury for the murder of Ambassador Maximilian Ophuls and returned to Bauchet Street to await trial. It was accepted by the grand jury that the special circumstances attached to the case made him eligible for the death penalty. If found guilty he would therefore be liable to execution by lethal injection unless he opted for the gas chamber, which was still being offered as an alternative method if the subject so preferred.

Shalimar the clown had initially refused legal representation but later accepted a court-appointed defence team led by the attorney William T. Tillerman, well known for his fondness for defending the indefensible, a brilliant courtroom performer, slow and weighty, reminiscent of Charles Laughton in *Witness for the Prosecution,* who first rose to prominence as a junior member of the team defending Richard Ramirez, whom the tabloid press renamed the Nightstalker, several years before. There were persistent rumours that Tillerman had been the "hidden hand" shaping the defence strategy in the notorious Menendez brothers trial, even though he was not a named attorney in the case. (Erik and Lyle Menendez were, like Shalimar the clown, inmates of cell block 7000, where, later in Shalimar the clown's captivity, the former football star Orenthal James Simpson would also spend some time.) When letters addressed to Shalimar the clown and written by Max Ophuls's orphaned daughter started arriving in large numbers at 441 Bauchet Street, it was Tillerman who saw the connection between these letters and his client's alleged nocturnal persecution by the so-called female demon, and so devised what became widely known as the "sorcerer's defence".

When the letter avalanche began Shalimar the clown was asked first by prison officials and afterward by his attorney if he wished to see them, was warned of their tone of exceptional anger and hostility, and was firmly instructed by William Tillerman not to reply no matter how strongly he wished to do so. He insisted on being given the envelopes. "They are from my stepdaughter," he told Tillerman, who noted that his client's English was heavily accented but competent, "and it is my duty to read what she wishes to say. As for answering her, it is not necessary. There is no answer she wishes to hear." The system worked slowly, and the letters were usually two or three weeks old by the time he received them, but that didn't matter, because the moment he read the first one Shalimar the clown identified their author as the female *bhoot* who had been pursuing him through his terrifying nightmares. He understood at once what Boonyi's child was telling him: that she had set herself up as his nemesis, and whatever the judgement of a Californian court might be she would be his real judge; she, and not twelve Americans in a jury box, would be his only jury; and she, not a prison executioner, would somehow carry out whatever sentence she imposed. It wasn't important to know the how or when or where. He braced himself for her nocturnal assaults, screaming through the sedation, but enduring. He carefully read her daily indictments, read them over and over, memorizing them, giving them their due. He accepted her challenge.

After the bombing of the World Trade Center in New York—eight years later this would be remembered as the first bombing—he sat across a table from his lawyer in a stinking meeting room and expressed his fears for his safety. Even in his maximum-security, solitary-confinement wing, it was a dangerous time in prison for a Muslim man accused by the state of being a professional terrorist. Shalimar the clown dressed up for his meeting with Tillerman, as finely as prison allowed, wearing his "bonneroos", prison-issue blue jeans and a prison-issue denim overcoat. There was a sign on the wall of the room saying HOLDING HANDS ONLY and another saying 1 KISS 1 HUG AT THE START 1 HUG 1 KISS AT THE FINISH. These messages did not apply to him. He avoided Tillerman's eyes and spoke in a low voice in halting but serviceable English. Men died all the time in the MCJ. The sheriff blamed budget cuts but so what, that didn't make anyone feel any safer. A convicted killer somehow managed to walk the halls at night and murder another inmate who had testified against him at his trial even though their cells had been on different floors. The other prisoners in their cells, six thousand of them, acted on gang instructions and turned their backs and saw nothing. News of such things reached Shalimar the clown even in cell block 7000. A Korean gang member was stabbed thirty times and stuffed into a laundry trolley and nobody found him for sixteen hours, until the laundry began to stink. A wife-beater had been kicked to death. Two hundred men had taken part in a race riot started by an argument about using a pay phone. In the argument one inmate was stabbed a dozen times. And now after the attack in Manhattan maybe a guard would leave a door to 7000 unlocked one night and some godzilla called Sugarpie Honeybunch or Goldilocks Ali or Big Chief Bull Moose or Virginia Slim or the Cisco Kid, some OVG—Old Valley Gangster—would wreak an American revenge. Tillerman shrugged. "Okay. I'll take it up." Then he leaned across the table and changed the subject. "Tell me about the girl." Initially reluctant to reply, Shalimar the clown yielded slowly to his lawyer's coaxing, and began to talk.

The case of the *People* v. *Noman Sher Noman* came to trial six months later at the Los Angeles County Superior Court at the San Fernando Valley Government Center in Van Nuys, before Judge Stanley Weissberg, who had been on the bench in the Simi Valley Rodney King trial, when the four LAPD officers were acquitted, precipitating the riots. He was a mild, professorial man in his middle fifties and seemed unshaken by the Simi Valley experience. Because of the heightened atmosphere created by the events in Lower Manhattan the security at the courthouse was unprecedented. Shalimar the clown arrived and left each day, shackled and chained, in a white armoured van surrounded by a police operation reminiscent of a presidential motorcade. Roadblocks, motorcycle outriders, police snipers on the rooftops, an eleven-vehicle procession. "We don't want a Jack Ruby situation here," the city's new chief of police, Willie Williams, told the press. What would he compare the operation to in terms of its scale, a reporter asked him. He replied with a straight face, "It's what we'd do for Arafat."

The court had initially summoned five hundred people for jury duty. To ensure a fair trial all five hundred had been asked to complete a hundred-page questionnaire, and on the basis of these questionnaires and the usual courtroom challenges twelve jurors and six alternates had been empanelled. Four men and eight women would try the case of Shalimar the clown. Their average age was thirty-nine. Tillerman had wanted a young jury with a female bias. He considered himself a student of human nature, and was certainly a barroom philosopher of the usual, disenchanted variety. It was his view that the young, believing themselves immortal, had less respect for human life and so were less likely to be vengeful towards a killer. And after all—this was the reasoning behind loading the jury with women—Shalimar the clown was a highly attractive man, and had a tragic tale of heartbreak and betrayal to recount. The crime of passion was not a legal category in California, in spite of which such extenuating circumstances could only help the defence.

The thirtysomething prosecutors, Janet Mientkiewicz and Larry Tanizaki, looked like baby-faced innocents next to the much older, more corpulent, worldly-wise Tillerman, but they were hardened lawyers who were determined to get their man. Tanizaki had privately expressed some doubts about the death penalty, knowing that many jurors didn't like imposing it, but Mientkiewicz bolstered his resolve. "If this isn't a hanging offence, nothing is," she said on the steps of the courtroom on the day of the pretrial hearing. Tanizaki and Mientkiewicz's greatest concern was that the defence might try to deny the crime. Strangely, even though the murder of Maximilian Ophuls had taken place on a bright, sunny L.A. day, there were no eyewitnesses. It was as if the whole street had turned its back on the event, just as the inmates of the MCJ had done on the night of the revenge killing. The prosecution had the fingerprinted knife, the bloodstained clothes, the motive, the opportunity and the evidence of Mr Khadaffy Andang, who was cooperating fully with the state. They did not have a witness to the crime. However, William Tillerman informed them at the pretrial hearing that his client would not deny responsibility for the death of Ambassador Ophuls; but he added that if the charge were not reduced from murder in the first degree, then a not-guilty plea would have to be entered. "My client is a severely disturbed man," he averred. What was he suffering from, Judge Weissberg wanted to know. "The effects," Tillerman solemnly replied, "of witchcraft."

A woman, my mother, died for the crime of leaving you, Kashmira wrote. A man, my father, died for taking her in. You murdered two human beings because of your egotism your amazing egotism that valued your honour more highly than their lives. You bathed your honour in their blood but you did not wash it clean it's bloody now. You wanted to wipe them out but you failed, you killed nobody. Here I stand. I am my mother and my father I am Maximilian Ophuls and Boonyi Kaul. You achieved nothing. They are not dead not gone not forgotten. They live on in me.

Can you feel me inside you mister assassin mister joker? At night when you close your eyes do you see me there? At night who is it that stops you sleeping and if you do sleep who stabs at you until you awake? Are you screaming mister killer? Are you screaming mister clown? Don't call me your stepdaughter I'm not your stepdaughter I am my father's daughter and my mother's child and if I'm inside you then so are they.

My mother whom you butchered torments you now and my slaughtered father too. I am Maximilian Ophuls and Boonyi Kaul and you are nothing, less than nothing. I crush you beneath my heel.

Early in 1993 she tried briefly to go back to work, her friends had urged her to restart her life, and for a time she had travelled up and down US-101, south to San Diego where the route began in Presidio Park and north as far as the Sonoma Mission, past the concrete bells hanging from their hook-shaped posts that marked the route of the old trail taken by Fray Junipero Serra in the 1770s, looking for the stories she wanted to tell in her projected documentary *Camino Real.* But her heart hadn't been in it and she abandoned the project after a few weeks. The underwear model got in touch and asked her to go out to dinner, which, under pressure from her girlfriends, she agreed to do, but even though he brought her flowers and wore a blazer and tie and took her to Spago and told her she was prettier than any of the movie actresses and tried not to talk about himself, she didn't make it to the end of the meal, she made her apologies—"I'm not fit for human company right now"—and fled.

She decided that the time had come to move out of her apartment, and returned to the big house on Mulholland Drive to live with her father's ghost. Olga Simeonovna, whose daughters had returned, moving into one of the building's many vacant apartments, gave Kashmira a loud, honkingly tearful farewell and promised she would "make it up there into the lap of luxury" whenever she could. In the lap of luxury Kashmira lived an increasingly reclusive life. The domestic staff was familiar with its duties and the household ran itself, there was food on the table three times a day and clean sheets on the beds twice a week. The heavily armed security specialists from the Jerome risk-consulting company went about their business silently and reported daily to the firm's operations executive vice-president. The day shift concentrated on the front and rear gates in the perimeter wall and the larger night-shift detachment patrolled the grounds with the aid of night-vision goggles and roving searchlights that made the house look like a movie theatre on the night of a red-carpet première. It was not required of Kashmira to give them orders. They, on the other hand, instructed her: in the use of the armoured panic room—actually the immensely long and mostly empty walk-in closet, built to accommodate a movie star's wardrobe, in which she kept her few, inadequately glamorous, clothes—and in the importance, should there be a "breach", of not trying to take on the intruder herself. "Don't be a heroine, ma'am," the Jerome guy said. "Lock yourself in here and leave it to us to do what it takes." There had recently been a scandal at Jerome. One of their top men had seduced two extremely wealthy women, both Jerome clients, one in London, one in New York. He gave both of them the same private love-name, "Rabbit", as in "Jessica", to minimize the risk of a pillow-talk slipup. But in the end he was caught out, and the discovery of his affair with the two Jessica Rabbits had led to lawsuits that badly damaged the firm's reputation as well as its profitability, and led to the introduction of draconian new rules of engagement that forbade the specialists from speaking to their "principals" at all except on professional business, and then always in the company of a third party. Kashmira had no problem with this. Detachment was what she wanted. On one occasion, when she asked a Jerome operative for a pair of night-vision goggles, "just for fun", he gave them to her surreptitiously, guiltily, like a boy meeting a girl for a secret assignation. "This'll just be between us, ma'am," he told her. "I'm not even supposed to look in your general direction unless I have to take down a bad guy standing behind you."

Sometimes in the middle of the night she awoke to the sound of a man's voice singing a woman's song and it took her a few moments to realize that she was listening to a memory. In an enchanted garden a man who loved her sang a melodious *lol.* Habba Khatoon's original name was Zoon, which meant the moon. She lived four hundred years ago in a village called Chandrahar amid saffron fields and chinar trees. One day Yusuf Shah Chak the future ruler of Kashmir heard Zoon singing as he passed by and fell in love and when they married she changed her name. In 1579 the emperor Akbar ordered Yusuf Shah to come to Delhi and when Yusuf got there he was arrested and jailed. *Come and enter my door, my jewel,* Habba Khatoon sang, alone in Kashmir, *why have you forsaken the path to my house? My youth is in bloom,* she sang, *this is your garden, come and enjoy it. The shock of your desertion has come as a blow to me, O cruel one, I continue to nurse the pain.* Yuvraj, she thought. Forgive me. I'm in a kind of prison too.

She swam in the pool, exercised in the private gym, worked out at home with a new personal trainer even though she knew it would hurt her friend the egg donor who had trained her for years, and played tennis on her own court, three times a week, with a visiting pro. When she did leave the premises it was to fight or shoot. Her body grew leaner and harder by the month, its spare tautness a testament to her relentless regimen, her rich woman's monasticism, and to the growing strength of her self-denying will. After a day's archery or boxing or martial arts, or a trip out of town to Saltzman's shooting range, she came home and retired wordlessly to her private wing, where she wrote her letters and thought her thoughts and kept herself to herself while the attack dogs on their leashes sniffed the air for trouble and the searchlights searched and the men in night-vision goggles roamed the property. She no longer lived in America. She lived in a combat zone.

The server carrying the subpoena summoning her to appear in the trial of her father's murderer as a hostile witness for the defence was intercepted at the gate to the property and then escorted to her quarters by Frank, the same Jerome operative who had given her the night-vision goggles. "This came, ma'am." It had to be some sort of practical joke, she thought, but it wasn't, her letters were coming home to roost, they were important exhibits in William Tillerman's case, and he wanted to question her about them. Tillerman had come up with a therapist named E. Prentiss Shaw who had developed a diagnostic tool for use with suspected brainwashing victims. The tool was a checklist that amounted to a form of psychological profiling. It was well known that Hamas chiefs in the Mideast used psychological profiling when selecting candidates for martyrdom. This was the age we lived in, Tillerman argued in court, an age in which our invisible foes understood that not everyone could be a suicide bomber, not everyone could be an assassin. Psychology was all-important. Character was destiny. Certain personality types were more suggestible than others, could be shaped by external forces and aimed like weapons by their masters against whatever targets were deemed worthy of attack. The Shaw profiling tool identified Shalimar the clown as a malleable personality of this type. Shalimar the clown screamed at night in his cell because he believed himself bewitched, Tillerman said. The defence presented as evidence over five hundred letters written by Ms India a.k.a. Kashmira Ophuls to the accused, letters which clearly stated her intent to invade his thoughts and torment him while asleep. One of the known associates of Ms. Ophuls, a woman of Soviet origins, actually was a self-described witch and member of the Wicca organization, as the testimony of a former fellow-resident of the apartment building on Kings Road, Mr Khadaffy Andang, would confirm. "Is it the contention of the defence, Mr Tillerman," Judge Weissberg interrupted, lowering his spectacles, "that sorcery exists?"

William Tillerman lowered his spectacles right back at the judge. "Sir, it is not," he replied. "But it is of no importance what you or I may believe here in this courtroom. What is important is that my client believes it. I beg the court's indulgence for what may seem like grandstanding, but this speaks to my client's extreme vulnerability to external manipulation. The defence will call witnesses from the intelligence community who will report on my client's presence over many years at various locations known to us as schools of terrorism, brainwashing centres, and it is our contention that in the matter of Ambassador Maximilian Ophuls my client ceased to be in command of his actions. His free will was subverted by mind-control techniques, verbal, mechanical and chemical, which gravely undermined his personality and turned him into a missile, aimed at a single human heart, which just happened to be the heart of this country's most distinguished counterterrorism ambassador. A Manchurian Candidate, if you will, a death zombie, programmed to kill. The defence will argue that the assassination may have been triggered by an unknown "sorcerer" or "puppet master" who has not been apprehended. After thorough conditioning the trigger moment would not even require the puppet and the puppet master to meet. The command could be given on the telephone, the conditioned response could be activated by the use of a commonplace word such as, oh, I don't know, *ba-*

nana, or *solitaire.* I am not sure, sir, if Your Honour and the members of the jury are familiar with the thirty-year-old movie to which I allude. If not, a video screening could easily be arranged."

"Far be it from this court, Mr Tillerman," Judge Weissberg said sternly, "to accuse you of trying to make a grandstand play. And yes: I saw the movie, and I have no doubt that the jury gets your point. However, this is murder one, Mr Tillerman. We will not be going to the pictures in my courtroom."

In the days that followed Tillerman's opening remarks the entire country was captured by his "sorcerer's" or "Manchurian" defence of Shalimar the clown. The classic movie was screened on network television, and plans for a remake were announced. The Twin Towers bombers, the suicidists of Palestine, and now the terrifying possibility that mind-controlled human automata were walking amongst us, ready to commit murder whenever a voice on the phone said *banana* or *solitaire* . . . it all made the new, senseless kind of sense, Tillerman could see it in the jury's eyes, and all the way through the prosecution's case he found assistance for his own. Yes, the accused was a terrorist, the prosecution said. Yes, he had been in some remote, scary places where bad people gathered to plot dark deeds. Under a number of work-names he had been involved for many years in the perpetration of such acts. On this occasion, however, the prosecution argued, the probability was that he had been flying solo, because of the seduction by the victim of the accused's beloved wife. When Janet Mientkiewicz proposed this, the vengeful husband theory, she actually saw the jury's eyes glazing over, and understood that the plainness of the truth was suffering by comparison with Tillerman's paranoid scenario, which was so perfectly attuned to the mood of the moment that the jury wanted it to be true, wanted it while not wanting it, believing that the world was now as Tillerman said it was while wishing it were not. "We may be screwed here," she confided to Tanizaki one night. He shook his head. "Trust in the law and do your job," he told her. "This isn't *Perry Mason.* We're not on TV." "Oh yes we are," she said, "but thanks for stiffening my spine."

It's dog eat dog up there in the Himalayas, ladies and gentlemen, the Indian army against the Pakistan-sponsored fanatics, we sent men out to discover the truth and the truth is what they brought home. You want to know this man, my client? The defence will show that his village was destroyed by the Indian army. Razed to the ground, every structure destroyed. The dead body of his brother was thrown at his mother's feet with the hands severed. Then his mother was raped and killed and his father was also slain. And then they killed his wife, his beloved wife, the greatest dancer in the village, the greatest beauty in all Kashmir. You don't need psych profiling to get the point of this, ladies and gentlemen of the jury, this kind of thing would derange the best of us, and the best of them is what he was, a star performer in a troupe of travelling players, a comedian of the high wire, an artist, famous in his way, Shalimar the clown. Then one day his whole world was shattered and his mind with it. This is exactly the kind of person the terrorist puppet masters seek out, this is the kind of mind that responds to their sorcery. The subject's picture of the world has been broken and a new one is painted for him, brushstroke by brushstroke. Like the man says in the movie you aren't going to see in Judge Weissberg's courtroom, they don't just get brainwashed, they get dry-cleaned. *This is a man against whose whole community a blood crime was committed that he could not avenge, a blood crime that drove him out of his mind. When a man is out of his mind other forces can enter that mind and shape it. They took that avenging spirit and pointed it in the direction they required, not at India, but here. At America. At their real enemy. At us.*

The Manchurian bubble burst, as Larry Tanizaki had promised Janet Mientkiewicz it would, the day Kashmira Ophuls took the stand for the defence. A hostile witness was always a gamble, and Tillerman's decision to field the Ophuls girl was, in Tanizaki's opinion, a weak choice, a choice that showed what a house of cards his case was. Under cross-examination by Janet Mientkiewicz, Kashmira revealed what Shalimar the clown had not told his attorney, what Tillerman's researchers had been unable to discover, what the usurpers of Pachigam did not know and the Yambarzals in Shirmal would not tell. In a single, brief statement, made with an executioner's calm, she unmade the defence's case. "That wasn't how my mother died," she said. "My mother died because that man, who also killed my father, cut off her beautiful head."

She turned to face Shalimar the clown and he understood perfectly what she did not need words to say. *Now I have killed you,* she told him. *Now my arrow is in your heart and I am satisfied. When the time comes to execute you I will come and watch you die.*

On the day after sentence was passed on him Shalimar the clown was moved by road to the California state prison at San Quentin where the men's death-row facility was located. Once again extreme security precautions were taken; he did not travel in the regular jail bus, and the eleven-vehicle motorcade with motorbikes buzzing beside it and helicopters tracking it from the sky looked, as it moved north past the silent concrete bells of the Camino Real, like a monarch's journey into exile, like Napoleon in rags on his way to St Helena. He remained impassive throughout the twelve-hour journey. His features had acquired something of the grey, pasty colour and texture of prison life and his hair was whiter and had thinned a little. He did not speak to the guards sitting beside and across from him in the white armoured van except once, to ask for a drink of water. He had the air of a man who had accepted his fate, and retained his calm demeanour while he was processed through the death-row reception centre, photographed, fingerprinted, given blankets and prison blues, and then led wearing waist chains to the adjustment centre or A/C to await classification. Here his possessions were taken from him except for a pencil and a sheet of writing paper and a comb and a bar of soap. He was handed a toothbrush with all but an inch of the handle cut off and some tooth powder. Then he was locked in a cage and stripped naked and the guards looked, as it was their habit to look, under his testicles and inside his bodily orifices, crack a smile, one of them told him, and he didn't understand until the guard grabbed him by the back of the neck and bent him over so they could inspect his rear. He was handcuffed and checked with a metal detector and taken to his cell. The guard yelled the cell number and the door opened with a great hiss because compressed air was used to open and close it. Then a tray slot was opened and he put his hands through it and his handcuffs were removed. All this he suffered without protest. From the beginning the guards were struck by his quality of stillness, *He was on some kind of meditation trip,* they said, and later, after he made his impossible escape, his captors were almost respectful, *It's like spaceships,* one of them argued, *if you don't see them you don't believe in them, but me and my colleagues here, we saw what we saw.*

Most of the men under sentence of death were sent to the East Block or the "North Seg"—the original death row, where the gas chamber was located—but those who were classified Grade B Condemned—the gang members, the men who had been involved in stabbings while in prison, the ones other inmates wanted to see dead in a hurry—had to stay in the A/C, where there were almost a hundred solitary confinement cells, on three floors. The classification committee decided that Shalimar the clown was a Grade-B prisoner because of the potentially large numbers of enemies he might find in the prison population. There were about thirty-five men in the North Seg and over three hundred in the East Block and violence and rape were commonplace and anything could be a weapon, a pencil stub could put out a man's eye. The men were let out for yard in groups of sixty or seventy and this was a dangerous time. If a fight broke out a guard might start shooting down into the yard and the risk of being hit by a bullet bouncing off the concrete walls was not small. The accommodation in the A/C was unpleasant even by the standards of death row but for a long time Shalimar the clown opted not to participate in yard. He remained in his cell, doing push-ups or strange, slow-motion, dancelike exercises for hour after hour or, for further hours at a time, simply sitting cross-legged on the floor with his eyes closed and his hands lying open on his knees, with the palms upturned.

His room was ten feet long and four feet wide and contained a bed made of a plate of steel and a stainless-steel sink and toilet. Twice a month the prison issued him writing paper, toilet paper, a pencil and some soap. He was not allowed to have a cup. He was given a container of milk for breakfast each day and if he wanted coffee he had to hold this container out through the tray slot and the guard would pour hot coffee into it. When the guard's aim was poor Shalimar the clown's hands were scalded, but he never cried out. The A/C was filled with the noises of a hundred condemned human beings and their smells as well. The men shouted and raged and made obscene remarks but they were also full of philosophy and religion and there were some who sang, *The days are coming when things will get better, First we must overcome the stormy weather,* and some who spoke fast and rhythmically in a kind of jailhouse rap, *I pace back and forth in a straight line, Thinking of nothing, trying to burn Time, The darkness cloaks the brightest of days, The chill in the bones is here to stay,* and many who called out to God, *Although I still sit in my cell, my new home, for hours and days upon end, I know in my heart that I'm never alone, 'cause Jesus is now my best friend.* The life of Shalimar the clown had dwindled to this, but he never ranted, nor did he sing, nor did he speak fast and rhythmically, nor did he call upon God. He took what was given to him and waited, when William T. Tillerman abandoned him and walked away he heard all around the voices of death row's most hated inmates telling him, man, took me four years to find an attorney to get my appeal lodged, that ain't nothin', motherfucker, took me five and a half, there were men who had waited nine years or ten, waited for justice they said, because many of them still protested their innocence, many of them had studied up and knew the statistics, the percentage of exonerations on death row was high, far, far higher than in the rest of the prison community, so God would help, if you trusted in God he would send down his love and save you, but in the meanwhile you just had to wait, you just had to hope your number didn't come up when some election-happy governor wanted a condemned man to fry.

On the wall of his prison cell a previous inmate had chalked a chemical equation: *2NaCn + H2SO4 = 2HCN + Na2SO4.* This, Shalimar the clown realized, was the true sentence of his death. "You don't need to worry about no ten years, pretty boy," one of the guards taunted him. "Brutha, in yo' case we hear ev'thing gonna be *expedite.*"

This turned out not to be true. The months lengthened into years. Five years passed, more than five years, two thousand slow, stinking days. The fabric of the prison was crumbling and so were its inmates. A rainstorm brought down chunks of the perimeter wall, injuring guards and prisoners. The men on death row grew older, fell sick, got stabbed, got kicked to death, got shot. There were many ways to die here that were not covered by the equation on Shalimar the clown's cell wall. After the third year he chose to come out of his cell and allow himself to be strip-searched and go outside wearing only his underwear and participate in yard and let what had to be come to pass. On the first day there were clumps of men staring at him, challenging him. He did not try to stare anybody down. He leaned against a wall and looked up at the giant green chimney stack sticking out of the gas-chamber roof. After the gas chamber was used the poison gas, the hydrogen cyanide, HCN, would be released into the atmosphere through this pipe. He turned his eyes away.

Men were playing cards at the two card tables. Other men were going one on one under a basketball hoop. He went to the chin-up bar and when he had completed one hundred chin-ups the basketball players stopped playing. When he had completed two hundred the poker school broke up. When he had completed three hundred he had everyone's attention. He dropped to the floor and went back to lean against the wall. People noticed he wasn't sweating. One of the most important Bloods came up to him. He was a big three-hundred-pounder and he was holding a sharpened plastic blade that had fooled the metal detector. The gang lord leaned towards Shalimar the clown and said, "No strongman stunt gonna save yo' terroris' ass now." Shalimar the clown's movements seemed unhurried but as a result of them the Blood King was in a painful armlock and Shalimar the clown had the plastic blade at his throat and before the guards could shoot he had pushed the Blood King away and tossed the blade into the yard toilet. After that he was left alone for a year. Then six men jumped him in a coordinated attack and he was badly beaten and fractured two ribs but he broke three men's legs and blinded a fourth. The guards held their fire. Wallace, the officer who had taunted him four years earlier, told him, "Only reason we didn't gun you down was, we waitin' to see you choke in that ol' gas cooker over there."

He had found a lawyer, a man named Isidore "Zizzy" Brown who was handling the cases of several of the poorest A/C inmates, and was one of the hundreds of death-row attorneys resident in the San Quentin area. There were meetings from time to time in the visitors' cage. At these meetings Shalimar the clown did not appear to be especially interested in the appeals process. One of the other inmates warned him during yard that his lawyer had a bad reputation. Apparently he had acquired his nickname by falling asleep several times in court. On one such occasion the judge had remarked, "The Constitution says everyone's entitled to the attorney of their choice. The Constitution doesn't say the lawyer has to be awake." Shalimar shrugged. "It doesn't really matter," he said. Five years passed and finally Brown told him an appeal date had been set. "Let it pass," said Shalimar the clown. "You don't want to appeal?" the attorney asked. Shalimar the clown turned away from him. "It's enough now," he said. That night when he closed his eyes he realized he couldn't see Pachigam clearly any more, his memories of the valley of Kashmir had grown imprecise, broken beneath the weight of life in the A/C. He could no longer clearly see his family's faces. He saw only Kashmira; all the rest was blood.

A man was executed at San Quentin that year. His name was Floyd Grammar and he was a diagnosed schizophrenic who talked to his food and believed that the beans on his plate talked back to him. He was on death row for the double murder of a business executive and his secretary in Corte Madera; after shooting them dead he had gone home and taken off all his clothes except for his socks and then stood out in the street until the police came. Nobody ever knew why he did it. He didn't know himself. Martians might have been involved. On the night before his lethal injection he believed that he had been granted an amnesty and so refused to fill out the last-meal request form. The guards gave him cookies and sandwiches and took him away. One hour later Shalimar the clown stood naked at his cell door while the guard named Wallace searched him before letting him go out to the yard. Wallace was in a good mood, a comical mood. Interest in the execution had been high. A media centre had been set up on the prison grounds and one hundred accredited persons had been given passes. "We on national TV, man," Wallace said, holding Shalimar the clown's testicles in his gloved hand. "But we just rehearsin'. The main attraction is when we do you. Today we just terminated some dummy. Call it a dummy run." Something broke inside Shalimar the clown at that moment, and naked as he was with his balls in the other man's hand he brought up his knee as fast as he could and hammered downward with both hands joined together and he pounded at Wallace for a spell until two other guards shot at him with wooden bullets and knocked him out. The guards gathered round him and kicked his unconscious body for several minutes, breaking his ribs all over again and damaging his back and injuring his groin so severely that he was unable to walk for a week and smashing his nose in two places and that was the end of his pretty-boy looks.

When he made it out to the yard again the Blood King beckoned him over. "You okay?" he asked. Shalimar the clown was limping slightly and his right shoulder hung lower than his left. "Yes," he replied. The Blood King offered him a cigarette. "You got some devil in you, terroris'," he said. "You need somethin', you ask me."

A sixth year went by.

Once the trial of Shalimar the clown had ended, Kashmira Ophuls became herself again. She telephoned her friends and apologized to them for her behaviour, she threw a party on Mulholland Drive to prove she wasn't crazy any more, she called up her old film crew and said, "Let's go to work." In the course of the next six years she completed *Camino Real,* took it to the major festivals, found a good home for it on television, and followed it with *Art and Adventure,* a dramatized re-creation of her grandparents' lost, prewar Strasbourg and its eventual destruction. At home, she revised the security agreement with the Jerome company, scaling down the level of protection to more conventional antiburglary levels. She also fell in love. Yuvraj Singh had followed her to America as he had promised he would, showing up on her doorstep looking a little ludicrous, carrying a bunch of flowers in a papier-mâché vase, a portrait of her face carved out of walnut, a selection of embroidered shawls and a yellow-and-gold chain-stitch rug, *You look like a walking flea market,* she said into her video entry-phone, then buzzed him in, and in her new, post-trial mood of euphoria lowered her defences and allowed herself to be happy and eased off on her weapons work and ring time and martial arts.

The relationship had its difficulties. She returned to Kashmir, to his enchanted garden, to be with him when she could, but he mostly needed to be there in the winter because the work of the craftsmen and craftswomen was winter work, the slow embroidery, the carving, and in that Himalayan winter the cold gnawed at her face and made her miss the Californian warmth about which she had always complained. Also there was the political situation; which did not improve, which deteriorated. War was often close, and he advised her to stay away. He was finding a growing market for his goods in the United States but still needed to be away for extended periods of time, and the fact that his absences seemed fine by her, that she matter-of-factly got on with her work and was happy to see him whenever he showed up, this was upsetting to him, he wanted her to mind his absences more, he wanted her to be more afraid for him, and especially to pine, because when they were apart he couldn't sleep, he said, the loneliness was overpowering, he thought about her every minute of every day, it was driving him crazy, no woman had ever made him feel this way. "That's because in this relationship I'm the guy," she told him sweetly, "and you, my dear, are the girl." This remark did not improve matters. However, in spite of the problems of an intercontinental love affair, and in spite of the fact that she seemed to dodge the subject of marriage whenever he tried to raise it, in spite of her gently pushing aside the box with the ring inside that he put on the table when he took her out for dinner on her thirtieth birthday, they were for the most part content with each other, so that when the letter from Shalimar the clown arrived it seemed anachronistic, like a punch thrown long after the final bell.

Everything I am your mother makes me, the letter began. *Every blow I suffer your father deals.* There followed more along these lines, and then it ended with the sentence that Shalimar the clown had carried within him all his life. *Your father deserves to die, and your mother is a whore.* She showed the letter to Yuvraj. "Too bad he hasn't improved his English in San Quentin," he said, trying to dismiss the ugly words, to rob them of their power. "He puts the past into the present tense."

Night in the A/C was a little quieter than the day. There was a certain amount of screaming but after the one a.m. inspection it quieted down.

Three in the morning was almost peaceful. Shalimar the clown lay on his steel cot and tried to conjure up the sound of the running of the Muskadoon, tried to taste the gushtaba and roghan josh and firni of Pandit Pyarelal Kaul, tried to remember his father. *I wish I was still held in the palm of your hand.* Abdullah had promised he would return from the grave in the form of a winged creature, but Shalimar the clown never looked to see if a tone-deaf hoopoe was hopping about somewhere, because it was his human lion of a father that he had loved and not some lousy orange bird. He summoned up the memory of his father finding birds under his skin, but Abdullah's face kept changing, becoming the contorted face of another bird-finder. Maximilian Ophuls. Shalimar the clown looked away. His brothers came into the cell to say hello. They were out of focus, like amateur photographs, and they soon disappeared again. Abdullah went too. The Muskadoon died away and the taste of the dishes of the wazwaan turned back into the usual bitter blood-flecked shit taste he'd grown used to over the years. Then there was a loud hissing noise and the cell door sprang open. He moved quickly onto his feet and crouched slightly, ready for whatever was coming. Nobody entered but there was a noise of running feet. Men in prison fatigues were running in the corridors. *It's a jailbreak,* he realized. There was no gunfire yet but it would start soon. He stood staring at the open cell door, transfixed by the empty space. Then the bulk of the Blood King filled the doorway. "You fixin' to reside on in this 'stablishment?" the Blood King asked. "Because in case you in'rested, we jus' arranged a early checkout time." Shalimar the clown did not ask how the doors had been sprung. The prison was crumbling and maybe some of the guards were for sale. It did not interest him. He ran.

Between the main building of the adjustment centre and the walled yard known as Bloods Alley there was a short outdoor passage enclosed by steel chain-link fencing and a solid steel roof. When the Blood King reached this passageway he produced from inside his overalls a gigantic metal cutter that impressed Shalimar the clown. The gang lord saw the *how?* on Shalimar the clown's face and grinned broadly. "My mama smuggled it in to me," he said. "Jus' baked it inside a cake." Now there were guards firing wooden bullets and the thirty or so men involved in the jailbreak began to fall. There were only three guards for the moment.

They would have pushed their panic buttons to summon sixty or more armed men but these were scattered around the prison buildings and it would take them a few minutes to arrive. Some of the prisoners attacked the guards. Shalimar the clown did not wait to see the outcome of the battle. He followed the Blood King through the opened fence and they ran. There was a wall to scale. They scaled it. Then they were moving along the top of the wall and a hundred yards ahead they could see a double row of fences ten feet apart and beyond the fences was open ground ending in water: the mouth of the San Pablo Bay. The sight of the dark water was intoxicating, the silent bay and the moon lying in it like treasure. Shalimar the clown began to move quickly towards the vision. The Blood King, wobbling desperately on the wall, called to him, sounding suddenly like a child being abandoned by his parent. "Where you think you goin'?" he yelled. "Wait up, brutha. Don't let me fall now. Don't you be lettin' me fall." The noise of gunfire was getting louder: more guns, much closer. "Those ain't no wooden bullets," the Blood King said. Then the front of his overalls exploded and his blood poured out and, looking irritated and young, he fell. Shalimar the clown turned away and ran faster. He was thinking about his father. He needed his father to be here with him, in sharp focus, Abdullah Noman in his prime. He needed to trust his father now. As long as he was held in his father's hand he could not fall. The top of the wall was the same as a rope. It was not a safety line through space. It was a line of gathered air. The wall and the air were the same. If he knew this he would be ready to fly. The wall would melt away and he would step out onto the air knowing that it would bear his weight and take him wherever he wanted to go. He was running along the wall as fast as he could run these days. It was fast enough. His father was with him. His father was running with him along the wall. It was not possible to fall. The wall did not exist. There was no wall.

There was no night at San Quentin. At night the state prison looked like an oil refinery. Banks of floodlights banished the darkness, illuminating the cell blocks, the exercise yards and Point San Quentin Village, outside the prison's main gate, where many correctional facility employees made their homes. It was on account of the brightly illuminated night that many guards and villagers afterward swore that they had seen the impossible, they swore to their friends and the police and the information media, and refused to budge from their story in spite of the universal scepticism, that a man had run flat-out off the corner of a walled area near the adjustment centre on death row and had simply taken off, had continued on his way as if the wall stretched out into the sky like the wall of China or such, had gone scooting up into the air just as if he were running up a hill, his arms stretched out, not like wings, really, more to balance him, or so it seemed. He ran higher and higher until the lights of the prison couldn't pick him out any more, and maybe he ran all the way to Paradise, because if he did fall to earth someplace in the neighbourhood then nobody in the San Quentin community ever heard a thing about it.

The coyotes had been busy. In many of the canyons there were reports of missing pets. Kashmira was happy that she had never wanted a lapdog or a canary, had never liked the idea of looking after a creature too stupid to fend for itself. She had always had a liking for solitude and with a dumb animal around you were never alone. Yuvraj was away and she was in bed watching the Lakers game with a glass of chardonnay in her hand and a bowl of freshly made popcorn on her lap. The century was ending, badly, of course, and she did worry about him, of course she did, though she wasn't good at showing it, there had been eleven weeks of Indo-Pak fighting around the Line of Control and people kept mentioning the nuclear option, of course she worried, but fear ate the soul, that was her way of thinking, the soul needed its owner to behave as if there wasn't anything to worry about, as if everything would be fine. She told Yuvraj this but he thought it was a failure of emotion on her part, sometimes she thought she couldn't live up to his love, she kept failing him, and how could he go on loving her if he thought of her as a failure, so this, too, would end badly, like the century, like the whole goddamn millennium. Too much chardonnay, she thought, stopping the downward spiral. Things were good. He was a good man. She loved him. There were Japanese lanterns hanging in the trees outside her window. Beyond and below them the city burned upward from the Valley. All that electricity used just to please her, just to provide her with this nightly bedtime extravaganza. She should shut up and eat her popcorn and watch Kobe's butt and then Leno's chin and then the new boy, Kilborn, the tall guy with the moue. Everything would be fine.

She had heard the news about the jailbreak of course. Everyone had heard the news. Yuvraj had called her from Kashmir, full of concern. She should call the Jerome people and restore the earlier, higher level of protection immediately, he said. The man Noman was ruthless and one guard at the gate and another patrolling the grounds with a single Alsatian might not suffice. Not even an Alsatian called Achilles, she asked, not even if it's the greatest warrior in history patrolling my lawn in canine form? He didn't laugh. I'm serious, he said. She did not make the call. Shalimar the clown was yesterday's man. She had already killed him and she wasn't afraid of ghosts. Nor was she anxious to ensnare herself again in the webs of maximum security. Nobody lasted long on the run after six years on death row. Let him run. He was hundreds of miles away and they would hunt him down soon enough.

Two hours later she woke up and the television was still on and the uneaten popcorn had spilled across her comforter. She tidied it up, put the bowl on the floor and used her master remote to turn off the TV and the lights. Damn it, she thought, now it will be difficult to get back to sleep. Maybe she should read. Maybe she should get up and go for a walk and say hi to Frank the risk consultant who was spending the night in the garden with the dog. It was already afternoon in Kashmir. Maybe she should call Yuvraj. She didn't know what she wanted. Tomorrow as usual a beautiful day would dawn, here in Paradise, in the city of the badass angels. She wanted to be asleep.

When the intruder alarm went off she looked at the zone monitor built into the wall beside her bed. That wasn't the gate or the perimeter wall. Somebody had tripped a beam inside the main house. The household had shut down for the night. The live-in staff were in their quarters at the far end of the lawn. They knew she valued her privacy and would not have reentered her wing without informing her. She had issued strong standing instructions regarding this. She was moving quickly now, grabbing her discarded jeans and sweatshirt and heading for the dressing room. A second alarm went off, also inside the house, closer to her bedroom. How could this be happening, she asked herself, the beams along the perimeter wall were unavoidable so whoever it was must have come in the main gate, and how could that have happened, unless the guard at the gate had been incapacitated, unless he had been knocked unconscious or killed so fast he hadn't been able to sound the alarm and then the intruder had just opened the gates and strolled in; and the Alsatian too, Achilles the Alsatian in the garden for whom she had a soft spot in spite of her personal no-pets clause because after all she was half-Alsacienne herself, was mighty Achilles also slain? Mighty Achilles and his buddy Frank? Were they lying on the lawn with arrows through their throats, because she had never bought that stuff about the heel, the throat was a better way to go, the throat was making sure. She was being a little hysterical, she knew that, and the memory of chardonnay was banging at her temples. Here was the key to the drawer where she kept the gun. Here were arrows and a golden bow. She should lock the dressing-room door, the armoured door, and push this button here that summoned the police. There was a monitor in the wall here too. A third zonal alarm had been tripped. He wanted her to know he was coming. He had come silently past her guardians but now that they were silenced he wanted her to know. There were always police cars cruising Mulholland Drive but they would not get here in time. She pushed the panic button anyway. Then she opened the box containing the circuit breakers for this part of the building and turned off the master switch. Here on this shelf were her night-vision goggles. She put them on. It was a while since she had gone regularly to archery class and her visits to Saltzman's shooting range had fallen off as well. Her shooting had always been a little wild. The arrow was her weapon of choice. She should lock the door of the safe room and wait for the cops, she knew that, but something got into her at her mother's grave and that was the thing in charge now and she wasn't going to argue with it. She drew an arrow from her quiver and took up her stance. The door of the night-black room was opening, and her stepfather was coming in, knife in hand, neither the knife that had killed her mother nor the knife that killed her father but a third, virginal blade, its silent steel intended just for her. She was ready for him. She thought about her mother's end by a Gujar hutment with hot food on the stove, and about her father's bloody slide down a glass door. She was ice not fire, and she too had a silent weapon. She would get one shot and no more, he would not allow her a second, and he was in the bedroom now, she felt him enter and then the night-vision goggles picked him out as he passed the open dressing-room door. He stopped moving suddenly, and she knew he had sensed a wrongness in the dark and was moving from attack to defence, switching modes from the inexorability of the hunter to the self-preserving wariness of the hunted. He turned his head, screwing up his eyes to try and make her out, to see where the black air gathered into a different sort of blackness. The cacophony of the alarm bells filled the air and was joined by the loud, approaching sirens of the police cars. He came towards the dressing room. She was ready for him. She was not fire but ice. The golden bow was drawn back as far as it would go. She felt the taut bowstring pressing against her parted lips, felt the foot of the arrow's shaft against her gritted teeth, allowed the last seconds to tick away, exhaled and let fly. There was no possibility that she would miss. There was no second chance. There was no India. There was only Kashmira, and Shalimar the clown.